PRAISE F(
TRACY (

Praise for *One Last Kill*

"Dugoni brilliantly folds murders past and present into his heroine's earlier cases and her troubled history."

—*Kirkus Reviews* (starred review)

Praise for *What She Found*

"Readers will eagerly await Tracy's next outing."

—*Publishers Weekly* (starred review)

"The fact that there's a truly gripping mystery, full of corruption, murder, and scandal, at the heart of the book to push and propel our protagonist into new realms is just the icing on the cake."

—Bookreporter

Praise for *In Her Tracks*

"Gripping . . . Fans of police procedurals will hope Tracy has a long career."

—*Publishers Weekly*

"Dugoni has produced one of his most shocking twists yet and Tracy, expertly developed over seven previous novels, is almost pared down here, in a refreshing, perspective-changing way."

—Bookreporter

Praise for *A Cold Trail*

"Tracy Crosswhite is one of the best protagonists in the realm of crime fiction today, and there is nothing cold about *A Cold Trail*."

—Associated Press

"Crime writing of the absolute highest order, illustrating that Dugoni is every bit the equal of Lisa Gardner and Harlan Coben when it comes to psychological suspense."

—*Providence Journal*

Praise for *A Steep Price*

"A beautiful narrative. What makes *A Steep Price* stand out is the authentic feel of how it feels to work as a police officer in a major city . . . another outstanding novel from one of the best crime writers in the business."

—Associated Press

"A riveting suspense novel . . . A gripping story."

—*Crimespree Magazine*

Praise for *Close To Home*

"An immensely—almost compulsively—readable tale . . . A crackerjack mystery."

—*Booklist* (starred review)

"Dugoni's twisted tale is one of conspiracy and culpability . . . richly nuanced and entirely compelling."

—Criminal Element

Praise for *The Trapped Girl*

"Robert Dugoni, yet again, delivers an excellent read . . . With many twists, turns, and jumps in the road traveled by the detective and her cohorts, this absolutely superb plot becomes more than just a little entertaining. The problem remains the same: Readers must now once again wait impatiently for the next book by Robert Dugoni to arrive."

—*Suspense Magazine*

Praise for *In the Clearing*

"Dugoni's third Tracy Crosswhite novel (after *Her Final Breath*) continues his series' standard of excellence with superb plotting and skillful balancing of the two story lines."

—*Library Journal* (starred review)

"Dugoni has become one of the best crime novelists in the business, and his latest featuring Seattle homicide detective Tracy Crosswhite will only draw more accolades."

—*Romantic Times*, top pick

Praise for *Her Final Breath*

"Absorbing . . . Dugoni expertly ratchets up the suspense as Crosswhite becomes a target herself."

—*Seattle Times*

"Another stellar story featuring homicide detective Tracy Crosswhite . . . Crosswhite is a sympathetic, well-drawn protagonist, and her next adventure can't come fast enough."

—*Library Journal* (starred review)

Praise for *My Sister's Grave*

"One of the best books I'll read this year."

—Lisa Gardner, bestselling author of *Touch & Go*

"Dugoni does a superior job of positioning [the plot elements] for maximum impact, especially in a climactic scene set in an abandoned mine during a blizzard."

—*Publishers Weekly*

"Combines the best of a police procedural with a legal thriller, and the end result is outstanding . . . Dugoni continues to deliver emotional and gut-wrenching, character-driven suspense stories that will resonate with any fan of the thriller genre."

—*Library Journal* (starred review)

A
DEAD
DRAW

ALSO BY ROBERT DUGONI

Hold Strong (with Jeff Langholz and Chris Crabtree)
The World Played Chess
The Extraordinary Life of Sam Hell
The 7th Canon
Damage Control

The Tracy Crosswhite Series

My Sister's Grave
Her Final Breath
In the Clearing
The Trapped Girl
Close to Home
A Steep Price
A Cold Trail
In Her Tracks
What She Found
One Last Kill
The Last Line (a short story)
The Academy (a short story)
Third Watch (a short story)

The Keera Duggan Series

Her Deadly Game
Beyond Reasonable Doubt

The Charles Jenkins Series

The Eighth Sister
The Last Agent
The Silent Sisters

The David Sloane Series

The Jury Master
Wrongful Death
Bodily Harm
Murder One
The Conviction

Nonfiction with Joseph Hilldorfer

The Cyanide Canary

A
DEAD
DRAW

ROBERT
DUGONI

THOMAS & MERCER

Text copyright © 2025 by La Mesa Fiction LLC
All rights reserved.

No part of this book may be reproduced, or stored in a retrieval system, or transmitted in any form or by any means, electronic, mechanical, photocopying, recording, or otherwise, without express written permission of the publisher.

Published by Thomas & Mercer, Seattle

www.apub.com

Amazon, the Amazon logo, and Thomas & Mercer are trademarks of Amazon.com, Inc., or its affiliates.

EU product safety contact:
Amazon Media EU S. à r.l.
38, avenue John F. Kennedy, L-1855 Luxembourg
amazonpublishing-gpsr@amazon.com

ISBN-13: 9781662524738 (paperback)
ISBN-13: 9781662524745 (digital)

Cover design by Damon Freeman
Cover image: © Cynthia Liang, © Kriengsuk Prasroetsung,
© Pikoso.kz / Shutterstock

Printed in the United States of America

To my father, William Dugoni, who instilled in me a love of old movies, including spaghetti Westerns and just about any other movie with Clint Eastwood or John Wayne.

Man is the cruelest animal.

—Friedrich Nietzsche, *Thus Spoke Zarathustra*

PROLOGUE

Seattle, Washington
Three Months Ago

If Erik Schmidt was worried, he didn't show it; not that Seattle detective Tracy Crosswhite could tell. Then again, Schmidt didn't know what was to come.

Crosswhite and Kinsington Rowe, her former partner on the Violent Crimes team, observed Schmidt from behind one-way glass in a room adjacent to the hard interrogation room on the seventh floor of Police Headquarters in downtown Seattle. With the door shut and the bright fluorescent lights radiating in the cramped, windowless interrogation room, the walls closed in quickly on a suspect, as could the thought of spending years in a room just like it.

Schmidt, however, looked like a man sleeping—eyes shut, head tilted back, blond hair falling to his shoulders, chest rhythmically rising and falling.

"Looks like a surfer, meditating," Rowe said as Tracy flipped through Schmidt's thick criminal file.

"Is he?" Tracy asked.

"Meditating?"

"A surfer."

"Not unless there's an inland ocean we don't know about." Kins explained that Schmidt had been born and raised in Springfield, Illinois. Kins sipped coffee from a porcelain mug, a Christmas gift from one of his now-grown sons. The mug was inscribed with the words "World's Greatest Farter!" The last word was corrected to say *"Father!"* "You want me to come in with you?" he asked. "Or watch from here?"

"Let me talk to him alone." Many male suspects would talk to Tracy before they'd talk to a male detective. A macho thing. "You can be the bad cop if we need it."

"I do like being the bad cop," Kins said and took another sip from his mug.

Tracy left the room. A moment later she pulled open the door to the hard interrogation room, crossed to the opposite side of the table, and sat in the chair across from Schmidt. His handcuffed wrists connected to a belly chain at his waist that continued to an eyebolt screwed to the floor. The furniture was similarly secured.

Schmidt exhaled forcefully, then opened his eyes, a piercing cobalt blue. His lips inched into a grin. "Tracy Crosswhite," he said, voice soft and deep. "Three-time Medal of Valor recipient and hottest detective on the Violent Crimes team. I'm honored."

Tracy and Schmidt had never met nor spoken.

"I don't work Violent Crimes anymore, Erik. I work Cold Cases."

"Erik." His grin widened. "First-name basis, Detective Tracy? I like that."

She shrugged. "Whatever you prefer."

"Erik is just fine." He looked around the room. "I assume your . . . *former* partner put me in here to make me nervous about spending time like this in a jail cell." He spoke to the mirrored glass. "Been there. Done that." Schmidt had spent a decade behind bars at the Walla Walla state penitentiary for drug possession and distribution. He redirected his attention to Tracy. "I actually enjoyed my time at Walla Walla."

"Did you?" Tracy said.

"You get a lot of 'me' time in prison. I took up yoga, meditation, tai chi." Schmidt, a shade over six foot two, appeared lean and muscular. "One learns a lot about oneself when one spends time alone—if one applies himself."

"Well, I'm glad you enjoyed it. You're looking at spending a lot more time there."

"How do you figure?" he asked, still grinning.

"I'm working on two murder cases, Julia Hoch and Bridgette Traugott." She'd inherited the cases from Art Nunzio, the Cold Case detective who had preceded her in that unit.

"Nice gals."

Hoch and Traugott had each been shot in the head in separate instances. With no physical evidence but the bullets, and no eyewitnesses, the two murders had sat dormant in Violent Crimes until Detective Moss Gunderson retired. Then the files were shipped to Cold Cases, seemingly for the duration.

Tracy wasn't surprised by the admission. Schmidt's file indicated he'd also made the same admission to Nunzio. "You admit you knew both women?"

"Of course. But you already know that. A detective came out to talk to me when I was at Walla Walla. Art something . . . I'm sure he made notes in a file somewhere. I've been down this road before, Detective Tracy."

"Go down it with me."

"Long time ago."

"When was the last time you saw either woman?"

He smiled again. "Are you interrogating me, Detective Tracy?" Something about his use of her first name made her skin crawl. "Rushing to ask me questions while I sit here on another manufactured drug charge before I've had the chance to call my attorney. You do know Bernard Gil is my attorney; right?"

"Never had the pleasure."

But Tracy knew of Gil. Everyone at SPD, and in the prosecutor's office, knew Gil, a highly successful and equally despised criminal defense lawyer who got good results for his clients, often by bending the rules, sometimes until those rules snapped.

"I'm sure the pleasure will be his, as it is mine." This time Schmidt ran the tip of his tongue over his lips.

Tracy had seen and heard just about every sexual innuendo, gesture, and crude joke, but something about Schmidt continued to make her itchy. "What do you remember about the last time you saw either woman?"

"I can't recall the details, I'm afraid. I was pretty torn up about the breakups."

"How torn up?"

"How does one measure a broken heart?" Schmidt never shifted his gaze from Tracy's face. "I loved those girls to death," he said. "'This world breaks everyone, and afterward, some are strong at the broken places.'"

"You just make that up?"

"*That* was the esteemed Ernest Hemingway in *A Farewell to Arms*. It means: What doesn't kill you makes you stronger. I also had a lot of time to read in the prison library." He shifted in his chair. "My turn. Why is a decorated homicide detective asking me about women I once dated, when I'm sitting in here on suspect drug charges?"

"Good question. The thing is, Erik, sometimes we detectives just get lucky."

"Do tell."

She sat back, crossed her legs. "The thing about a fired bullet, Erik, is it is as distinct to a particular gun as a fingerprint is to a person."

"Is it now?"

"And we have your gun."

"I was curious about Detective Rowe's charade, storming my home at three in the morning."

"Curious?"

"The basis for his entering my abode. I'm not a criminal defense lawyer, but I do believe a detective must demonstrate probable cause to a judge to justify a search warrant on a law-abiding citizen's home." He opened his palms and lifted his arms from his lap as far as the chain would allow. "A man's house is, after all, '*his castle and fortress.*' Sir Edward Coke."

"You really did spend time improving yourself."

"The prison library has a wealth of knowledge."

"So, guess who owns the gun we matched to the bullets that killed Julia Hoch and Bridgette Traugott, Erik?"

Schmidt paused for just a moment. *Got you,* Tracy thought.

"Well, I don't think we'd be sitting here having this conversation if they didn't match to the gun Detective Rowe took from my house this morning; would we?"

"Not likely."

Schmidt sat up and leaned forward. His voice hardened. "Which raises the question previously postulated." He turned his head and glared at the one-way glass. "What probable cause did Detective Tough Guy have to search my home and take the gun? Why would he assume it was *my* gun and invade the sanctity of *my* home while I slept?"

Tracy waited until Schmidt turned back. Tracy shrugged. "I'm not here to talk about those details."

"No?"

"I'm here to determine if you want to talk to me about Julia Hoch and Bridgette Traugott."

"I told you. Past history. Talk to my lawyer."

It was clear Tracy wasn't going to get anywhere. She stood. "If you change your mind, Erik, and suddenly remember something more, have your lawyer call me. You're going to be looking at two counts of murder one, and forever is a very long time. You show some compassion to the families of the victims and, maybe, I can get the prosecutor to go easy on you at sentencing."

"We're already at sentencing? I think we have a long way to go before we get to sentencing."

"We'll see." She started for the door.

"Do you know what else one can do in the prison library during the hours of tedium reshelving and pulling books?" Schmidt said. "One can make himself a good friend."

"Can he?" Tracy said. She stopped at the door and looked back. "Well, I guess you'll have that to look forward to when you return."

"I'm afraid not," he said. "Ed's dead."

Tracy felt a cold shiver run up and down her body.

Schmidt turned his head, a hard stare, this time without the grin. "Surely you remember Edmund House?"

Tracy felt her face flush at the mention of the man who nearly thirty years earlier had killed her sister, Sarah, and subsequently had tried to kill Tracy.

"Oooh," Schmidt cooed. "You do remember. I can see just the thought of Ed still makes you hot."

Walk out. Leave. He's goading you.

Schmidt faced away from her. "Ed never stopped talking about *you*—like a freight train rolling down tracks when he got going on the subject of Detective Tracy. And then . . . you came to see him. Imagine that. Ed came back to the library from the visitors center that day and said it was an honest-to-God miracle; you, a homicide detective, believing him innocent and determined to get him a new trial." Schmidt laughed and it sounded like Edmund House's laugh.

Against the advice of the voice in her head telling her to leave the room, Tracy walked back to Schmidt, placed her hands flat on the metal table, and leaned down. Too close. She could smell the acidic odor of his breath and the sharp, sour smell of his perspiration. She'd smelled that same foul odor on House, in the mine shaft above Cedar Grove, just before she'd killed him. "The only thing Edmund House got was a grave. And I put him there."

"Oh, I know that too," Schmidt said softly. "I know that too well."

Leave. The voice continued to urge her.

She straightened and again moved to the door.

"Ed hoped you would be a better lay than your sister; Sarah, was it?"

Tracy saw red. Waves crashed in her head, the sound deafening. Schmidt's voice came as if from down a long tunnel. "He said you were the one he wanted all along, but your sister was a feisty one."

Tracy had her hands around Schmidt's throat. He'd gripped her wrists and pulled her down close, laughing now, mocking her. She felt and heard Kins enter the room, struggling to pry them apart, succeeding, then hurrying her out the door and back to the adjacent room.

Schmidt cackled through the speakers as the door slammed shut. "I guess you're both feisty, Detective Tracy."

Kins shut off the speaker. "Are you all right? Tracy? Hey?"

She stopped pacing and looked at him, breathing heavily, her adrenaline pulsing through her body.

"Shit," she said, then swore repeatedly while chastising herself for letting Schmidt get to her. "I'm sorry, Kins."

"Don't be. He's an asshole. And you couldn't have known." He, too, swore. "Neither of us knew."

She sucked in air, as if she was drowning.

"I thought you said I'd be the bad cop." Kins chuckled, but it was, she knew, nerves.

She looked back through the glass. Schmidt grinned at the window, then shifted his gaze to where the camera was mounted in the corner of the interrogation room. Though the speaker was off, she heard what he said.

"Gonna make for great theater, Detective Tracy."

CHAPTER 1

The Present

Tracy gave up trying to fall back to sleep and got out of bed, walking across her darkened bedroom to her walk-in closet. She slid the door closed before she turned on the light, so as not to further disturb Dan. Her husband had been busy at work with mediations, arbitrations, and trial preparation—sleep at a premium, and he wouldn't be thrilled with being awakened at four in the morning, again.

She pulled off her damp shirt and tossed it into the laundry basket with the half dozen others from this week. She'd have to do the wash. She slid on padded bike pants and a sports bra. Her bike shoes were downstairs in the workout room with the Peloton bicycle.

Her night sweats were a product of her night terrors, which started shortly after her confrontation with Erik Schmidt in the hard interrogation room at SPD headquarters three months ago. She had initially tried to work through the terrors, but being awakened at four every morning and unable to get back to sleep took its toll on being a good mother, spouse, and detective, especially when Daniella, their almost-four-year-old daughter, was cranky. Tracy got tired of being tired and called her counselor, Lisa Walsh. She'd first seen Walsh after a childhood friend shot herself in Tracy's presence. Walsh had diagnosed her with situational PTSD and anxiety—with occasional panic attacks. She explained then that Tracy's PTSD was deeply rooted in guilt she felt after Edmund House's abduction and murder of her sister, Sarah, in 1993, and her father's subsequent related suicide. Her own confrontation with House during the winter of 2014, when Tracy had nearly died, had exacerbated those issues.

During months of therapy, Tracy had learned to meditate, worked out rigorously, and used other anxiety-reducing techniques like box breathing and counting. Gradually, she had returned to feeling "normal" or at least like her old self, though Walsh had warned Tracy that she'd never be "cured."

Walsh had apparently been correct, as this morning and the preceding others so precisely illustrated.

And that thought depressed her.

She hated succumbing to the anxiety, because it made her feel mentally weak. Walsh had tried to allay those concerns during their sessions. "It's your mental toughness that has allowed you to better control your situation this time," she'd said.

"It's embarrassing," Tracy had replied. "It's hard enough to do this job. I can't break down in tears because I spilled my coffee."

"Did you break down in tears because you spilled your coffee?" Walsh had asked.

"You know what I mean," Tracy had said.

"Tracy, everyone is dealing with something. None of us are immune. Some people just do a better job masking their issues. You'd be surprised at the number of police officers I see on a regular basis." Tracy wouldn't be. She knew the job stresses, more amplified now than ever before. "As well as the many high-level, successful professionals who seek my help,"

Walsh continued. "To seek help does not mean you . . . or they . . . are weak. It takes courage to admit you need help, and strength to then seek it. In other words, you're 'normal.'"

Maybe.

She put on a sweatshirt, turned off the light, and slid open the closet door.

"Was wondering how long you were going to stay in there," Dan said from the darkness. "You have another episode?"

"Don't use that word. It sounds like I'm losing my mind."

"I didn't mean it that way."

"I know."

"Did you have another nightmare?"

"Yes," she said, not elaborating.

"Could you recall it?"

"Not really." She could. It was a version of the same nightmare. She'd seen Edmund House in her prior night terrors, but now House became Erik Schmidt, sitting in the hard interrogation room, laughing at her. Baiting her. Two psychos for the price of one. Lucky her.

"Did you try writing it down when you got up?" Dan asked, which had been another of Lisa Walsh's suggestions.

She didn't want to get into it. "It was too late. I didn't remember it."

"What are you doing now?"

"Thought I'd ride the bike."

"It's four fifteen in the morning."

"I am aware," she said. She sighed. No need to take it out on Dan. "Hoping the exercise will exhaust me, and I can catch a couple more hours sleep before the shoot this morning."

"Thought the shooting test was last week."

"That was the qualification test."

"What's this?"

"Something new the brass wants to introduce every few years, and the Guild agreed to."

Each year, SPD officers and detectives were required to pass a firearms test using their duty weapons. This year the brass added a "shoot or no shoot" course. The intent was to reduce officer-involved shootings through practical exercises, but a fine line existed between slowing an officer's deadly force decision to give her sufficient time to correctly assess the threat and slowing it so much it got her killed.

"How's it differ?"

"The targets don't move in the qualification test. In this course they do."

"My wife—the badass."

"Go back to sleep. You're delusional."

"I'll be dreaming of Tracy Crossdraw." She had used that name in her teens when competing in Cowboy Action Shooting competitions. "Wearing her chaps and cowboy boots, her six-guns resting on her hips."

She waited until it was clear Dan wasn't going to continue dressing her. "You're delusional and horny."

"I'm a guy."

In their workout room, Tracy put on her bike shoes, clipped in, and picked a forty-five-minute workout. Her Peloton instructor wasted no time getting her heart rate elevated, urging her and the rest of the class from their bike seats for a three-minute climb at maximum effort. Tracy lifted her water bottle, squeezed a stream into her mouth, and pushed through the pain and her stress. The annual qualification test was never stress free, especially for bad shooters and aging officers with worsening eyesight. This morning, tensions would be heightened for all the officers. The shoot/no-shoot course was an unknown. They'd been told only that it would consist of one hour in the classroom and three hours on a course designed by their training coordinator, "Crazy Joe" Mazy. Mazy had studied at the FBI Academy near Quantico, Virginia, where an FBI agent first built a tactical, urban training city known as Hogan's Alley. The city consisted of a bank, hotel, pool hall, homes, and other businesses and shops. The training was designed to simulate real-life circumstances officers might encounter—active shooters, hostage situations, domestic violence calls, and other dangerous scenarios.

In Seattle, Mazy had created his own versions of Hogan's Alley. While Seattle didn't have the budget to build a city, Mazy could be creative. He designed alleyways using black plastic attached to two-by-fours. Officers progressed through the alleys, stopping to shoot around, over, and under obstacles. Along the way, the officer might encounter "pop-out" or "pop-up" targets on mechanical arms or ambiguously dressed dummies. The officer needed to quickly assess the target as a lethal threat—one holding a gun, knife, or other weapon—or benign, such as a person holding a cell phone, wallet, radio, small child, or some such thing.

Tracy had never failed a shooting test of any kind. She'd grown up in a shooting family. Her father, a doctor and student of the Old West, had enrolled her and her sister, Sarah, in Single Action Shooting Society competitions in their teens. They learned to shoot revolvers, lever-action rifles, and period shotguns at metal targets in reenactments of infamous Wild West shootouts.

It had been a bucolic childhood—until Edmund House came to town, Sarah disappeared, and no one and nothing was ever the same.

CHAPTER 2

The weather wasn't cooperating, which wasn't unusual during spring in Seattle. After the gray, damp fall and winter months, Seattleites ready for sunshine could be bitterly disappointed when spring rain came instead of spring sunshine. They called June "Junuary." The gray dampness this particular morning added to Tracy's gloomy mood after having another aborted night of sleep.

She entered the Seattle Police Athletic Association's range office and saw the anxious faces of officers waiting to take the qualification exam this morning. Shooting in dry conditions could be difficult for some; shooting in a cold rain was difficult for all. But Tracy had been taught to train in a way that replicated whatever variables she might encounter. She'd shot in rain, sleet, even snow, weather so cold she could hardly feel her fingers. She'd learned to mentally block out the conditions she couldn't control and to focus on the variables she could.

Some of the officers inside the cramped, squat, concrete building tried to disguise their nerves with gallows humor, conversation about the Mariners' chances this season or their golf games, and by dishing out jabs and ribbing. But Tracy had assessed enough competitors over the years to know their tells when they were anxious.

Tracy spoke over the din. "I was hoping for snow today."

The others laughed, then let her have it. She took their ribbing, hoping it might loosen some of them up. Being atop the shooting pyramid for twenty years didn't mean much to her anymore, but it did to others, especially the female officers, who believed Tracy's notoriety gave them greater credibility among their male colleagues. She spotted a shooting protégé, Katie Pryor, in a corner of the room pretending to sip coffee from a paper cup. Working in the two-person Missing Persons Unit, Pryor didn't have much officer camaraderie. Tracy approached with a nod to the cup. "Decaffeinated, I hope?"

Pryor managed to smile. "I'm nervous enough as it is," she said in a soft voice. "What brings you out? You already qualified."

"Crazy Joe's shoot/no-shoot course. I need to grab some ammo."

Years ago, Pryor had sought Tracy's help after failing to achieve 75 percent on her qualification test and getting sent back to remedial training. Pryor's problem was not uncommon. She flinched as she pulled the trigger, which lowered the front sight of her gun barrel. Tracy had helped her break the connection between her brain and flinching by having her state out loud, as she shot, "Front sight. Squeeze."

"You've been putting in the time?"

"Twice a month," Pryor said.

"Then you'll do fine. Remember, get your shooting hand as high up on the grip as possible, but don't hold it too tight. No white knuckles. Breathe to help you relax. Squeeze the trigger with the pad of your finger. Don't get too much finger into the trigger or you'll pull the shot. Be deliberate. You'll think you're going too slow, but with all your adrenaline, you'll be going faster than it feels. Slow is smooth. And smooth is fast. You can't miss fast enough to win a gunfight."

"Thanks, Tracy. And good luck to you as well."

Tracy made her way to the counter. Ordinarily, ammunition was provided after the armorer inspected each qualifier's gun, but today her gun would be checked at the rifle range where Mazy had set up the decision-making course. Virgil greeted Tracy with a smile from behind the counter and handed her a box of .40 S&W ammo without her asking.

"First group," Virgil said. "I heard Crazy Joe put together something good for you all, especially in this weather."

When she had competed in Cowboy Action Shooting tournaments, Tracy had rolled her own ammunition, at her father's tutelage. Doc Crosswhite believed in being authentic to the Old West. Ammo was also expensive—especially given the number of rounds the family shot practicing and competing. But her father's primary reason for reusing brass casings and bullets was specificity. By putting a precise amount of gunpowder in each cartridge, he ensured consistent muzzle velocity, thereby optimizing accuracy, reducing recoil, and increasing shot-to-shot speed.

Tracy stepped outside and raised the hood on her jacket against the rain. It had increased in intensity, and the wind had also picked up. Variables beyond her control. As she drove to Rifle Range #1, the retort of pistols mixed with the familiar barking of dogs in the nearby SPD K-9 kennel. She parked and entered the building at the front of the rifle range, greeting officers and detectives seated at tables or milling about, drinking coffee. A cadre of training instructors stood at the front of the room—including John Sievers, their range master that morning.

While the officers' shooting scores were not officially ranked, a quick visual survey revealed those testing were, historically, the best shooters in the department. It had to be purposeful, to increase tension, perhaps. The officers present in the room included her Violent Crimes captain, Johnny Nolasco, who sat at the table closest to the front. Tracy took a seat at the table at the back.

Sievers gathered their attention and went through updates for use of force standards, recent legal cases decided and their ramifications, and other important legal precedents. He touched upon pending cases within SPD and police departments around the nation. As always, he discussed safety protocol and the four rules of shooting. *Every gun is loaded. Never point a gun at anything you're not willing to destroy. Finger off the trigger until your sights are on target and you've made the decision to shoot. Identify your target* and *what is beyond your target.* When Sievers had finished, he turned the class over to Joe Mazy.

Mazy looked like a 1960s NASA engineer in black-framed glasses, a crew cut, and a short-sleeve white shirt with an honest-to-God pocket protector.

"What I've tried to simulate for you today is a real-life scenario you might encounter, though hopefully not. I'm going to throw a few wrinkles at you to test how you respond. Remember, you will not be timed during this exercise. We want you to move deliberately and fluidly. Do not rush, but do not belabor your assessments. At the end of your session, you must defend and justify your decisions to your firearms instructor."

The firearms instructor would follow each shooter through the course to ensure the officer did not break the 180 and shoot in any direction but downrange.

"You will remain in the classroom with the blinds lowered. No one sees the shoot course or knows what to expect, just as in real life. After you finish, you will move to a covered area to be debriefed, then watch your fellow officers. You can learn from observing, as well as shooting.

"This combat shoot is the longest I've ever constructed." Mazy smiled. "Yes, I am proud of it. I used every bit of the one-hundred-yard range. You will start in a patrol car, as if arriving upon a scene. Only then will you be given further information. Any questions?" Mazy gave a mischievous smile. "I hope you enjoy it."

Sievers held up a clipboard. "The order of shooters has been chosen randomly. First up, Captain Johnny Nolasco. I'll put this clipboard on the wall so the rest of you can prepare as your turn approaches."

Tracy looked at the list. She'd be twelfth. The intensity in the room picked up as each officer left. Those remaining heard multiple rounds being fired. Tracy counted forty-two rounds when Nolasco shot, and as many as fifty for other officers. That meant the combat shoot included knock-down targets, possibly a dueling tree—steel plates on a swivel arm officers shot to swivel the plate from one side to the other. She also heard long-range rifle shots.

Varying distances, difficult angles, as well as moving targets made combat shoots challenging. In Cowboy Action Shooting competitions, the targets were metal, stationary, and usually within ten to twelve feet. Speed took priority over precise accuracy; you weren't penalized if your shot was not in the center-of-mass zone. During police quals, the paper targets outlined center-of-mass zones, and the shooting distances were as far as seventy-five feet.

As Tracy's turn approached, she prepared physically and mentally. She'd worn jeans and thick-soled police boots, slid on an SPD baseball hat and pulled her ponytail through the back, then slipped on a light rain jacket over her Tru-Spec Level 2 body-armor T-shirt. Last, she put on her outer vest with a MOLLE system to carry extra magazines, a radio, handcuffs, a CAT 7 tourniquet, and a Spyderco Endela folding knife.

Again, train as if it's the real deal.

Sievers handed her three loaded Glock 23 thirteen-round magazines when her name was called. She slid on shooting glasses, inserted earplugs *and* noise-cancelling earmuffs that allowed for conversation but cancelled out noises over a certain decibel, like gunshots. She stepped outside. The weather had not improved with time. The clouds were ominously dark, and though the rain had lessened, it now slanted sideways in the strong wind.

After exchanging pleasantries, Sievers said, "You ready?"

"Ready," Tracy said, confident.

"Load and make ready."

Tracy unholstered her Glock 23 duty pistol, locked the slide back, and loaded one of the spare mags into the mag well. She slingshotted the slide forward and press checked to make sure the round had seated in the chamber. She then reholstered the Glock in her Safariland Level II holster and rotated the secondary retention/safety hood in place.

"All right. Get seated in the patrol car." Tracy did so. "Here's your scenario."

Over the car's radio, dispatch reported multiple shots fired in a neighborhood, possible casualties, a possible hostage situation. Dispatch reported two officers on scene, but dispatch had lost radio contact with the officers, and the shooter or shooters were unaccounted for. It was a "help the officer" call, meaning all available officers were to drop what they were doing and immediately respond. There was no waiting around for backup.

Tracy stepped from the car and deliberately approached a second patrol car parked perpendicular to Hogan's Alley, the driver's door open. A dummy in a police uniform lay on the ground. Suspecting an ambush, Tracy used the apex of the car and the open door as cover to conduct a quick scan and saw what she had suspected, a paper target—a bad guy with a gun. Shoot. She squeezed two center-of-mass shots. About to step around the car, she saw two metal pepper-popper knockdown targets low to the ground. Bad guys. Shoot. She dropped to the wet ground, aimed in a prone position from beneath the patrol car, and fired three shots to knock down the two targets. She rose to a kneeling position, quickly scanned in a 360, and conducted a tactical reload to bring her Glock back up to full-ammo capacity. She placed the partially expended magazine in her cargo pocket in case she needed the rounds later in the fight.

She got to her feet and moved forward to the first blind alley, her Glock held firmly in an isosceles stance, which allowed her to smoothly traverse left and right, like a tank turret. She stepped deliberately down the narrow corridor. The black tarps flapped and rustled in the strong wind. Raindrops on her shooting glasses obscured her vision, but removing them would be grounds for an immediate disqualification. The visor of her ball cap helped divert the rain.

Weather was a variable to deal with, not to control.

She stepped around a corner, encountered another bad guy holding a pistol to the head of and using the hostage as a shield. Shoot. She put one round in his forehead, swiveled down the alley, and encountered a dummy with a hoodie pulled over his head. She quickly scanned his hands, saw a shiny object in one of them. Cell phone. No shoot.

She stepped past him.

She felt the adrenaline rush, like when a runner's high kicked in, and took slow, deliberate breaths. A failure to breathe caused hands and arms to shake from a lack of oxygen. She turned another corner. Another dummy. This one wore body armor and held a pistol-caliber carbine. Shoot.

She heard a click. No bang. The loudest sound a police officer heard was a "click" when she expected a "bang."

Malfunction drill.

Sievers had put a dummy round in her magazine with the live ammo.

She slid back behind the barricade for cover, slapped the bottom of the magazine hard against the heel of her hand, racked the slide to clear the dummy round from the chamber, and loaded a live round from the magazine. She turned the corner a second time and fired at the dummy. Center-of-mass shots. One to the head. Two to the chest.

She moved forward, down another narrow alley, head swiveling left and right, her Glock sights fixed wherever she gazed. The rush of blood echoed in her muffs along with the sound of the rippling canvas. Rain blew across her field of vision. She turned another corner.

A target popped out from behind the barricade—a Crazy Joe specialty. This man held a Glock pistol with a thirty-three-round extended magazine. Shoot. She smoothly and rapidly squeezed the trigger three times, two to the body and one to the forehead. She performed another tactical reload behind cover, then took two deep breaths to oxygenate her blood and steady her arms.

She stepped forward.

Another figure flipped into her view down the alley. A woman. Unarmed. No shoot.

She stepped past.

A third target, a man with a scruffy beard, large muscles. Something in his hand. Tracy nearly pulled the trigger. A plastic water bottle. No shoot.

She kept her trigger finger indexed along the slide of the Glock and moved again.

Target four popped up from the ground. He held a small Smith & Wesson J-Frame revolver. Shoot. Body. Body. Head.

Water dripped from the brim of her soaked hat. She shook her head to clear her vision, rocked her elbow to her side, ejected the magazine onto the ground, grabbed her emergency spare mag from her vest, and slapped it hard into the grip.

The rush of blood in her ears grew louder.

Another dummy.

A light burst, as in her nightmares.

Edmund House held a gun, but the barrel aimed to Tracy's left. She turned. Sarah. Just eighteen. Captive. Ratty clothes. Hair unkempt. Face covered in dirt.

Her adrenaline spiked.

She felt dizzy. Disoriented. Off-balance.

Breathe. Breathe! Tracy squinted hard, shook the vision.

House evaporated.

A man in blue jeans and a white T-shirt. Unarmed. No shoot. She moved.

Target six. Another flash of light.

Erik Schmidt in his chair. Laughing. He raised a gun.

Too slow. Too far behind in the OODA—observe, orient, decide, act. She didn't raise the barrel in time.

Schmidt pulled the trigger.

"No!" Tracy's Glock spit casings, one after the next, after the next . . . and the next, until her slide locked back on an empty chamber.

Her instructor's voice came as if echoing down a tunnel. Tracy ripped off her muffs. Her instructor shouted. "Unload and show clear, Detective. Unload and show clear. End ex! End ex! The exercise is over."

Tracy dropped her arms to the low-ready position, unsure what had just happened, but confident it had not been good. She looked at her Glock and saw that she had shot to slide lock. She ejected the empty mag from the grip, showed Sievers the chamber was empty, dropped the slide, and reholstered her now-empty pistol.

The rain fell in sheets. The plastic tarps sucked in and billowed out, like sails on a ship during a storm. In front of her, hanging on a wooden arm, was a target riddled with fourteen .40 caliber holes. She stepped closer.

A man. Unarmed.

Not a bad guy.

No shoot.

CHAPTER 3

A fog lifted. Her vision cleared, as did her mind. Realization hit hard.

She'd shot an unarmed target.

An innocent civilian who held a walkie-talkie.

Her instructor, perhaps more shaken and shocked than Tracy, looked pale. He asked if she was all right. She wasn't, not completely.

"What just happened? Justify your shots."

She couldn't. She couldn't tell him she saw Edmund House then Erik Schmidt. "I . . . I saw a gun." It might explain why she had fired but certainly not why she'd emptied her magazine.

She and her instructor exchanged uneasy glances, uncertain body language. He spoke into his radio. Within seconds, Sievers arrived, along with Joe Mazy, to discuss what to do. Tracy had not completed the shoot. They, too, considered the target, riddled with holes when there should have been none. Sievers addressed the instructor. "What happened?"

The instructor shook his head. He didn't know.

Mazy said to Tracy, "What did you see?"

"I saw a lethal threat. In the dark . . . the rain . . . I thought it was a gun, not a radio."

"Why did you fire to slide lock?" Sievers asked. It was a legitimate question.

Tracy didn't have an answer. "I don't know."

"It's your job to know—for each and every shot you fire," Sievers said.

She nodded. "I know."

An uneasy silence ensued.

"Why don't you take a break?" Sievers nodded to the officers who had completed the course and now stood beneath a pop-up tent watching her with morbid curiosity, Johnny Nolasco among them.

"I don't . . ."

"I've seen this before," Mazy said. "We all know your shooting abilities, Detective. Take a break. We can slot you in at the end of the day. Give you time to clear your mind."

She nodded, but her mind and body felt numb. Mazy continued to speak. She wasn't clearly processing what he had to say. She'd seen Edmund House. She'd seen Erik Schmidt. She'd seen Sarah.

But they hadn't been there.

Sarah was dead. Tracy had seen her bones unearthed in the mountains above Cedar Grove. She'd put House in a grave. And Schmidt remained incarcerated in the King County Jail, arraigned for the murders of Julia Hoch and Bridgette Traugott. He was going to prison for the rest of his life.

"I know what you're thinking," Sievers said. He didn't. "I've been there. We've all been there." No. They hadn't been. "Let it go. Don't let it get inside your head. Come back fresh."

Tracy turned for the tent. Her colleagues fixed on her as she walked past. She didn't stop beneath the canvas with the others. She didn't want to talk about what had happened. She hit the gate in the cyclone fence.

When she reached her Subaru she climbed inside, started the engine. Classical music filled the car. Her father had taught her to listen to the scores before competitions, to feel the tempo, how the notes did not rush to a crescendo but built gradually. He taught her to similarly let the shooting scenario naturally build to its crescendo, to the moment requiring her peak performance, then to allow the decrescendo, the gradual decrease in intensity and tempo to the end. Then and only then should she assess and evaluate how she had done—to judge whether she could have done better—never *during* the competition, when she needed to be singularly focused.

She turned off the music. The rain pattered hard on the roof of her car. The curtain of gray hung over the industrial buildings as if smothering them. Tendrils reached down from the dark sky like ghostly fingers.

She backed her car from the parking space, windshield wipers slapping, and drove down the narrow road. It would have been surprising had Tracy missed one of her shots, though it did happen, even to her. No one was perfect. She could rationalize and make excuses for such an occurrence. She was getting older. Reflexes slowed. Eyesight worsened. Age and priorities required changes. It happened to her father. He had two daughters to raise, to devote his time to, along with his wife and his medical practice. He no longer had the time to practice shooting the way he once had. What time he did have, he devoted to Tracy's and Sarah's shooting, until they'd surpassed him.

Tracy, too, was no longer the young woman she'd once been. Her eyesight, once 20/10, had slipped to a mere mortal 20/20. She felt her aches and pains getting out of bed in the morning, her back stiff. Her hands could no longer loosen the lid on some jars. She could no longer do as many push-ups, sit-ups, or pull-ups as she'd done as a young woman. Pregnancy had added stubborn pounds. Her six-pack stomach had vanished.

And she'd been all right with that.

Because she, too, had different priorities. She had a husband and a child. She would not sacrifice them to practice her shooting—to feed her ego.

She would have shrugged off an imperfect shoot.

She would have been happy to pass her crown to a younger officer, maybe another woman.

But this was different.

She hadn't just missed a shot.

She hadn't just failed to achieve a perfect score.

She'd been disqualified.

But it was worse than that.

So much worse.

Tracy knew from the look in her instructor's eyes how utterly horrific it had been. She couldn't hide it from them—or her colleagues. Crazy Joe Mazy said he'd seen it happen before, but his eyes betrayed his words. It wasn't just the shooting of an unarmed civilian. It was the violence Tracy had inflicted, the number of kill shots—limited only by the magazine's capacity. She hadn't neutralized a threat.

She'd obliterated an innocent civilian.

And she had no rational reason for having done so.

———

She parked in the secure lot on the sixth floor and crossed to Police Headquarters downtown, entering the seventh floor. The familiar murmur of detectives' voices mixed with the television news. The smells, too, were the same—coffee, microwaved popcorn. Everything remained the same.

Except it wasn't.

She'd contemplated going home. But what then? Daniella would be in preschool. Therese, their nanny, would be working at the art gallery—flexible hours so she could pick up and care for Daniella until Tracy or Dan returned home. Dan was in Kent, handling a domestic violence case. She didn't want to sit at home alone thinking about the morning. Work had always been her refuge.

She slipped into her office, closed the door, and leaned her head against the wood, eyes closed. She inhaled and exhaled deeply. Box breathing. Four seconds in. Hold four seconds. Release four seconds. Hold four seconds. Repeat. She felt herself gradually calm.

She opened her eyes to the black binders lining her shelves and teetering on her desk. Each represented an unsolved murder. She refused to call them cold cases. It sounded like the victims had been forgotten. So many. Even with all the advances in genetic testing and scientific analysis. In her three years in her current position, she had solved dozens of cases, but more kept coming in her door, a cruel assembly line that never stopped. Always more work to do.

On days like this, she was grateful for the distraction.

A knock on her office door caused Tracy to look to the corner of her computer screen: 5:10 p.m. The entire afternoon had passed in a blur. "Come in," she said.

The door opened. Vic Fazzio's hulking figure filled the doorway, the top of his coiffed hair just a few inches beneath the six-foot-eight-inch door sash. Faz and Tracy had worked for a decade together on the four-person Violent Crimes Section's A Team, occasionally as partners. With both her parents and Sarah, her only sibling, deceased, Tracy largely considered Faz and Vera, his wife, the closest thing she had to family.

"You're here," Faz said in his familiar, strangely warm, gravelly voice.

"All afternoon, apparently. The day got away from me."

Faz looked uncomfortable. Consoling was not one of his better skills. "Wondering if you have time for a drink before heading home. Vera's at her book club tonight, which means I'm on my own. If you're up for it, we could eat at Fazzio's. I haven't seen Antonio in a while." Antonio was Vic's only child, a chef, who named his Italian restaurant in Fremont after his father.

"Not tonight. I'm anxious to get home to Dan and Daniella. Thanks though."

"Okay," he said. "Just thought I'd check."

"I appreciate it."

"Okay," he said again, still not leaving. Starting to look very uncomfortable.

"Something else?" she asked, teasing him now.

He sighed. "Look, I'm sure this is none of my business, but there's a rumor going around the section—"

"Only the section? I assumed it would be all around the department by now."

"So, you know?"

"If we're talking about the same thing. Yes, I was there."

"You okay with it?"

"What are they saying?"

Faz motioned to the door, and she nodded. He closed it behind him. "They say you shot up the shoot/no-shoot course. Emptied your magazine at an unarmed target."

"Who says?" She doubted highly it was John Sievers or Crazy Joe Mazy. Maybe her captain and longtime nemesis, though their relationship had improved after they'd been forced to work a serial killer investigation together. "Nolasco?"

"Haven't seen him, but I don't think so. You know how it is, Tracy. Nothing is sacred around here. Rumors start flying."

"What else are they saying?"

"It's not important what they're saying."

"It is to me," she said.

He scratched the stubble on his chin, then pulled his tie loose. He and his partner, Delmo Castigliano, were old school. Both still wore a suit or a sport coat and tie. Faz said if he respected the job, people would respect him. The only concession he made was for his feet. He wore black tennis shoes. "Just what I said—that you emptied your clip on an unarmed civilian."

"Target. Don't make it worse than it is."

His eyes widened. He waited for an explanation. Tracy had none to offer. "What happened?" he asked.

She wasn't even sure she was going to tell Dan what had happened. She didn't want him to worry about her. She didn't want anyone to worry about her. Telling a colleague, though, someone who had experienced what she was experiencing, might help. Faz had suffered PTSD after being held captive and beaten by the drug dealer Little Jimmy. He wouldn't judge her. He wouldn't think her crazy or assume she was coming unhinged. He knew this job took years off an officer's life, and inflicted unseen psychological and physical injuries that could be as debilitating as a bullet, and just as painful. She motioned to the chairs across her desk. Faz sat.

"You remember the incident I told you about a few months ago? The one in the hard interrogation room—"

He leaned forward, eyes wide. "What, did you have like a flashback or something?"

She was right. Faz did know. "I don't know what you'd call it. I didn't see a man holding a radio. I saw Edmund House. Then I saw Erik Schmidt. I saw a gun and . . ."

"And what?" he asked.

"I haven't admitted this, not even to myself, and certainly not out loud."

"Okay."

"I saw Sarah."

Faz sat back. "Oh, Tracy. I'm sorry."

"I thought it was in my past, Faz. I thought with the counseling . . . But I still think of Sarah—every day—"

"Nothing wrong with that."

"And for the most part . . . I don't dwell on the negative—what happened to her. I've locked that in a box, and I've forgiven myself for not driving home with her that night."

"You couldn't have known. If you had been with her, you might both be dead."

"Maybe."

"But you're worried now because you had it under control and now you don't."

He knew. "I'm scared . . . for Daniella . . . and Dan."

"I know how you feel. After I had my incident, I thought it was behind me also. But it wasn't. Not entirely. Vera would wake me in bed and tell me I'd been moaning, yelling, sleep talking. I thought I was going crazy. Finally got some help. Now, when I get the thoughts, see Little Jimmy, I tell him he can come along for the ride, but he's got to sit in the back seat and keep quiet. I don't acknowledge him. Eventually, he faded. Never gone though. Not completely."

"That's where I thought I was headed, Faz. I thought I was past the guilt I'd once felt, the feeling that I'd abandoned Sarah."

"This is just a blip because of that piece of shit, Schmidt. He'll get tried and sent away, this time for good, and you'll be able to put him in your rearview mirror, the way you did House."

She smiled. "From your lips to God's ears," she said, though she felt anything but certain that would be the case.

CHAPTER 4

Tracy and Dan spent a relaxing evening at home, which is what she needed. Dan had resolved his domestic violence case and arrived home first. He relieved Therese, made Daniella dinner, and started chicken cacciatore over brown rice, a recipe Antonio had shared with him after a meal he and Tracy enjoyed at Antonio's restaurant.

Tracy opted not to tell Dan about the shoot/no-shoot fiasco. She didn't want to spoil their evening. That, and Dan was busy with other cases. He did not ask her about it; Tracy passing her shooting tests had become perfunctory.

After dinner, Tracy went through Daniella's nighttime routine before bed, getting her showered, into her pajamas, and reading to her from a book. Her daughter, tired after preschool and a trip to the park, went down easily.

Tracy returned to the family room, where she and Dan watched an episode of one of several different television series they enjoyed. Weeknights weren't ordinarily for romance, not after a long day at work, fighting rush-hour traffic to get home, scrambling to get dinner made and feeding both dogs, as well as Roger, Tracy's cat. Then, after dinner, they alternated between cleaning the kitchen or performing Daniella's nighttime routine.

But this night was different.

Tracy needed to be loved. She'd been unable to release her tension at work or, as she ordinarily could, when she entered the peace and serenity of their home. And that made her angry. She'd be damned if she was going to let Erik Schmidt, or the memory of Edmund House, invade their sanctuary.

When Dan climbed into bed to read, Tracy went into the bathroom and put on a hint of perfume. She didn't give him time to protest being too tired or to argue that morning would be better. This night, their passion was akin to armed combat, each moving in rhythm with the other, a familiarity to their touching, squeezing, even a few well-placed bites. And when they'd finished, they lay on their backs panting from exhaustion and struggling to catch their breath.

Dan said, "Where did that come from?"

"It's always been there," she said.

"Yeah? Tell me the secret to getting it to come out and play more often."

"No secret," she said. "Just love me."

"Well, that's easy." He rolled to her and wrapped her in his arms until she fell asleep, this time without waking to her nightmare.

In the morning, Tracy got to SPD early, but she couldn't avoid everyone. She got looks and nods, though nobody said anything directly to her, which was worse than them just asking her what had happened.

When she reached her office, her desk phone was ringing.

She recognized the number on the console. "To what do I owe the pleasure?" she asked.

"I wish it was pleasure," Rick Cerrabone said.

Cerrabone, a senior prosecutor in the King County Prosecutor's Most Dangerous Offender Project, MDOP, was the lead attorney on the two murder charges pending against Erik Schmidt for the shootings of Julia Hoch and Bridgette Traugott. "Erik Schmidt just secured a hearing on a motion to suppress the evidence Kins obtained executing the search warrant that led to Schmidt's arrest."

"On what grounds?"

"Schmidt's arguing that the test fire of his weapon was an unlawful search without a warrant, violating his Fourth Amendment rights."

Obtaining Schmidt's Beretta pistol and test-firing it had been fortuitous. Two police officers had responded to a call reporting a Caucasian male brandishing a gun in a downtown Seattle parking lot. Upon arrival the officers found Schmidt sitting in his gold Corvette, advised him of his Miranda rights, and obtained his consent to search his car. The officers found a Beretta pistol shoved between the console and the driver's seat, along with $3,000 in cash—an amount usually associated with drug dealing—but no drugs. Based on the two witness statements, they arrested Schmidt for displaying a firearm to intimidate and for unlawful possession of a weapon without a license.

Before the gun was returned to Schmidt following the dismissal of the misdemeanor charges, Maria Fernandez, Kins's partner since Tracy had moved to Cold Cases, knowing Schmidt was a person of interest in the murders of Bridgette Traugott and Julia Hoch, took Schmidt's gun to Barry Dillard. She asked Dillard, head of the Washington State Patrol's Firearms and Toolmarks division, to test-fire the Beretta and send the bullet and the casing to the National Integrated Ballistic Information Network (NIBIN) maintained by the ATF—the Bureau of Alcohol, Tobacco, Firearms and Explosives. The markings made on a casing and on the bullet as it passed through the gun barrel were as unique to that gun as a fingerprint was to a person. If the ATF matched that bullet or casing to another shell or bullet with the same markings stored in the ATF system, it meant the same gun had been used in those crimes, and a detective was one step closer to finding the suspected shooter.

The test-fired bullet matched the bullets that killed both Hoch and Traugott, leading to the probable cause for Kins to secure the arrest and search warrants SWAT had served on Schmidt.

"He's also moved for a Franks hearing, contending Kins obtained the warrant by knowingly or recklessly offering false information to Judge Samantha Lee."

"Sounds contrived," Tracy said. "Sounds like perfunctory, bullshit lawyering by Gil. Any specifics?"

The Franks motion was one of a cadre of pretrial motions criminal defendants brought. The Supreme Court case, decided in 1978, allowed defendants to challenge a detective's affidavit in support of a search warrant. If a defendant was successful in proving some impropriety, which was rare, the judge could throw out some, or all, of the evidence seized pursuant to the execution of that warrant, jeopardizing the case.

"I thought so, too, but we have a couple of things working against us. A big one being David Chen has been assigned to hear the motion."

Tracy groaned. In the prosecutor's office and at SPD, Chen was considered a jurist who leaned far to the defendant's side of the courtroom, a place where he had once sat as a defense attorney prior to becoming a controversial judge. On a scale of one to ten of preferred judges, Chen was a negative four.

"Dare I ask what's the second thing?"

"In this instance, Chen's going to have a lot to work with."

CHAPTER 5

Thursday morning, Kins and Fernandez and Tracy met outside Judge Chen's courtroom at King County Superior Court. Cerrabone, who had a natural hangdog look about him, looked worse than normal. The bags under his eyes were darker and more pronounced, and his nose could have led Santa's sleigh.

"You don't look well," Tracy said. It was an understatement.

"I'm not," he said, voice hoarse. "But it's not Covid. I tested. Just a bad head cold. Hit me hard last night. I didn't sleep much, despite pumping my body with cold medicine. Just made me sick. My sinuses feel like they're about to burst."

"Ask for a delay," Kins said.

"Tried. Gil opposed it, said this was another attempt to delay the hearing, a violation of his client's constitutional rights. Bullshit, bullshit, and more bullshit. Chen agreed."

"Do me a favor when we get in there," Kins said. "Ask for a dozen sidebars and cough all over both of them."

Inside the courtroom, Tracy had to step past Schmidt, already seated at counsel's table in a red jumpsuit with black stenciling to indicate a high-security jail prisoner. His hands were cuffed to a bellyband around his waist.

As Tracy passed, Schmidt smirked. "We going to wrestle again, Detective Tracy?"

Tracy ignored him. Kins did not. He leaned across the table, getting in Schmidt's face. "The only person you're going to be wrestling with is the devil, Schmidt."

"Detective, do not speak to my client," Bernard Gil shot back. In his forties, Gil had sharp, angular facial features, thick black hair, and what Vic Fazzio called "animated eyebrows" that furrowed, rose, and dove as he spoke, earning him the nickname "Groucho" at SPD.

"Counselor, tell your client not to address the detectives, and we won't have a problem," Cerrabone said.

Gil adjusted black onyx cufflinks on his monogrammed shirt cuffs. He wore tailored suits. Cerrabone wore off-the-rack suits and shirts to project an everyman appearance. "Tell your detectives that when a person in custody requests his lawyer, it means they are not to speak to him without his lawyer present, and it won't be an issue."

Cerrabone leaned in close, and Tracy, anticipating what was to come, almost laughed. "I'm sorry, what was that?" He coughed several times. Gil stepped back as if to avoid a blast of pepper spray.

At the State's counsel table, Tracy took the seat as far from Schmidt as possible. The gallery behind them and the jury box across the room were empty.

Just after nine, at the bailiff's beckoning, they all rose as Judge David Chen entered the courtroom and climbed the steps to his bench. Chen was small in stature but had earned his nickname "the Chihuahua" because he latched on and was difficult to shake free. He'd developed a staunch reputation for vigorously representing underserved communities when he had practiced law, including several cases against the Seattle Police Department for racial profiling, constitutional rights violations, and the improper use of force.

"Good morning, ladies and gentlemen," Chen said. "We are in Superior Court this morning to hear evidence on defendant's motions to suppress evidence unlawfully seized. I have read the briefs submitted by both sides." Chen shuffled his papers, tapped the bottoms to align them, and sat forward, looking like a kid seated at his father's desk.

"First, defendant seeks suppression of evidence secured from the Seattle Police Department's test-firing of his gun while it was in their possession. The defendant asserts that test-firing the weapon was unrelated to the two misdemeanors with which he was charged when the gun was seized, thus it required a separate search warrant. Since a separate warrant was not obtained, the search was not supported by probable cause."

Chen set the document aside and read from another. "The government argues the test-firing of the gun was a routine administrative procedure conducted by the Seattle Police Department while the firearm was lawfully within its possession." He cited several cases from the brief. "All right, Mr. Gil, does the defense wish to call any witnesses?"

Gil pushed back his chair and stood, his trademark pen in hand. "The defense calls Officer Laurence Kepler, who was subpoenaed to be present in court here today."

"The bailiff will bring in Officer Kepler," Chen said.

The bailiff did so. Kepler was built like a refrigerator. Bald, he entered in his navy-blue uniform. The bailiff swore him in before he sat. After preliminaries, Gil established that Kepler and his partner responded to a weapons call in a parking lot on Capitol Hill.

"Would you tell the court the nature of that call?"

"We didn't know the nature of the call, other than two witnesses saw a man with a gun. The call was made to 911. My partner and I responded."

"Did you subsequently come to understand the nature of the call?"

"We could deduce it pretty easily," Kepler said.

"Would you deduce it for the court today?" Gil said, smiling.

"Two women sitting at a window in their office overlooking a parking lot noticed a Caucasian male seated inside his car displaying a firearm. At one point the man exited his car and waved the gun at a Black male."

"What did you and your partner do?"

"We spoke to the two women, who identified the suspect as a man seated in a gold Corvette. Then we drove around the block so the suspect would not see us entering from Broadway and parked perpendicular to his front bumper to keep the car from leaving. We approached and asked the suspect and his passenger, a woman, to exit the car."

"Is that suspect in the courtroom today?"

Kepler pointed. "The defendant seated beside you."

Chen said, "Let the record reflect that the witness has identified Erik Schmidt, the defendant."

"Did the defendant do as you asked and exit the car?"

"He did."

"And the passenger?"

"Not as compliant."

"What do you mean?"

"She was mouthy. She wanted us to show them a warrant . . . and made other statements less polite."

"Did she eventually get out of the car?"

"After the defendant told her to 'Shut the eff up and get out.'"

"What did you do next?"

"We handcuffed both the suspect and the passenger, standard operating procedure for officer and civilian safety, then advised the suspect, Mr. Schmidt, of his Miranda rights and asked whether he had a weapon on him."

"And his answer?"

"He said he had a 9-millimeter Beretta firearm between the console and the driver's seat of his car. We asked if he would provide oral and written consent allowing us to search his car, and he agreed to provide both."

"What was next?"

"We conducted the search and recovered the gun and three thousand dollars in cash. We asked if the defendant had a CPL, and he said he did not."

"A concealed pistol license?"

"Correct. We arrested the defendant, brought him to the King County Jail, and booked him." Kepler recited the municipal criminal code for each offense.

"Were those charges felonies or misdemeanors?"

"Misdemeanors."

"Thank you, Officer Kepler. I have no further questions."

As Gil retreated to his seat, Judge Chen said, "Mr. Cerrabone?"

Cerrabone stood and approached the lectern, squinting as if the fluorescent lights hurt his eyes. "Officer Kepler, did you appear in court to testify against the defendant on the charges you mentioned?"

"I was prepared to testify, but I was told the prosecutor had to dismiss those charges when the two witnesses refused to appear because they feared the defendant."

Gil rose. "Objection. Irrelevant. Speculation. Hearsay. Move to strike the defendant's understanding as to the basis for the dismissal."

"Sustained and so stricken," Chen said.

Cerrabone gave a small head shake and said, "No further questions."

"Mr. Gil, call your next witness."

"The defense calls Detective Maria Fernandez."

Fernandez was heavyset with a stern look that earned her the nickname "the Principal" in the Violent Crimes Section. After preliminary questions, Gil got to work. "After the firearm was taken from Mr. Schmidt's car, what was done with it?"

"The gun was catalogued and submitted to the Evidence Unit."

"Did it remain at the Evidence Unit until being returned to Mr. Schmidt?"

"Not the entire time. No."

"Why not?"

"I checked out the firearm and took it to the Washington State Patrol Crime Lab, specifically the Firearms and Toolmarks section."

"For what purpose?"

"I asked the section to test-fire the weapon, then enter the bullet and the shell casing into the National Integrated Ballistic Information Network, or NIBIN, maintained by the Bureau of Alcohol, Tobacco, Firearms and Explosives."

"Did you obtain a search warrant to have the recovered firearm test-fired or to have the bullet and shell casing submitted to the ATF?"

"No."

"Did you request Mr. Schmidt's permission, either verbally or in writing, to have the bullet and shell casing submitted to the ATF?"

"No."

Gil asked about and Fernandez explained the database's purpose.

"And presumably it thus leads law enforcement to the particular person who owns the firearm that fired the catalogued bullet and shell casing, but not necessarily to the person who fired the weapon; correct?"

"Correct."

Gil nodded. "The defense has no further questions."

"Mr. Cerrabone?"

Cerrabone stood and approached the lectern, brow furrowed. "When you checked the firearm out from the Evidence Unit and took it to the Washington State Patrol Crime Laboratory, did the gun remain in the Seattle Police Department's custody?"

"Yes, it did."

"Was Mr. Schmidt still in the custody of the Seattle Police Department?"

"No. Mr. Schmidt had been released."

"Did a trial ever take place?"

Gil stood. "Objection. Relevance."

"I'm seeking to establish whether legal proceedings were pending," Cerrabone said.

"Then ask that question," Chen said.

Cerrabone did.

"The legal proceedings were still pending," Fernandez said.

Cerrabone sat.

"The case against Mr. Schmidt was dismissed; was it not?" Gil said, not bothering to rise from his chair at counsel's table.

Cerrabone looked as though he might stand and object, then refrained.

"It was dismissed," Fernandez said. "When the witnesses declined to testify."

Gil smiled, as if amused by an insolent child, and let her answer go.

"Does the defense wish to call any further witnesses?" Chen asked.

"No, Your Honor," Gil said.

"Are the parties willing to submit this argument on the briefs and evidence submitted?"

"Submitted," Cerrabone said.

"Submitted," Gil agreed.

"Then I am prepared to rule." Chen laid down several pages on his desk. "To determine whether a Fourth Amendment violation has occurred, this court must ask first whether the government's conduct amounted to a search within the meaning of the Fourth Amendment; and second, whether that search was reasonable. Here, the Seattle Police Department had lawfully seized and controlled the weapon. It was a search." Chen cited several cases as authority. "Second, the search was reasonable." He cited more authority. "For this reason, the defendant's motion to suppress evidence is denied. The order of this court shall be entered forthwith."

Tracy let out a sigh of relief, though Schmidt's second argument remained pending.

Chen set aside the papers and picked up others. "We will now take up the defendant's motion to suppress evidence for a warrantless arrest without probable cause." Gil wasted no time calling Kins to the witness stand.

Kins looked nervous, which was unusual; he enjoyed the confrontation with the defense attorney during cross-examinations, confident in the thoroughness of his investigations. Tracy chalked up his nerves to the potential ramifications of the hearing. If Chen found Kins had secured the warrant based upon knowingly false or recklessly misleading statements, he could suppress all evidence seized pursuant to the tainted warrant, including the recovered gun—known as "fruit of the poisonous tree." Cerrabone would have to dismiss the murder charges, and Schmidt would walk from the courtroom a free man.

After preliminaries, Kins said in answer to a question, "ATF confirmed the bullet test-fired from Schmidt's gun matched the two bullets recovered from the bodies of Julia Hoch and Bridgette Traugott, two women murdered in Seattle. With that information, I put together a warrant to arrest Mr. Schmidt and to search his home and his car for the gun."

"With a supporting affidavit; correct?"

"Correct."

Gil put the request for a warrant and Kins's supporting affidavit onto the computer screen and had him authenticate both as the application submitted to Judge Samantha Lee.

"Upon securing the arrest-and-search warrant, did you attend the operation to execute that warrant and to arrest Mr. Schmidt?"

"I'm the person who put the handcuffs on him." Kins looked and sounded defiant. Tracy glanced at Schmidt, who no longer grinned. He had a dark expression, staring at Kins, the two men like prizefighters trying to intimidate the other before the bell for round one.

"What agency within the Seattle Police Department did you use to execute the warrant to arrest Mr. Schmidt and search his home?"

"I asked that SWAT execute the warrant."

Gil read from a sheet of paper. "'A highly trained tactical team which provides 24/7 response to various high-risk situations such as barricaded persons, active shooting scenes, high-risk search warrants, crowd-control during large-scale disturbances or riots, sniper incidents, and terrorism threats'? That unit?"

"I considered Mr. Schmidt a high-risk search warrant," Kins said, cutting through Gil's crap.

"And you represented to Judge Lee in your affidavit that Mr. Schmidt was a high-risk suspect; did you not?"

"I did."

"Detective, did Mr. Schmidt have a criminal record?"

The question, as phrased, was a mistake. Gil clearly meant a criminal record for a violent crime. Kins jumped on it.

"He'd served time in the Army brig and was dishonorably discharged from the military for smuggling heroin and cash out of Iraq, and he'd been convicted of drug possession with intent to distribute and served a decade at the Walla Walla state penitentiary. Beyond those criminal convictions, he was a suspect in the murders of Julia Hoch and Bridgette Traugott. So yes, he had a criminal record."

Gil acted as if the answer were no big deal and not the roundhouse punch it had been. If nothing else, it demonstrated Kins was not a mouse to toy with. "Let me rephrase my question, Detective. Had Mr. Schmidt been *convicted* of any violent crimes?"

"Define violent crimes."

Gil smirked as if amused by the answer. "Let's go with violent crimes as it is defined by the Washington State Criminal Code as set forth in Title 9A of the Revised Code of Washington."

"I don't believe he'd been convicted, but in making my assessment, I consider every threat, including those 'not proven.'" Kins made air quotes with his fingers.

"Going back to the NIBIN report." Gil picked up a document while changing subjects. "The report states, very clearly, that 'NIBIN leads are inconclusive, and that a microscopic comparison by a trained ballistics expert is necessary for confirmation, *before* the report can be used as the basis for a search or arrest warrant.' Did you get confirmation from a trained ballistics expert, Detective Rowe?"

Kins looked like he was swallowing whatever it was he wanted to say, before he responded, and Tracy knew why Cerrabone had been so concerned. "No."

"No? But in your affidavit supporting the warrant, you represented to Judge Lee that you had obtained confirmation; didn't you?"

"I did not say that."

Gil held up the report. "You stated, unequivocally, in your sworn affidavit, that, quote, 'The gun owned by Mr. Schmidt is the same gun that fired the bullets that killed Julia Hoch and Bridgette Traugott.' Close quote. Did I read that correctly?"

"I never stated to Judge Lee that I obtained expert confirmation, which is what you asked."

Why the hell not? Tracy asked silently.

"No, you certainly did not," Gil said, and as Cerrabone rose to object, the defense attorney quickly added, "The defense has no further questions of Detective Rowe."

Cerrabone made his way to the lectern, and Tracy watched with growing concern. "Detective Rowe, in preparing your affidavit, was it your intent to mislead Judge Lee in any way?"

"No. Of course not."

"Can you explain why you did not get a firearms expert to confirm the NIBIN findings in its report?"

Tracy had worked a decade with Kins. He had always had the results certified, succumbing to the adage "Better safe than sorry." His not doing so in this instance struck Tracy as out of character.

"I understood confirmation was necessary *if* the NIBIN report expressed any uncertainty in the match. Here, the report gave no indication of uncertainty. Just the opposite. It found two 'matches.' The bullets that killed Julia Hoch and Bridgette Traugott matched the bullet test-fired from the gun Mr. Schmidt owned and had in his possession. Expediency was critical here. The gun had already been used, to our knowledge, in two murders."

Cerrabone did his best, but Tracy knew Kins's failure to get NIBIN confirmation from a firearms expert left Cerrabone with few arrows in his quiver.

CHAPTER 6

When the parties submitted the matter, Judge Chen broke for a brief recess. Outside the courtroom, Tracy walked the courthouse hall to where Kins stood, Fernandez apparently in the bathroom. Tracy said, "That was kind of rough."

"Yeah," Kins said.

"I thought you handled it as well as possible." Kins shrugged. Tracy continued. "Especially since you weren't the one who failed to get confirmation; were you?"

Kins stared at her a long moment. Then he blew out a breath and shook his head. "I assumed Maria did it. She was the one who had the gun test-fired and submitted the bullet. When we got the match, I thought she had handled it, as you would have. I didn't know she hadn't until Gil brought the motion. It was too late for me to do anything about it then."

"Why didn't she get confirmation?" Tracy asked, befuddled and worried.

"She has a little girl who's sick, Tracy, in and out of the hospital. They're running a series of tests but haven't yet definitively determined what's wrong with her. Maria has been spending nights with her at Seattle Children's Hospital, not getting much sleep, then coming into work."

Tracy certainly could empathize with Fernandez having more pressing matters on her mind, but . . . "Why doesn't she take a leave?"

"She has two other children at home, and her husband lost his job. She's the sole breadwinner."

"You'll get suspended, Kins. And if Chen suppresses the evidence, Schmidt will walk, and the brass will want a scapegoat."

"Look, I'm sick about the thought that Schmidt might walk for the killing of those two women, but I'm not worried about me. I'm a big boy. My three sons are grown. One is out of the house and the other two are close. Shannah recently got a promotion at work and is making good money. We'll be fine. Maria needs the job more than I do. I'd appreciate it if this went no further. This is my decision. I'm prepared for the worst."

"I won't say anything." Fernandez walked back toward them. "Let's hope it doesn't come to that."

The parties returned to the courtroom. Judge Chen wasted no time retaking the bench. He again shuffled papers, though this time with more urgency, looking eager to rule. He sat forward. "This hearing is to decide defendant's Franks motion. The court finds that certain statements made by Detective Rowe in his affidavit in support of the warrant were either intentionally false or made with reckless disregard for the truth."

There it was. Blunt and to the point. Tracy silently cursed.

"The NIBIN report definitively states its findings are not conclusive and are to be confirmed by a ballistics expert. To suggest to the court that such confirmation was obtained, in the absence of any such confirmation, was false, and this court cannot construe the statement as anything but intended to lead Judge Lee to believe he had confirmed the NIBIN findings with a ballistics expert. Even if Detective Rowe's intent was *not* to mislead Judge Lee, this court finds his statements were made with reckless disregard for the truth."

Chen had just cut off a possible avenue of appeal.

"Detective Rowe's statement that he believed confirmation was only necessary if the NIBIN report was uncertain is not credible."

And now a third avenue. He'd also just called Kins a liar.

"The report clearly does not state confirmation is optional or limited to certain situations. Nor is Detective Rowe's statement credible that he believed an urgent need existed requiring the immediate arrest of Mr. Schmidt. Mr. Schmidt was arrested in his home in the middle of the night by the SWAT Unit. No evidence was presented that Mr. Schmidt had learned of the warrant for his arrest, or that he was making any attempt to flee or to destroy evidence."

Chen was making his ruling bulletproof.

"For these reasons, the defendant's Franks motion is granted."

Cerrabone lowered his head, then took out his handkerchief and blew his stuffy nose. Fernandez also looked sick. Kins sat with his chin up, gaze fixed on the jurist who'd just called him a liar.

Chen continued. "If a defendant proves an affidavit supporting a search warrant was invalid, then the evidence obtained *must* be excluded." He cited a Ninth Circuit Court of Appeals case as authority. "It is also well settled that the 'exclusionary rule' provides that: '*All* evidence seized during an unlawful search cannot constitute proof against the victim of the search.'

"Therefore, this court is without discretion and must exclude *all* evidence, direct and indirect, obtained as a result of Detective Rowe's false affidavit."

Tracy clenched her teeth. Schmidt was going to walk.

"Let me conclude by saying this court takes no pleasure in rendering its opinion and fully understands the ramifications of this ruling, but this court must make difficult decisions if it is to protect the Fourth Amendment. In my thirty years of practice and during my years on this bench, I have never witnessed a more egregious display of police misconduct in misleading a jurist. No need existed, Detective Rowe, for your deception. Your failure to undertake the simple tasks of confirming the NIBIN results, whether negligent or a deliberate attempt to mislead, is a direct cause for my ruling today."

With that final deflection, no doubt intended by Chen to wash his hands after he'd just set a murderer free, he rapped his gavel and descended from the bench.

Tracy looked at Kins. She knew him well enough to know he was chewing nails and spitting mad. Fernandez and Cerrabone were also easy to read; they each looked like someone had died. Gil and Schmidt stood, shaking hands. Schmidt slapped Gil on the shoulder, then looked past him to Kins. The two men again stared at one another until Schmidt smirked and shifted his gaze, finding Tracy. He made a gun with his index finger and thumb.

Then he mimed pulling the trigger.

CHAPTER 7

Later that afternoon, Tracy, Kins, Fernandez, and Captain Johnny Nolasco sat in the conference room of Chief of Police Marcella Weber on the eighth floor of Police Headquarters. Tracy being summoned to Weber's office came as a surprise to everyone, given she had not been part of the detective team that obtained or served the search warrant. Still, she didn't put anything past Weber, with whom she had a volatile truce.

Little was said as Weber made them watch the news conference Bernard Gil held on the courthouse steps, his freed client, Erik Schmidt, standing at his side. The media in attendance pulled no punches, implicating the Seattle Police Department and noting that Kins's malfeasance had jeopardized the resolution of the Julia Hoch and Bridgette Traugott murders. Equally unsurprising, the media found members of both women's families, who leveled their criticism at SPD about the years it had taken to get to this point—and now the failure to bring either case to closure.

"This case demonstrates the fragility of the justice system when renegade police officers disregard the truth in favor of false and convenient narratives tailored for expedient results," Gil said. "It is a disgusting example of vigilantism and Old West justice involving a rope and a tree branch, as this recently obtained video of decorated Violent Crimes detective Tracy Crosswhite assaulting Mr. Schmidt while he was handcuffed and in custody further illustrates."

The television footage switched to the grainy video of the hard interrogation room, where Tracy grabbed a handcuffed Schmidt. She now knew why Weber had summoned her.

"As a result of these egregious breaches of Mr. Schmidt's constitutional rights and state law, Mr. Schmidt has authorized my office to file a civil rights lawsuit against King County, the Seattle Police Department, and detectives Rowe and Crosswhite, believing it to be his responsibility to do so, so that other law-abiding citizens do not suffer a similar fate."

Weber, dressed in her police uniform, hit the power button on the remote control and shut off the television. In her sixties, she looked younger with a pixie haircut and few wrinkles or strands of gray. This morning, she simply looked pissed. She'd been looking for an excuse to get rid of Tracy since Tracy had uncovered enough evidence to know Weber had been involved in police corruption early in her career, though not enough evidence to prove it.

Weber put the remote control down and addressed Kins first. "We'll be issuing a statement today in response to Mr. Gil. You are suspended pending the outcome of an internal investigation. The Professional Standards Bureau has been notified and will ensure the investigation's transparency." She next directed her gaze at Fernandez. "Detective Fernandez, since you do not appear to have had any involvement in the wrongdoing, you are free to leave and return to your duties."

Finally, Weber fixed her gaze on Tracy. "Detective Crosswhite, I'm curious why an incident report was not written up regarding what we all just witnessed in the hard interrogation room."

Tracy was about to answer, but Nolasco spoke first. "Detectives Rowe and Crosswhite provided me with verbal reports," he said, though Tracy had not told Nolasco of the incident. "I initiated an internal investigation and obtained the video. Based on my investigation, I opted against suspending Detective Crosswhite."

"Why?" Weber asked.

"Because you did not view the entire incident and what led up to it. While Detective Crosswhite acknowledges she should not have grabbed Mr. Schmidt under any circumstance, I believe in this instance, she showed considerable restraint."

Weber's eyebrows arched. "Considerable restraint?"

"That's right," Nolasco said. "Mr. Schmidt initiated the confrontation by telling Detective Crosswhite that Edmund House, the vicious killer of Detective Crosswhite's sister, told him in prison that she had been a good fuck prior to his strangling her."

Nolasco's language was out of character, especially to the chief of police, and, Tracy speculated, clearly intended for emphasis.

"After my investigation, which included a review of the entire tape, I determined Mr. Schmidt had not requested an attorney prior to being questioned. Therefore, Detective Crosswhite was justified and prudent in her attempt to speak with him regarding the two murdered women. Both cold cases are under her control. I wrote her up and placed a written reprimand in her file, but determined a suspension was not warranted."

Nolasco handed Weber several documents.

Tracy sat in stunned, uncertain silence. Nolasco, her longtime nemesis, had not only stood up for her, he'd lied to the chief of police.

After a long moment, Weber said, "And you believe this reprimand is sufficient?"

"I do. I can't say that any of us, under similar circumstances, would have demonstrated restraint."

Weber had clearly entered this meeting intending to suspend Tracy. She now looked pissed and upset she would be unable to do so.

"I've asked Detective Crosswhite to take a few days off—what we can ostensibly call a temporary leave—until the fallout from Bernard Gil's publicity stunt has passed," Nolasco said.

"And what do we tell the press in the interim?" Weber looked at her watch. "In less than an hour?"

"Tell them an internal investigation is being undertaken, and that appropriate disciplinary action will be taken."

Weber pursed her lips. She looked to be swallowing a bitter pill. Weber turned to leave the conference room but stopped at the door. She turned back and directed her comment to Tracy. "Given your celebrity stature, the press will seek you out for comment. I am ordering you not to speak to the press. I would suggest you do as your captain has suggested and stay away from the office and the telephones until this blows over."

Weber left the room. Those who remained did not immediately speak. After a beat, Nolasco said, "Kins, let the union know you'll need legal counsel. Turn in your credentials and your service pistol. Fernandez, you will return to duty. Crosswhite, go home."

"For how long, Captain?"

Nolasco made a face to indicate he didn't know.

"I have cold cases I'm working."

"Two less now," he said with bitterness.

Kins departed. Fernandez followed. Tracy lingered. After she and Nolasco had solved a serial killer investigation, Tracy had let Nolasco take credit. She wondered if his actions today were a quid pro quo.

"Captain?" she said.

He raised a hand. "I know Kins is covering for Fernandez because her daughter is sick, and she's been distracted but needs this job." He shook his head. "And I didn't lie to Weber. Kins told me about the incident with Schmidt in the hard interrogation room when it happened. I wrote up the incident report and put it in your personnel file in case we needed it. I can't protect you in the civil lawsuit, however, if it goes anywhere."

"I understand. Thank you, Captain."

Tracy started to leave, but Nolasco's question stopped her, catching her off guard. "What happened at the shoot/no-shoot course?"

She wasn't about to tell him what had happened, not in any detail. "I screwed up," she said.

He nodded. Their relationship also remained an uneasy truce. "I'm just saying that, after the failed task force . . . I had some trouble dealing with that, with all those cases I didn't solve. You might want to talk to somebody."

"I appreciate the advice, Captain."

"Because I don't think we've heard the last of Mr. Schmidt or Bernard Gil."

She thought about that for a second. "I don't either," she said.

CHAPTER 8

Tracy returned to her office on the seventh floor but not to pack up and head home. Not yet. This wasn't over. Not in her mind. She wasn't about to let this go. That wasn't in her DNA. Schmidt was a killer. He'd screw up. He'd make a mistake. She just needed to be around to know it or to find one he'd already made. She'd check the files again, see if she could work other angles, get him before he killed again.

She pulled the Hoch and Traugott binders off her shelf, hard copies of materials she could also access on the police computer system, and slid both binders into her briefcase. She left her office and made her way to the Violent Crimes Section's four bull pens. When she stepped into the A Team's bull pen, three of the four desks were empty. Fernandez sat at her desk talking quietly on her personal cell phone, which had a Mariners baseball case cover. Tracy tried not to eavesdrop but deduced from what she heard that Fernandez was talking to her husband about their daughter at Children's Hospital. When she hung up, she closed her eyes for a moment, looking as if she was fighting back tears.

Tracy said, "Maria?"

Fernandez turned quickly, her reaction confirming she had been unaware of Tracy's presence. "Tracy. I was just following up on some reports."

"No worries. Listen, I thought with Kins out for a while you could use a little help. I'd like to take a look at Schmidt's military records when they come in."

"They're here," Fernandez said. "Came in yesterday afternoon."

Fernandez handed Tracy a thick file and looked about to say something more, but Tracy, not wanting to make Fernandez explain, quickly said, "I'll have a look and let you know what I find. You should get home, Maria, to your family." She left the bull pen.

Outside, in the parking structure, Tracy made a phone call as she walked to her car. She'd been told to take time off, but she hadn't been suspended. She could read Julia Hoch and Bridgette Traugott's files again, but Art Nunzio, her predecessor in the Cold Case Unit who had initially worked the two cases, had once driven to Walla Walla to speak to Erik Schmidt. Nunzio professed to having an eidetic memory, and Tracy hoped he could remember something to help her. She wanted more than just facts on a page; she wanted Nunzio's impressions.

She hit traffic on Interstate 5, but far less than the congestion that would bottle up both I-5 and I-405 later in the afternoon. From I-5 she took State Route 518 west past the airport and made her way through the city of Burien, eventually descending Maplewild Avenue, which wound to the tip of Three Tree Point, a beach enclave. Upon retiring, Nunzio had bought a narrow, three-story house on the south side of the point, across from a strip of beach. Colorful flags, strung over the road to beach cabanas, fluttered in a light breeze. Nunzio's view, on clear days like this afternoon, was of fishing boats tied to buoys floating on Puget Sound's blue water. In the background, islands seemingly stretched the entire eighty miles to Mount Rainier, looming majestically on the southern horizon.

As Tracy parked and stepped from her car, Nunzio came out his front door, greeted her, and grabbed a tackle box, large fishing rod, and a cooler from his garage.

"Thought we'd take advantage of the day," he said. "That, and Carole doesn't like it when I talk police business."

"I'm sorry to disturb your retirement, Art."

"Retirement isn't all it's cracked up to be."

"Bored?"

"When I see news stories like the one today. I have a good suspicion that's the reason for your call. Here, hold this." He handed Tracy the rod and tackle box, and they made their way down the beach to a rowboat with a small engine. Tracy waited on the beach while Nunzio used the boat to retrieve a silver-and-blue North River fishing boat and drove it to shore. Despite what he'd said, retirement looked like it suited him, as it did most police officers. He looked relaxed in cargo shorts, flip-flops, sunglasses, and a white baseball cap. The locks beneath his cap nearly reached his shoulders and blew in the breeze.

Within minutes, they'd loaded the supplies, and Nunzio helped Tracy onto the boat. The aluminum hull slapped the water as he drove from the point to join a procession of fishing boats trolling parallel to the shoreline. The light breeze made the temperature comfortable and carried the briny smell of salt water and sea life.

"What are we trying to catch?" Tracy asked from a bench seat.

"Peace and quiet and some sunshine," Nunzio said. "And, if we're lucky, a couple of silver salmon, which are running at the moment."

"How's your luck been?" Tracy pulled out sunglasses and slipped them on to cut the sun's reflection on the water's surface.

"I'm getting better with experience," he said. "Carole found this house about a year ago, and the sale included the boat and all the equipment, as well as the owner's fishing knowledge, so I guess I'm a fisherman now. Carole thought it a good way to keep me out of her hair."

"Is it working?"

"We'll see. The neighbors are always willing to share their knowledge. I assume that's the reason for your call. For me to share a little knowledge?"

"Thought it better than reading case notes again."

Nunzio opened the cooler and popped off a Corona bottle cap, handing the bottle to Tracy. "Sorry. Forgot the limes."

"Not a problem." Tracy sipped her beer and watched Nunzio set up the gear. "You need help with the poles?"

"My fishing buddies tell me a pole is the thing nude dancers swing around and politicians manipulate. These are fishing rods."

"Sounds like a man who knows what he's doing."

After rigging the rods, Nunzio connected the fishing line to a cannonball-sized weight connected to a downrigger, dropped the weight into the water, and lowered it to a depth where his fish-finder indicated the fish were swimming. Then he grabbed himself a beer, sat on the boat's edge, and used the trolling engine's extended throttle to control their speed and direction. He spoke over the sputtering motor. "So . . . what happened with Kins? Schmidt's attorney skewered him . . . and you, on the courthouse steps."

Tracy explained to Nunzio what had happened, though she didn't break Kins's confidence about Fernandez.

"Doesn't sound like Kins. I remember him being thorough, doing things by the book."

"I'm hoping to find another angle to go after Schmidt for the murders of Hoch and Traugott. How did you put the connection to Schmidt together in the first place?"

Nunzio told her Hoch, just twenty-seven years old when murdered, had become addicted to opioids after she had knee surgery at eighteen years of age. Her addiction to oxycodone led to heroin, and heroin had led her to hell.

"Where she met the devil himself," Tracy said.

"She hid her addiction from her family, but by twenty-two she'd flunked out of college. Her family got her into a detox program, then inpatient rehabilitation, counseling, therapy, group sessions. It cost a small fortune, but she'd made it out. She'd beat the devil."

"But the devil doesn't give up that easily," Tracy said.

"He never does. She relapsed."

Tracy blew out a held breath, sensing how close Hoch had been to surviving.

"Her family was unable to afford another round of expensive treatment and tried tough love," Nunzio said. "She ended up on the street, bummed her way to Seattle, and, at some point, met Schmidt."

"Easy pickings for a predator who could provide her a fix."

"Her family lost track of her. She'd sold her cell phone for drugs. No one knew where she was. A brother contacted Katie Pryor in the Missing Persons Unit. They found a last known address and did a door knock. Found her inside an apartment. A bullet in the head."

Tracy knew Bridgette Traugott's story was similar. She listened as Nunzio explained how Traugott came from a broken home. Her father left when she was a kid. Her mother was an addict. Traugott lived with her grandmother for a while, but her grandmother had one steadfast rule. No drugs.

"Traugott broke it. Her grandmother kicked her out. She, too, found her way to Seattle. She, too, was preyed on by Erik Schmidt. She, too, had disappeared, yadda, yadda, yadda. Anyway, the similarities were there. Just didn't see them right away."

"So how did you piece it together?"

"I pulled Traugott's file one day as I was getting ready to retire, routine review, and saw a photograph Traugott had sent a friend in a text message—a picture of her new boyfriend."

SPD didn't yet have facial recognition technology back when Hoch and Traugott were killed, and Erik Schmidt's mug shot would not be in the database for another two years—when he and his Army buddy, Tim Herman, were convicted of possessing large quantities of drugs with intent to distribute.

"I took a shot and filed an affidavit saying I was attempting to locate a witness in a missing person case and needed a warrant."

The Washington State Legislature put limits on the use of facial recognition software if the reason for the request was inconsistent with or violated civil liberties such as personal privacy. It did permit the use to try to identify a missing person.

Nunzio smiled. "I sent the photograph off to the lab and asked if they could help identify the guy in the picture. Honestly? I wasn't optimistic. I was shocked when I got a hit on Erik Schmidt's mug shot when he got pinched for distributing. Now the bells started ringing because of the similarities between Hoch and Traugott's circumstances. I asked ATF to compare the bullet that killed Traugott to the bullet that killed Julia Hoch."

"And you got a match."

"A hundred percent."

"File notes indicate you made a drive out to Walla Walla and spoke to Schmidt. Wondering if you can give me your impressions?" Tracy asked.

"I made the drive on a Friday, and after, Carole and I made a weekend out of it. Spent a couple of days golfing and wine tasting. Schmidt was very bright. Very charming. Also, very calm."

Most sociopaths and psychopaths believed they were smarter than everyone else and were often very bright.

"He admitted he and Traugott had dated after I showed him the photograph, but he said she told him she was leaving Seattle to travel. Said he hadn't seen or heard from her since she'd left. Because he was being so forthright, I decided to ask him about Julia Hoch. Without a photograph, I expected he'd deny knowing her."

"But he didn't."

"He admitted they'd also dated. Said much the same thing as with Traugott. Said she told him she was leaving for Florida, and he hadn't seen or heard from her either."

"So, he claimed to not know they were dead?"

"That's what he said. There was something else he said though. Something that I never forgot."

"What?"

"He looked at me with these hard blue eyes, stared at me like it was a blinking contest, and said, 'I loved both those girls to death.'" Nunzio shook his shoulders. "Still sends a chill up and down my spine. It was as if he was admitting to killing them both and challenging me to prove it."

Tracy had felt the same thing when Schmidt made the statement to her, and she knew the look Nunzio was describing. It was the look Schmidt had leveled at Kins on the witness stand, then at her before he mimed pulling the trigger on a gun. Like this was all just a game, a competition, and neither Kins nor Tracy could beat him.

Nunzio tossed his empty beer bottle in a bucket. "Anyway, I got the command from on high to devote my remaining time to solving cases with DNA evidence so we could give families some closure and get a little positive PR."

Tracy had received the same marching orders from the brass, specifically Chief Weber. "Did you ever look further into Schmidt's background in the military, or before he went in?"

Nunzio shook his head. "Didn't have those records, and, like I said, I had my marching orders, and those orders became your orders. Sounds like the best chance you had to nail Schmidt went south when Chen threw out the evidence." He shook his head and sounded like he'd never fully let the two unsolved cases go. "The same gun. *Man, you had him.*" Nunzio checked the fishing line. Then he said, "So where do you go from here? Any other leads? DNA evidence on either of the two bodies?"

"No. Nothing like that. I feel kind of like the way you described fishing. I'm just throwing out lines in a vast and deep body of water and hoping to get a bite."

CHAPTER 9

Tracy and Nunzio got skunked fishing, but they'd had a couple beers and enjoyed a glorious day of sunshine on calm waters. Even without a fish to bring home, it felt like a successful venture. It was all very Zen, enjoying the journey and not focusing on the result. Unfortunately, Tracy didn't have the same luxury. Her career remained a results-based profession, and she needed something else to pursue regarding Schmidt and his murders of Julia Hoch and Bridgette Traugott. Yes, the two women had been drug addicts, but in her mind, that only made them more vulnerable. Schmidt had preyed on that vulnerability the way Edmund House had preyed on Sarah's vulnerability. No wonder the two men became fast friends in prison. It made Tracy all the more determined to get Schmidt.

When she arrived home, Therese's car sat parked in their circular drive close to the front door. Daniella, still strapped in her car seat, slumbered, a baby monitor in the seat beside her. Rex and Sherlock, their two Rhodesians, kept a watchful eye on the car. They got up when

Tracy approached, acting as if she'd been gone for days instead of hours, competing to get their sides and rear ends scratched.

"Good dogs," Tracy repeated several times, then commanded each to sit. "Watch Daniella." The dogs dutifully complied.

She stepped inside. Roger, her aging cat, jumped onto the pony wall that separated the front entry from the staircase upstairs, purring and rubbing up against her. It wasn't love. He wanted to be fed. Roger was more regular than the clocks in their home. Tracy dropped her keys into a bowl, picked him up, and petted him as she walked into the kitchen.

Therese stood in the pantry. "I was just about to get dinner started, Mrs. O," Therese said, using her moniker for Tracy's married name. "Daniella is zonked in the car. Fell asleep on the drive home."

"I saw. Let's not let her sleep too much longer," Tracy said. "I'll never get her down tonight."

"She's had a full day, that one. She ran all around the park this afternoon."

"Dan outside?" she asked.

"He's upstairs," Therese said. "Said he came home early to get in a quick run before dinner. Too beautiful a day to waste it. You should join him."

Tracy felt the two beers she'd had, and her motivation to exercise waned. "You sound like you've had a long day also. I can take over dinner duties."

"Don't be daft. Daniella's sleeping and the sun is shining. You don't get opportunities like this often, the two of you home early at the same time. Better to take advantage of it while you can."

Therese was right, and Tracy could use the exercise to relieve her stress, though she could also use a nap. She knew what would be better for her. Despite the relaxing time on Nunzio's boat, her neck and upper back remained stiff from the stress of the past few days. "You sure you don't mind?"

"Not in the least."

She climbed the stairs and found Dan on the bench seat at the foot of their bed, slipping on his running shoes. "Hey," he said. "Thought I heard you come in. You up for a run?"

"Or a nap," she said.

"Hmm." He stood and wrapped his arms around her waist. "What has gotten into you?"

"I spent a luxurious afternoon drinking beer on a boat on the Puget Sound."

He dropped his hands. "So . . . when you said 'nap' you really did mean 'nap.'"

She shrugged.

"Nope." He shook his head. "Too late to sweet-talk me now, sister. Get changed. We're going on a run."

"Rats," she said. "Give me a moment to change."

Ten minutes later, they walked and stretched as they made their way to the trailhead a short distance from the back of their house. Over the years they had scouted out several defined routes of varying lengths and chose the route depending on how they both felt that day.

"What do you feel like?" Dan asked as they reached the trailhead.

"A nap," Tracy said. "But barring that, nothing too strenuous."

"Do tell about this boat."

"It was work related."

"I need work like that."

"I'll explain on the run."

They set out at a controlled pace, just trying to get their muscles warm and loose. When she'd caught her wind, Tracy told Dan almost everything—the results of the hearing, her meeting with Weber, Kins's suspension, and Nolasco's act that saved her from a similar fate. She'd again omitted the results of the shoot/no-shoot test.

"I'm surprised you didn't have a heart attack on the spot," Dan said, breathing hard and still working to catch his breath.

The run soothed her. She smelled the trees and the grass. Birds, unseen, chirped. Tracy explained how she'd used the afternoon to visit Nunzio and tried to run down anything she could to pursue Schmidt for the murders of Bridgette Traugott and Julia Hoch.

"Anything?"

"It doesn't look good."

"But you're not going to let this go."

She didn't answer, but he knew what her answer would be.

"How much time off did Nolasco suggest you take?"

"I'm supposed to lie low until the storm passes, which could take a while based on the articles Nunzio said he'd seen over the internet, which I assume will be in tomorrow morning's metro section and maybe on the nightly news."

"Makes Kins dead in the water. You know that, right?" Dan said. "Prosecutors won't put him on the witness stand in another case when he can be impeached so easily."

"I know."

"Doesn't sound like Kins," Dan said.

"It wasn't," Tracy said, and she explained.

"Admirable, but . . ."

"I'm more worried he's going to retire and not bother with all the BS anymore." More and more eligible officers were calling it a career and finding other lines of work.

They continued jogging, quiet for a few minutes. Finally, Dan said, "Any thoughts on what you're going to do with your time off?"

"At present? Go back over the two files, review Schmidt's military records, see if I can come up with anything. I also want to take a drive out to Eastern Washington and talk to someone who knew Schmidt in the Army and in prison."

"Thought you were suspended?"

"Nope. Just told to stay away from the office until the storm dies."

"You're not going to let him walk; are you?"

"Not if I can help it," she said.

After getting Daniella down for the night, Tracy slipped into the home office she and Dan shared.

"How late will you be?" Dan asked. He was in his pajama bottoms and a Bob Marley T-shirt.

"Not too late," she assured him.

"I'll read for a bit."

She set a cup of chamomile tea, which helped her to relax, on the desk pad, and turned on the Tiffany lamp, then pulled out Schmidt's military records that Maria Fernandez had provided. A quick perusal through the file indicated the records were divided into three sections: Schmidt's service records, his medical records, and his disciplinary records—his court-martial and the time he'd spent in the brig for smuggling heroin and cash back to the US. She read his service records first, taking notes on one of Dan's yellow legal pads.

Schmidt entered the Army straight out of the Marmion Academy in Aurora, Illinois. Having not heard of it, Tracy looked it up online and read that Marmion was a private college preparatory school for young men that emphasized academic excellence, leadership development, and spiritual formation. Schmidt entered the academy's four-year Army Junior Reserve Officers' Training Corps (JROTC). It all seemed a bit incongruous with the psychopath Tracy now knew, but she also knew from other cases that antisocial behavior often didn't get triggered until the person reached late teens and sometimes early twenties.

Schmidt, she read, had been a part of the academy's competitive rifle team and had participated in various shooting events and tournaments. That caught her eye, and she scribbled the word *shooter* in her notes, then circled it and wrote *Age 14*. It was about the age she had been when her father first entered her in shooting competitions. She flipped to Schmidt's military records. Schmidt completed basic training and advanced airborne and Army Ranger training at Fort Moore, Georgia. He'd been assigned to the 3rd Ranger Battalion of the 75th Ranger Regiment and served four years as a rifleman, sniper, and reconnaissance specialist.

Tracy wrote *sniper* beneath *shooter,* but it wasn't until she read the next paragraph that she felt her blood run cold. Schmidt had been selected to join the Army Marksmanship Unit, where he joined the Action Shooting Team, competing in various pistol and rifle events around the country.

Anyone who participated in competitive shooting knew of the Army Marksmanship Unit—an elite shooting team. Some of its members had competed in the Olympics and were generally considered the best of the best in the competitive shooting world.

Tracy typed "Army Marksmanship Unit" into a search engine and wrote down the name of the AMU's commanding officer, First Sergeant Tony Reed. Reed had led the unit for more than twenty years—which would have included the years Schmidt had been a member of that unit. Tracy hoped the first sergeant might remember him.

And know what the hell had happened to him.

She checked the clock on her computer. It was just past 10:00 p.m. in Seattle, meaning it was one o'clock in the morning at Fort Moore, Georgia, home of the AMU.

She'd call Reed in the morning on the drive to Eastern Washington.

She shut down the computer, turned off the desk lamp, and walked the dark hall to peek inside Daniella's room. The night-light cast a blue glow on the walls and furniture. Tracy walked into the room and looked down at her daughter, asleep on her back in her new "big girl" bed. Daniella had kicked off her pink comforter with the farm animals and had stretched out, long and lean. When had her daughter grown so much? And what was to come next? The crib was in the spare bedroom, but Tracy now thought it highly unlikely it would be used again. Her biological clock was not just ticking, it approached being antiquated for having babies. Beyond that, raising children took the type of energy young people could muster, especially after a long week of work. Though she and Dan worked out often, Dan frequently and rightly warned, "Don't let the old man or the old woman in!"

Nature had a way of creeping in on its own.

She kissed her daughter and pulled the blanket over her, then walked into her bedroom. Dan breathed heavily.

In the walk-in closet she changed into her nightclothes, then made her way in the dark to the bathroom to brush her teeth and get ready for bed. In the bedroom, she gently pulled back the covers and slid quietly beneath the sheets.

"What time is it?" Dan asked, his voice gravelly.

"After ten," she said.

"Sorry," he said. "I was reading and couldn't stay awake."

"My fault, not yours. The time got away from me."

He rolled toward her and put an arm around her. "Everything all right?"

"Everything is fine," she said.

She lay on her back, her mind going over what she'd read about Schmidt and the AMU Action Shooting Team.

That had been twenty years ago.

About the time she'd last competed.

She thought again of what Art Nunzio had said, about the feeling he had when he interviewed Schmidt, that the man had been challenging him. It again reminded her of the look in Schmidt's eyes when he'd squared off with Kins in court, then with her—seemingly issuing the same challenge.

She'd thought his pulling the trigger was an idle threat.

Maybe not.

CHAPTER 10

Tracy awoke before sunrise and was on the road for the long drive east to the Walla Walla state penitentiary. She called the AMU at Fort Moore and left a message for Tony Reed—the first sergeant who led the unit. She then waited until a more reasonable hour, when she was outside of Cle Elum on Interstate 90, to make the difficult calls to Julia Hoch's brother, Robert, whose name and number she'd found in the case file, and to Bridgette Traugott's friend. Traugott's grandmother had passed on. She had no living family members.

Traugott's friend was upset, but nothing like Robert Hoch, who got on the phone spitting mad and let Tracy know it. She allowed him to vent, then told him the purpose of her call was to let him know she wasn't giving up on the case, though she could not provide him anything specific to pacify him. She provided her name and telephone number but doubted she would hear from him, unless she found some way to implicate Schmidt.

As she neared the turnoff to Yakima on Interstate 82 east, her cell phone rang, a 706 area code and number she recognized as the number she'd earlier called for Fort Moore, Georgia. She answered the phone and identified herself.

First Sergeant Tony Reed sounded young, his voice high pitched, not the crusty voice of an all-business sergeant she had expected of someone who'd led the AMU for decades.

"Sergeant Reed, thank you for calling me back."

"Not a problem. And you can drop the 'sergeant.' Tony is fine. Let me guess. You're calling about one of my former unit members, Erik Schmidt."

"You recall him."

"You're not the first person to call."

"No? Someone else?"

"A prison psychiatrist called me from Eastern Washington some years back wanting to know about Erik."

"The Walla Walla state penitentiary?"

"Hard to forget that name. It's like Sing Sing, just outside of New York."

"Do I detect a New York accent?"

"They've tried to convert me here in Georgia, but it's tough to beat the Bronx out of a man."

"You must be a Yankees fan," she said, seeking some common ground, unsure Reed would talk openly about a shooter he'd trained being accused of two murders.

"I bleed pinstripes," Reed said. "You?"

"Washingtonian—born and raised."

"Ken Griffey and Edgar Martínez just about killed me in the 1995 divisional series," he said, referencing the game that eliminated the Yankees from the baseball playoffs that year. "I'd love to talk baseball, but I get a sense that's not why you called. I took the liberty of doing an internet search on Erik Schmidt after I received your voice mail. Looks like he was in trouble again but managed to wiggle free."

"He is and he did, for now anyway."

"Damn shame what happened to him."

"Can you fill me in? I have a lot of gaps, and that's one of them. What happened to him?"

"I can try. Where would you like me to begin?"

"At the beginning . . . when you first met him. First impressions. If you noticed a change and, if so, when? And any theories you might have. Those sorts of things. I'm curious why a man would go from an esteemed unit like the AMU to running drugs."

"You and me both. I have my hunches though."

"I'd love to hear them."

"Okay. But first, you know about the AMU?"

"I know shooting," Tracy said, hoping again to cultivate common ground and build camaraderie. "I won several state shooting championships back in the day."

"What kind of shooting?" Reed asked.

"Pistols, single-action revolvers, rifles, shotguns."

"Single-action shooting competitions?"

"Out west we're more partial to Cowboy Action Shooting," Tracy said. "You know it?"

"I've been active with the Texican Rangers in Ringgold, Georgia. They have monthly matches. I can't make them all—it's a five-hour car ride—but I try to make a few each year just for fun. My wife and I make a weekend of it, take the dogs, and drive over in the RV. Are you still active?"

"With a three-year-old and a full-time detective job? No chance."

Reed chuckled. "I hear you. My three are grown and out of the house, but my daughter competes, so we spend that time together. All right, enough bullshitting. Let me get back to Erik Schmidt. I assume you have his military file?"

"I do."

"Medical records?"

"Yes, though I haven't had a chance to review them in any detail."

"Okay, you said from 'the beginning.' This is from the beginning."

Tracy sat back to listen as she ascended I-82 and saw the picturesque, treeless northern slopes of Horse Heaven Hills.

"Erik was one of the best shooters I ever trained. Period," Reed said. "He had the intangibles you just can't teach. If you've won championships, you know what those are."

Tracy did. The ability to tune out all distractions and focus just on the shooting.

"Nothing fazed him. He had a heart rate that rarely reached the sixties even during competitions, and he had the mental discipline to be the best. Confidence bordering on cocky. There wasn't a shot he didn't believe he could make."

Tracy could relate, but the truth was, Reed was describing her sister, Sarah, more than Tracy. Tracy had what it took to be the best—*if she worked hard at it*. Sarah's talent had been innate, and that sounded like the talent Reed was describing he'd seen in Schmidt.

"Beyond his natural ability, he trained hard, in all weather conditions," Reed continued. "Didn't matter if it was a driving rain or bitter cold, Erik was at his best."

Which begged the question: "So, what happened to him?"

"Well, I'm not a psychiatrist, but if you ask me, the intangibles that made him so good also broke him."

"How's that?"

"That drive to be the best can be crippling if not tempered," Reed said. "Nothing less than perfection is ever good enough. There was always that one shot he could have made but missed. A lot like golf. Frustration starts, then frustration becomes anger. It can screw with your head."

Tracy knew what Reed was getting at. Her father had warned both her and Sarah about dwelling on the negatives after a competition and instead taught them to focus on the positives.

"I think that need to be perfect was largely the result of Erik's father, Colonel Bob Schmidt."

"Sounds like his dad was a taskmaster." Tracy knew of such fathers who drove their children to be what they themselves could not be, whether at shooting or some other sport.

"'Iron Bob' was a great soldier, but a son of a bitch of a man," Reed said. "He was decorated multiple times for battles in Iraq and Afghanistan, and he was a strict and demanding leader who expected nothing but excellence and obedience from the men he commanded—and his son. You saw *The Great Santini*?"

"Pat Conroy's book was better."

"Iron Bob made Lieutenant-Colonel 'Bull' Meechum look like a cream puff."

"Ouch. Did Erik's father teach Erik to shoot?"

"He did. Iron Bob was a champion shooter himself, and from everything I could glean, he wanted Erik to be the best and drove him hard," Reed said. "Enrolled him in the ROTC program in high school and demanded they train him rigorously. I know he had Erik competing at a very early age, and from what I subsequently learned, he punished him harshly for mistakes or failures."

"Punished how? Verbally?"

"Hmm . . . ," Reed said, perhaps considering the Army code not to shit on another soldier. "I guess I can't defame a dead man—Iron Bob died of a heart attack at fifty-six. I was told the punishment was both verbal and physical."

Erik Schmidt stepped away holding the belt buckle to commemorate his second-place finish in the Illinois state shooting competition. At fourteen, he was the youngest competitor in his age division, which maxed out at nineteen. Having finishing second, he had qualified for the 1995 national team. But he felt sick to his stomach. He'd missed a target in his final stage, costing him points. Worse, the miss had so unnerved him, he had difficulty getting the pistol sights aligned on his next target, costing him precious seconds.

"Hey, Erik."

Erik turned and saw Hayes Bolton jogging toward him. Hayes held the silver belt buckle awarded for first place. Upon reaching Schmidt, Hayes said, "Congratulations, man. You had some great rounds. Especially given your age." Hayes was eighteen. "Anyway, I just wanted to say it was great to finally beat you. You're the best, man." Hayes stuck out his hand.

Erik was the best.

Just not today.

And that was a problem.

Erik shook Hayes's hand. "Thanks. And congratulations. You . . . you deserved it."

Hayes put a hand on Erik's shoulder. "You can't win them all. I'll see you at nationals."

"See you," Erik said.

As Hayes turned and jogged across the dirt lot to where his parents, siblings, and girlfriend stood waiting, all smiles, Erik let out a sigh. He felt the acidic burn up the back of his throat and forced it down. He didn't want to throw up. He turned to where the cars had parked and saw his father sitting in the truck cab, watching. His father had left the spectator area the minute Erik had finished his final stage; he didn't wait to watch the other shooters or the awards ceremony. Erik rolled his cart holding his guns and ammo across the dirt and gravel to the bed of the truck. His father did not get out to help him lift the cart into the bed, though it was heavy. He had to lift it from the ground, then lean it onto the tailgate and slide it in.

If he could have walked home, he would have. He didn't care how many miles it would be. The longer the better, he knew. This was the worst moment—getting into the truck after a competition, listening to his father analyze every shot, what Erik had done wrong, where he had lost time.

And that was after Erik had won.

He jumped down from the bed and slammed the tailgate closed, then made his way to the passenger side, opened the door, and pulled himself up onto the bench seat, putting the belt buckle beside him and securing his seat belt.

His father wasted no time backing up, dust and rocks spitting from the tires as he sped out of the lot.

They drove in silence. That was worse than getting yelled at. He glanced over at his father's hands on the steering wheel. No white knuckles. His father drove with the window down, a cigarette dangling between his fingers. Though his posture looked relaxed, Erik couldn't really tell; his father wore dark sunglasses, an Army ball cap pulled down low on his brow.

Maybe today would be different. Maybe he hadn't drunk too much yet.

His father flicked the cigarette butt out the window. "Tell me what that was all about," he said, eyes never leaving the road.

"I missed, Sir. I rushed my shot. My aim was too high when I squeezed—"

"I saw you miss. I was there . . . with all the other parents."

Only he hadn't been. Not really. His father never sat during any of Erik's competitions. He never spoke to any of the other family members. He stood some distance away from the bleachers.

"I want to know what that was in the parking lot."

"Hayes wanted to congratulate me, Sir."

"Congratulate you?"

"Uh-huh."

His father turned and looked at him.

"I mean, yes, Sir."

"For losing."

Erik didn't respond.

"He wasn't congratulating you, boy. He wanted to let you know he beat you, except he didn't really win. Did he?"

"No, Sir."

"No, sir. You lost. He was just fucking with your head. Because you're going to face him again, in other competitions. He's seeking a mental edge. He's trying to make you weak. Make you think about missing another target, then having to slow to find—"

"He just congratulated me!"

The backhand was swift and hard, striking Erik across the nose and mouth, drawing blood. It trickled from his nose, and he tasted the familiar metallic tang down the back of his throat.

His father handed him a handkerchief. "Do not get blood on the seats of my truck," he said. "And do not interrupt me when I am talking." After a long moment of silence, his father said, "Who are you?"

"Erik Schmidt, Sir."

"Who?"

"Erik Schmidt," he said raising his voice.

"And who am I?"

"Colonel Bob Schmidt, Sir."

"That's right. Schmidt is my last name, and my father's last name, and his father, and his father. You understand? Your name is our *legacy. The Schmidts are winners. But not today. Today, the Schmidts are losers. Today you disgraced my last name. What have I told you?"*

"When I compete, I compete for all of us, Sir."

"That's right." His father grabbed the belt buckle from the bench seat and tossed it out the window. "You do not, ever shake the hand of a man you lose to, and do not accept anything except winning. We do not accept

losers in this family. We do not accept losing. In battle, you either win or
you die. Do you want to die?"

"No, Sir."

"Do you want to be a loser your whole life?"

"No, Sir."

"When we get home what will you do?"

"Practice, Sir."

"Why do we practice?"

"To get better, Sir."

"Wrong!" His father slapped the steering wheel. "Why do we practice?"

"To win, Sir. We practice to win."

———

"Bob would come to competitions," Reed was saying. "And I will tell you I never heard him praise or encourage Erik, but he did criticize and belittle him. He always asked about the shots Erik missed, not those he made. In my opinion, he instilled in Erik a fear of failure that ultimately broke him."

"Okay," Tracy said, "but a lot of people fail and walk away. They don't start running drugs and killing young women."

"Agreed. And I'm getting to that."

"Okay. Sorry to interrupt."

"I don't think Erik joined the AMU for himself as much as for his father. Iron Bob made it clear he wanted Erik in the unit. I capitulated, because I thought Erik needed the unit and, frankly, he was very good, as I've said. But as calm as he appeared shooting, I don't think Erik ever enjoyed it much. From what I learned, though far too late, Erik tried to cope with his low self-esteem, anxiety, and his depression by drinking and smoking pot. Worked for a while, I guess, but as we all know, that eventually catches up to a person; makes things worse, not better. He also started to have headaches—migraines. I learned this after the fact. I didn't know he had nightmares and hallucinations, but I was subsequently told he did."

"Hallucinations?" Tracy said.

"It's in his medical records. His scores declined, though Erik never would admit he was sick or weak. He knew what that would mean."

"Disappointing his father," she said, rhetorically.

"He kept pushing himself harder and harder, and his shooting got worse and worse. The more he lost, the more he self-medicated, and the more irrational and impulsive his behavior."

"Such as?"

"We had incidents in the unit of stealing, lying. Guys in the unit found their weapons tampered with before competitions. They accused Erik. He denied it. Didn't matter. They didn't trust or like him."

"Anything proven?"

"It didn't exactly get that far."

"No?"

"After one of the competitions, when Erik again had flamed out, one of the guys in the unit who had his rifle tampered with rode him hard. Erik went berserk. Beat the hell out of him. Others said Erik might have killed him if they hadn't pulled him off. He got sent to the brig, but Iron Bob stepped in, said Erik would volunteer to go to Iraq. Erik was given a summary court-martial and thirty days."

"That wasn't in his Army file."

"No. It isn't."

"His father?"

"I assume. But I couldn't keep him in the unit anymore. He was impacting the rest of my shooters. It wasn't just the aggravated assault, though that was the straw that broke the camel's back. As I said, Erik had become impulsive and acted without considering the consequences. He became emotionally detached when he shot, which is initially what made him so good but now made him dangerous. I didn't want to put a gun in his hand for fear of what he might do. Turns out I didn't have to. When he got out of the brig Iron Bob shipped him to Iraq." Tracy heard something in the first sergeant's voice. Regret? Guilt? Disappointment? "And Iraq is where the wheels fell completely off the cart."

"You referring to his court-martial?"

"Before that. You know anything about the Battle of Karbala?"

"No."

"Here's the *Reader's Digest* version. Hundreds of Iraqi forces ambushed a US Army convoy transporting fuel and supplies near the city. Schmidt was in that convoy. The enemy hit the convoy with rocket-propelled grenades, mortars, and machine-gun fire, and it eventually became close-quarter combat. Hand-to-hand fighting. The convoy managed to escape the city with the help of air support and reinforcements but suffered eleven killed and thirty wounded. Erik was one of the wounded. At an inquiry to determine what had gone wrong, some of the soldiers said Erik killed a dozen Iraqi soldiers and as many, or more, civilians. They said he killed indiscriminately, without thought or remorse, that they were all just shooting targets to him."

Tracy saw the shooting target of the unarmed civilian in which she'd put fourteen bullets.

"Anyway, I'm told it was while Erik was recovering in the hospital that he first met another soldier, a drug runner."

"Tim Herman."

"Is that the name? He was older. Midtwenties. Erik was vulnerable. Not an official diagnosis, but I think he was looking for anyone who didn't just see his faults."

"Like his father," Tracy said.

"Like his father. Anyway, this guy, Herman, cultivated a friendship and eventually recruited Erik to smuggle heroin and a lot of cash home. Erik got caught and sent to the brig. He was court-martialed and dishonorably discharged. So, what exactly happened to Erik? As I said, I'm not a psychiatrist, but the guy I heard about and read about in the news—the one running drugs, the one who killed Iraqi citizens indiscriminately, and the one suspected in the murders of two young women? That is not the young man who first came to me, and who I trained to shoot. But something happened to him. What, I can't say for certain. Drugs? Alcohol? An inherent defect in his character that made him snap under all the stress? I don't know. Maybe that psychiatrist in Walla Walla knows why."

Tracy couldn't temper her curiosity—the competitor in her—nor could she dismiss Schmidt's gesture in the courtroom. "You said Schmidt was one of the best you ever trained."

"Maybe *the* best when he was atop his game."

"How good was he?"

"I still have some clips I pulled up when the psychiatrist called. If you want, I can send them."

"I'd be grateful," Tracy said, and she provided her email.

"I'll get those to you as soon as we hang up. I have a favor, however."

"Shoot."

"If you ever do find out what actually made Erik go off the rails . . . what happened to him, well, I'd like to know if there's anything we can do out here . . . in our training . . . to make sure it doesn't happen again."

"Fair enough."

Tracy thanked Reed for his insight and hung up, then she sat back. She'd had more than her share of experience with psychopaths and serial killers. The Cowboy, who'd killed sex workers, and the Route 99 serial killer among them. Police psychiatrists described each man the way Reed had described Schmidt. Adept liars, smart, and impulsive men who did not consider consequences. Emotionally detached.

Ten minutes after disconnecting the call, Tracy's phone pinged—an email, as promised, from First Sergeant Reed.

She was about to find out how good Schmidt had once been.

She pulled off the highway at the next rest stop and stepped from her car to stretch her legs and pulled up the first of the two videos. Schmidt looked nothing like the man in the hard interrogation room. In the video he wore a black ball cap tight on his head, not a strand of hair seen beneath it. Shooting glasses covered his eyes, but his facial features still had the sharpness of youth. A black T-shirt clung to the muscles of his arms and chest. Tracy knew enough about shooting to quickly recognize the video captured a timed accuracy exercise. Schmidt shot over, under, and around obstacles at targets on a shooting range. He moved from target to target, shuffling his feet, each step certain, without hesitation, never a wasted movement. His shoulders were low and relaxed. His arms formed a triangle with the gun barrel at the apex. He kept his eyes downrange as he moved from cover to cover, hunting targets. He fired what looked to be a 9 mm Beretta M9A1, which was a standard-issued military sidearm back then.

Schmidt shot so quickly, and so accurately, it looked like the video had been sped up. He dropped one target after the next, puffs of dirt exploding in the hillside behind each one. He ejected one magazine and locked the next in place cat quick, not losing any time between shots. A range officer in a red shirt followed behind him, holding up a shot timer, recording the time stamps of all the shots fired.

When Schmidt had finished, he remained at the ready, arms still forming the perfect V from his chest. His head swiveled left to right and back again, like a tank turret, checking his six and hunting his next target.

The official directed Schmidt to unload and show clear. He did so, then reholstered his pistol. Having done so, Schmidt turned but he did not look at the official, who was holding up Schmidt's shot time. He looked directly into the camera with the same intense gaze Tracy had seen in the glare he had leveled at Kins in the courtroom, the gaze

Nunzio had described, one she had seen in other competitors, a look she herself had been accused of when she competed.

"Confidence bordering on cocky," Reed had said.

A challenge, Nunzio had said.

Schmidt considered himself the best.

And he dared anyone to prove otherwise.

The video ended.

Tracy didn't load the next video; she didn't need to.

She already knew the answer to her next question.

She couldn't beat Schmidt, not even on her best days.

And her best days were far behind her.

CHAPTER 11

With little traffic and her foot heavy on the accelerator, Tracy reached Walla Walla quicker than anticipated. She turned north on State Route 125, a two-lane highway that headed away from the town, and saw the state penitentiary rising above flat fields. The prison had once housed Washington's death-row inmates, like House, and had been the site of executions before the state supreme court abolished the death sentence. The façade, a red brick, reminded Tracy of the prison depicted in Stephen King's short story *The Shawshank Redemption*. Razor ribbon spun across the top of the walls, and light stanchions poked over modular cellblocks, each block separated by high cyclone fencing and overseen by armed guards in towers, indicative of the violent prisoners housed there.

At the facility entrance Tracy noted the address—1313 13th Avenue—and again wondered if anyone had ever considered all the thirteens to be a bad omen for a prison's address. In contrast to the bleak landscaping surrounding and leading up to it, the entrance to the 540-acre facility looked like the gated entry to a Kentucky horse farm, with waist-high white fencing, light stanchions, and a white sign arching over the road stating:

"Entrance to Penitentiary Grounds." Furthering the peaceful illusion, green lawn spotted with Douglas fir trees spread like a carpet to the outer prison walls.

At the visitor's check-in, Tracy provided her credentials and secured her gun and cell phone in a locker, as per protocol. A woman came out to take her to the office of Mark Schoen, the prison psychiatrist.

Schoen greeted Tracy in a comfortable office that revealed little about the man. His desk and shelving held no family photographs or knickknacks to indicate hobbies. Schoen looked to be midforties, with dark hair but for distinguished gray at the temples. A lean build indicated he worked out.

He smiled. "Can I get you a cup of coffee or tea?"

"Thank you, but I had my fill on the drive."

"I thought it would be good for us to talk before Mr. Herman is brought over." Round tortoiseshell glasses, a collared shirt beneath a black cashmere sweater, and gray slacks gave Schoen a professorial look. In earlier phone calls to the prison, Tracy requested to interview Tim Herman outside the prison walls, not in the visitors center. She told the warden the fewer eyes and ears the better. She hoped Herman would be more willing to talk in a private setting.

Tracy sat in a chair across an expansive wood desk, and she and Schoen spoke about Schmidt. "Can you offer some insight into him?"

"Well, I wasn't here when he arrived, but I took a look at his file to get caught up." He reiterated much of what Reed had told her, but Tracy let him speak because her father had once told her *You don't learn anything talking.*

"Erik resented his father, but he also craved his approval and his attention," Schoen explained. "When he didn't get it, he pushed himself, until he finally had a psychotic break that ended his military career and almost cost him his life."

Tracy noted Schoen's use of Schmidt's first name. "What can you tell me about his break?"

"Erik said he was injured in an ambush while in Iraq and hospitalized."

"And do you think that is when he had his break from reality?"

"I do."

Tracy was more inclined to believe Reed, and what she'd learned from her past experiences with psychopaths. Schmidt's father might have been a precursor to his son's problems, but not necessarily the cause. If anything, he was more the trigger who released an antisocial personality disorder already present.

"What do you mean by a break from reality?"

"A break from reality is a term used to describe a condition called 'psychosis.' Psychosis is a mental state that involves losing touch with reality and having problems with thinking, perception, and emotions. People who experience psychosis may also have hallucinations—sensory experiences such as hearing voices or seeing things that are not there."

Internally, Tracy wondered if her past traumatic experiences were converging to cause her to suffer a break from reality. If that was the reason for her hallucination and for her night terrors. Try as she might, she couldn't completely dismiss the possibility—or the fear it caused.

"They may also have delusions—false beliefs they firmly hold despite evidence to the contrary, such as believing they're being followed by secret agents, or that they have special powers," Schoen continued.

"Is it caused by stress?"

"A number of things can cause or contribute to it—certainly extreme stress or trauma, a mental illness such as schizophrenia or bipolar disorder, physical illnesses such as brain tumors or infections, substance abuse caused by alcohol or drugs."

"What do you think caused or contributed to Erik Schmidt's psychosis?"

"Certainly, the stress and trauma caused by his father, the strain he experienced in the AMU to be the best, and, of course, what happened to him in Iraq."

"How do you treat it?"

"Medication and psychotherapy can help people manage symptoms and help the person cope with their challenges."

"How were Schmidt's symptoms managed while he was here?"

"With the proper medication and counseling. Erik's file indicates he was a model prisoner while here."

Tracy doubted it, from what Tony Reed had described on the phone, and knowing that Schmidt and Edmund House had become friends. She thought it more likely Schmidt had pulled one over on the prison psychiatrist and his staff.

The phone on Schoen's desk rang. He picked up the receiver, spoke for a moment, then hung up. "Tim Herman is here. They're putting him in a room down the hall."

"Thanks for helping make it happen."

"Anything else I can tell you?"

"Schmidt's squad leader in the AMU said he thought Schmidt's break happened before Iraq. He spoke of an incident in which Schmidt snapped and beat another soldier in his same unit, that Schmidt might have killed him had others not stopped him. He said Schmidt had become callous and emotionally detached, impulsive, cold. What do you think of that?"

"Well, if the allegations you spoke of are true, and I have no reason to think they're not, and given what I know of Erik, you're describing someone very bright, manipulative, and violent. Those are classic traits of someone with an antisocial personality disorder."

"A psychopath."

"You're familiar with the term and the traits."

"More than I'd like to be."

"It isn't an official diagnosis, but . . . Yes."

CHAPTER 12

Tim Herman waited in a windowless conference room. He'd been told he would see a prison psychiatrist in preparation for his upcoming parole hearing, at which time he was expected to be released, more than two years after Erik Schmidt's release.

When Tracy walked into the room, Herman, seated at the conference room table, did a double take, clearly expecting Schoen, and clearly intrigued. With gray hair, wire-rimmed spectacles, and a studious face, Herman didn't look like a drug dealer. He wore the prison's khaki short-sleeve shirt and long pants, and tennis shoes. A photo key card identified him as an "offender."

"Who are you?" he asked—more curiosity than irritation in his tone, but also a prisoner's suspicion and cynicism.

Tracy nodded to the prison guard. "You can leave us," she said.

The guard, who'd been told Tracy would speak to Herman alone, said, "I'll be right outside the door. There's a button."

Tracy nodded. Herman watched the guard leave, like a kid watching a parent leave on his first day of school, uncertain in whose care he was being left. He turned back to Tracy and said, "What's going on?"

Tracy pulled out a chair and sat at the head of the table, Herman on her left. "What's going on is I have some questions for you."

"Who are you? A cop?"

"I'm a detective. That's all you need to know."

"I was told I was meeting with a prison psychiatrist for my parole board hearing."

"Plans change."

"What do you want?"

"Some information."

"About?"

"Erik Schmidt."

Herman didn't react, at least not visually. He sat back in his chair and folded his hands in his lap. "I'm not a snitch."

"I know. That's why you've been in here longer than Schmidt, who sold you out as the drug-ring leader."

"I *was* the drug-ring leader."

"Then I guess there's good reason for you to still be here."

Herman looked around. "Is that why you brought me here under false pretenses? So I wouldn't look like a snitch? You thought I'd be more inclined to talk to you?"

"I thought you'd be inclined to talk to me about Schmidt because he blamed you for the drug running, because he's been out making money using your contacts, but that's just me. I'm vindictive," Tracy said.

Herman grinned. "Nothing in it for me?"

"Revenge is often a powerful motivator."

"I'm too old for revenge. I'm done doing time here or anywhere else. What's done is done. I want to get on with my life."

"That's big of you. I can help make sure your parole hearing goes without a hitch."

"I'm getting out. I'm told it's a done deal."

"Funny how sometimes those done deals get undone."

Herman's eyes narrowed, uncertain. "You can't do that."

"I'm not here to bust your balls, Mr. Herman. As I said, I'm just looking for some information on Schmidt, particularly while he was in here."

Herman gave a cautious smile. "Okay. You're right. There's no love lost between me and Erik, but I don't want him to know I told you anything. I want nothing to do with him once I'm out."

"No? Why not?"

"Because he's fucking crazy."

"Is that an official diagnosis?"

"One based on experience. You don't want to get on his bad side. He gets this . . . crazed look when you're in his crosshairs. I don't want any part of him."

Tracy was certain she'd seen it. "I'm just looking to confirm a few things. Did Schmidt work in the prison library?"

Herman's brow wrinkled in thought. "I seem to recall he did."

"Did you ever hear him talk about a prisoner named Edmund House?"

Herman leaned back in his chair, his eyes still searching for Tracy's angle. Then he got a *holy shit* look on his face. Not quite a grin but inching in that direction. "You're her; aren't you?"

Tracy played dumb. "Her?"

"You're that detective; the one that got House the new trial. The one that got him out. Tracy . . . something. That's your name. Tracy . . . something." Herman gave a nervous chuckle while shaking his head. "It all fits. House described you to a T, man. Tall. Blonde. Good looking. He said you thought he was innocent. You had a sister; right? House killed her, but you thought he was innocent."

Tracy felt her insides roiling. "What can you tell me about the relationship between House and Erik Schmidt?"

Herman looked like he wanted to keep talking about the irony of their meeting, but maybe Tracy's body language and facial expression convinced him that wasn't going to happen. After a pause, he said, "He talked about you all the time. House, I mean. He talked about you like you were his girlfriend."

Tracy didn't react. Inside, her stomach churned.

Herman laughed again but not derogatorily. He sounded amazed that things were suddenly full circle. "He said you were the one he wanted, but he took your sister because she was driving your truck. He figured, what the hell; maybe he could have you both."

"You knew him then, House?"

Herman again caught himself. "I mostly knew of him. I mostly stayed the hell away from him—and from Schmidt." Herman shook his head. "Guy was a psychopath and steroid user. Schmidt too. They both scared the hell out of me and ninety percent of the other guys in here. It's the reason Schmidt initially befriended House."

"What is?"

"House's reputation. Then he developed his own, after House died. He took a page out of House's book. Why the hell would you get a guy like that a new trial?"

Erik Schmidt looked up at Edmund House walking into the library at the Walla Walla state penitentiary following visiting hours. He thought House looked bewildered, though with an impish grin on his face, adding to the intrigue. House had never had a visitor to the penitentiary; he had no living relatives or friends, at least outside the prison, so the fact that anyone had visited him had piqued both their interests. A lack of friends had been the reason Erik had been able to get in House's good graces. Erik had connections inside and outside the facility, and the ability to get things that prisoners, like House, needed. He had initially gravitated to the pumped-up steroid user, serving a life sentence, for protection; other prisoners didn't want any part of House, which made him someone good for Erik to know. He never anticipated it would evolve into a genuine friendship, but it had.

"You look like the cat that swallowed the canary," Erik said.

"I might just be that cat," House said. He sat at one of the tables. Erik sat across from him. House never worried about other prisoners overhearing his conversations and snitching on him. To do so would be a death sentence.

"Who came to visit?" Erik asked.

"A criminal defense attorney named Dan O'Leary, and Detective Tracy Crosswhite."

Erik thought it had to be a joke—Ed fantasized about Detective Tracy Crosswhite often, but judging by the persistent, perplexed expression on House's face, Erik knew it was no joke. Now he was bewildered. "She want you to confess to killing her sister?"

House laughed—a chuckle like he couldn't believe it himself.

"What?" Erik said, starting to think again that maybe House was pulling his leg.

"She thinks I'm innocent." House looked at Erik with that deep, penetrating gaze. "She thinks I'm honest-to-God innocent."

After a moment of disbelief, Erik managed to ask, "Why?"

"Because she says the evidence doesn't make sense, just like I told that piece-of-shit attorney who defended me. It didn't make sense, not the way the prosecution and that big-shit chief of police were spinning it. She's apparently been pursuing this for twenty years, and she is convinced the Cedar Grove Police Department is guilty of corruption and deceit and has perpetrated some kind of cover-up to protect the real killer." House laughed again, but this time it was a wicked giggle.

"She said that?" Erik asked. "She said she thought you were innocent?"

House nodded. "She did."

Erik almost couldn't believe the magnitude of what was transpiring. House had been convicted in 1993 for the kidnapping and murder of Sarah Crosswhite, the detective's sister, though they'd never found the body. The jury had sentenced him to death, which was commuted to life as Washington State wrestled with the constitutionality of the death penalty.

"They found her body," House said. "They found her sister's body."

"I thought you said you buried her in an area just before they built a dam and created a lake."

"Apparently they took down that dam, said it interfered with the salmon migration, and the lake receded. They found abandoned cars, the foundations of structures, all kinds of shit. Two hunters found bones their dog had unearthed. Detective Tracy is convinced her sister's remains support my defense, and the attorney believes we have grounds for a new trial." House started laughing again. "They wanted my blessing to prepare a motion for a new trial. Said I could be back in the courtroom this summer."

Erik shook his head. Now he laughed. "That's unbelievable."

"Ain't it though?"

"Do you know what this means?"

"Hell, yeah, I know what it means. It means I've been right all along. Tracy Crosswhite has a thing for me, always has."

"If you get out, you can get what you've always wanted. You can get Tracy Crosswhite," Erik said.

House nodded, but quickly lost the grin.

"What?" Erik asked.

House drummed his tattooed fingers on the table. "I'm just wondering if there could be some catch; you know?"

"What kind of catch?"

"I don't know. Just thinking no way this comes with no strings attached."

"Maybe it does."

House seemed to give this some thought. "When did luck ever shine down on me or my family?"

House had told Erik during their many hours together that his great-grandfather, Charles House, had once owned a mining claim worth millions of dollars but had it stolen from him, then had been shot to death. And like Erik, House's father beat the hell out of him every chance he got, ridiculed him. It was one of the things that deepened the bond between the two men.

"Guys like us . . . we don't get breaks like this," House said.

"Maybe it's time we did. Maybe you're overdue for a break like this."

"Maybe," House said again, though he didn't sound convinced.

"What are you going to do?"

House shrugged. "What can I do?" Then he smiled and chuckled. "I'm going to ride this out. See where it takes me."

"What can you tell me about House's relationship with Schmidt?" Tracy asked Herman again.

Herman shook his head. "All right, I get it. You want to know about Schmidt and House? Fine. I'll tell you what I know. My perspective. Schmidt *worshipped* House. And, no, that is not too strong a word. It's like Schmidt finally found someone who understood him and didn't judge him. What's that saying . . . They were thick as thieves."

"What about you? I thought you were close with Erik."

"Nah. That was strictly a business opportunity. When it went badly, Erik blamed me."

"Erik ever talk about his father?"

"Said how much he hated the son of a bitch, how his father had always judged him, and nothing Erik did was ever good enough. In prison, Erik might have initially befriended House for protection, but pretty soon he lived and died on just about everything House said and did. If House told Erik to read a book, Erik read it. If House told him to do something, get him something, Erik did that also."

"For protection."

"House was huge—and certifiable. He scared the shit out of most everyone in here except Erik. You did not want to get on that guy's bad side, but over time, I think Erik's motivation changed."

"Changed how?"

"He found a kindred spirit, man. Crazy birds of a feather. Erik was like . . ." His gaze shifted to the ceiling. "How would I describe it?" Herman lowered his gaze to Tracy. "Okay. You ever see that Looney Tunes cartoon with the two dogs, Spike and Chester?"

"Spike and Chester?"

"Spike was this big old bulldog with a hat, and Chester was a terrier, small and jumpy, always following Spike around and hanging on his every word."

"That was Erik?"

Herman nodded. "That was Erik."

"What was in it for House?"

"Erik was one of those guys who could get things, and House made it known no one was to screw with Erik, and let me tell you, with his long blond hair, there was more than one guy who would have."

"That was it?"

"Not quite. As I said . . . not sure how to put it."

"Spike and Chester?"

"It was like House became Erik's big brother . . . or . . . I don't know. They weren't that far apart in age but . . ."

"A father figure?"

Herman nodded. "Something like that. It's like he wanted to be House. Crazy shit, I know, but that's how I would describe it."

Tracy felt nauseated. "Did Erik ever mention Julia Hoch or Bridgette Traugott while he was in here?"

Herman shook his head. "Not to me. Who are they?"

"Girlfriends."

"Did he kill them? Is that what you're trying to find out?"

"He never mentioned them to you?"

"No. But if he had, I'm not certain I would have told you."

"Because Erik is crazy."

"He got crazier in here, especially after you killed House. His whole demeanor changed."

"Changed how?" Tracy asked.

"It's like I said. He became House."

———

Erik lay on his bunk in his cell, smiling up at the ceiling. Ed had done it. Word had spread quickly on the cellblock that the jury in his retrial had set him free and found that Ed House had been the subject of a police conspiracy. Just like Detective Tracy had said. It had been all over the news. Ed had even been on television, seated at a press conference with the defense lawyer.

Lady Luck had finally found Ed.

Hell, maybe a little of that same luck would rub off on Erik as well, and he and Ed would be out together. Until then, Erik would miss Ed's pearls of wisdom and their philosophical discussions on life. Erik never had anyone to talk with like that before, to bounce ideas off of, or to just hang around and soak in knowledge. Ed understood Erik in a way Erik's father never had. He accepted Erik for who he was.

He wondered what Ed was up to with his newfound freedom. He liked to imagine him lying by a big hotel pool, a drink in his hand—Captain

Morgan and Coke—and Detective Tracy, as Ed liked to call her, lounging poolside beside him with that long blonde hair and equally long legs.

He just hoped Ed could resist his burning desire to kill his first lawyer, as he'd said more than once that he'd do if he ever got out.

Tim Herman stuck his head in Erik's cell. He looked uncertain, tentative. "Hey. You hear the news about House?"

"I heard," Erik said. "The bastard is free. Seemed so unlikely. But it was just like that detective said it was."

"No," Herman said. "The more recent news."

"More recent?" Erik sat up.

"Shit, man. You don't know? House is dead. I'm sorry to be the one to tell you. I know you were close."

Erik stood from his bunk. "What the fuck did you say?"

"I said House is dead, man."

Erik saw red. Liar. Herman was lying. He crossed the cell in a flash and had Herman by the throat, pressed up against the wall in his cell. "You're a liar. You're lying."

Herman grunted and shook his head. "No, man. I'm not lying," he managed, voice hoarse from Erik pinching his larynx. "It's all over the news. See for yourself. They found his body in a cave. He apparently took that detective there, the one he was always talking about."

Erik released his grip and stepped back, too stunned to speak. He started to breathe heavily, unable to catch his breath. His eyes watered.

Herman rubbed his throat and tried to clear it, grunting several times. "Sorry, man."

"Get out. Get out!"

Herman quickly left.

Erik didn't want to hear it. He didn't want to be consoled. He didn't want to accept Ed was dead. He wanted to feel the pain. He wanted to feed off of the pain.

He screamed and tore his cell apart, upending the bed, knocking down the shelves, the few books there, until, exhausted, he collapsed onto his bunk, now numb.

When he'd received word that his father had died of a heart attack, he'd celebrated. The only thing that would have been better was if Erik had been there to watch the man suffer.

He'd never felt pain the way he now felt it. Never knew loss the way he now knew it.

Then he remembered something Ed had said.

Ed had said it was too good to be true, that there had to be some kind of catch, some reason for Detective Tracy to be trying to get him a new trial. He said good luck didn't happen to guys like him or Erik.

Ed had been right.

The reason Detective Tracy got him a new trial wasn't because she fancied him or thought him innocent. She'd lied to him. She believed him guilty all along. She hated him for having killed her sister, and what she wanted was the chance to kill him. Maybe she thought she'd achieved that when Ed got convicted and had been sentenced to death. But then Ed had his sentence reduced to life in prison.

And maybe she couldn't stand it, knowing Ed was still alive and her sister dead.

"She killed him," Erik said. She couldn't live with the fact that Ed wasn't going to die after all, not by lethal injection. So she cooked up a reason to get him a new trial, hired an attorney, and lied to Ed. It was all just a lie, to get him out. To kill him.

Erik wiped at tears streaming down his cheeks. His father used to beat him when he cried, told him to swallow his pain, to never display his weaknesses. Said people took advantage of weakness. That's what Detective Tracy had done. She'd preyed on Ed's weakness—every prisoner's weakness. Ed's desire to get out, and that desire overcame his common sense that was telling him something wasn't right, to trust that instinct.

Erik had another thought. With Ed gone he had no protection. Just the specter of Ed maybe coming back to prison had been enough to keep him safe. Not any longer.

Ed was dead.

But Erik had learned. He'd learned a lot about how Ed carried himself, made others believe he was crazy. So be it.

He reached between the wall and the edge of his bed and found the shiv Ed had given him to protect himself while Ed was away being retried. He grabbed his blond hair, which made him think of Detective Tracy and her long blonde hair, twisted it into a tight ponytail and secured it with a rubber band. Then he put the shiv to the band and sawed off the ponytail, holding it in his hand.

He'd keep it . . . He'd keep it as a reminder of Detective Tracy.

———

"After House was gone," Herman said, "Erik took on more and more of the guy's personality. He had this long blond hair that he cut off after Erik died. Nearly shaved his head. Then he started lifting weights. Guys left him alone because he became volatile. You never knew what he might do. What might set him off."

"Did you see anyone set him off?"

"You," Herman said. "Schmidt blamed you for House's death. He believed you got House a new trial just so you could get him out to kill him for what he'd done to your sister. Did you?" he asked. "I mean, I could understand if you did." He grinned.

Tracy wondered if Herman was now screwing with her, enjoying himself. "Did Schmidt ever say anything about getting even . . . for House?"

"At the end, I really couldn't tell you. The crazier Erik got, the further away I stayed, like everyone else. But it's like you said, about revenge." Another grin. "It can be a powerful motivator, Detective Tracy."

CHAPTER 13

After the prison guard escorted Tim Herman from the conference room and shut the door, Tracy bolted from her seat, pacing the room and repeatedly flexing her fingers. She'd been clutching them in a ball in her lap below the table to keep them from shaking. They now felt thick and stiff, like she'd sprained the joints. Adrenaline coursed through her system, seeking a release. She hadn't thought it possible Edmund House could ever again find his way back into her life. But he had.

He'd come back. In the form of Erik Schmidt.

Maybe that's why she'd seen them both at the firing range.

She thought of the parallels between the men, and she wondered if that's what House had also seen in Schmidt—if House had seen himself, before he went to prison and discovered steroids and the weight yard. The Edmund House who had come to Cedar Grove had also been lean and muscular, with long hair and a one-hundred-and-twenty-watt smile that could charm the devil, or in Sarah's case, a young eighteen-year-old girl. Schmidt had charmed Julia Hoch and Bridgette Traugott in the same way and, like House, and all the other psychopaths, he didn't need a reason to kill, just an opportunity. House and Schmidt were vile and cruel predators, without consciences, unable to feel others' pain and suffering. Cold. Reptilian.

And Schmidt blamed Tracy for House's death.

It explained that morning, months ago, in the hard interrogation room, how he knew so much about her. House had filled him in.

He talked about you all the time. House, I mean. He talked about you like you were his girlfriend.

She thought again of the video of Schmidt on the shooting course, and his stare into the camera, and of the look he'd given her in the courtroom when he'd mimed pulling the trigger.

Not an idle threat.

He knew from House of Tracy's shooting prowess. He knew she had been, at one time, the best in the state. Schmidt's act had been an unmistakable challenge, perhaps to avenge House's death.

And now Schmidt was out, free.

Tracy had a sudden urge to get home, to protect Dan and Daniella, overcome with a feeling of impending dread. She wanted to pack the car and get her family away from Seattle, away from Erik Schmidt.

Herman's warning about revenge rang in her ears.

It can be a powerful motivator, Detective Tracy.

She hurried from the conference room, stopping just long enough to thank Mark Schoen for making the interview happen and promising to send him details of her conversation with Herman.

"Did you get what you needed?"

"More," she said.

She quickly retrieved her cell phone and gun from the locker and exited the building, greedily sucking in the fresh air. She fought against an urge to run. She got into her car and unlocked the screen on her cell phone to call home. Her message and email icons indicated multiple missed messages and phone calls. Far more than normal.

Something was happening.

Fear engulfed her.

A numbing sensation made her hands so cold she had trouble pressing the buttons.

She checked the voice mails first. Each from Vic Fazzio. He asked her to call him. Nothing more. She checked the text messages. Each from Faz. Again, he asked Tracy to call. Didn't say why. Between the lines she deduced he didn't want to upset her without the chance to speak to her.

She thought of Dan.

And of Daniella.

She called Faz back. When he answered she didn't bother with pleasantries. "Faz? I just got back in the car and you're blowing up my phone."

"Are you sitting down?"

"I told you I'm in the car."

"Pull over."

"What? Vic, you're scaring me. What the hell is going on?"

"Pull over, Tracy."

"I'm in a parking lot. I haven't even started the car. Tell me what it is?"

"There's been an accident."

Tracy did her best to stay within the speed limit on the long drive back to Seattle, but her thoughts would drift, and she'd look down at the speedometer and realize she was exceeding eighty miles per hour. Faz had provided few details in her initial call to him, but he had updated her as he got more information on what had happened and the injuries Kins had sustained.

Faz said Kins had been involved in a multi-car accident at an intersection while driving home from the Roanoke Bar on Capitol Hill. Tracy felt guilty but, for a brief moment, she had felt relief that nothing bad had happened to Dan or Daniella.

Faz explained that according to the first officer on the scene, Kins had blown through a stop sign at an intersection and his car had been T-boned by a delivery truck. The forty-mile-an-hour impact had sent Kins's BMW careening across the intersection, where a second car hit the rear passenger side, hurtling the vehicle, and Kins, into a concrete wall.

Faz told Tracy the BMW sustained so much damage that emergency responders had to use the Jaws of Life to extract Kins from his car. He'd been taken to the Harborview emergency room, the only level-one trauma center in the Pacific Northwest, meaning his injuries, including a head injury of unknown severity, were life-threatening.

"How bad is it, Faz?"

"They aren't yet certain of the extent of the blunt-force injuries to his internal organs," Faz said. "They think his head struck the windshield, because the glass was shattered and he'd cut his forehead, but since he's unconscious they haven't yet determined if he suffered a traumatic brain injury. They do know he fractured his right tibia, and his wrist."

After the update, Tracy called Therese and Dan, told them what had happened and not to expect her home until very late. Then, subscribing to the adage of better to be safe than sorry, she called the Redmond Police Department, identified herself, and asked to have a patrol car sit on her house. She told them she didn't want the officer to go inside the house or engage the people living there unless they engaged him first. The sergeant she spoke with said they'd pull Schmidt's mug shot and ensure the officer watching her house had it, as well as the specifics Tracy provided on Schmidt's gold Corvette.

When she finally reached downtown Seattle, Tracy found Jefferson Street lined with multiple police vehicles. She double-parked and hurried into the emergency room entrance. Faz and Del met her in the hallway as agreed, away from Shannah and their three boys. Her Violent Crimes partners looked like Italian bodyguards—tall, big-boned men dressed in slacks, loafers, and loose-fitting, short-sleeve shirts. They fidgeted in the hall like expectant fathers.

"Let's walk," Faz said. "All that sitting has made me stiff." They stepped outside the emergency room entrance onto Ninth and Jefferson. The temperature was mild. "He's out of surgery and in the recovery room," Faz said, "but they're not letting anyone in to see him, not even Shannah."

"What have they said about his injuries?"

"Still too early to tell," Faz said. "But the doctors haven't sugarcoated it, nor are they being cautiously optimistic."

"No, they are not," Del agreed, sounding worried.

"They're most concerned about the injuries to his chest and head, whether he sustained damage to his internal organs."

"They've confirmed he hit the windshield?"

"He had a cut and was bleeding from his forehead," Del said. "So . . ."

Tracy took a deep breath.

Del said, "Listen, given Kins's familiarity with that intersection, it being so close to his home, we decided to call in Joe Jensen in TCI." Jensen was a sergeant in the Traffic Collision Investigation Unit.

"We want Joe and his team to determine if maybe there was something wrong with the car, something to explain why Kins would have blown through an intersection he knows well," Faz said.

"Why would you think it was a mechanical issue?" Tracy asked.

Del said, "The police on scene were speculating about that, or maybe that Kins had a heart attack or some other medical emergency, because they did not find skid marks to indicate he'd even tried to hit the brakes."

That bit of information gave Tracy pause.

"They also aren't ruling out alcohol either," Faz said. "Given the circumstances, Kins being recently suspended and getting excoriated by the media."

"And his coming from the Roanoke," Del said.

"No. No way," Tracy said.

"According to Shannah, Kins was with old football teammates from when he played at the UW," Faz said.

Tracy emphatically shook her head. "Kins and his boys had . . . have a deal to never drink and drive. Kins agreed to pay for any Uber or taxi, without question or punishment. There's no way he would have violated that agreement, the trust he established with his sons."

Faz shrugged.

"Joe said he has to wait until the investigators are finished," Del said. "When they are, he'll have the car towed to the VPR and look it over personally." The Seattle Police Department's Vehicle Processing Room was located at a satellite facility on Myrtle Street not far from the Washington State Patrol Crime Lab.

"It's unlikely to be a mechanical issue," Tracy said. "Kins treated that car like it was a family member."

"We said the same thing," Faz said.

Del said, "Look, if need be, we can also get CSI involved."

"But let's see what Joe finds out first," Faz said.

Del checked his watch. "I got to make a call home," he said, pulling out his cell phone and stepping away.

Faz wrapped an arm around Tracy. "Hey, it's going to be okay," he said. "They have the best doctors in the world working on him."

She felt shattered, and Faz, who knew her as well as anyone, sensed it. "Something else going on?"

"Let's just focus on Kins. That's enough for all of us."

"Hey, if something is going on, you can tell Faz."

Tracy told Faz about her conversations with Sergeant Tony Reed and Tim Herman.

"And?" Faz asked.

Tracy said, "According to Herman, Schmidt thought of House like a big brother. Maybe a father."

"Crazy birds of a feather . . ." Faz grunted. Then his gaze narrowed. "What else has you shaken? I know you."

Tracy let out a breath of air. "Herman said Schmidt believes I got House a new trial to get him out so I could kill him for what he did to Sarah."

"That's crazy shit."

Tracy told Faz what else Herman had said about Schmidt taking on more and more of House's identity, about him possibly seeking to avenge House's death, about revenge being a strong motivator.

"If you're worried, we can get a car out to your house."

"I already did."

Faz's eyes narrowed. "You don't think Schmidt could have had something to do with this; do you?"

"I'm just wondering . . . I saw the look between Schmidt and Kins in court. It was the same one Ed Nunzio told me about when he interviewed House in prison. Schmidt was issuing a silent challenge. It was dark, menacing."

"That's a long way from this."

"No skid marks," she said. "A car Kins cares for religiously. Just doesn't make a lot of sense, Faz." Kins had executed the warrant, put the cuffs on Schmidt. And he'd been Tracy's partner for more than a decade. "There might be something else, another reason."

"What other reason?"

"Something more personal."

"Meaning what?" Faz asked.

"Meaning me," she said.

"You think he'd go after Kins to get at you?" She heard skepticism in Faz's voice.

"I think it's possible," she said, and she told him why, what she had learned from Sergeant Reed and Tim Herman. She felt sick, thinking that Kins was clinging to life, maybe because of her.

"Let's not start internalizing what's happened here. Kins might have just fallen asleep or had a medical emergency. Maybe he was distracted from all the shit that's been going on." Faz raised a hand before she could protest. "Not drunk. I heard what you said, but maybe he was thinking about the suspension, and whether it was worth putting up with all this bullshit anymore, and lost focus. It could have been any number of things."

"Maybe," she said, looking down the sidewalk. Del lowered his phone and walked back toward them.

Del's eyes darted between Faz and Tracy. "It's worse than we thought."

"What?" Faz said.

"Worse how?" Tracy asked.

"Jensen just called me back. He said somebody cut the brake line on Kins's car, right up near the brake caliper."

Tracy's knees weakened.

"When Kins stepped on the brakes, he blew brake fluid all over until he was just stepping on air. Joe is sending somebody out to look farther back from the intersection, which is when, he suspects, Kins's brake pedal went all the way to the floor."

"Is he sure?" Faz asked. "Could it have been cut in the accident?"

"I asked him that." Del shook his head. "He got under the car with a flashlight. Said this was unequivocally a cut. If he finds brake fluid before the intersection, that also rules out the crash as a cause."

Faz gave Tracy a knowing look.

"Ask Joe if there are any traffic cameras in that area," she said. "And let's get officers to canvass the area looking for cameras on the commercial businesses and residences that maybe could have picked up something. Call CSI—the fingerprint unit. Have them go over the car."

Del said, "Hey, I got this. Joe is on it." He looked from Tracy to Faz. "What do you think is going on here?"

"We don't know anything yet. Not for certain," Faz said.

"Screw that. Kins was my bull pen mate for more than a decade. If we're going to wage war on somebody, I want in."

Tracy explained to Del what she'd explained to Faz. "It was just a hunch, a feeling—"

"But not now," Del said. "Not with Joe confirming a cut."

Faz turned to Tracy. "Let's suppose you're right, and we strike out on getting any camera footage. How are we going to prove it was Schmidt?"

"I don't know," Tracy said. "Given recent events, we can't knock on Schmidt's door and start asking him questions about where he was last night without something more."

"Let's talk to Maria. Maybe someone else has an ax to grind against Kins," Del said.

Del could do so, but Tracy had already ruled out that possibility. A criminal going after a cop was rare. Most understood that to wage that war would bring the wrath of an entire police force down on them. Beyond that, there was the timing to consider. For something like this to happen so close in time to the recent events in the courtroom could not be dismissed as mere coincidence. They could rummage through other files, consider other criminals Kins had put away who were now out, but they couldn't dismiss the most likely.

"I'm going to call home, make sure everything is all right," Tracy said. She also wanted to let Dan know why a patrol car with a uniformed officer was sitting at the end of their cul-de-sac. "Del, let's start with any video footage from any cameras in that area. Maybe we get lucky and get an image or a license plate we can use."

"Maybe," Faz said, but in a tone that indicated he'd also thought this through, and he did not believe that would be the case.

Neither did Tracy.

After calling home and explaining to Dan why there was a patrol car parked in the street leading to their long driveway, Tracy spent time with Shannah and their sons, then sat and waited for news. As the night progressed, more family and friends arrived, and the doctor treating Kins came out to tell Shannah they would keep him unconscious for the night. Tracy, Del, and Faz decided to give the family some space and left the hospital. Faz walked Tracy to her car, and they both checked the ground beneath it for any fluids before she got in.

On the drive home she'd checked her rearview mirror frequently to make sure she wasn't being followed, even took a couple wrong turns, including one down a street she knew to be a dead end.

Nothing suspicious.

Her address was not listed anywhere, and she used her married name except at work, and she had their mail delivered to a PO box, but with the internet, she didn't put it past anyone motivated to dig up her address.

And Schmidt, according to Herman, was very motivated.

When Tracy arrived home, she relieved the uniformed officer. She was armed, and with Rex and Sherlock as an alarm, no one was getting inside their home.

Dan greeted her at the door with a hug and asked how she was doing.

Tracy set her things on a barstool in the kitchen and took off her coat. "I'm okay. Tired."

Dan moved around the kitchen island to the refrigerator. "Are you hungry? I can heat up some pasta."

Tracy shook her head. She'd split half a sandwich with Faz, but she didn't have much of an appetite despite having eaten little all day. "I just need to unwind a bit before I try to sleep."

"Any further updates on Kins?" he asked.

"He's out of surgery and in recovery in ICU. We're told they'll keep him unconscious. We won't know if he suffered a traumatic brain injury until they wake him, but they said a CT scan and an MRI did not show fractures, bleeding, blood clots, or swelling. All positive signs." Then she said, "Let's talk."

She told him in greater detail what she'd learned from Tony Reed at the AMU and Tim Herman at Walla Walla, though she didn't get specific about Schmidt seeking revenge. She also told him what Joe Jensen had determined about Kins's car.

"We have officers looking for traffic cameras and cameras mounted on buildings and residences in that area. We'll check all the video for Schmidt, his car, or anyone else near Kins's car. Until and if we get that video, we don't know much and can't do a lot."

"But for a defendant to do this would be rare, and there's no other explanation as to who would have cut his brake lines."

"There could be, but . . ."

"But it would be rare, and the timing of this can't be ignored," Dan said, knowing this from having defended criminal suspects.

"I don't think so either."

"What do you suggest?"

"I have time off and I was thinking maybe we use it to get away, until they figure out what actually happened."

"I've been thinking the same thing."

"We could go up to Cedar Grove." Tracy wanted to get her family away from Seattle and Schmidt, but she also had been thinking about Cedar Grove since she watched the video Reed had sent her of Schmidt shooting. "We can pack up in the morning and get out of here after I check on Kins."

"I'm busy as hell at work; I'll have to go back and forth to Seattle, and I have depositions in San Francisco for an upcoming trial. I don't like being away, especially not knowing what is going on."

"We'll bring Rex and Sherlock with us," Tracy said. "Best alarm system in the world. And I'll talk to Roy Calloway first thing. Ask him to have a police presence drive by our house."

Dan sighed. "You really did think this through; didn't you?"

Tracy smiled to ease Dan's concern, but she knew it had little effect. She was worried also. "Better safe than sorry; right?"

CHAPTER 14

Early the following morning, Shannah called Tracy at home with good news. The doctors had removed Kins's breathing tube and revived him from deep sedation. Though he was groggy and initially confused by his surroundings, he was responsive to questions asked, recognized her and his sons, and said he recalled the car accident in some detail, including that his brakes had failed. He seemed more upset the BMW had been totaled than he did about his current medical condition.

It sounded just like Kins.

Shannah said the hospital had limited guests to family only, and only during certain hours. "But I told them Kins has a sister."

After she and Dan packed the car to leave town, Tracy stopped at the hospital. Dan and Therese remained in the car with Daniella, Rex, and Sherlock. "I'll be quick," she said.

Faz again greeted Tracy in the hallway, sipping coffee from a paper cup. "Del and Fernandez are outside with Nolasco. He wants to talk."

Tracy headed outside with Faz.

Del said, "I just gave Captain an update. Joe has footage from a camera on the exterior of a pizza place across the intersection and just up the street from the Roanoke Bar. The video speaks for itself." Del punched the keypad on his cell phone, then turned it horizontal so Tracy and the others could view the snippet Jensen had sent over. The video was poor quality, taken after dusk. The lights of cars driving along Tenth Avenue further distorted the images.

"Kins parked just up the street from the entrance to the Roanoke," Del said. "That's his car, there, on the left."

After several seconds, a man, presumably, though it was hard to be certain, walked around the corner from East Miller onto Tenth Avenue. He had a hood pulled over his head and his hands in the pockets of the sweatshirt. A surgical mask further obscured his face. Since the Covid pandemic, no one would have given a man in a mask a second look. When he reached Kins's BMW, the man turned his head and looked behind him, then dropped out of sight. In less than a minute, the figure popped up and continued up the block.

"Shit," Faz said speaking for all of them.

Del said, "Jensen said there's no ambiguity. The brake line was cut."

"You think that was Schmidt?" Nolasco asked Tracy.

"Can't tell. Could be . . . or somebody doing his bidding," she said.

Nolasco looked to Del. "What about other video—other cameras on any of the apartment buildings that might provide a closer look, or maybe where this person came from or went to, a car he got into?" Nolasco asked.

Del explained that officers continued to canvass the area. "But so far, the nearest apartment building is a block away, and the camera only covered the sidewalk and walkway leading to the entrance. Joe's looking for traffic footage near Schmidt's home, trying to determine if we can prove Schmidt left his house, maybe track him driving around Capitol Hill close to the time of this video."

"We can't let him get away with this, Captain," Del said. "We let the criminals start picking us off, none of us is going to be here long."

"I'm not about to let anyone get away with anything," Nolasco said. "And I agree, the timing certainly points to Schmidt. But we need to be smart about how we go about proving this. We can't give Bernard Gil the chance to raise more hell about police harassment. The brass is pissed enough." He looked at Tracy. She waited for the verbal undressing telling her to stay away from Schmidt. "Are you all right?"

"Captain?"

"Faz told me the guy in the prison said Schmidt holds you responsible for House's death. Are you worried about your safety?"

"I guess I should be," Tracy said. "Not for me but . . ."

"But for Dan and your daughter," Faz said.

"We can have a police presence at your home," Nolasco said.

"All respect, Captain, but for how long?" Tracy asked. "Dan and I talked this over last night. We're leaving town for a while, going up to our house in Cedar Grove."

"Then do it," Nolasco said. "Today. Tomorrow. But do it. At least until we get a better grip on what's going on here." He spoke to the others. "I'll look into putting Schmidt under surveillance. You two"—he gestured to Del and Faz—"determine if there's any video around his residence, and pull every traffic camera and any other type of camera between his driveway and the bar. Talk to employees working in the stores around that area—determine if there are any dog walkers or regular runners, anyone who might have seen the guy in this video."

"We have CSI going over the car," Del said. "Hoping maybe for a fingerprint."

"Anything and everything," Nolasco said. "Off the books for now. I don't want the brass to get wind of anything we're doing, but I want the son of a bitch in this video." He looked at his watch. "I have meetings. Somebody keep me informed on Kins's condition and anything else you learn." He turned and left.

They stood for a moment. Uncertain. Then Faz said, "I'm going to pop down and see my goddaughter before you take off. Anything comes up? You don't hesitate to call. Capisce?"

"Capisce," Tracy said.

Fernandez remained. She looked pained. "Shit, Tracy, I'm sorry. This is my fault."

A part of Tracy, the cop in her, was pissed Fernandez had not obtained the ballistics confirmation. If she had, Schmidt would be heading back to prison, this time for the rest of his life. Exactly where he belonged. Instead, Kins was in the hospital, and she was worried about the safety of her family. The thought of Daniella made her think of Fernandez's little girl, seriously ill and in the hospital, and whatever bitterness Tracy held melted. "Don't think that way, Maria, and don't take the blame for what Schmidt has done. How's your daughter?"

Fernandez gave a grim smile, worried eyes. "They ran more tests yesterday afternoon and confirmed it's cancer."

"Oh, Maria—"

"But the doctors said this is a very treatable form of leukemia. It's not great news . . . but . . ." She shrugged and looked to be on the verge of tears.

Tracy put a hand on her shoulder. "But it's good news. So take it. And don't hesitate to take time off, Maria, to be with your family."

"I won't," she said. Fernandez gave another small shrug. "You watch your back."

Tracy intended to.

She went into the hospital to say good-bye to Shannah and tell her she wouldn't be by for a while.

"Kins asked to talk to you," Shannah said.

Tracy stepped past a uniformed officer stationed in the hall outside Kins's door and entered the room to a bell dinging from one of his machines. She moved quickly to the monitor at the side of the bed, worried the bell indicated something serious that required a nurse or doctor. Kins turned his head and opened his eyes. "It's just my heart rate," he said. "Push the button on the screen in the lower left-hand corner and it will shut off."

"Should I call someone first?"

"I'm on medication and occasionally my rate gets too fast. Usually when a pretty, young nurse enters."

"I'm flattered," she said.

He gave her that boyish grin, but he looked tired, and he sounded hoarse from the tube that had been down his throat.

"I won't stay long. I know the doctors want you to rest."

"Doctors," Kins said. "What do they know? I was told family only. Are we related now?"

"I'm your long-lost sister."

"I always wanted an older sister."

"I can see you haven't lost your sense of humor, and that it hasn't improved. I'm going to be heading out of town, so I won't see you for a few days."

"You worried?" he asked.

She didn't want to rile Kins and said, "Dan thought it best to take advantage of the time off and head up to the house in Cedar Grove."

Kins seemed to ponder this, clearly not buying her proffered reason.

"Place is yours and Shannah's . . . and the boys . . . If you want some place to rest and recuperate when you get out of here. There's fishing and hiking up there. And peace and quiet."

"Sounds ideal . . . But the boys can't get the time off from school and work like they once could. And I don't see myself hiking anytime soon." He took a moment to inhale deeply, as if short of breath. "Things change," he said, now sounding nostalgic. "That's the downside of having kids when you're young. They go off on their own, and you have to find different things to do without them."

"They've all been here, Kins. With Shannah. Every minute."

"I know," he said. "Shannah told me about all the support. I'm grateful." He became quiet again and shifted his attention back to her. Then he said, "You'd tell me. If there was something more to all this. You'd tell me; right?"

She knew what Kins meant.

"You know I treat that car better than myself. Never put anything in it but the best, get it looked over at least once a year."

"I know," she said.

"No way my brakes failed just like that. One minute the car is slowing, the next I got nothing. Pedal hits the floor and I'm flying downhill toward that intersection. I should have pulled the emergency brake, but I was too slow and too damned shocked."

She just didn't want his machines to start beeping again, but she also didn't want to lie to him. "You don't need to worry about that stuff right now, Kins. All you need to focus on is getting better and getting out of here."

"But somebody is worrying about it; right?"

"Yeah. Somebody is worrying about it. Somebody is all over it. We all got you covered, Kins."

He nodded. "Schmidt?"

"No evidence we can use. Not yet. But we're working on it. Nolasco green-lighted it."

Kins smiled, but it quickly faded. "Maria know?"

"Yes and no," Tracy said. "She knows somebody screwed with your brake line."

His eyebrows arched in question.

"Del got TCI involved and they found a video. Too far and too grainy to identify the person who dropped down under your car, but we're working some other angles. I told Maria it wasn't about you, that it was personal between me and Schmidt."

"I appreciate it."

"She got some news on her daughter. Good and bad."

"Yeah?"

"Cancer, but a very treatable form of leukemia."

He shook his head. "She doesn't need anything else on her plate."

"It's a nice thing you did, Kins. You paid a hell of a price to protect her."

"You would have done the same for me."

"Good partners look out for each other. You were the best."

"Don't start writing my obituary," Kins said. "I ain't done yet."

"No?"

"Thought about private sector, but . . ." He let out a long breath. "Too many Erik Shitheads still out there. Now he's just pissed me off."

"Glad to hear it," she said.

"You get that son of a bitch, Tracy, and if he gives you the chance, don't hesitate to save the taxpayers money on another trial. You hear me?"

"I hear you." The monitor started to ping again. Tracy smiled. "The doctors told us not to get you excited. I think I better leave before all those monitors start pinging."

CHAPTER 15

Cedar Grove was like taffy, either being stretched toward progress or contracting back to the way it had always been. At present, it was again being stretched, so much so that it hardly resembled the town in which Tracy and Dan had grown up. Instead of just the one traffic light, which had dangled from a black wire strung across Market Street and swayed violently with each wind gust, now the city had half a dozen lights mounted on signal poles. Wider sidewalks had been poured downtown, and the antique streetlamps and storefronts refurbished. At least one remnant of Tracy's and Dan's past remained. They drove beneath the cast-iron sign that stretched over Market Street and signified the entrance to the city.

WELCOME TO CEDAR GROVE
WASHINGTON'S MINING CAPITAL

Mining hadn't been conducted in Cedar Grove in more than a hundred years, and the city had never been Washington's mining capital, but good PR never let the facts get in the way. Tracy knew the town's truth from her father's tutelage, and from having researched and written a paper on the city's history while in high school. In the 1840s, miners discovered gold, copper, and coal in the mountains, and Christian Mattioli later founded the Cedar Grove Mining Company. He'd built the initial miners' houses and the businesses that became the town. It had been a lucrative venture, until the mine stopped producing. Mattioli, the mining company, and half of Cedar Grove's residents departed. Those who stayed were hardy blue-collar workers without a lot of other options.

Tracy's father, seeking to get out of Seattle after Tracy's birth, searched for a small-town experience for his daughter and moved his family to Cedar Grove to be a country doctor. He bought the abandoned Mattioli mansion atop a hill overlooking the city, then refurbished its Brazilian wood floors, Italian marble, and mahogany-paneled walls and bookshelves. He also restored its chandeliers to their original luster. In his spare time, he taught Tracy and Sarah to fish, to hunt, and to hike the North Cascades. He'd made growing up in the mountains, with its rivers and lakes, special. Tracy and Sarah had every intention of raising their families in Cedar Grove.

Then Sarah disappeared.

Her father, overcome with grief, took his own life.

Her mother became a recluse.

And everything and everyone in town changed.

Decades later, when Tracy came home to bury her sister's newly discovered remains, Market Street had looked like a ghost town. Businesses had been boarded over. Stray newspapers blew down sidewalks and gathered in the empty storefronts. She and Roy Calloway, Cedar Grove's sheriff for decades, had reminisced, but not fondly.

"What happened to my town, Tracy? What happened to our town?" Calloway had once asked.

"I don't know, Roy."

"It feels like the devil walked here in 1993 and spread evil. So much evil."

That devil had been Edmund House.

But Cedar Grove stretched again when Covid hit the cities. Young professionals with money looking to work remotely in vacation settings had found the peaceful town in the mountains, with its fresh air and proximity to rivers and lakes. After the pandemic, many families had stayed. New restaurants opened. A microbrewery was established. A pastry and coffee shop filled the vacant space where once there had been the thrift store. The corner drugstore remained, as did Hutchins' Theater. Kaufman's Mercantile Store, a large brick building, became to the yuppies what it had once been to the miners—a source of needed supplies, this time outdoor recreation, for fishing, biking, hiking, and camping. Residents said a developer would be putting in an eighteen-hole golf course and building houses along the fairways.

As Dan drove past the corner of Second Avenue and Market Street, Tracy glanced at the entrance to the Cedar Grove Police Department. The one-story metal-and-glass building wasn't part of any renovation project, not with Roy Calloway chief. Calloway was a throwback, a salmon who had gone back to his birthplace, where he would eventually die. He liked things fine the way they had once been, although he had, at least, allowed an upgrade to their police vehicles: new SUVs with computer consoles and all the other bells and whistles.

At home, they unloaded Rex and Sherlock, who raced around the expansive front lawn for a bit. Dan got them fed while Tracy, Therese, and Daniella got settled. Then they all headed out to Grandma Billie's Bistro to eat comfort food.

Grandma Billie's also looked to be stretching. Since Tracy and Dan's last visit, the bistro had added a covered outdoor dining area, complete with strung lights and lanterns.

"You see," Dan said. "I put in a patio and now everyone is jumping on the bandwagon."

Tracy laughed. "Maybe we should set up tables and serve food to offset the cost."

"We do serve food," Dan said. "Cooked by the best *bar-be-cue* and homemade-pizza chef in the Pacific Northwest."

"I think somebody's head is about to explode," Therese said from the back seat.

"Let him live in his fantasy world," Tracy said. "It could be worse. He could drive home with a Porsche 911."

"About that," Dan said.

"No," Tracy said. "No room for Daniella."

"Or me," Therese said.

The closest parking space was down the street from the restaurant. Business was good at Grandma Billie's. Tracy got out of the car and looked up and down the block for anything suspicious. On the drive up, she'd checked her side mirror frequently and had Dan make a couple unplanned stops, once professing to need a bathroom break and the other at Whidbey Pies to pick up a blackberry pie. She did not detect anyone following them.

They stepped beneath the gray awning that stretched over a pop-out façade and glanced at the written menu in the curtained window. A slate chalkboard beside a refurbished iron bench advertised the evening specials.

Dan pulled open the door, causing familiar bells to jingle, and they stepped inside. Tracy went last, again taking another gaze up and down the block.

"You coming?" Dan asked, noticing her looking.

She smiled. "Just admiring all the changes."

They hung their coats on a coatrack inside the front door. Tracy took a moment to breathe in the smells—fried chicken, chicken pot pies, macaroni and cheese, mashed potatoes, and fresh pies, a Grandma

Billie specialty. The smells were Pavlovian. They brought her back to good times, when her family would come to the restaurant to celebrate special occasions, and they'd all delight at a candle flickering in a piece of blueberry pie with vanilla ice cream. Everything felt magical.

"What happened to my town, Tracy? What happened to our town?"

"I don't know, Roy."

Elle, one of Grandma Billie's two granddaughters who now owned and ran the bistro, personally greeted them, giving them both a hug. "Tracy, Dan. So good to see you."

Dan reintroduced Therese.

"And look how big this little one is getting," Elle said, sidling up to Daniella, who was dressed in a red dress with a cape and white tights. Daniella turned her head and hid her face behind Dan's legs.

"Are you shy?" Elle squatted to tickle Daniella's side. "Are you shy? Are you shy? What a beauty."

"Looks just like her mother," Dan said.

Therese laughed. "I think he's buttering you up, Mrs. O, for that Porsche."

"Not working," Tracy said.

"I saved your table," Elle said to Dan, who had made the reservation.

"You have a table?" Therese said. "I'm impressed. You must be important."

"They are," Elle said. "I think of you both as BMT."

"BMT?" Tracy and Dan said simultaneously.

"Before my time. Original residents."

"I don't know whether to be flattered or to feel old," Tracy said to Dan.

"I'll be flattered. You feel old."

Elle led the four of them through the restaurant's dozen tables. The interior looked like a country home, which it had once been, the tables draped with white tablecloths. Red candles flickered beneath Tiffany chandeliers. Mid-nineteenth-century wall mirrors hung alongside assorted mining tools. While the restaurant remained the same as when Grandma Billie ran it, Tracy didn't recognize a single face at the other tables. Definitely not a BMT among them.

"Let me tell Hannah you're here. She wants to say hello when she gets a break," Elle said. "And she will just love this little cutie."

As they looked over the menu, Hannah came out from the kitchen in her white chef's jacket, greeting them and making a fuss over Daniella.

"Things are changing around here," Hannah said. "But this time they're taking their time and making them more organic. They have a plan in place."

"Certainly not the way things were when we grew up here," Tracy said to Dan. "A lot more people."

"We're *too* busy," Hannah said. "I'm looking for help in the kitchen. If you know of anyone . . ."

"I'll keep my ears open," Tracy said.

"And speaking of old times, you heard the Mattioli mansion sold?"

The news surprised Tracy. She'd never contemplated buying her childhood home—too many ghosts—but it still stung a bit to know it now belonged to someone else. "When?"

"I couldn't tell you. I heard about it a little while ago."

Her father had successfully petitioned to have the mansion declared a historical landmark, so although the property had gone into foreclosure after Tracy's mother passed away, it had not been torn down. The bank likely hoped Cedar Grove's revitalization and growth would attract a potential buyer at a fair price. Apparently, it had. After her initial surprise, Tracy was pleased the mansion had been bought and hoped the new owners were a family that would enjoy the home, and the acreage surrounding it, as she and Sarah once had.

"Enjoy your dinner. Try the pork chop. It's to die for . . . And you, little one," she said to Daniella. "What do you like to eat?"

"Macaroni and cheese," Daniella said.

"Then I'm going to make you a special plate," Hannah said.

After Hannah returned to the kitchen, Tracy thought again about her childhood home—all the wonderful moments she'd experienced growing up there. After Sarah's abduction and her father's suicide, Tracy had never spent another night in the mansion.

She didn't want to go home again. Didn't want to linger in the past. A fresh start was the better way to go.

"Tracy?" Tracy looked up. Dan and Therese were staring at her. "You okay?" Dan asked.

"Fine. Why?"

"I asked what you were going to have."

"Oh, I'm sorry. I was just reminiscing. I never pass up Grandma Billie's chicken pot pie," she said.

Therese closed her menu. "That settles it."

Daniella also closed her menu. "That settles it," she said, causing them all to laugh.

Tracy looked back down at her menu, then back to Dan, who continued to watch her.

He knew her well.

CHAPTER 16

Their first morning in Cedar Grove, Dan wanted to run the mountain trails to their old swimming hole, but Tracy was anxious to talk to Roy Calloway and had something else on her mind. First, she drove downtown with Therese and Daniella. The community had put in a new play structure in the central square amid the lawn and cedar trees. The play structure looked formidable, with a pirate ship complete with climbing ropes, a sliding pole, and slides. The structure also included swings, a teeter-totter, and rocking horses. Daniella loved it.

There being many mothers, nannies, and a few fathers present, Tracy told Therese she had a quick meeting and crossed the street to the Cedar Grove Police Department. She pulled open the glass doors and encountered a female officer seated behind bulletproof glass. This was new. Tracy held her police credentials to the glass and said, "Is Roy Calloway in this morning? He's an old friend."

"Roy is out fishing a few days."

"Probably why I couldn't reach him on his cell. What about Finlay Armstrong?"

"He's acting chief. Let me tell him you're here."

A moment later a buzzer clicked, and Tracy pulled open a metal door. Also new. Armstrong met her in the hallway. "Tracy Crosswhite. What brings you back to our fair town?"

Finlay looked good. He'd regained weight he'd lost when his wife, Kimberly, was killed in a house fire. His gray hair now made him look distinguished, and his facial features again had the sharp edges that, along with his hazel eyes, had once attracted the attention of the girls in their high school class.

"Dan and I wanted to get away. Brought Daniella and the nanny up as well."

"How long you here for?"

Tracy grimaced. "Tough to say. I'm on a break from SPD. Long story, but good timing."

"Roy's gone fishing for a few days."

"I heard. When did you redo the lobby with the bulletproof glass and secure door?"

"About a year ago. We got new police cars, too, and a new communications system."

"How does Roy feel about all the changes?"

"You know Roy. He refuses to check in, and he insists he be buzzed in the minute he enters. But I think he's liking the new cars and coming to terms with all the bells and whistles."

"Look, I know you're probably busy as acting chief, so I won't keep you. I stopped by because I have a favor to ask."

"Let's step into Roy's office."

Finlay closed the door behind them and slid behind the desk. Tracy sat in a chair across from him. On the wall behind Finlay was the sign Calloway had hung the day he took office, decades ago.

RULE #1: THE CHIEF IS ALWAYS RIGHT.

RULE #2: SEE RULE #1.

To Finlay's left hung the rainbow trout Calloway had caught on the Yakima River that his wife, Nora, had framed.

"The more things change, the more they stay the same," Tracy said.

Armstrong glanced at the trout. "Tell me about it. I've already accepted that someday I'll come in here and find Roy has passed sitting at his desk, with his boots still on. So, tell me what can I do for you? You know Roy would have my hide if I turned *you* down for anything."

Tracy explained the situation in Seattle with Erik Schmidt. She handed Finlay a copy of Schmidt's recent mug shot with a physical description and another of his gold Corvette and license plate. "I don't want to be paranoid, but we have some evidence Schmidt cut the brake lines on another detective's car. But his real grudge is against me."

"What about?"

Tracy explained her visit to Walla Walla and conversations with Tony Reed and Tim Herman.

"Geez," Armstrong said. "Will we ever be rid of that guy House?"

"I don't know, Finlay. I'm starting to doubt it."

"I'm sorry, Tracy. I assume you want us to keep an out for this guy, Schmidt?"

"If you would. I was hoping maybe you could put your deputies on alert, have them keep an eye on the house, and if they see any strange cars, stop and check it out?"

"Sure. I can do that. I can have a deputy sit at your house if you like."

"I don't want to alarm Dan or Therese any more than I have, and I don't want them to feel like prisoners. We came up here to get away from all the crap. I'm not going to let Schmidt or anyone else make us live that way. I just want to be prudent and have a police presence . . . in case."

"I assume you're carrying?"

She raised her fleece, showing her Glock. "I'm well armed, and we brought Rex and Sherlock with us to sound the alarm if needed." She let out a held breath and had to fight back her emotions. "I'm sorry, Finlay, I just . . ."

"Hey, don't be. I understand. This is your family we're talking about. And excuse me for saying so, but this guy seems to have you spooked. That's unlike you."

She thought again of Julia Hoch and Bridgette Traugott. She thought of Edmund House and Sarah. "I'm hoping it's just a precaution," she said, "and we never have to worry about it. But if your men encounter Schmidt, let them know he'll likely be armed, and he's unlikely to miss."

After dropping Therese and Daniella back home for Daniella's nap, Tracy spoke to Dan, who'd returned from his run. She told him about the deputy who might be stopping by to check on the house, so he wouldn't be surprised, then said she was going to run a second errand.

She'd first thought of Mason Pettibone, who had been her shooting instructor as a young woman, when she'd failed her shooting test, but she started to seriously consider contacting him after she watched Erik Schmidt's AMU shooting video. She no longer believed Schmidt's pointing his finger at her and pulling the trigger was just bravado. Not after what Nunzio had said and after what had happened to Kins. She saw it as Schmidt issuing a challenge, one she could not, at present, win.

Pettibone had trained Tracy, Sarah, and their father to shoot with speed and accuracy. Beyond the physical aspects, Pettibone taught shooters the mental aspects, tips to help them relax, to be singularly focused, and to more easily slip into the shooting zone. Between Tracy, her sister, and their father, Pettibone had trained three Washington State

Champions. She wanted to determine if he could help her—maybe not to shoot as well as she once had, but to shoot as well as possible, though she hoped it didn't come to that. "Whatever increases your sense of security, I'll support," Dan said.

Pettibone lived across town from where Tracy had grown up, but not far from Dan's parents' home. Back then, that side of town had been considered the side where the poor people lived. When they had been kids, Tracy had teased Dan as coming from "the wrong side of the tracks." She stopped when she'd visited his home and realized how poor his family was.

Pettibone lived out here for a different reason. He needed the acreage to ensure his neighbors' safety, and for noise control. Neighbors didn't want to be on the wrong end of a stray bullet, nor did they want to hear the pop-pop-pop of guns firing all afternoon and into the early evening—when Pettibone returned home from work and had time to give his lessons.

Pettibone had been a do-everything attorney in Cedar Grove when Tracy's father was the town's do-everything doctor. He'd made a living drafting wills and trusts, power-of-attorney documents, leases, and legal papers needed for the purchase and sale of homes. He probated estates, mediated divorces, and prepared advanced-care directives. He also had a sense of humor. His cowboy name, "Loophole Pettifogger," combined a legal term with a derogatory term for a lawyer who handled trivial legal matters. Pettibone said it was better to make fun of himself than have others do it for him.

Pettibone had long since given up his law office in downtown Cedar Grove, though he still lived in the one-story rambler he'd owned when Tracy trained with him. She did not, however, know his phone number or if he even used a landline any longer. But she could drive to his house darn near blindfolded.

His property abutted the North Cascades, and he'd constructed a shooting range in his backyard with several shooting lanes where he trained students on gun safety and basic shooting techniques. Some just wanted to improve their shot for hunting deer and elk. But for those who wanted to compete, he'd also re-created shooting scenarios, based on famous Old West gunfights.

She parked the truck in Pettibone's driveway. Grass sprouted from cracks in the cement and in his wife's once-pristine flower beds. Monica had passed away a couple years ago. Behind the home, the North Cascades' steep and rugged topography made for a picturesque backdrop. The house sat in a V-shaped valley surrounded by jagged ridges and mountain peaks from which foliage grew at every angle and from seemingly every crack. Ribbons of fog could make the mountains appear eerie and mysterious, but to Tracy it was like seeing an old friend. She, Sarah, Dan, and their friends spent their summers all over those rugged mountains—exploring for hidden waterfalls, steep cliffs, and pools in which to swim. Tracy recalled training on clear mornings, when sunlight flowed over the peaks and swept into the valley, as beautiful as any sunrise she'd ever seen.

She stepped along concrete pavers leading to the front door beneath a small eave, rang the bell, then stepped back. A small dog yapped inside, followed by Mason's familiar, deep voice commanding the dog, who he'd apparently named Lucille.

"Hush, Lucille. Hush now."

When the door pulled open, the dog, a miniature white poodle, dashed out and jumped up on Tracy's shins, then put her paws in the air and danced on two legs. Tracy got another surprise, and another indication why, perhaps, you couldn't go home again. Mason Pettibone stood with the help of crutches propped beneath each armpit. On his left foot he wore a pointed cowboy boot. As for his right leg, his jeans were folded back at the knee, where the lower portion of his leg had apparently been amputated.

He broke into a surprised grin. "Tracy Crossdraw." He used her cowboy name, and his voice brought a smile to Tracy's face. Mason had called all of his students by their Cowboy Action names. Tracy's father had been "Doc" and Sarah "Kid." "I'll be damned. To what does an old codger like myself owe the pleasure?"

"Hi, Mason. So good to see you. How are you?" Tracy stepped forward and gave him an awkward hug, worried she might knock him off-balance.

"Well, I've been better," he said with a light chuckle. "Come on in. Lucille, get down now. Get down. She gets excited when we have visitors."

"She's adorable."

Pettibone shuffled backward and Tracy stepped into a small, tiled foyer, Lucille still prancing on two legs like a circus performer. Tracy had never actually been inside Pettibone's home. She'd always accessed the shooting range in his backyard by walking along the side of the house.

Pettibone closed the door. Now in his early eighties, his skin was marked with age spots, and the vibrant blue eyes Tracy recalled had lost some of their luster. His hair had thinned and turned a distinguished silver, as had his bushy eyebrows and handlebar mustache—with a triangle of hair beneath his bottom lip. He wore what Tracy recalled him always wearing: a black T-shirt from a single-action shooting competition, this one from the Texas Black Powder State Championship in Groesbeck, Texas, and blue jeans with an oval, silver belt buckle engraved with a bareback horse rider.

"What happened?" she asked, figuring since he'd raised the subject it was better to get the obvious out in the open and not pretend she was blind.

"Diabetes," he said. "They keep hacking off pieces of me. Started with neuropathy in my foot, which led to an untreated ulcer. By the time I got in for treatment they had to take a couple of toes, then the foot. They were worried the infection could spread to the bone, so I finally just told them to take the damn lower leg. I look like one of those old Civil War veterans you see in the photographs."

"I'm sorry," she said.

"It is what it is," he said. "Had two good legs for eighty-two years. I'm not going to look a gift horse in the mouth." He smiled broadly. "But enough about me. What brings you out here? I'm tickled as punch to see you."

They discussed family for a few minutes.

"You know I lost Monica two years ago," Pettibone said.

"I heard after the fact, when I last made a trip up here, otherwise Dan and I would have been at the funeral. You got our card, I hope."

"I'm sure I did, but that time is a bit of a blur. Me and Lucille are getting along just fine though, aren't we, little one?" The dog ran around, looking up at him expectantly. "My daughter, Celia, divorced some time ago, and she, my granddaughter, Lydia, and Lucille here moved in. I figured no sense having all these rooms go to waste, and it's nice to have family looking after me."

"I've been meaning to bring Daniella around, but Dan and I don't get up here as often as we'd like, both of us still working, and usually we're rushed."

Pettibone waved off her apology. "Big-time Seattle homicide detective." He smiled. "We're all proud of you up here. Do you still compete?"

"That's something I wanted to talk to you about."

He looked surprised. "Okay. Well, come in and sit." He was better than adept at moving about on his crutches and looked to still be in good shape.

The interior was spotless, a beige carpet unblemished, the furniture a matching set. Taking up nearly the entire wall behind the sofa was a large painting of a cattle roundup that looked, from the expansive blue sky, to be somewhere in Montana.

Mason made his way to a recliner, laid his crutches down on the carpet, and hopped a couple times to his seat. Lucille sprang into his lap and circled a bit before settling down. Tracy sat on the sofa across from him, a coffee table between them.

"Well, tell me what brings you out here? I'm more than a little curious."

"My shooting. I want to take lessons again—while I'm here," Tracy said. "Are you still teaching? I mean, with the leg and all."

"Don't need my leg to teach, but Tracy, your family already exceeded all my expectations—and knowledge. I taught you everything I know. You had the intangibles that made each of you champions."

"I might have at one time. I'm not so certain anymore."

She told him what had happened on the shoot/no-shoot course, the missed targets, and her hallucination. She did not tell him that watching the video of Schmidt had initially triggered a competitiveness in her that had once made her one of Washington's best shots, or that she had a premonition, perhaps a maternal instinct, that Schmidt would challenge her, and she wanted to protect those she loved. She wanted to be at her best, if it came to that.

"Let's start with the physical aspects," he said. "We're all getting older, and we aren't as young as we once were. When's the last time you had your eyes checked?"

"Every year. I'm no longer 20/10 but I'm still 20/20."

"Okay. No cataracts?"

"No."

"No tremors in your hands? Nothing like that?"

"Nothing."

"Okay, so it's mental."

Tracy laughed. "Well, I'm hoping it's nothing too bad."

"I just mean it's not physical. Going back to the hallucination, can you describe it?"

"Edmund House."

Pettibone grimaced as if hit by a sudden pain. Those, like Pettibone, Finlay Armstrong, and Roy Calloway, who had been living in Cedar Grove when Edmund House initially came to town would never forget him. Pettibone squeezed the triangle of hair beneath his lip. "Have you had these hallucinations before?"

"I started having some difficulties after I came back here in 2013, when House was retried, and we had the confrontation in the mountains, but I saw a counselor for it. Got some help. Things were good for a while."

"Did this counselor have any explanation for it?"

"She says that my subconscious is triggering my repressed memories of Edmund House. She said it's similar to PTSD."

"Yeah, but why now? Did she have any idea?"

"It might be related to another case I'm involved in regarding a drug dealer in Seattle. He looks the way House once looked when he was young. This man has also killed two women, but because of a legal technicality, he's still out there. I recently spoke to some people who knew him and learned he'd been in the Army Marksmanship Unit at Fort Moore, Georgia."

"The AMU?" Pettibone whistled. "They're some of the best shooters out there. Grand Master caliber."

"This guy has had a long fall from grace." Tracy told Pettibone Schmidt's background and said, "He was sent to Walla Walla, where he became close with House."

Pettibone raised his eyebrows.

"In fact, I was told by someone who knew him in prison that Schmidt blames me for House's death, believes it was premeditated, that I got House out of prison to kill him for what he did to Sarah."

"I can certainly see why that would cause you nightmares."

"But what happened on my shooting test wasn't a nightmare. I was awake. The last target I saw was House, not of a man holding a radio."

Tracy decided not to go any further; not to tell Pettibone that Schmidt had threatened her and, she believed, tried to kill Kins. But he sensed it anyway.

"I guess the real question, Tracy, is, are you in any danger?"

"I don't know, Mason, but I don't want to leave anything to chance either. I spoke to Finlay about having a police presence, and I want to be as prepared as I can be, were anything to happen."

"Okay. But are you here to compete, or do you foresee a possible scenario where this guy . . . Schmidt might come after you?"

That was a tricky question to answer. She didn't want to lie, but she didn't really know. "At the moment, I just want to get back to the basics; if I can get faster and more accurate, all the better. I'm hoping the more I shoot, the faster I'll begin to process information, without thinking too much, and let my instincts take over."

It was a phrase Pettibone had frequently used when he'd been training her and Sarah.

Clear your head. Don't think about the process. Don't dwell on the shot you just fired, focus on the shot you are about to take.

"You're serious about this."

"I wouldn't be here if I wasn't," she said.

"Well, if you're serious about becoming faster and more accurate, you're going to have to be open to some new forms of training and, given my situation"—he gestured to his amputated leg—"an instructor who can train you."

"I have all the confidence in the world in you, Mason."

"Maybe, but this type of training is well beyond me. Come on. Easier for me to show you than to try to explain it. I don't understand it myself."

He'd certainly piqued Tracy's curiosity.

He helped the dog down from his lap and onto the carpet, where Lucille again bounded and pranced. He grabbed his crutches and, after a moment of shifting and sliding to the edge of his seat, he was back on his foot. Rather than move toward the front door, he made his way down the hallway, Tracy following. He stopped outside a closed door and knocked. "Lydia? Lydia, may I come in?"

He got no answer.

"Earphones," he said, giving Tracy a look, then reached and turned the door handle, pushing the door in.

A young woman sat facing one of three computer monitors. The overhead lights were off, and the window shades pulled, further darkening the room. She wore headphones as her fingers and hands moved rapidly across a keyboard and manipulated a computer mouse. On the screen, figures moved at warp speed and bright lights flashed.

"My granddaughter. Her cowboy name is 'Lightning Strike.' Nobody, and I mean *nobody*, comes close to her speed and her accuracy."

CHAPTER 17

Lydia turned her head, saw her grandfather and Tracy, and abruptly stood, removing the earphones and setting them on the desk. "Sorry, Grandpa. I didn't hear you come in." She eyed Tracy with suspicion.

"Nothing to be sorry about, Lydia. I wanted to introduce you to someone. This young woman here is Tracy Crosswhite," Pettibone said. "I taught her how to shoot when she was younger than you."

"Oh wow," Lydia said, suddenly animated and smiling brightly, but not making solid eye contact.

Lydia looked to be late teens, maybe early twenties, tall and lean like her grandfather, nearly Tracy's height. She'd pulled her strawberry-blonde hair into a ponytail and looked at Tracy with blue eyes. It was, to Tracy, like looking at Sarah as a young woman, when Tracy had last seen her. And it gave her pause.

"Really nice to meet you, Ms. Crosswhite. Did you have a cowboy name?"

Tracy shook the image of Sarah. "Crossdraw," she said. The faint sounds of classical music permeated the room, coming from speakers on the desk.

"Crossdraw," Lydia said. Her gaze shifted to the ceiling. "Tracy 'Crossdraw' Crosswhite. Won three consecutive Washington State shooting championships. At eighteen years of age, she was the youngest competitor to win the title until her sister, Sarah 'the Kid' Crosswhite, took the crown at seventeen. Shoots the Uberti 1873 Cattleman Colt Single-Action .45 revolver with a 5.5-inch stainless steel barrel and simulated-pearl grips. Wears a red bandanna, turquoise bolo tie, black Stetson, suede dustcoat, and cross-draw holster."

Tracy was both impressed and perplexed. Mason had no idea she was coming to his house, which meant Lydia had no opportunity to look Tracy up on the SASS website, let alone time to memorize her shooting biography. The young woman had sounded like an infomercial, repeating Tracy's information verbatim. Tracy glanced at Mason, who hid a sheepish grin.

He flexed his eyebrows. "Lydia likes to read my back copies of the Washington State Single Action Shooting Society magazine, and just about any other shooting magazine or website she can get her hands on. I might have told her to read up about you and your sister, given your similarities in age when you were both winning competitions."

"This was recent?"

"No," he said with a chuckle. "Months ago. Maybe years."

Tracy redirected her gaze on Lydia, still perplexed. "You're a hundred percent accurate. That's amazing."

Lydia's broad smile expanded, but again Tracy noticed she broke eye contact. She also rocked from the balls of her feet to her heels.

"Your grandfather says you also compete?"

"My cowboy name is Lightning Strike. Grandpa helped me choose it. I won my first Washington State championship last year."

"How old are you, Lydia?"

"I'm eighteen. Almost nineteen. My birthday is September twenty-fifth. I'm a Libra, like my mother."

"Did you attend Cedar Grove High School?" Tracy asked.

"Homeschooled," Mason interjected. "Lydia graduated four years of online college last year at the University of Washington."

"College?"

"College," Mason repeated.

"That's . . . also amazing," Tracy said. "What did you study?"

"I created my own major," Lydia said. "I received degrees in applied physics and computer science. I finished first in my class and achieved a perfect score on my final exams."

"Remember what we discussed, Lydia," Mason said.

"Oh, sorry, Grandpa. Modesty. Don't be too proud or confident about oneself or one's abilities. Don't talk too much about yourself. Others will think you're bragging. It can make them feel bad."

"It's okay," Tracy said. "I'm glad to hear you did so well." She wanted to ask what Lydia intended to do with her majors, but she got a sense that was not something contemplated, given she was at home in the middle of a workday.

"What do you do, Ms. Crosswhite?" It sounded like something rehearsed, something Lydia had been taught to ask others.

"You can call me Tracy," she said. "And I'm a police detective."

"Oh wow," Lydia said, looking genuinely intrigued and impressed. Again, her gaze flickered up and to the right. "A police detective is a specialized law enforcement professional responsible for investigating crimes, gathering evidence, and identifying suspects. Their expertise in investigative techniques plays a crucial role in solving criminal cases and ensuring justice. Here are some key duties typically associated with the job of a police detective."

"Lydia . . . ," Mason said.

She looked at her grandfather. "Sorry, Grandpa. Would you like to hear the key duties associated with the job of a police detective, Tracy?"

"Not right now, Lydia, but thank you," Tracy said.

"Tracy here wants to take up competitive shooting again, and I told her you would help to train her—on your computers—using some of your video games."

"Oh wow. That would be awesome. I would really love to help you train." She stepped to a shelf. "I have *Halo Infinite*, *Call of Duty: Warzone*, *Dota 2*, *Valorant*, *League of Legends*, and videos that simulate famous Western shootouts and enhance the skills necessary to be a competitive shooter." She smiled at her grandfather, and Pettibone nodded. "Grandpa got me those games." Her voice again changed. "These games allow you to experience the thrill and challenge of dueling with other gunslingers in various scenarios and settings. Examples of such games are *Gunblood*, *Call of Juarez: Gunslinger*, *West of Dead*, *Desperados* . . ."

"Lydia?" Mason said.

"Sorry. Focus. Engage with others."

Tracy had no idea what she was in store for, though she trusted Pettibone. And she was intrigued how a video game could increase her speed and accuracy on the shooting course. "That sounds terrific, Lydia. I would love to train with you."

"Do you want to get started?" Lydia moved toward her computer.

"No. Not today," Tracy said. "How about tomorrow? After I take my daughter to the new park downtown?"

"That would be totally perfect," Lydia said. "Does your daughter want to learn to shoot also?"

"Someday. She's not quite four years old."

Lydia stuck out a hand at a perfect ninety-degree angle. "I'll see you tomorrow, Tracy Crossdraw."

Tracy shook her hand, a strong grip. "I'll see you, Lightning Strike."

Tracy and Mason exited the room. Mason closed the door, and they made their way back down the hall to the small entry. "So," Mason said, still wearing his sheepish grin. "What do you think of my granddaughter?"

"She's brilliant," Tracy said.

"It's called 'scripting.' Lydia recalls passages she reads just once, verbatim. And she can repeat lines from TV shows and movies she watches. Celia had Lydia tested when she was young. She's autistic with mostly low support needs. Some people say, 'She's on the spectrum.' When she develops an interest in a specific topic, she will learn everything about it—like shooting and video games. You might have noticed her rocking on the balls of her feet?"

"I did."

"She'll also rub the pads of her fingers together or rub her hands on her thighs. That's called 'stimming'—self-stimulatory behavior. It helps her to maintain her focus when she moves out of her daily routine."

"I'm sorry. I would have called but didn't have your number."

"No. It's good for Lydia to break from routine. It teaches her that things don't always go as planned and that's okay."

"Her father's not in the picture?"

"He moved out of state following the divorce, supposedly for a job. I think Lydia embarrassed him, and he couldn't handle it. Couldn't live with the responsibility."

"She's lucky to have you."

"Celia works two jobs, so . . . I've stepped in to help. I've done a lot of my own research and talked with Lydia's counselors and parents of children on the spectrum to try to ease Celia's load."

"You're a good man, Mason."

"You're kind to say so, but I'm also not going to be around forever. Lydia needs to socialize more and learn to live on her own. That's tough for me, given my one leg. But we're working on things here at home."

"Why was she homeschooled?"

"You might have noticed that Lydia struggles with social cues like body language and emotional expressions. She tends to say what is on her mind, unfiltered and without considering the context or the company.

She can be blunt, but it is never intended to be hurtful. Other kids didn't understand. She also has a tendency to repeat things, though more when she was younger. Kids who don't understand do what kids do."

"I get it," Tracy said. "She's also beautiful."

"Both a blessing and a curse. The boys . . . they weren't always honest about their intentions, and Lydia . . . well, she didn't always understand."

"I'm sorry," Tracy said.

"Social situations, like school, became a source of anxiety for Lydia, which led to withdrawal and avoidance. Lydia likes to keep to a predictable routine. We do try to limit her time on the computer, however, or she would immerse herself in those worlds and her imagination."

Tracy had wondered about that. "It's so dark in there. Does she get outside?"

"Every day. Also, part of her routine. She's sensitive to light, so she wears sunglasses outdoors. She used to come out to the shooting range with me in the afternoons when we would train, and we used to go on walks together in the mountains." He nodded to his right side. "Before the diabetes got my leg."

"Who gets her out now?"

"Celia does her best, but working two jobs, and weekends, well, she doesn't have a lot of time to spare. Lydia gets out around here. We planted a garden out back, and she helps me with that." He chuckled. "Actually, I help her now. She knows more about gardening than I ever did."

"How did you get her to compete in SASS, given her need for routine?"

"Actually, you and Sarah had a part in that."

"We did?"

"I wanted her to know that she could do it and do it well. So, I had her read up on your championships and your times. The tinted shooting glasses, earplugs, and noise-cancellation earmuffs also helped. Along with a lot of gentle persuasion."

"What's the future hold for Lydia?"

"Uncertainty. I take her to see a therapist in Bellingham who is helping her overcome her anxiety in social situations so she can hopefully live on her own someday. Many high-functioning people like her do."

"Does she drive?"

"No. I've tried teaching her, Celia has also, but . . . it's a challenge to get her to concentrate because there is so much stimuli when one drives. She just needs more exposure. I am teaching her to grocery shop, how to put gas in the car, and we take her to some large events like rodeos to try to acclimate her—well, we did until my surgeries. The hope was she'd progress to living in an apartment and manage her own finances, so people don't take advantage of her. An advantage and disadvantage of computers is Lydia can do just about everything online now: shop for groceries and supplies, buy books—she loves to read—get my prescriptions, buy clothes. Everything is delivered. She never has to leave the house."

"Never thought of it that way, but I guess making everything easier also makes us more isolated."

"And the more isolated we become, the more alone we are. I can tell you from experience. Some days I get up and don't have a clue what I'm going to do with my day, and that can be scary and depressing. I'm glad to have Lydia. Helping her helps me."

"I appreciate your help also, Mason."

"It gives me a purpose."

"Why not just train on the range, like I once did?"

"You'll see. Computers require fast-twitch muscles and increase the speed of your decision-making. You will have a lot of stimuli coming at you and learn to filter out the irrelevant. You'll better understand when you go through some of Lydia's games. I was skeptical, but Lydia made a believer out of me. Computers can't cover it all, though, the recoil of the gun, the anticipated violence that can make the best of us flinch and throw our shots off. So, she trains on both. At least she did. How long are you in town?"

"Indefinitely. Long story, but I'm on a bit of a break from the police department. Not sure when that break might end."

"All right. Well, how about we set up times to train on the computer *and* on the range that hopefully won't interfere too much with your family time."

"Dan is only going to be here a few more days. He needs to take care of some business back in Seattle but will come up on the weekends."

"What about your daughter? You're free to bring her along."

"She's a handful. Much like Lucille. She'd be into everything, and I wouldn't be able to concentrate. I have a nanny to help me out."

"Okay. Tell me how to best get ahold of you and we'll get lessons set up."

As they exchanged cell phone numbers, Tracy said, "I want to pay you, Mason. And Lydia. I hope that is clear."

"I won't accept your money. I hope that is clear. As I said, this will get me out of bed in the morning and give me something to truly look forward to."

Tracy said, "Maybe we can incorporate my paying Lydia into her learning to manage her finances."

Mason smiled. "Now you're talking my language. Okay, I got a proposition for you. You can pay Lydia. As for me, I'd be grateful if you would take Lydia into town with you every so often while you're here. Maybe take her grocery shopping or shopping at the mercantile store. Get her out and around others. Give her some exposure to new experiences."

"It's a deal," Tracy said. "And something that I'll look forward to."

Tracy showed herself to the door. Outside, she made her way to her truck. Just being here brought her back to those days many years ago when she'd come with Sarah to train and afterward her father would pick them up in the truck. Mason Pettibone was a tie to her past.

She looked back at the house. Flashes of light flickered behind the curtain covering the window of Lydia's room.

She thought of Lydia, and of Sarah. And she wondered if they could have been similar in more ways than just their physical attributes.

CHAPTER 18

At home that evening, after Daniella's nighttime routine and putting her down for the night, Tracy walked outside to the detached garage and turned on the overhead fluorescent lights. They flickered before reaching full power, illuminating her Ford F-150 she'd inherited from her father and kept in Cedar Grove so they'd have two cars, if needed. The lights also shone on Dan's workbench and the woodworking tools and equipment he'd inherited from his father. Dan had used the tools and the equipment to gut and rebuild his parents' home. He'd contemplated bringing the assortment of saws and the drill presses down to their Redmond home but always came up with an excuse not to do so. Tracy believed his reluctance was likely out of deference to his father, who spent his life and his career in Cedar Grove doing cabinetry and other woodwork.

Tracy moved to a corner of the garage and pulled off a paint tarp, revealing the rugged carts her father had helped his two daughters build. The wooden carts looked very much like the baby stroller Dan and Tracy pushed Daniella in when they took her on runs. Her father had used wheelbarrow handles and small bicycle tires to construct the frames, then fashioned a box with vertical slots to the frames. Within the boxes, Tracy and Sarah could slide their rifles and shotguns. The bottom of the cart was a square storage box. Tracy and Sarah had placed their pistols and their ammo there, as well as bottled water and snacks when they'd competed in tournaments.

Tracy had decorated her storage box with decals from the many shooting competitions she and Sarah had attended. She knelt and opened it, expecting it to be empty, but inside she found Sarah's blue bandanna. The shock caused her heart to ache and her eyes to quickly water. She picked it up. Something fell and hit the bottom of the box with a dull thud. She lifted out the object and had another shock when she held it up to the light. She'd won the silver-plated buckle at the 1993 Washington State Cowboy Action Shooting Championship—though her victory was only because Sarah had purposefully missed a target during the competition. Sarah didn't want Tracy to lose and be upset. Unbeknownst to Tracy, her boyfriend at the time, Ben, had a diamond ring in his pocket, a dinner reservation, and plans to propose. It was the reason Tracy had not driven home with Sarah after the competition, the reason Roy Calloway had found their truck abandoned along the county road leading back to Cedar Grove the morning after the competition.

The last time Tracy ever saw her sister.

The last time she'd ever competed.

"Stubborn as a mule," Tracy said, referring to her sister, though the phrase applied equally to herself. They both had refused the buckle—Tracy because she knew she hadn't won it, and Sarah because Tracy refused to take it. Tracy had thrown it in the truck bed, where Calloway found it the following morning. After Edmund House had been convicted, Calloway had returned the buckle. Tracy forgot she'd stored it with her sister's bandanna in the rugged cart.

Tracy shook the welling tears, then carefully wrapped the buckle in the bandanna and put it back in the cart box.

On pegs along the garage wall, Dan had hung Tracy's canvas duster, her sister's black Stetson cowboy hat, and Tracy's red bandanna and bolo tie. Beneath the clothing, he'd built a shoe rack for the Nocona cowboy boots she'd worn in competition. Her father had purchased the boots for both his daughters on a trip to El Paso, Texas. Tracy's boots had a hint of red in the stitching, Sarah's a hint of turquoise. Tracy had kept her gear for the same reason Dan had kept his father's woodworking machinery. Nostalgia. She told herself someday Daniella might use it, *if* she wanted to compete, but really, she held on to it because she couldn't bring herself to get rid of it. She never in a million years had thought she'd be putting the clothes on again, but Mason demanded his students practice in the gear in which they competed. It was one less variable for them to worry about.

Tracy stepped beyond her father's reloading press to the gun safe bolted and concreted to the garage-floor slab. The nearly six-foot fire-resistant steel safe weighed close to five hundred pounds and held Tracy and Sarah's collection of guns, as well as Dan's hunting rifles and shotguns. She put her fingertips on the biometric pad. The door clicked open to more of her past. Her two .45 Colt replica revolvers, her .32-20 Winchester center-fire rifle with lever and exposed hammer—the rifle some said won the West—and her replica 1887 lever-action 12-gauge shotgun. The rifle, used mainly to hunt small game, weighed less than rifles others used in competition. Her father believed the lighter weight made it easier for his two daughters to aim and to handle the recoil.

"I wondered where you'd disappeared to."

Tracy startled, turned, and nearly pointed one of her pistols at Dan. He sprang backward about three feet, like a cat. It took Tracy a moment to catch her breath. "Geez, you scared me."

"I scared *you*? Shit. I'm glad you hadn't loaded anything," he said. "You're awfully jumpy."

"It's night, I'm in the garage alone, and I hear a man's voice. Yes. I'm jumpy. I'm also trained. You're lucky I wasn't carrying."

"Schmidt?" he said.

She shrugged.

He walked over to where she stood and eyed the rugged cart and clothing. "But you're not really alone; are you? You're surrounded by memories. Is that what's making you jumpy?"

He had a point. "Maybe it's where I focused my attention."

"Good memories or bad?"

Another shrug.

"It's hard; I know," he said softly. "Is that the reason you want to take lessons again? Good memories competing from your past. Or more recent events."

"It was a lot of good times, up until it wasn't."

"You're serious though?"

"I am," Tracy said.

Dan exhaled audibly.

"Just taking precautions, Dan. Hey, it could be something fun for the two of us to do together?"

He smiled. "I'm not sure I can fit another hobby into my schedule at the moment, but it would be fun to watch you compete again, Crossdraw."

She smiled back. "Maybe we'll both be watching Daniella compete someday."

"We have a few more years. I think the pistols are bigger than she is. Pettibone must be excited to have you back."

"I think he's more eager than I am."

"From what you've told me, I can see why. Sounds like it could benefit his granddaughter as well."

"It could. She's a beautiful girl. Mason said the boys come sniffing around but for all the wrong reasons. I hope we don't have that problem with Daniella."

"Her mom's a police detective with loaded guns. I think the boys will be discerning."

A thought struck her. "Why did you come out here?"

"I was also looking for . . . a hammer." Dan reached above his workbench and took a hammer from a peg on the wall.

"You were, huh? For what?"

"Hammering."

"Anything in particular?"

He smiled. "Just checking to make sure you're okay. I know this place has a lot of ghosts. For me also."

"Cedar Grove has ghosts. But this place, our home, has only good spirits." She smiled at the recollection of the first time she'd come to the remodeled house, after they'd both been away for years. "You do remember the first time we made dinner. You were still remodeling. Do you remember teaching me the golf swing?"

"In every bone in my body."

"Good. Why don't I put these away and we go in? You can teach me again."

CHAPTER 19

The following morning, with Dan at home and a deputy making frequent drive-bys of the house, Tracy drove to Pettibone's. He opened the door, grinning like he held a secret. "She's been hard at work preparing for you."

"I hope it's not taking her away from anything important."

He looked at Tracy from beneath those bushy eyebrows. "Are you kidding? She's like a kid in a candy store. Spent yesterday getting her room all set up for you. Even cleaned up the clutter. Then she went outside and went to work on getting the steel plates set up on the range for tomorrow's first stage."

"Any hints on what that might be?"

"The 'professional,'" he said. "Do you recall it?"

"Can't say I do."

"Straightforward. Nothing too complicated. A few Nevada sweeps, but mostly just basic, timed shooting."

"I'll look it up on the internet. Looking forward to it."

"Tomorrow, you come dressed in your cowboy gear."

"I remember. Went through much of my stuff last night. Not sure what still fits—after twenty years and a baby." Tracy looked around. "What smells so good in here?"

"Lydia made a quiche for me last night, and my daughter left detailed instructions explaining how to put a piece in the microwave." He made a face. "I lost a leg. Not my mind."

"You didn't say that to her."

"No. I'm a good patient. 'Yes, dear' and 'No, dear' with a lot of thank-yous mixed in. She's my guardian angel. And she can cook. She's teaching Lydia."

Tracy thought of Hannah's need of help in the kitchen at Grandma Billie's, and filed that possibility away. Lydia had to walk before she could run.

Lydia came down the hall with an expression like she held the same secret as her grandfather and couldn't wait to see Tracy's reaction. She wiped the smile from her face. "Good morning, Crossdraw." She looked and sounded all business.

Tracy raised her hand and tipped the brim of an imaginary Stetson. "Lightning Strike."

"I've set up a station for you." She spoke to her grandfather. "Are you done?"

"Social graces . . . ," Mason said.

Lydia's eyes widened. "Right. Sorry, Grandpa. Can we get started, please?"

Mason gave Tracy another knowing glance, then said, "I'll get out of your way. I have the finishing touches to put on the shooting stages before tomorrow."

Stages in Cowboy Action Shooting were the sequence of shots the shooter would make with her pistols, rifle, and shotgun in a re-creation of a Wild West shoot-out while being timed. Accuracy wasn't as difficult as the police qualification test. Speed decided between shooters.

Lydia escorted Tracy down the hall to her closed bedroom door. "Shut your eyes," Lydia said. Tracy had no idea what to expect but played along. Lydia held her by the elbow and escorted her into the room. "Open them."

Mason wasn't kidding about Lydia having put in a lot of work. She'd picked up and organized much of the clutter. She'd also moved one of her computer screens to a separate table and brought in an ergonomic chair. Tracy noticed Lydia had a movie poster on the wall— Gene Wilder rising from a colorful hat surrounded by colorful streamers from the movie *Willy Wonka & the Chocolate Factory*. Books, dozens of them, filled a bookshelf, many titles Tracy recognized. The Harry Potter series. The Twilight books, as well as some classics. *The Count of Monte Cristo*. *The Old Man and the Sea*. *The Great Gatsby*. *To Kill a Mockingbird*. *The Red Badge of Courage*.

Tracy had grown up a reader. She and Sarah read for hours at night with a flashlight under their bedcovers, including many of the classics Lydia had also apparently read.

"You've read a lot of books, Lydia."

"I have. I have read a lot of books."

"I'll bet I can guess your favorite." Lydia's eyes widened in anticipation. Tracy ran her fingers along the spines and stopped at *Charlie and the Chocolate Factory*. She pulled it out and held it up. "This one?"

"Yes!" Lydia said, sounding and looking elated. "How did you do that?"

Tracy smiled. "I am a detective," she said.

Lydia beamed. "Yes. You are a detective. A very good detective."

"We better get started."

"You sit here." Lydia held the back of the chair she'd brought in, and Tracy sat.

On the table was a computer mouse and a keyboard. The mouse pad was blue with a gold lightning bolt above the words "Lightning Strike." It reminded Tracy of the cover of the superhero comic books she and her sister used to buy at the mercantile store.

"I'm not taking your mouse pad; am I?" Tracy asked.

"That's the best mouse, and you need the best."

"Why is the mouse important?"

"The mouse is your pistol."

"I don't understand."

"You will." Lydia moved like a whirling dervish, talking as she did. "I'm going to train you the way my grandfather trains you, but on the computer. Fast-twitch, small movements for improving accuracy and increasing speed and judgment."

Mason Pettibone used to say much the same thing—teaching an efficiency of movement to reduce time and mistakes, as well as to improve accuracy.

"I've picked out several FPS video games," Lydia said.

"FPS?"

"Sorry. First-person shooter. Video games that simulate the experience of shooting from the shooter's perspective—that's you. You're behind the gun barrel. I chose single-player mode. Meaning it will be you against a computer-generated outlaw."

"I hope I don't disappoint."

"Grandpa says you were his best student. He said your sister was a colt that couldn't be broken, but you were a Thoroughbred that ran straight and true."

"Sarah was very spur of the moment, that's true. I tended to follow the book."

Lydia smiled like she'd found something she'd lost. "That's the way I am. Spur of the moment. I'm like Sarah. A colt that couldn't be broken. Was Sarah on the spectrum also?"

The honesty of Lydia's question, and her self-awareness, surprised Tracy, but she realized Mason and Celia couldn't hide Lydia's diagnosis from her. She was too bright. Until she'd met Lydia and talked to Mason, Tracy had never considered whether Sarah might have been on the spectrum, but while in the garage going through her things the prior evening, the possibility had dawned. Sarah, too, had been wicked smart, and when she became focused on something, like shooting, she became almost obsessed with learning everything she could. And she had been very, very good. People didn't initially use terms like "on the spectrum" and "Asperger's." Back then, people said things like "different" or "she's a pistol" or "she's something" to describe Sarah. Sarah had died so young, there really hadn't been time to get her idiosyncrasies diagnosed. Tracy had always considered her sister to have been one of a kind.

She had been that. And more. "I don't know," Tracy said. "Maybe."

"We're going to start with *Gunblood*," Lydia said, fidgeting at the computer. "It tests your reaction and accuracy in nine rounds of one-on-one duels. You choose a gunslinger . . . Actually, I already chose one for you."

"I'm sure you chose well."

"The game is simple to understand. You shoot your opponent before they shoot you."

"That's it?"

"That's never it."

"Okay, what else?"

"Maintaining focus is important because when you win, you move up a level. At each level your opponent is quicker on the draw and more accurate, and your odds of survival decrease."

"How do I fire? Why don't you show me? I think it will be easier."

Tracy stood from the chair and Lydia sat at the terminal and hit "Play." The game came to life. Lydia chose a female character standing in profile, a short distance from a male gunslinger, also in profile. When a timer on the computer screen counted down from three to one, Lydia moved the mouse, just a twitch, as she had said, then tapped the left-click button to fire her revolver. The outlaw took two shots to the skull and hit the ground. Lydia's character twirled her gun and holstered it. She'd registered twenty-seven points for accuracy and quickness.

"I hardly saw what you did."

"Second round is starting," Lydia said. "Watch the mouse."

The second outlaw appeared, and the game indicated the degree of difficulty had increased by 10 percent. The countdown followed. Lydia vanquished the second outlaw just as quickly, a shot to the chest and another to the head, then beat the third through the eighth outlaws as well. Throughout, Lydia kept up a running instructional.

"With practice you learn not to think but to react," she said, and Tracy recognized the phrase as another Mason Pettibone staple she had carried with her.

"And the game slows down," Tracy said.

"Yes!" Lydia said, excited. "It does. The game slows down. Grandpa says that."

Tracy had similar experiences in competitions, when she stopped thinking and simply reacted.

The ninth-level outlaw was spitting fast off the draw, but Lydia vanquished him. A sign congratulated Lydia as being the most feared gunslinger and posted her score.

Lydia stood so Tracy could sit.

"It's so violent," Tracy said.

She and Dan would keep Daniella away from the computer, as well as cell phones, for as long as possible, the glorification of violence being a chief reason. Their friends with older children scoffed and said, "Good luck."

"That's a misconception," Lydia said without hesitation. "Video games are not about violence."

Curious, Tracy asked, "What are they about?"

"Competition. You have to figure out the puzzle at each level before you can move up to the next level. That's why my mind is so tired after competing. It's a lot of concentration. And don't think of the characters you shoot as real people," Lydia added.

"What should I think of them as?"

"Grandpa says metal plates, but I like to think of them as robots. You defeat the robot, they get repaired in the shop, and come out again when you start the next game."

"Like the movie *Westworld*," Tracy said.

"There was a movie?" Lydia said, sounding amazed. "I saw the television series with Anthony Hopkins and the gunslinger, Ed Harris."

The movie starred Yul Brynner as a robot gunslinger at a Wild West–themed amusement park. Because of a glitch in the programming, Brynner goes on a killing spree.

"There you go," Tracy said. "I didn't know a TV series existed."

The competitor in Tracy made her almost believe she would not only reach the ninth level, but better Lydia's score. The pragmatist told her it was not possible, even if she had played the game many times. "I'm ready," she said.

Lydia stood beside her and held a Pocket Pro shot timer over Tracy's shoulder. "Grandpa thought we should simulate the game like in a Cowboy Action Shooting competition."

The timer was a handheld device that emitted a beep, signaling the shooter to start, recorded the time of each shot and the intervals between shots, as well as the shooter's total time.

"Shooter ready?" Lydia asked.

Shooters in competition could say a line to indicate their readiness to shoot. Some shooters used lines from movies. Tracy had traditionally used a line from what she considered the best Western movie ever made, *True Grit*. John Wayne, as a one-eyed US marshal named Rooster

Cogburn, faces off against a gang of outlaws in the climactic gun scene. Just before charging his horse into the group, he shouts at an outlaw who has insulted him to fill his hand and calls him a son of a bitch.

Sarah had used a line from Wyatt Earp in the movie *Tombstone* when Wyatt warns his enemies that he's coming and he's bringing hell with him.

Tracy decided to use Sarah's line.

Lydia hit the "Play" button. Tracy's hand jerked, causing the mouse to twitch. Her character spun and flexed spasmodically, her shots off target. The gunslinger shot her three times, killing her character.

Game over.

"Well, that was anticlimactic," she said.

"Don't get discouraged," Lydia said.

"Right. Practice makes perfect," Tracy said.

"Wrong," Lydia said "'Perfect practice makes perfect.'"

"I stand corrected," Tracy said dutifully, recalling those were also Pettibone's words when he'd been working with her and Sarah.

"You're going to stand?"

"No. It's just an expression, Lydia."

"Shooter ready?" Lydia said, again all business.

"You tell them I'm coming, and hell's coming with me," Tracy said.

The game counted down from three to one, Tracy moved the mouse and fired. This time she landed one shot before she was shot and killed.

"That was better," Lydia said.

"Not if I'm lying on the ground about to be buried six feet under."

"Do you want to take a break?"

Tracy shook her head. The competitor in her refused to give in or give up. "No. Let's go again."

Using Lydia's suggestion, Tracy did not focus on her opponent's speed but her speed. At the end of an hour, she had reached the fifth level. She simply wasn't fast enough to reach the next level. She was also mentally exhausted.

"When you master *Gunblood*, we'll move to a different game with better graphics and more variables. Are you working with Grandpa now?" Lydia asked.

"No. I need to get home to my daughter and husband," she said. "Would you like to meet them sometime?"

Lydia looked caught off guard. Tracy had hoped asking the question without preface would prevent Lydia from overthinking and keep her from getting anxious. Then she noticed Lydia touching the tips of each finger to her thumb—stimming, Mason had called it. "I . . . I don't know if I can."

"Okay. No problem. Whenever you'd like. I know they'd like you."

"How?"

"Because you remind me of someone. Perhaps tomorrow, after I shoot on the range."

"*We* shoot on the range," Lydia said with a wicked smile. "Didn't Grandpa tell you? We'll be competing."

CHAPTER 20

The following morning, another glorious day of cornflower-blue sky and bright sunshine, Tracy dressed in her full cowboy gear. Everything felt snug, and her cowboy boots pinched her toes. She wore Wrangler jeans; a gray, long-sleeve shirt with snaps; her black leather vest, tight across her back; and her traditional red bandanna, bolo tie, and duster. She tossed what had been Sarah's hat onto the front seat of her truck. Her Stetson was lost in the mine shaft where she had her final confrontation with Edmund House.

As Dan helped her load her rugged cart into the Ford bed, they noticed a police SUV drive slowly past the house. The deputy gave them a look.

"That your doing?" Dan asked.

"Just being cautious," she said.

"I'm glad," he said. Dan did his best John Wayne impersonation, hands hooked to his beltline, leaning at an angle and speaking in an affected accent. "Well, pardner. Wah-huh. Them pilgrims won't know what hit 'em."

She smiled, thankful for his humor. "You're a dork."

"Yes, ma'am, but I'm your dork." He dropped the accent. "What time will you be back?"

"Couple hours, tops."

"Beautiful morning. The birds are out, and the fish are biting."

"And how would you know the fish are biting?"

"How could they not be? Thought we could take Daniella on a hike, have a picnic. Venture to the lake and cast a few flies."

"Sounds like a plan," she said.

On the short drive to Mason Pettibone's, with the window down, the cool mountain air hummed through the truck cab and brought the smell of the evergreen trees. She'd never appreciated the beauty of Cedar Grove when she'd lived here. She didn't know any different.

But she did now, and she tried to take notice each time she visited.

She felt excitement—though it was also possibly nerves. Sarah never had nerves before competitions. On drives she would bounce on the truck seat between Tracy and their father, talking and making observations—perhaps another indication Sarah had been on the spectrum. Maybe.

As she drove, Tracy went back through the things she could remember about her lessons. She'd spent time in the backyard working on her stance, cross drawing and dry firing her empty pistols to get a better feel for the trigger pressure. She rolled onto the balls of her feet, gripped the gun handle firmly against the pad between her thumb and index finger, ripped the gun from the holster, rocked her right elbow to her side, and thrust the gun forward until it was at the apex of her two arms, the barrel pointed at the target downrange. She wrapped her supporting hand around her shooting hand on the grip and pushed forward with the shooting hand while the support hand applied rearward pressure—tension to lessen muzzle flip, which allowed for faster on-target follow-up shots.

Her holster work needed practice—she was slow pulling the pistols and, on occasion, exceeded the 180, the muzzle of her gun pointing too far to the side—a safety violation that would disqualify her from any competition.

After greetings, Pettibone led her around the side of his house to the backyard. Lydia walked out with them. Gone was the young girl with the bubbly personality eager to please. This morning, Lydia was all business, the same demeanor Sarah could summon when she walked to the first station to compete. Dressed in black jeans and boots, a red bodice over a black, long-sleeve shirt, Lydia looked even more like Sarah. Noise-cancellation earmuffs hung around her neck, and red-tinted shooting goggles covered her eyes.

This woman was singularly focused.

When Tracy saw the shooting range, it took her back twenty-five years in an instant. The three ten-foot Old West storefront facades from her youth were more weathered than when she'd been young. Paint had peeled or worn thin in spots, and dry rot looked to have invaded some of the studs. Over the storefronts hung hand-painted signs: **HOTEL & SALOON**, **GENERAL STORE**, and **WELLS FARGO BANK**. Tracy and Lydia would be shooting through the storefront windows, as if inside the buildings. They could also step to the side to fire—if they could not align with a steel plate shooting from the window.

"The range isn't what it once was," Pettibone said apologetically. "I just can't work on it the way I once did, but Lydia here has been working on the setup, and it's in pretty good shape."

Lydia looked at them and gave a quick nod.

"It looks just like I remember it, and it feels wonderful to be here again. I feel like I'm home," Tracy said.

"You and me both, Crossdraw. You and me both." Pettibone looked to get a bit misty eyed, and Tracy realized how much this meant to him, to feel useful again. "Well, let's get started," he said. "I thought it best that you have someone to compete against. That always seemed to bring out the best in you during competitions—if I remember correctly," Pettibone said.

He did. Tracy did her best when competing against Sarah, the very best. Tracy turned to Lydia. "I'm looking forward to the challenge, Lightning Strike."

Again, Lydia nodded. "Likewise, Crossdraw."

As Pettibone explained the first stage, Tracy slipped on her holsters. The imitation-pearl grips faced inward. Her shotgun-shell ammunition belt fit snug above them.

"First stage is 'the professional,'" Pettibone said. Tracy had looked it up the night before. "Ten rifle, ten pistol, six shotgun," he said, meaning the number of shots with each weapon. "Rifle. Nevada sweep from either end. Double tap the center target each pass." Tracy would shoot the three steel plates left to right and back, putting two bullets in the center target each time she swept past it, for a total of ten shots.

"Ten pistol shots, also Nevada sweep. Third station, six shotgun shots, knock 'em down."

Tracy noted two metal targets on the left and four on the right that would knock over when hit. Any target that remained standing at the end of a round was a miss—the shooter penalized five seconds.

"Any questions?"

Lydia shook her head.

So did Tracy.

"I thought I'd let Lydia go first. Give you a chance to see the scenario."

Tracy declined that invitation. She didn't want Lydia's time in her head while competing. "If it's just the same, I'd like to go first."

Tracy slipped on her shooting muffs and her yellow-tinted glasses. She had loaded her pistols, shotgun, and rifle upon arrival and staged the shotgun in the third storefront window. She carried the loaded rifle with her to the first window, barrel pointed to the sky.

"Visualize each shot," Pettibone said.

Tracy took the moment to do so. She didn't want to be thinking. She wanted to act instinctually.

"Set your feet."

She took her position and toed the ground. When shooting the shotgun and rifle, she remained square to the target and lowered her dominant eye to align the sight at the end of the barrel.

Pettibone stood behind her and held the timer close to her ear. This morning, he would fill multiple roles—range master, timer, and judge.

"Take a deep breath and exhale. Don't hold your breath. Regulate your breathing. Empty your mind with the first shot. Don't think. React."

Thinking slowed down a shooter.

"The designated line is 'Here they come, boys,' but you can use one of your own. Your call."

Tracy nodded. After a calming breath, she said, "You tell them I'm coming. And hell's coming with me."

The buzzer beeped.

She picked up her rifle and pumped the lever, her eyes sweeping from one target to the next.

One shot first plate.

Two shots middle plate.

One shot third plate.

Repeat on the sweep back.

She set down the rifle and moved to the next window, feeling the familiar adrenaline rush return like an old friend. Pistol shooting is where she had excelled in competition, where she made up or increased the time gap on her opponents. She drew her pistols across her body and shot with both hands at the three steel plates.

Right hand. Cock. Fire.
Left hand. Cock. Fire.
Right hand. Cock. Fire.
Left hand. Cock. Fire.

She settled into the familiar. Smoke filled the stage windows and brought the smell of burned gunpowder, sulfur, and charcoal. It was a rush. She felt like she was twenty-two again.

She set the pistols down and moved to the final stage, picking up the shotgun. The barrel ripped twice. Two targets dropped. She pumped the fore-end, ejecting the spent shell casings and loading the chamber with a fresh shell. The shotgun held seven rounds total.

She fired again. The third target did not go down. Miss.

She fired again, dropping it.

The fourth target dropped.

She missed the fifth target.

Shit.

Don't panic. Composure.

She knocked down the fifth, but she was now out of shells and still had a target left to knock down.

She pumped open the action while reaching for two spare shells from the belt around her waist. She managed to insert one shell into the chamber, but the second hit the rim of the magazine tube and dropped to the ground.

Now she could panic.

Grab another shell, or close the action and pray she dropped the target?

The smart move was to load two shells, but it took more time. She ran the pump action forward, pulled another shell from her belt, loaded it into the magazine, took aim, and dropped the sixth target.

She set the shotgun down and closed her eyes.

Not good enough.

Not even close.

"Time: 27.18," Pettibone said. "Unload and show an empty chamber." Lydia held up two fingers. Tracy had missed two targets, a ten-second penalty. "Total time, 37.18."

Tracy grabbed her guns, barrels pointed to the sky, and stepped back, disappointed and discouraged, but refusing to let it show on her face or in her posture.

"Okay. We've got some work to do. The big problem was the shotgun. Rifle and pistols were good. We can do a few things to decrease your time, eliminate some unnecessary movement," Pettibone said. "That's why we're here. Lydia, shooter ready?"

"Ready," Lydia said after she'd prepared her guns. She shouldered her rifle but kept the barrel in the low-ready position. She toed the ground, spread her feet shoulder width, and squared her shoulders to the target.

"On the beep."

Lydia looked downrange. "Best get off the range, boys. There's a Lightning Strike coming."

Pettibone hit the timer.

Lydia smoothly and rapidly fired, worked the action, and fired again. Tracy watched, mesmerized. The young girl's hands constantly moved. She pumped the rifle lever so fast Tracy could hardly distinguish between the individual "tings" of the bullets hitting the plates. In a blur, she lowered the rifle and drew her pistol with her right hand. Her left hand slapped the hammer five times in rapid succession, the ping of the steel plates, again, almost indistinguishable. Five shots. She holstered that weapon and pulled the second pistol, repeating the process. In a whir she had the shotgun, and in seconds the six targets were down.

Pettibone glanced at Tracy. "I guess you both like a little competition." He said to Lydia, "That's your best score on this stage, Lightning Strike: 20.25 seconds. You almost broke twenty seconds."

And she'd almost cut Tracy's time in half.

CHAPTER 21

Dan stepped to the counter and eyed The Daily Perk's fresh-baked pastries while enjoying the earthy aroma of its freshly ground coffee. He confirmed the presence of one remaining cinnamon-raisin pastry, with two people in line ahead of him. The coffee shop had been a part of Cedar Grove's initial downtown revitalization, and it had survived the subsequent recession because, well, people always needed a good cup of joe and a pastry, regardless of their bank accounts. It was a guilty pleasure.

Dan limited himself to two pastries a week when he came up on vacation. Tracy wouldn't go that far. She had one pastry—on Saturday.

Though initially pleased by Tracy's sudden urge to take shooting lessons, it also worried him. Dan couldn't dismiss what had happened to Kins. He knew it had Tracy rattled, enough that she wanted Dan and Daniella far removed from Seattle. He wondered if his wife's desire to improve her shooting also had something to do with Schmidt. He'd have a tough time getting that out of her.

Tracy internalized too much and wasn't good about asking for help, even when she needed it. Given what she'd been through in her life, the tremendous losses she had suffered, he understood that was not easy for her. Guarded, she often tempered or even withheld information. Her motive was earnest—to protect Dan and Daniella from the evils of the world—but it often left Dan in the dark.

He worried his wife was preparing for some confrontation with Schmidt she believed inevitable.

And that frightened him.

"You come here often?"

Dan turned. The question came from the man standing behind him in line. Like all the others sitting at the half dozen tables or outside beneath the green-and-white striped awnings, Dan didn't recognize him. He wasn't what Elle at Grandma Billie's called BMT, though he also didn't appear young enough to be one of the Gen Xers or bourgeois bohemians who brought their laptops and tablets and cell phones and focused on screens rather than the majestic views. Dan could relate to the man's cargo shorts, T-shirt, and flip-flops—dressed for comfort, not to impress.

"More often than I probably should," Dan said.

The man smiled. "That's a good sign."

"Best pastries anywhere around here," Dan said. Then he chuckled. "Also, the only pastries anywhere around here. At least within a forty-five-minute drive."

"I'm learning that also," the man said.

"You're new in town?"

"Very. Bought a home here and still getting moved in."

"What street?" Dan said.

"Still learning those. Everyone calls this place the Mattioli mansion."

Dan chuckled. "No kidding."

"You know it?"

"Too well. That was my wife's childhood home. We heard someone purchased it just the other night at dinner."

"I guess word travels fast in a small town."

"Among those of us who grew up here. Well . . . welcome." The man in front of Dan moved up to the counter and Dan took a step forward. The cinnamon-raisin pastry remained.

"You live here?" the man asked.

"I grew up here. I live in Seattle now."

"What brings you back?"

"I kept my parents' home for when we want to get away."

"Ah. Sentimental. Another good sign."

The man offered his hand. "William Kenmore. I guess I should know your name if we're going to be neighbors."

Dan returned the grip. "Dan O'Leary."

The man in front of Dan moved to the side, and Dan greeted the familiar young woman at the counter. "Hey, Mr. O'Leary. What will you have this morning?"

"I'll have the last cinnamon-raisin pastry and a latte."

Emily rang Dan up, and he moved to the side to await his drink order from the barista. Kenmore ordered at the counter and stepped back to wait alongside Dan.

"Are you planning to live here in Cedar Grove full-time, then, William?" Dan asked.

"No. Like you, I have a place in Seattle. Found this place on a visit passing through."

"Passing through?" Dan said. "I didn't know Cedar Grove passed through to anywhere."

Kenmore laughed easily. "It does seem to be a bit remote. I guess that's why some like it though. They think it's hard to get to, keeps out the riffraff."

"It did," Dan said. "Not anymore. Not on the weekends at least."

"Ouch," Kenmore said.

"I didn't mean you."

"I thought about renting, but this house is perfect for my needs. The real estate agent said the mansion was once owned by the man who built the town?"

"Christian Mattioli," Dan said. "He discovered gold, copper, and coal in the mountains and founded the Cedar Grove Mining Company."

"I was told he didn't discover it as much as he stole it from those who did."

"That might be true. Anyway, when the mines stopped producing, Mattioli left, and the house sat vacant for decades until my wife's father bought it. He restored the mansion and made it pretty much the center of life in Cedar Grove. For many of us anyway."

"That's a lot of pressure, Dan. Though, again, not sure why anyone would want to make a thief and a liar the center of anything."

Dan was not sure of Kenmore's intent and not interested in pursuing it. "You got a family, William?"

"I do," he said. "A wife and two young girls."

The conversation stalled uncomfortably while they waited for their orders. To fill the dead space, Dan said, "You have hobbies, William? The fishing and hunting around here are some of the best."

"Never had the patience for fishing. I do like to hunt though."

"What do you hunt?"

"Anything on four legs . . . or two," he said.

The comment seemed odd. "What do you hunt on two legs?"

"Bigfoot." Kenmore grinned. "Sorry, I guess that was a poor attempt at humor."

"Well, if you find one, you'll have won the lottery," Dan said. "In the interim, you'll have better luck hunting black-tailed deer and elk."

"You hunt then, Dan?"

"Not seriously. I always had trouble looking a deer in the eyes after I shot it."

"Huh. I've never had that problem. Maybe I just don't look deeply enough," Kenmore said. "Or care. Why hunt if you're not going to shoot something?"

Dan looked to the barista, hoping his was the next drink order. "Mostly now it's a good excuse to get out and exercise and do a little target practice," he said.

"Ah, you're a shooter?"

"Not really. My wife is though."

"What kind?"

"She grew up competing in Cowboy Action Shooting. It's—"

"I know it. I've competed in all kinds of shooting tournaments. Did your wife have a cowboy nickname?"

"Crossdraw," Dan said. "How about you? Wait. Let me guess. Billy the Kid."

"Nah. Ain't a kid no more. 'Wild Bill' suits me better. What is it you do, Dan?"

"I'm an attorney."

"Any particular kind?"

"Mostly criminal defense."

"No kidding. Mind if I ask about the town? Since you know it so well?"

"No, not at all."

"Before I bought the mansion my real estate agent said she had to disclose that a previous owner killed himself in the house. She said he shot himself. Would that have been your wife's father?"

Again, Dan thought it an odd thing to ask in a casual conversation, particularly because the real estate agent was not accurate. "I'm not aware that Washington law requires disclosure of a death on a property— natural causes or violent."

Kenmore made a face. "No? I guess my agent was just being vigilant. You can appreciate that; can't you? You have that kind of obligation to your clients also; don't you? To be honest and vigilant?"

Dan didn't know what to make of the question. "Do you mean diligent? Vigilant means to pay attention to one's surroundings for potential signs of danger."

"I know what it means, Dan."

Dan smiled, but Kenmore did not. The conversation had shifted. Dan regretted correcting him. "Sorry, I didn't . . ."

"Mean to imply that I was stupid?"

Dan needed to get out of this conversation. He willed the young man making the coffees to call Dan's name.

He did. "Tall latte. Dan O?"

"That's me." Dan picked up the white bag with his pastry and grabbed his latte.

"I wouldn't have figured you as a latte guy," Kenmore said. "Isn't that a woman's drink?"

"William?" the barista called out. "Double-shot espresso."

"That's me." Kenmore grinned. "Wild Bill. Nice talking with you, Dan."

Dan started for the door.

"I guess we'll be seeing one another," Kenmore said. Dan turned back. "Around town, I mean. It being so small and all. Maybe do a little hunting, Dan O? I could teach you to get past your hesitation to pull the trigger."

CHAPTER 22

Following her shooting lesson with Mason Pettibone, Tracy returned home and backed the truck down the gravel drive to make it easier to unload her rugged cart. Dan, Daniella, and Therese ran around the lawn with Rex and Sherlock in hot pursuit. The two dogs barked for the sheer joy of being outside, and Tracy knew how they felt. Being outside all morning had invigorated her.

She stepped down from the cab. Dan knelt beside their daughter on the lawn and pointed to Tracy. "Who's that? Who is it?" he said.

Daniella cried out, "Mama's home from shooting" and ran over as fast as her little legs would propel her, but not faster than Rex and Sherlock, who knocked her down in their hurry to greet Tracy. She fended them off and picked up her daughter from the lawn, swinging her and causing Daniella to squeal with laughter.

"How's my little girl?" Tracy said, hugging her tight and kissing her cheek. "Did you have fun at the park?"

As Daniella filled Tracy in on the pirate ship she climbed at the park, and the horses and the swings, Dan went to the truck bed and lowered the gate. "Made you something. Hold on." He went into the garage and returned with two-by-ten planks with metal claws on one end that he hooked onto the bumper of the truck, creating a ramp. Then he climbed into the bed and rolled Tracy's rugged cart down the two-by-fours to the ground. "Thought it would be easier for you when I'm not around."

"Somebody has been ambitious."

"How did the shooting go, Crossdraw?"

"A little rough," Tracy said. "Mason says I have a lot of rust to kick off. Sorry I'm a bit late. Mason gets going and he can run on a bit."

"I got a lunch packed and Daniella's backpack is in the car. Just need for you to get changed. Or do you plan on hiking in that costume?"

"Not a costume, Dan."

"Excuse me."

"I'll quickly change." She handed him her coat, hat, and red bandanna, then went inside, drank a large glass of water, and changed quickly into shorts and a T-shirt. Her hiking boots were by the front door.

Back outside, Dan had loaded Daniella in her car seat, put the two dogs in the back, and started the Subaru.

Tracy approached Therese, who lay on the lawn. "Aren't you coming?"

"Not me," she said. "I'm not going to be the fourth wheel in this family picture. You spend time with your husband and daughter. Mr. O has told me all about the hike. Maybe I'll take Daniella up another time when you're shooting."

"Plans to go anywhere?"

"No. I thought I might do a little painting on the porch and enjoy the afternoon."

Therese had become adept at her painting; several of her works hung in both homes.

"Why don't you paint out back? Much better view of the mountains." Tracy saw a police SUV drive past the house and felt better about leaving Therese at home.

"Must be something going on," Therese said. "That's the third time I've seen that police car pass the house."

It gave Tracy comfort. "Anything comes up, just dial 911 and ask for Finlay Armstrong."

Therese gave her a queer look.

Tracy said, "You know me. It's my nature to worry."

Therese said, "Go. Enjoy your family time." She smiled. "I'll paint out back."

"Thank you," Tracy said.

When Tracy reached the car, Dan said, "Thought we could explore around Racehorse Falls. The hike is not too strenuous, and we can relax by the falls and have a picnic. Are you game?"

"I'm game," she said.

They drove to the junction of State Routes 9 and 542, then east to Mosquito Lake Road. Along the route, Daniella peppered them with "why" and "what" questions about the trees, where they were going, and just about everything else. Her verbal skills were more advanced than most three-year-olds because Therese spoke with her constantly. So much so that every once in a while, Tracy detected an Irish brogue, or Daniella would respond to a question with the word "grand."

When Dan saw the large boulder marking the turnoff, he drove up a dirt-and-gravel road, eventually parking behind a line of cars extending from the entrance to the trailhead. Hiking had become a big weekend adventure all throughout the Northwest.

Tracy sat on the edge of her seat, door open, and laced up her hiking boots, while Dan put Daniella into the backpack and adjusted the straps. Tracy loaded her backpack with food and drinks, and they set off, Rex and Sherlock forging a path. Both dogs were well behaved on the trail. Dan had taught them to heel and to sit when other hikers passed going up or down the path. The size of the dogs caused some concern, but their obedience seemed to alleviate most. The temperature was warm with a touch of humidity beneath the canopy of trees that emitted a chorus of birds and the rhythmic thrumming of a woodpecker. Ironically, given the number of cars, they saw few people on the trail.

Tracy and Dan's intent was to access the middle and upper falls. As they drew close, Tracy heard the hypnotic rush of water. When they reached the top of the falls, Tracy spent a few minutes pacing to recover her breath. The dogs also paced, tongues hanging from the sides of their mouths. "Phew," Tracy said. "I'm out of hiking shape."

Dan agreed. "You're not the only one," he said with a nod to Rex and Sherlock. "The altitude takes some getting used to you; doesn't it?"

"Yeah. Let's go with that."

They spent a few minutes enjoying the view and got a kick out of Daniella when the breeze shifted and blew the spray from the falls into their faces. They found a flat spot to picnic near the middle falls, and Tracy helped Dan with Daniella, then set up lunch. Rex and Sherlock drank water from a bowl brought by Dan, then lay in a patch of grass with shade.

Dan had brought a sourdough loaf, cold cuts, cheeses, and fruit. Tracy tore off a piece of bread and handed it to Daniella to gnaw on, periodically giving her drinks of apple juice from her sippy cup.

Dan ripped off a hunk of bread, opened it, and made sandwiches, handing the first to Tracy.

"So how was *your* morning?" Tracy asked.

"Interesting," Dan said with a chuckle. "I met the guy who bought the Mattioli mansion."

"The guy Hannah mentioned? Where?"

"He was behind me in line at The Daily Perk."

"I hope you didn't get a pastry. That would be one beyond your allotment for the week."

"What? Me? I have the willpower of a Navy SEAL."

She took a bite of her sandwich, then asked, "How did the subject come up?"

"He asked what to order, said he was a new homeowner, and eventually we got to his having bought the Mattioli mansion."

She said, "So, who is he?"

Dan took a bite of his sandwich and swallowed, drinking from his water bottle. "His name is William Kenmore. Also said he competes in shooting. Even asked your cowboy name."

"Huh. That was a long time ago. How old is he?"

"I'd say around our age. Midforties."

"Did *he* have a cowboy name?"

"Wild Bill."

She shook her head. "A lot of 'Wild Bills' and 'Billy the Kids.' What does he do for a living?"

"Not sure. I didn't ask. To be honest, I got a weird vibe from the guy."

"Weird how?"

"He said his Realtor had to disclose the fact that a prior owner had shot himself in the mansion."

Tracy didn't respond. She didn't like to think of those dark days.

"The thing is," Dan said, "Realtors don't have to disclose that. Not in Washington State. The law doesn't assign any loss in value to property due to a death, natural or otherwise."

"Did he have an explanation?"

"He said maybe the Realtor was being 'vigilant.' And when I asked if he meant 'diligent' he got offended, said he wasn't dumb, and insulted my drink choice. Said a latte was a woman's drink. That pretty much ended the conversation."

She laughed. "Really?"

Dan nodded. "Truly."

"He didn't bruise your male ego; did he?"

"It's pretty fragile," Dan said. "I am surrounded by women."

"Are you complaining?"

"Not in the least."

She set her sandwich down and looked out at the waterfall for a spell. Then she said, "We should stop by, welcome the family to Cedar Grove."

"Maybe," Dan said. Tracy heard reluctance in his voice.

"You don't want to?"

Dan shrugged. "We don't live here anymore. I don't really see the point."

"To being friendly? He really did bruise your ego."

Dan nodded to Daniella, whose head had fallen forward. "Somebody is a sleepyhead." Their daughter had soggy breadcrumbs around her lips and was still holding on to the hunk of bread she'd been gnawing on.

"Let her sleep," Tracy said. "We can go when she wakes. It's peaceful out here." She pulled out two paperbacks from her backpack, handing one to Dan.

"Just what I was looking for." He lay back and put the paperback over his eyes. "A sunblock."

CHAPTER 23

Dan returned to Seattle Monday morning, and Tracy spent the week getting up early, rushing off to Mason Pettibone's house to work with Lydia on the computer one day and Pettibone on the shooting range the next, then hurrying back to be with Therese and Daniella. Her shooting times and her accuracy were both improving. Pettibone said it was like anything a person did as a child. It was just a matter of muscle memory. And having Lydia to compete against pushed Tracy's innate competitiveness.

She spoke to Shannah just about daily. Shannah said Kins continued to progress in his recovery, was out of ICU, and eager to get home. Shannah said the doctors were surprised and pleased Kins didn't have a head injury and, in the scheme of things, that he had been lucky.

"Doesn't surprise me," Tracy said. "He's always been a hard head."

Shannah said they hoped to get him home by the end of the week. The hospital wanted to keep an eye on him a few more days before they discharged him.

"We'll have a strong police presence when he goes home," Faz said when Tracy called to fill him in and ask for an update on the investigation. "We've canvassed the area around the Roanoke, but so far we haven't had any luck finding a camera that shows Schmidt or his car in that area that night. In fact, traffic cameras near Schmidt's home don't indicate his car ever left."

Faz said they did document that a red Jeep, registered to Schmidt's girlfriend, left the garage earlier in the evening before Kins's accident. "The passenger seat was empty, but Schmidt could have been lying down in the back of the car, then got out somewhere on Capitol Hill. We're trying to track the Jeep's movements, but Nolasco is sensitive about us confronting Schmidt, or his girlfriend, and asking questions without something more."

"What about the civil case?"

"Cerrabone says Bernard Gil is making noise about taking depositions, but Cerrabone thinks he's just posturing for a settlement. Nothing is imminent with Kins in the hospital."

"How much is he asking for?"

"Two million."

"Unbelievable."

"How are things up there?" Faz asked.

"Quiet," Tracy said. "Everything is good."

"You being careful?" he asked, as he did during each of their conversations.

Tracy put her hand on the holster holding her two Colts. She had her Glock in the glove compartment of the car. "Locked and loaded," she said.

Friday, Tracy booked a double session—one with both Lydia and Pettibone so she could spend the weekend with Dan when he returned. She waited to leave the house until she saw the Cedar Grove police vehicle pull up and park at the end of the driveway, a change in routine she had requested of Finlay Armstrong until Dan had returned from Seattle. She also felt better with Rex and Sherlock in the house.

Tracy turned on the radio and listened to a country music station as she made her way to Pettibone's. Initially skeptical, she better understood the logic of the computer training—the quick-twitch muscles and the hand-eye coordination it promoted, as well as how it sped up her shoot/no-shoot decision-making. She was also better understanding Lydia's instruction that Tracy take each level one at a time and not look ahead to the next puzzle or think back about a previous mistake. Stay in the present and solve the puzzle before her. Then and only then think about the next level. It was similar to her shooting range training. She'd learned to focus on the variables she could control while ignoring those she could not.

It also seemed to be working. She was processing information more quickly and responding organically. That improvement translated to lower times on the range and improved accuracy. Pettibone said she was trusting what her eyes saw and what her brain processed. She'd successfully completed the ninth stage of the *Gunblood* duels, and she had lowered her time on the range to under twenty-five seconds: 24.88 seconds.

Tracy pulled into Pettibone's driveway, and he met her at the door. "She's waiting for you," he said. "Has a new game for you."

"Before I go in, I wanted to run something by you. We're making progress," Tracy said. "Getting to know and trust one another."

"I think so too," Pettibone said. "She says she maybe wants to be a detective."

"I'd like to take her grocery shopping with me when we're done—if she'll go."

"That's always the question with Lydia, but it's worth a try."

Tracy smiled. "I was also thinking, she's so good at these games. Maybe she has a future in it; maybe she could test games for companies before they go to market—tell the company what's right about it and what's wrong. I don't know that world, but I would think it would save them a lot of money marketing a bad game."

"It's not a bad thought." Pettibone pinched the triangle of hair beneath his lower lip, a habit when thinking. "Actually, it's a very good thought. I'll look into it. What we'd really like, though, is for Lydia to get some human interaction outside the house."

"Got a couple of thoughts on that as well," Tracy said, but she didn't get the chance to elaborate before Lydia's door opened and the young woman stepped into the hall.

"Crossdraw. I thought I heard you come in. We have a lot of work to do."

"Got to go," Tracy said to Pettibone.

"I'll be outside getting your stages set up for the afternoon," he said.

Inside Lydia's room, Tracy moved to her seat at her terminal. Lydia started to give instructions before Tracy's butt hit the mesh of her chair.

"Different game. *Outlaws*. It's also a first-person-shooter game. Your character, Marshal James Anderson, uses a shotgun, a rifle, and revolvers. He can also use dynamite—but that's not relevant here," Lydia said.

"Tell me the story's plot," Tracy said.

Lydia slipped into her infomercial voice, and she looked up and to the left. "*Outlaws* was released April 7, 1997. Your name is James Anderson and you're a retired US marshal. You come home after a trip to the general store to find your wife, Anna, dying from a gunshot wound and your daughter gone.

"You learn that railroad baron Bob Graham has hired several outlaws, including Matt 'Dr. Death' Jackson and 'Slim' Sam Fulton, to force people in the county to sell their land to him. When Anna refused to sell their land, Dr. Death shot her, kidnapped your daughter, and burned your home to the ground. After burying your wife, you pick up your guns and set out to find your daughter. You travel the Old West dueling Graham's hired outlaws."

Tracy felt a twinge in the pit of her stomach; the game's premise hit a little too close to home. She asked, "How did you choose this game?"

"I thought it would be good for SASS training. Why? Don't you like it?"

"No. I think it's . . . Why don't I just get started and you can help me through the first few levels."

"Okay," Lydia said, and she pressed the "Start" button.

The graphics weren't great, but the music was reminiscent of the gritty spaghetti Westerns Tracy had watched as a young girl with her father, movies produced in Europe by Italian filmmakers like *A Fistful of Dollars* and *The Good, the Bad and the Ugly*. Both starred Clint Eastwood.

After an hour, Tracy had reached her limit and didn't want to be worn out for her afternoon session on the range. As she prepared to leave, she said, "I'm going into Cedar Grove to grab some lunch before working on the range. Would you like to go with me? We could have lunch together."

She expected Lydia to come up with an excuse not to go. Surprisingly, the young woman did not. "Okay," she said. They walked to the front room where Pettibone waited. "Lydia and I are going to the market. I have some shopping to do, and then we're going to have lunch before my training session in the afternoon."

He glanced at Tracy, who wore her best poker face and silently urged him to do the same. Pettibone, who understood Lydia better than anyone, said, "Okay."

Lydia stepped out the front door first but turned back to Pettibone, and, for a moment, Tracy thought she might change her mind.

"Would you like soup, Grandpa?"

"I'd love soup," he said. Then Lydia walked down the path to the waiting truck. Tracy glanced back at Pettibone. His eyes widened to illustrate both shock and approval.

In the truck cab Lydia seemed at ease. "I like trucks," she said. "I think I'd like a truck."

"You'll want to get snow tires if you live up here," Tracy said.

"I don't drive," Lydia said. "But I need to learn."

"Why do you need to learn to drive?"

"I have to move out of my grandfather's house," she said.

The comment surprised Tracy. "Why do you have to move?"

"I'm an adult. I can't live with my mother and my grandfather forever. I have to live on my own. My grandfather will die someday, and so will my mom." Lydia spoke like she was reciting facts, which, in a sad sense, was true. Her voice was without emotion.

"I can teach you to drive my truck. I taught my sister to drive. Sarah was younger than you, but she was persistent."

"A colt that couldn't be broken," Lydia said quickly. "I think I'd like your sister."

"I think so too," Tracy said.

When they reached Cedar Grove Market, Tracy pulled out a shopping cart, thinking that having Lydia push it would give her something to do and keep her out of her head. They went up and down the aisles, and Tracy picked up items more for the purpose of comparing the prices and telling Lydia about the decisions she was making. Lydia seemed more interested in the people around them and finding the soup counter.

"Chicken noodle," Lydia said when they had arrived. "Grandpa likes chicken noodle." They picked up a tall container and brought their groceries to the checkout line.

The owner of the store, a Mr. Cunningham, greeted them, and Tracy introduced Lydia as Mason Pettibone's granddaughter, then made casual conversation about the weather.

Lydia told the man they were going to have a picnic. "We bought sandwiches. And soup. Chicken noodle for my grandfather."

Mr. Cunningham smiled, then said to Tracy, "I'm sorry we're a bit slow today at checkout. Our bag boy got a full-time job in Seattle and yesterday was his last day. Hard for us to keep them. It's usually a summer position."

"What is it that a bag person does?" Tracy said with a nod to Lydia. She'd been in the store earlier in the week, learned of the possible position, and mentioned Lydia to Cunningham. He seemed more than willing to give her a shot at the job. The trick was to interest Lydia.

Cunningham explained the job's responsibilities and the pay. Tracy looked at Lydia, but she couldn't read the young woman's interest. She thanked Cunningham, then she and Lydia went outside to a picnic table to eat their lunch. As they ate, discussing various subjects, Tracy said, "Sounds like the store could use some help with a new bag boy."

Lydia didn't respond.

"Would you have any interest in maybe trying out that job?"

"I'm a girl, not a boy."

"I'm sure Mr. Cunningham would make an exception. I was just thinking that earning money would help you save, for when you have to move out."

Lydia didn't respond, and Tracy, mindful of Pettibone's instruction that decisions had to be Lydia's, didn't push it. She had another idea to help Lydia socialize.

"My husband is in Seattle working this week. He's a lawyer. I'm at home with my daughter, Daniella, and her nanny, Therese. We're going to have a 'girls' night' tonight."

"What's a girls' night?"

"We girls are going to watch a movie and eat popcorn. Would you like to come over and watch the movie with us—just the girls?"

Lydia's finger rubbing started again. "I don't drive," she said. "And my mother has to work nights."

"I could pick you up and bring you home after the movie."

Lydia's gaze shifted between the cars passing on the street and the people walking past their table. "I have to watch my grandfather at night."

"I'll have you home early. But this is totally your decision, Lydia. I just thought you might like the movie." Tracy got the idea from the poster in Lydia's room and the book on her shelf. Casually, she said, "We're going to watch *Wonka*."

Lydia's eyes got big. Her voice went again to infomercial. "*Willy Wonka and the Chocolate Factory* is based on the beloved 1964 children's novel by British author Roald Dahl, *Charlie and the Chocolate Factory*. The story features the adventures of young Charlie Bucket inside the chocolate factory of eccentric chocolatier Willy Wonka." She redirected her gaze to Tracy. "I have read the book seven times, and my mom bought me the movie."

"Well, this movie is the story of Willy Wonka as a young boy. How he grows up to become the chocolatier and own the factory. Would you like to see how he became the chocolate man?"

"Yes!" She nearly shouted her answer. "Yes. I would like to see the story of Willy Wonka as a young boy and how he grows up to be the chocolate man."

Tracy smiled at the young woman's sweet naïveté, which was beautiful, but she also understood how it could be worrisome for her mother and her grandfather.

On the range that afternoon, Pettibone made the session particularly challenging. The first station was a solitaire sweep that required Tracy to shoot four targets, firing one less shot on each pass:

1-2-3-4-1-2-3-1-2-1. The second session was the chimney sweep, shooting at three targets stacked one above the other, moving up and down several times: 1-2-3-2-1-2-3-2-1.

Tracy did well. Her best time again being just under twenty-five seconds.

"You're improving," Pettibone said. "Remember, don't let your feet get too close together, keep them shoulder width so you maintain a solid base. Get your upper torso weight forward, and your butt back, and keep your eyes out over your sights. Also, at times you're holding your breath."

"Getting better, huh?"

Pettibone smiled. "Hard to change an old dog."

CHAPTER 24

On her drive home, Tracy called Therese to check in and tell her she'd grab a few things for girls' night—popcorn, ice cream, and various toppings. She also wanted to speak to the store owner without Lydia present to find out how he felt about possibly hiring her, having now met her.

She parked in an angled spot outside Cedar Grove Market and stepped down from the cab, pulling her shirt down to cover the micro 9 mm pistol at her hip. As she went down an aisle a familiar voice called out.

"What, you don't stop in and say hello when you come into my town anymore?"

Tracy turned to the familiar voice. Roy Calloway, Cedar Grove's chief of police, filled the aisle the way Faz filled her office doorway. He wasn't wrong about it being his town, and it had been since Tracy was young. Roy had tried retirement, briefly, but it didn't suit him.

"I heard you were out fishing," she said.

"Just got back this afternoon. How long you been in town?" He lumbered with a pronounced limp. A bear trap set in the mountains by Edmund House had snapped his right ankle when he went searching for Tracy. He looked like he'd just got off the water, dressed in jeans, a long-sleeve shirt, boots, and a fishing vest.

"About a week."

Calloway's face, once hard edges to complement chiseled features, had become soft creases with age. His hair showed almost no vestiges of its once-brown color.

"I'll give you a pass this time. Finlay said you were on a hiatus."

"Didn't know I was in town, huh?"

Calloway said he had spoken to Finlay and learned of Tracy's situation.

"Is that what brought about the desire to train with Mason again?"

"Figured it can't hurt," she said.

Calloway made a face, as if struck by a pain, but Tracy knew it was likely a memory they had both tried and failed to forget. "Is this town ever going to be rid of that guy . . . his memory?"

"I hope so, Roy."

He changed the subject. "Looks like you're picking up dessert."

She told him about girls' night and Lydia.

"She's a pistol; ain't she?"

Tracy paused. "Does she remind you of anyone, Roy?"

"I might have said you when you were that age, but to be honest, she's more Sarah than you. She certainly shoots like your sister did; I daresay she might even be faster."

"I think you're right. I was just wondering. Lydia's mannerisms are a lot like I remember Sarah's. You think Sarah could have been on the spectrum also?"

"That's above my pay grade. She was a pistol though. That's for sure."

Talk of her sister and her youth made Tracy think of the mansion. "Finlay tell you someone bought the Mattioli mansion?"

"You know news like that travels fast up here," Calloway said.

"Anyone met the family?"

He shook his head. "Just heard it sold. Didn't know a family bought it. Hope that's the case. It would be good to see a family enjoying it again. How do you feel about it?"

Tracy shrugged. "Same as you. I've been ready to let it go for a while, and I'm glad it sold to a family. Dan ran into the man who bought it in The Daily Perk. Said his name was William Kenmore, and he had a wife and two daughters."

"Huh," Calloway said. "Then you know more than I do. If you're curious, check with Atticus. I would think the sale of the Mattioli mansion would warrant an article." Atticus Pelham was the editor and owner of the *Cedar Grove Towne Crier,* always on the hunt for a story to fill the paper's pages. "If Atticus doesn't know about it, Margaret will," Calloway said. "She knows what I'm wearing before I do." Margaret covered soft news around Cedar Grove.

"No reason to snoop around. I'll just stop by the house before I head home."

"Well, where's the fun in that?" Calloway said, making Tracy laugh. "I'll go with you and introduce myself. Let them know who runs this town."

"Give me a minute to pay," Tracy said, "and I'll meet you outside."

At her truck, Tracy loaded her girls' night supplies on the floor of the cab and backed the Ford from its parking spot. Calloway followed. Once out of town, the road wound into the mountain, and the size of the houses and the yards increased. Tracy drove on autopilot, slowed when she saw the wall surrounding the property, and turned at the river-rock gateposts. She felt a wave of nostalgia as the truck crested the sloped driveway to what had once been her home. She recalled the first time her father described their new home. He said Christian Mattioli had enlisted an architect all the way from England to design a two-story, Queen Anne–style home that would be the tallest and grandest in Cedar Grove. Tracy thought of it as a castle.

The house's bones didn't look much different than the last time Tracy visited, nor did the yard. The flower beds, once tended to regularly by her mother and filled with perennials, were still just dirt. The weeping willow that had once stood in the center of the yard had been felled by a disease and the stump finally removed.

No cars were parked in the driveway. The yard showed no indication of two girls having played there. She saw no toys or bicycles lying unattended.

Calloway pulled up on her driver's side and spoke through his lowered passenger-side window. "It still looks abandoned. You sure Dan said someone was living here?"

"That's what he said."

"Maybe the guy said he'd bought the property, but they hadn't moved in yet."

"Maybe." She shut off the engine. "I'll go knock on the door."

Calloway pushed from the car as Tracy stepped down from the cab. They walked across the gravel drive sprouting grass and dandelion weeds. The front walk led to the portico entrance. At the cathedral front door, Tracy rang the bell and listened to the familiar chimes echo inside.

"Sounds empty," Calloway said. Tracy thought so too. She tried to look through the colored panels on the side of the door, but the stained glass blurred the images inside.

"Let's go to the front lawn," Calloway said. "We can look in the picture window."

Tracy followed Calloway across the overgrown front lawn to the picture window. The four corners of the large window were also stained glass. They cupped their hands and pressed against the panes to peer inside. The dust and grime on the interior of the window provided more blurred images, though Tracy could envision the Brazilian hardwood floors and the box-beam ceilings her father had redone, as well as the wainscoting and the crystal chandeliers.

"No furniture," Calloway said. "Not that I can see anyway."

"I don't see any either."

They circled the house and looked through a few other ground-floor windows, coming to the same conclusion. As they walked back to where they'd parked their vehicles, Tracy looked up at the second-story windows that had once been her and Sarah's bedrooms. She thought she saw a flash of white in her bedroom window, and it made the hair on her arms tingle.

Calloway must have noticed her reaction because he also looked. "You see something?"

The window was clear. "No," she said. "I . . . No."

Calloway slid into his SUV with some effort. Age and injuries had slowed him. "I'll stop off at the paper and talk to Atticus on my way home, if he's still there. If I hear anything, I'll let you know."

Calloway backed down the driveway, leaving Tracy standing outside her truck cab. She looked around the yard, then turned back to the house and glanced again at the upstairs window.

Was it another hallucination? Was she now seeing things that weren't there?

Maybe, but the hair on her arms continued to stand, and she now felt a chill she could not shake, a feeling like she wasn't alone. Not wanting to linger, she slipped into her truck cab and descended the driveway but took one last look in her rearview mirror.

She saw only the dust from her tires.

No ghosts.

CHAPTER 25

Friday evening, Tracy returned to Mason Pettibone's, and he answered the door with a wistful smile. "Lydia is so excited she's hardly stopped talking about girls' night," Pettibone said. "I haven't seen her this animated since I don't know when. And this afternoon, after you finished up on the range, she made me drive her down to the grocery store to fill out an application to be a bagger. Are you behind that?"

"Maybe," Tracy said. "But I left it up to Lydia, as you suggested."

Mr. Cunningham had told Tracy he knew and understood Lydia's situation and said the store could accommodate her as much as needed. His youngest son had Down syndrome and had worked at the store for several years before he, too, had moved on.

Before Tracy could ask Pettibone anything else, Lydia came out of her room and down the hall. Tracy had told her to dress comfortably, and she wore yellow sweatpants and a gray hoodie. Pettibone's eyes got a little watery when they said good-bye, Tracy telling him, for Lydia's sake, she'd have her back by 10:00 p.m.

"I heard you went to Cedar Grove Market," Tracy said in the truck cab.

"I filled out an application to work at the market as a bag girl. The job is for a bag *boy*, but since I'm a girl, Mr. Cunningham said it would be okay if we called it a 'bag *girl*.'"

Tracy smiled. "That's terrific, Lydia."

"Why?"

Tracy stifled a smile. "When do you start?"

"I work a floating schedule that changes each week. My mother will pick me up and drive me home after she gets off work. Grandpa will drive me to work. Until I learn to drive on my own."

"I'm so proud of you."

"Why?"

Again, Tracy had to stifle a smile. "No reason," she said.

When they reached her home, Tracy said, "I forgot to tell you that I have two dogs."

"Grandpa has a dog."

"Yes, but these are big dogs, and their bark can be a little scary to people who aren't used to big dogs."

"Why? Do they bite?"

"No. No, they don't bite. They're very friendly. Are you going to be okay with that?"

"Yes. I am okay with your dogs being friendly."

Rex and Sherlock did not disappoint, as rambunctious as ever, but Lydia didn't appear to be the least bit scared. To their delight, she rubbed their backs and scratched each behind their ears. "Lucille loves to be scratched behind her ears," she said.

Therese came into the room holding Daniella's hand. "Lydia, this is Therese," Tracy said.

"It's wonderful to meet you, Lydia," Therese said. "Mrs. O has spoken highly of you."

"You talk funny," Lydia said.

Tracy smiled. "Therese has an accent."

"She has an Irish accent. I heard it on a television show. It sounds like a song," Lydia said.

"You're right," Therese said. "I'm from Kinvara, a town in County Galway. And I love that you think my voice sounds like a song."

"Galway is a picturesque bay located on the west coast of Ireland," Lydia said in a perfect Irish accent. "It lies between County Galway in the province of Connacht to the north and the Burren in County Clare in the province of Munster to the south."

"Have you been there?" Therese asked.

"No," Lydia said matter-of-factly.

"Lydia has a very good memory for things she watches on TV or reads about," Tracy said.

"I should say," Therese said. "It's like listening to a Rick Steves travel book."

"And this little girl hiding behind Therese's leg is my three-year-old daughter, Daniella," Tracy said. Daniella took Tracy's fingers and stared up at Lydia.

"Is she going to be part of girls' night?" Lydia asked.

"She is, for a while. Then she has to go to bed."

"A three-year-old child typically requires eleven to fourteen hours of sleep within a twenty-four-hour period, including naps. Establishing a consistent sleep schedule is essential for their well-being."

Tracy and Therese shared a smile. "We certainly try," Tracy said. "I bought pizza. Should we eat before we watch the movie?"

"You said on girls' night we'll eat popcorn and watch *Wonka*," Lydia said.

"I did and we will," Tracy said. "But first we eat pizza for dinner. Okay?"

Lydia shrugged. "Okay."

Lydia was inquisitive, and Daniella quickly warmed to her. It made Tracy both happy and sad. She couldn't help but think Sarah would have been a wonderful aunt. After dinner, Lydia lounged in a beanbag chair close to the television, and it didn't take Daniella long to climb onto the bag beside her.

"Well, I guess we're chopped liver, Mrs. O," Therese said under her breath.

When the movie started, Lydia sat up and crossed her legs. Daniella imitated her posture. Lydia focused on the television with an intensity that rivaled her attention to the computer simulations. It was as if she was absorbing every scene and every line. Her facial expressions were limited, but every so often she smiled warmly, and it brought another smile to Tracy's face, reminding her of those times when she and Sarah would sit next to one another on the floor to watch *The Wizard of Oz*.

When the show ended, Tracy drove Lydia home. "What part of girls' night did you like best?"

"The part I liked best was the song," Lydia said and commenced singing "Pure Imagination."

Tracy was amazed at Lydia's pitch and tone. "You have a beautiful voice, Lydia. Do you like to sing?"

"I like to sing."

Tracy pulled into the driveway and Lydia stuck out her hand. "Good night, Crossdraw."

Tracy shook her hand. "How about when we're competing, I'll be Crossdraw? Otherwise, you can just call me Tracy; okay?"

"Okay, Tracy. When we compete, I'll be Lightning Strike. Otherwise, you can just call me Lydia." With that, the young woman stepped from the truck and walked to the front door.

Mason Pettibone opened the door, smiling as Lydia made her way. Tracy waved and he waved back. After Lydia stepped past him and went inside, Pettibone mouthed, "Thank you," and put his hand over his heart.

Tracy backed down the driveway to the county road, smiling inside as she made her way home. She felt like maybe she'd been given a second chance with Sarah. Crazy as that sounded, it made her feel good to help Lydia to develop, and she hoped she'd be able to do enough that the young woman could achieve her goal of living on her own.

Headlights flooded the inside of the cab. Tracy quickly flipped the rearview mirror up to cut the glare and looked in the side mirror. The car behind her had come out of nowhere, its high beams on. "What the hell? Where did you come from?"

Had she slowed down, thinking of Sarah and Lydia?

She checked her speed. Forty miles per hour.

Her pulse ramped up, as did her adrenaline.

She touched the Glock holstered at her hip and looked again in the side mirror to determine the make of the car, color, or maybe get a license number, but with the headlights blinding her, and no streetlights, and little ambient light, she couldn't make out the type of vehicle or the color, though it looked like an SUV. She looked to the front bumper but did not see a license plate.

Time to find out if this was deliberate.

She pressed down on the gas pedal. The car remained close. She slowed and the car slowed. She pulled to the left to allow the car to pass, keeping her hand on the Glock, but the car also slid to its left, remaining behind her. She slowed. The car slowed. She sped up. The car sped up.

"Let's see what you want," Tracy said.

She hit her brakes hard and swung the truck cab around so the truck partially blocked the road. The car, too, hit its brakes, but then quickly turned down the intersecting side road. Tracy couldn't fully turn the truck on the narrow two-lane road without going into a ditch on either side. By the time she corrected, punched the gas, and turned, the taillights were barely visible, the car now traveling at a high rate of speed.

About to follow, she thought of Therese and Daniella at home. That was where she needed to be.

She turned the truck back to the county road and drove quickly toward home.

When she arrived, the lights in the house were off but for the front porch light and a light in the kitchen window. She checked her rearview and side mirrors, didn't see any headlights or a car, and exited the cab. She took a deep breath and realized she was perspiring; trickles of sweat rolled down the side of her face and beneath her armpits. She kept her eyes on the road as she closed and locked the cab door, then walked to the porch. At the front door she inserted a key in the deadbolt, heard a car engine, and quickly turned, drawing her Glock but holding it at her side.

A Cedar Grove police vehicle driving past the house braked suddenly, no doubt considering the darkened figure standing at Tracy's door.

Tracy reholstered the Glock, waved, and stepped down onto the front lawn as the driver got out. "Tracy?"

"Finlay."

"Everything okay?"

"I'm not sure. I was just tailgated by a car with its high beams on."

Finlay approached. "Did you get a license plate number or make and model of the vehicle?"

"No. The headlights were too bright."

"Where was this?"

Tracy told him where the encounter occurred.

"Okay. I'll sit here for a bit and get on the radio about the high beams. Could be kids out horsing around. I'll let you know if I hear anything."

"Thanks, Finlay."

"No problem. You have a good night."

Finlay got back into his car and pulled it to the shoulder. Tracy looked again at the darkened road and thought of the Mattioli mansion, the white flash she thought she'd seen in what had once been her bedroom window but which turned out to be nothing.

The road, too, was empty.

She had perhaps imagined the white flash, but she definitely had not imagined the car.

CHAPTER 26

Sunday, Tracy walked into the house after taking Daniella to the playground. Dan sat on the couch watching an early morning Mariners baseball game. He'd returned from Seattle to spend the weekend with them but had to fly to San Francisco in the morning to take depositions in advance of a trial. Tracy would drive him to the Bellingham Airport in the morning so she and Therese would continue to each have access to a car.

He picked up Daniella and kissed her, playing with her for a few minutes. "I'm just taking a break to catch a few innings of the game," he said to Tracy, sounding defensive. He'd been up early working and had declined accompanying Tracy and Daniella to the park. "They're on a road trip back east this weekend playing the Yankees."

"Are they winning?"

"Tied in the eighth inning."

"I meant to tell you I ran into Roy in the market the other day."

"How's he doing?" Dan asked, gazing back at the television.

"Still working too much, though he'd just got back from a fishing vacation."

"No doubt at Nora's insistence," Dan said.

"He looks good. He's lost weight and is moving better. Anyway, I asked him about the new owners of the Mattioli mansion."

"What did he say?"

"He said he'd heard the rumors also, and he and I took a ride out there to meet them."

"Uh-huh." Dan put Daniella down and glanced between Tracy and the television. "Did you meet Wild Bill?" he said sardonically.

"No." She sat Daniella at the table and got her a bowl of grapes she'd cut in half. "It looks like the house is still empty."

Dan turned, looking and sounding puzzled. "Empty?"

"No furniture, at least. No cars or bikes in the driveway either. Windows are still grimy. Roy was wondering if maybe the new owner said he'd bought the house but *hadn't* moved in yet?"

Dan raised his eyebrows and slowly shook his head. "Boy, I could have sworn he'd said he and his wife moved in with their two daughters. I don't know. I guess he could have said they *were* moving in." He turned his head again when the announcer's voice rose, indicating Julio Rodríguez had hit a three-run home run. Dan pumped his fist. "Yes!"

"Go watch your game," she said. "I'll put Daniella down for her nap after she has her snack. Did you get your flight for tomorrow morning?"

"Yeah. Not too early. Nine a.m."

"I want to stop at the cemetery on the way out and put flowers on our families' graves."

"We should, shouldn't we? It's been a while," he said. "I'll make dinner tonight for getting you up early tomorrow to drive me."

"We're barbecuing a pork loin," she said. "And you love barbecuing almost as much as you love the Mariners. Don't try to fool me, Dan O'Leary. I know you like a well-worn book."

"A spicy romance, I hope."

"Not trending that way."

The following morning, Tracy and Dan got on the road early. Therese and Daniella remained fast asleep. Outside, the air held the aroma of pine trees, though an easterly breeze also brought the pungent smell of skunk cabbage. Tracy felt reassured when a Cedar Grove Police SUV drove past the house.

Dan threw his bag on the bench seat but kept his laptop to review his deposition questions and exhibits on the drive to the airport. Before getting into the cab, he looked at the police car and sighed. "We can't live our lives like this, Tracy."

"It's not forever."

"No? How long is it for?"

"It's better to be safe than sorry."

"Than sorry?"

She blew out a frustrated breath. "We're going to be late if we don't get going."

The Cedar Grove Cemetery had existed longer than the town, though no one knew the first burial date. The original graves—miners or family members of miners—had been unmarked or marked only with stones. Volunteers had enclosed the grounds with wrought-iron fencing, tended to the upkeep, and dug the graves.

"We could apply for permission to be buried here, since we were born in town," Tracy said as she navigated the one-way road. Because of the limited size of the cemetery, the city council had passed an ordinance requiring residency in Cedar Grove for burial.

"Morbid," Dan said, his eyes on his computer screen. "I don't want to think about that. And don't put me underground. Put my ashes on the mantel so I can watch sports for eternity."

"Ashes on the mantel? Now who's being morbid?"

The O'Leary grave site was situated beneath a Chinese maple Dan had planted when he'd buried his mother. She had tended to the one in their garden and had always loved the vibrant colors in the fall and spring. After a brief visit, they walked to the Crosswhite plot atop the knoll overlooking Cedar Grove. Though it was technically a two-person plot—their father had expected Tracy and Sarah would someday be buried beside their spouses—the city council had permitted Tracy to bury Sarah's urn with her parents' coffins. The family tombstone included her father and Sarah's cowboy names: "Doc Crosswhite" and "The Kid."

Tracy put a bouquet of flowers in the slots on each side of their tombstone, then knelt and picked at strands of grass where the mower couldn't reach, tidying the plot. She and Dan said a quick prayer—her mother would have told her not to linger over the dead, but Tracy couldn't help but wish they all remained alive. Her family would have doted on their granddaughter and niece. Dan's parents also. They were two orphans, she and Dan.

As Tracy turned to leave, she caught sight of a name on the weathered tombstone to the immediate right of her family's plot. She stepped closer; the four chiseled names had been worn with time.

"What did you say that guy's name was?"

"Who?" Dan said, looking back, then, "What the hell?"

Tracy felt her blood run cold. Dan stepped closer to the tombstone.

William Kenmore

The tombstone also included the names of Kenmore's loving wife, Abigail, and their two daughters, Elizabeth and Frances. All four had died on the same day: June 12, 1865. The girls were not yet teens.

"This is weird," Dan said. "The guy I met said he had a wife and two little girls."

"Seems an odd coincidence. Maybe he's an ancestor?" Tracy said.

Dan shook his head. "He said he fell in love with the town passing through one day."

"Passing through? To where?"

"That's what I said."

Tracy said, "You said you got a bad vibe from the guy?"

"Yeah. Sort of."

"Bad how?"

Dan shrugged. "I don't know. Just a vibe you get. You know. The guy seemed off."

"What did he look like?"

"Why does that matter?" Then Dan's eyes widened. "Do you think it could be the guy from Seattle? Schmidt?"

"I don't know. But this . . . ," she said, motioning to the tombstone. "Like I said, seems an odd coincidence."

Dan thought for a second. "Midforties. Short hair. Fit. Blue eyes."

It could have been Schmidt, except for the hair, but hair could be cut. Tracy's mind went back to the shooting video of Schmidt when he'd been in the AMU. He'd had short hair then, though he wore a ball cap.

"What color was his hair?"

"I'm not sure. He had a hat on. How would he know you're here?"

Tim Herman at Walla Walla had told her Schmidt spent hours with House working in the prison library, that Schmidt knew about Tracy getting House a new trial. He'd said House had been obsessed with her. He could have told Schmidt everything about Tracy—where she had lived in Cedar Grove, her parents, Sarah, that Tracy had once been a competitive shooter.

"I need to make a call," she said.

"What? To whom?"

"Roy."

Tracy pressed her cell phone to her ear.

"Tracy, do you think the guy I met could have been Schmidt?"

"I don't know, Dan." Her call connected. "I'll explain in a minute."

"Tracy," Dan said.

"Roy? It's Tracy Crosswhite. I need a favor. I need you to get a car out to my house."

"Finlay said we have a car driving by every twenty minutes," Calloway said.

"I know. I know. But this morning I'm taking Dan to the airport. Can you have someone just knock on the door and make sure everything is okay? Therese and Daniella are home, though likely still asleep or just getting up. The dogs are with them."

"Absolutely. I'll do it myself. What's going on?"

"Just ask her if anyone has called or stopped by asking about me or Dan. Anything unusual."

"Sure. I'm on it. But why? Tell me what you think is going on."

"I don't know. Maybe nothing. But I might have found William Kenmore. Maybe."

"The guy who bought the Mattioli mansion? Where?"

"The Cedar Grove Cemetery."

"What?"

"I'll explain later. Just get out to the house, please, and call me when you do. I have to get Dan to the airport." She was about to disconnect, then thought of something else. "And Roy?"

"Yeah."

"Do me another favor. Ask Atticus to pull old copies of the *Towne Crier*."

"For when?"

"Tell him to start with June 12, 1865. Probably on microfiche, if the paper goes back that far."

"What's the significance of that day?"

"According to the tombstone, William Kenmore, his wife, and his two daughters all died on that same day. I want to know if anything exists that explains how they died."

CHAPTER 27

As they walked back to the truck, Tracy said, "Could have misheard the guy—"

"I didn't mishear him."

"Yesterday you said you could have."

"Yesterday I hadn't seen the tombstone," he said.

"Maybe the guy was passing through to visit his relatives here."

"We both just agreed there is no passing through Cedar Grove."

"Just let me make another call," Tracy said, frustrated.

"To whom?"

"To Faz."

They got back into the truck cab. Tracy reached Faz and asked if he and Del would make a run by Erik Schmidt's house and find out if he was home. She knew she was putting them in a difficult position with the pending civil action against SPD by Schmidt and his attorney, Gil, but Faz, predictably, didn't hesitate. He, too, asked her what was going on, and when she told him what she knew, he said he and Del were already headed out of SPD to their car and would do a door knock. Tracy thanked him and disconnected.

"Where are we going?" Dan said as she pulled from the cemetery.

"I'm taking you to the airport."

Dan protested. "No. Turn the truck around and go back home."

"We don't have any evidence the man in the coffee shop was Erik Schmidt, or that he bought the mansion. Why would he buy the mansion, Dan? It wouldn't make any sense."

"I don't care. I want to get Therese and Daniella out of here."

"The two dogs are home. No one is getting in uninvited, and Calloway is closer and will get there more quickly. Until then, let's not panic."

Dan wasn't happy or pacified, but he acquiesced. They continued toward Bellingham in an uneasy silence, both waiting for Tracy's phone to ring. Every so often, Dan told her to turn the truck around, and she would again have to talk him off the ledge.

Calloway called back first, as he got into his SUV following a personal visit to the home. "I'm sorry it took longer than expected."

"Everything okay?"

"Your nanny said everything was grand. No phone calls. No knocks on the door. Nothing unusual. Everything is fine, Tracy."

"You didn't scare her," Tracy said.

"The dogs might have . . . they have an intimidating bark, but she gave no indication she was scared," Calloway said. "I told her I was just stopping by to say hello and to see your daughter. She said you were taking Dan to the airport and invited me in for a cup of coffee. I'll head over to the newspaper when it opens and talk to Atticus. He goes to work later on Mondays. And I instructed my deputies to increase their drive-bys and report back anything unusual until you return. They have the mug shot you gave Finlay of this guy Schmidt and the information regarding his car. Tell me again his beef with you?" Calloway said.

Tracy explained it to him.

"What would he be doing up here? *If* he's up here?"

"Nothing good," Tracy said. "*If* he's up here. I made a call to SPD and asked that someone run by his house in Seattle and determine if he's there. I'll let you know what I hear."

"Okay. I'll keep you updated as well. And if we see him around town, I'll run his ass out of here."

"He hasn't done anything to break the law, Roy."

"Like I give a shit. If he's up here harassing one of my citizens, I don't need more than that."

Calloway did, but Tracy wasn't about to argue with him. She disconnected but was already thinking: *Run him to where?*

As they continued, uneasily, toward Bellingham, Faz returned Tracy's call. She also put him on speaker for Dan to hear.

"What did you find out?" she asked.

Faz's gravelly voice came over the phone. "Inconclusive. Schmidt's girlfriend answered the door. She said Schmidt was sleeping, and if we didn't have a warrant we were trespassing. She told us to leave."

"You didn't see him?"

"No. But she said he was there, and his Corvette was parked in the driveway. Unfortunately, our hands are tied. We can't do much more at this point."

"Not ten minutes after Faz and I did the door knock, we got a call from Nolasco," Del chimed in. "He said he got a call from Cerrabone, who said that prick Gil called him and said SPD was harassing his client without a warrant, and if it didn't immediately cease and desist, he'd be filing additional charges and taking the matter up with the press and the brass."

Tracy bit her tongue. "Don't do anything else that could get you in trouble."

"Screw them. We both got in enough years to retire on a full pension," Del said. "And Nolasco has our backs on this."

Faz cut in. "On my way back to the car I put a chalk mark on Schmidt's back passenger tire, then notified the uniforms in that area to pass by his house frequently and let us know if that car leaves or is moved."

"What about the girlfriend's Jeep?"

"Could be in the garage. Don't know," Faz said.

Tracy wasn't going to take out her frustration on them. "Thanks, guys. I appreciate you putting your asses on the line."

"You okay up there?" Faz asked.

"I'll keep you posted."

"You need anything, you call us," Del said. "Faz and I will come up there and get things settled the Sicilian way."

Tracy disconnected. She didn't know what to say to Dan. She would have felt better if Del and Faz had actually seen Schmidt, but . . .

"I don't feel right about leaving," Dan said. "Let's go back home. I'll move to have the trial postponed."

"Until when?"

"Until I know my family is safe."

"We're just speculating it might be Schmidt, Dan."

"You asked Finlay to keep an eye out for him."

"It's just a precaution. You heard Roy. They're safe, and he'll look after them until I get back."

"You said you think this guy killed two women?"

"Women he dated. Not random women like the two House killed."

Dan shook his head and let out a burst of air. "I don't like this, Tracy."

"I don't either, but I also don't want to live in fear, Dan. And I'm not going to run. Where are we going to run to? Seattle? He lives in

Seattle. This is our sanctuary, Dan. And I'll be damned if I'm going to let Schmidt, or the specter of Schmidt, take that away from me."

Dan was quiet. Too quiet. In a soft voice he said, "It's not just about you, Tracy. Not anymore." She looked over at him. His eyes watered. "We're a family. You, me, Daniella, Therese. It's about all of us. It's about keeping all of us safe."

"Schmidt lives in Seattle, Dan. We can't run from one place to the other. Not forever. I'm not going to do that. I'm not going to let him do that to our family. Let's wait—"

"Until when?" he said.

"Until we know more."

"Until then what do you propose?"

"Just what we've done. The dogs are home. And Roy is on alert. You get on that plane to San Francisco and do your job. Let me do mine."

"What does that mean?"

"You heard both phone conversations. I have deputies watching the house until I get back, and Faz and Del have cars going by Schmidt's home. I'll take it from there."

"*We'll* take it from there," Dan said. "We're a team, Tracy."

"No." She shook her head, and before Dan could protest, she added, "Not in police matters, Dan. No. We're a family, absolutely. But this is *my* job."

"That affects all of us."

"If it were a legal matter you'd handle it."

"I don't like the look in your eyes, or their color."

"I can't change the color—"

He spoke over her. "They're gray, Tracy, and I know what gray means. It means you're pissed off and you're itching for a fight."

"I'm not itching for anything, Dan. And I'm not going to do anything that would put Therese or Daniella in danger. Not ever. You just heard me taking precautions. I'm giving you my word."

"What about you, Tracy?"

"What about me?"

"Can I have your word that you won't do anything that puts *you* in danger?"

"I'm a homicide detective, Dan. Sometimes it comes with the territory."

"And sometimes you seek it out."

She shook her head, both hurt and frustrated. "You think I asked for this? Do you think I asked for any of this?"

"No, Tracy—"

"Do you know what I'd give to have my sister back?"

"Anything."

"No, Dan. Not anything. I wouldn't give you back or Daniella. You're my life now. You're my family. I didn't ask for things to turn out this way, but I'm damn sure not going to regret the good things I have in my life because of what happened. I have you and Daniella. I'd go through every shitty damn thing I've been through again, and I still wouldn't trade places, not with anyone in the world."

They finished the drive in silence. When Tracy pulled into the Bellingham Airport and parked outside the terminal, Dan didn't move to get out of the cab.

"You're going to miss your flight," she said.

"I'm sorry about what I said before. I know you didn't seek out any of this."

She wiped tears from her eyes.

"Just promise me you won't do anything stupid," he said.

She turned and looked at him. He smiled—the same big, goofy smile he'd always given her when he tried to make up, since they'd been kids. "You're an idiot; you know that?" she said.

"Yes, but I'm your idiot."

She smiled. "I'm not about to do anything stupid," she said.

Dan checked his watch, and for a moment she thought he might refuse to go. Then, reluctantly, and punctuated with several swear words, he got out of the truck cab. He grabbed his briefcase and his suitcase, put them on the ground, then leaned in across the seat and stared Tracy in the eyes. "You call me. As soon as you know anything."

"You have my word."

"I don't know what I would do without you or Daniella," he said.

"You're not going to have to ever find out," she said. "And I'll put your ashes on the mantel so you can keep an eye on us after you're gone."

Dan didn't smile. He kissed her, then said, "Morbid." He gave her another serious look. "You call me. Anything comes up. You call me."

Tracy nodded. *Anything she couldn't handle.*

He closed the door, picked up his things from the sidewalk, and walked to the glass doors, turning back one last time to look at her. He mimed putting a phone to his ear. Then he disappeared inside the terminal.

Tracy pulled from the curb. She'd had another idea on their drive to the airport, a way to determine who had, definitively, purchased the Mattioli mansion. She called Roy Calloway first to ensure everything was okay.

"Everything is fine. Finlay checked in a minute ago. He's sitting at the house and said everything looked fine. No strange cars or men around. And I got ahold of Atticus. He's going to go into the newspaper early to see what he can find on the microfiche, if it goes back that far. You know him. He's excited to have a potential news story. You on your way home?"

"I'm going to stop off at the county building department while I'm here and determine who bought the Mattioli mansion."

"Good idea. Keep me posted," Calloway said. "I got your house covered."

Tracy disconnected and made her way to Grand Avenue and the Whatcom County Courthouse, a modern multistory brick-and-glass building with a tall rotunda and colonnade entrance. She parked on a street lined with trees and made her way inside, eventually finding the county assessor's office. Having arrived just before the office opened, she was first in line. She filled out forms on a table, then met with a young woman, showing the woman her SPD credentials and telling her the nature of her business. The woman invited Tracy behind the counter to a chair beside her desk while she sat at a computer terminal tapping her keyboard and moving her mouse.

After a moment she said, "According to our paperwork, that piece of property hasn't sold. The bank still owns it."

"Could it have sold recently, and you don't yet know about it?"

"Possibly, but it would have had to have sold really recently."

Tracy thanked her and left. She thought again of the white blur she'd seen in her bedroom window, and of the tombstone, then told herself not to start chasing ghosts.

Though in a sense, she already was.

CHAPTER 28

Therese put Daniella's go bag in the Subaru beside her child carrier backpack "That bloody bag weighs more than you do," Therese said to Daniella, who sat in her car seat.

"Why is the bag bloody?" Daniella asked.

"It's just an expression, love," Therese said. "Because the bag is red."

"And blood is red. I saw it when I had my owie."

Daniella kept asking Therese if they were going to the playground. She'd fallen in love with the pirate ship. But Therese wanted to go on the hike Mr. O'Leary had told her about, the one with the waterfalls. "Since you woke up early, I thought we could go on a hike and see the waterfalls your mommy and daddy took you to see. Would you like that?"

Daniella clapped her hands and told Therese about the water spraying her in the face.

"Today we're going to get some fresh air and get you tuckered out, so you'll nap this afternoon and be a bright little ball of sunshine when your mommy gets home."

"I don't want to take a nap."

"You can sleep with Rex and Sherlock on your bed. How's that?"

"Okay," Daniella said.

Therese waved the two dogs into the back. They didn't have to be asked twice. Then she double-checked to ensure she hadn't forgotten anything before she backed down the driveway and drove toward downtown Cedar Grove. She drove past the playground, which prompted a series of questions from Daniella about playing on the pirate ship.

She drove out of town, and when the GPS on her phone indicated Therese had driven roughly seven miles, as Mr. O had instructed, she checked for traffic in her rearview mirror before slowing to scan the edge of the road. Mr. O had said the turnoff to the dirt-and-gravel road was marked by a large boulder.

Daniella squealed and Therese looked in the mirror. Rex had stuck his head over the seat, licking Daniella's face. She almost missed the boulder.

"There's the boulder, just where your daddy said it would be," she said to Daniella. "Aren't you lucky to have such a smart mommy and daddy?"

Daniella commenced with another string of questions that Therese answered, only to get additional "Why?" questions.

The car bounced and rattled on the dirt-and-gravel road, causing Daniella to laugh and Therese to slow. Two-tenths of a mile up the dirt trail, as Mr. O'Leary had instructed, she looked for his next landmark, a fence made of limbs from the surrounding trees that marked the start of the trailhead. "And there is the fence." Therese parked alongside another car in the pullout. "Easy peasy," she said.

"Easy peasy," Daniella repeated.

"Looks like we might have company."

"Who?" Daniella said.

"I don't know who. We're going to have to find out."

"Why?"

Therese stepped from the car and inhaled the fresh pine fragrance and took in the beauty of the mountains. She noted the cairns Mr. O'Leary said served as trail markers—stones stacked in a pyramid shape along the trail edge by hikers and hunters to keep from getting lost.

Daniella wanted to walk, but Therese told her the trail was steep and she could walk when they reached the top, and play in the water, which seemed to appease her, at least for the time being. She let the dogs out of the back to do their business, then lifted Daniella into the backpack, and she fit a sunhat on the little girl's head after Daniella's mild protest stopped when Therese put on a similar hat. She then slathered Daniella's arms and legs, and her own, with sunscreen.

"We Irish don't exactly tan," she said. "We don't want to look like lobsters; do we?"

"What's a lobster?" Daniella asked.

Therese lowered to one knee, fit the straps over each shoulder, stood, and shrugged to get the weight to rest on her hips. Daniella was not so light anymore. "Are you ready for an adventure?"

Therese started up the incline behind the two dogs. Mr. O'Leary said the hike was under four miles round trip, but with 1,500 feet of elevation gain—much of it at the start of the hike. Therese hoped she was up to the task, particularly with thirty-five pounds on her back.

"Should get our heart rates up and the blood pumping at least," she said.

"My blood is red," Daniella repeated. "I saw it when I got an owie."

⬤▬

Tracy removed her cell phone from her back pocket as she walked to the truck in the parking lot, intending to call Therese to tell her she was on her way home, when the phone rang in her hand. Roy Calloway.

"Roy?" she said.

"Tracy," Calloway said. "I was just talking to Finlay. I don't want to alarm you."

Too late.

———

Therese had just started to feel like maybe she'd bitten off more mountain than she could climb. Her thighs and calves burned, and the back of her shirt beneath the backpack clung to her perspiring skin. She'd kept a brisk pace. She wanted to reach the falls, spend some time there, and be home before Mrs. O returned around eleven o'clock. Therese stopped for a drink of water, handing Daniella her sippy cup over her shoulder. Rex and Sherlock also dutifully stopped.

She took a deep breath and considered her watch. Based on how long Mr. O'Leary had said it would take to reach the falls, it couldn't be much farther.

"Be a shame to come this far and not actually make it; wouldn't it?" she said to Daniella. "But you are not as light as you once were. You're a big girl now."

"I'm a pirate," Daniella said.

About to resume her hike, Therese heard heavy footsteps thudding on the trail above them and saw the brush move. A middle-aged man wearing a red bandanna and holding hiking poles appeared from around a bend, then a woman right behind him. The two hikers greeted Therese with smiles.

"I was just wondering how much farther it is to the falls?" she asked.

"You're nearly there," the man said. He stopped and used his poles to point. "It's just around the corner. Maybe another two-tenths of a mile to the lower falls."

"What about the middle and upper falls?"

"It gets pretty steep," the man said. "And honestly, you aren't going to see anything much different than the view from the lower falls. If you want the exercise, go for it; if you're just looking for a little serenity, the lower falls will be fine."

Mr. O'Leary had said the same thing.

"Serenity works for me," Therese said. "Sounds like we should push on, then."

Therese continued up the trail, which steepened, then flattened, and started a downward slope. She heard the rush of the falls and, as she neared, felt the cool mist. Daniella felt it also and wanted out of the backpack. "Almost there," Therese said.

They came to a pool of crystal-clear water, and Therese stared up at the falls. The water cascaded over several different levels before hitting the pond of granite rock, then flowed into the creek and continued down the mountain.

Therese saw the flat area Mr. O'Leary had mentioned near the shallow pool, out of which Rex and Sherlock drank greedily. She wanted to get Daniella off her back and give her shoulders a break as much if not more than Daniella wanted to get down. She'd let Daniella play in the water for a bit, though she anticipated the water temperature would be a deterrent. Then they'd have a picnic and relax before heading down the trail, timing their arrival home just as Mrs. O'Leary returned from taking Dan to the airport.

She laid out a beach towel and several containers of food but, as she'd suspected, the little girl wanted to play at the pool.

She took off Daniella's tennis shoes and socks, and they walked to the pond's edge. Rex and Sherlock, now seated, watched them but otherwise had no interest in going in the cold water.

Daniella put her feet in the water, then pulled them out, squealing. "It's cold," she said.

"Not like the warm baths your mommy gives you; is it?"

Daniella squatted and played at the water's edge, Therese beside her. Therese wet a rag and ran it over her neck and face, the cool water refreshing. Daniella wanted Therese to do the same to her so Therese dipped the rag again, but this time she caught the reflection of something in the water, the image distorted by the ripples she and Daniella had created. At that same moment, both dogs growled.

Therese lifted her head.

A man in hiking boots stood on a boulder on the other side of the pond, looking down at them with a sharp grin.

"Looks like you found the best spot," he said.

———

Tracy rushed to her truck, speaking to Calloway on the phone as she did. She kicked herself for not having told Therese to stay at the house until she returned home, but she'd still been asleep and . . . Screw that. She should have woken her.

This was worse. Much worse. "I thought a deputy was sitting on the house?" she said.

"He didn't get that message. He was doing frequent drive-bys."

"How long ago did he notice the car missing?"

"He drove past the house every twenty minutes, so it could not have been long. He called me from his car and said the Subaru was not in the drive. So, we know the nanny drove them somewhere."

Not necessarily, but Tracy wasn't about to get into semantics. "Have your officers check the park. Daniella likes the new play structure—the pirate ship. I'm going to try to reach Therese. Don't hang up."

"I sent Finlay to the park first thing. He said he didn't find them or the car there. He's heading downtown to see if maybe she went to The Daily Perk, or possibly to do some shopping. This might be nothing."

"Just hold on, Roy."

Tracy kept Roy on the line and called Therese. With each ring that Therese did not answer, Tracy's anxiety spread. Her call went to voice mail. She disconnected, Roy still on the line.

"She isn't answering her phone. That is not like her," Tracy said. She was breathing heavily, unable to catch her breath, and having trouble remaining composed. "It's Schmidt," she said.

"Who?"

"William Kenmore. I just came from the county assessor's office. No one has purchased the Mattioli mansion. It hasn't been sold, Roy. Dan didn't mishear the guy. The guy lied."

"Why would he choose the name William Kenmore?"

"Why would he say he bought the mansion? I don't know, Roy," she said, voice rising. "Maybe because Kenmore and his family are buried next to my family's plot and he knows I lived in that house. He's screwing with me."

"I understood others also heard the mansion had been sold."

"Like you said Roy, rumors travel fast in Cedar Grove, but the house hasn't sold. It was a lie. He's in town. Schmidt. Oh God. You have to find my little girl, Roy."

Calloway swore. "All right. Can you think of anyplace else your nanny might have taken her?"

"I don't know where else, Roy. The library? Maybe? Or on a run. We have a jogging stroller in the garage. The code for the garage door is 2288."

"I'll have it checked out. Hang on."

As Calloway spoke into his car's radio, Tracy's mind raced through various other scenarios and quickly dismissed the thought that Therese had gone on a run. Dan had mapped out several runs of various lengths around the house. There would have been no need for Therese to take the car.

"Wait. Therese wouldn't have taken the car if she'd gone on a run."

"What?"

"Therese wouldn't have taken the car if she'd taken Daniella on a run. She would have gone from the house. And she'd still be in cell range."

"Okay, anyplace else?" Calloway asked.

Tracy fought to maintain focus. She came upon a slow-moving car on the two-lane road, moved the truck to the left to see around it, then swerved back when she saw a car quickly approach from the other direction. "Are the dogs home?"

"I don't know."

"Find out. If she took Rex and Sherlock, she likely is hiking." That thought triggered another. "And Dan told Therese about a hike he and I and Daniella did close to home. It could also explain why she didn't answer her phone. She could be out of cell range."

"Where?" Calloway sounded as frustrated as Tracy. No doubt thinking of that horrible morning when they couldn't find Sarah after finding their blue truck abandoned along the side of the county road.

"The falls outside Cedar Grove. Dan and I hiked it the other day, and he told Therese about it. The trail that follows Racehorse Creek. A large boulder designates the turn off the county road."

"I know it," Calloway said. "I'm on my way. I'll call you as soon as I get to the trailhead and let you know if I find your car. If you think of anything else, call me and I'll radio Finlay."

"I'm going to try to reach Therese again."

"If she's up the mountain, she'll be out of cell phone range, but give me her number so I also have it."

Tracy did. "Roy?"

"Yeah."

"Don't let anything happen to them."

"On my life," he said, but he'd said the same thing to Tracy's father, when Sarah had gone missing, and she had never returned home.

CHAPTER 29

Therese took a step back from the water's edge, taking Daniella by the hand. The man wore camouflage pants with multiple pockets and a tight tank-top T-shirt that stretched across the muscles of his chest, shoulders, and biceps. Tattoos ran up and down both arms from his shoulders to his wrists. He also wore a floppy camo hat and glasses tinted yellow. They weren't sunglasses. They looked like the safety glasses she'd seen Mrs. O'Leary wear when she went for her shooting lessons.

Protruding over the man's right shoulder was the muzzle of a rifle. On one hip, a holster held a pistol. Strapped to his other leg was a long knife.

"Sorry," he said. "I didn't mean to startle you."

But something about the man's grin and the tone of his voice did not sound genuine. The words were friendly, but his appearance was anything but, and Rex and Sherlock had alerted, both now on their feet, growling.

"That your little girl?"

Therese put down the rag and picked up Daniella. The man stepped down from the boulder and across others, approaching. The two dogs barked. The man stopped.

"They're so much fun when they're that age; aren't they? Not like teenagers who sass you back no matter what you tell them."

Therese found her tongue. "You have daughters?" she asked. The fact that the man was a father might give her a small measure of comfort.

"Two," he said. He stepped down from the final boulder and came closer.

Now Rex and Sherlock moved between the man and Therese and Daniella, continuing to bark. Therese shifted Daniella to her other hip, away from him.

"They don't seem to care for strangers either," he said, though he didn't sound or look intimidated.

"You live near here, then?" Therese said.

The man came around bushes, now just a few feet from Therese. Rex and Sherlock moved closer still, continuing to bark, and the man stopped. Instinctively, Therese took a step back, and felt cold water seep over her hiking boot.

"Careful," the man said. "You don't want to hike in wet boots and socks. Good way to get a blister. I just moved my family to Cedar Grove. You?"

"Just visiting," Therese said.

"Do I detect an Irish brogue?" Therese didn't answer. The man's attention again found Daniella. "Beautiful girl," he said. "Can't really say she looks like you though. Must look like her father." He turned his head in each direction. "Is he here?"

Therese felt her knees go weak. She spoke, but her words were rushed and did not sound confident. "He wanted to go on a bit further, to the top. I'm sure he'll be back any minute."

"I'm sure," the man said.

"I passed a man and a woman on the trail coming up," Therese said. "They should be here any minute also."

"You must have been huffing it." Therese didn't respond. "Because I didn't see anyone. I wonder how I missed them? I saw a man and woman going down the hill, and just the two cars at the trailhead." He looked about. "You're smart to come up on a weekday. I'm told these trails get busy on the weekends, but you can walk for miles up here on a weekday and never see another soul. Not one. You're all *alone*." His last word was pointed.

"I'm not alone," she stammered. "My husband—"

"Isn't here," the man said. "You're not married." He nodded to her hand. "I have very good observation skills. No wedding ring. My guess, from your brogue and lack of a wedding ring, is you're the nanny. Am I right?"

Therese didn't answer.

"Hey, I don't blame you for lying. You're up here alone and a strange man startles you. I'd expect you to say you were up here with your husband, or friends, but in this case . . ." He shook his head and shrugged. "We both know that's a lie. You're all alone."

He took another step forward and put out his hand. Rex lunged at him, and the man stepped back and raised his hands. "Let me start over. My name is William Kenmore. Though my friends call me Wild Bill." He waited a beat. Then he said, "Are you my friend?"

A phone rang. They both looked to Therese's backpack.

"Are you going to answer that, *Therese*?"

Therese felt her stomach lurch. "How did you know my name?"

"Like I said, I'm an observant man. And would this little girl be Daniella? She is a golden beauty; isn't she?"

Therese said, "What do you want?"

"That's a tough question for me to answer. Justice might be the best word."

"Why the guns and the knife?"

"You could say I'm hunting," he said. "Thought I'd come out here and contemplate the future. How do you like Cedar Grove, Therese?"

"You didn't tell me how you knew my name."

"I'm a person who likes to know things. It can be useful. I know all about that mansion on the outskirts of town—who built it, how they got the money, who has lived in it."

Therese's eyes widened. Tracy had grown up in the mansion on the outskirts of town.

"You know it too. I can tell by the look on your face," he said.

"You met my employer. At the coffee shop in town."

Kenmore put a hand to his chin as if thinking, though Therese had a sense the man knew immediately she was talking about Dan. "About my age? Curly, blondish-brown hair with flecks of gray? Wears wire-rimmed glasses."

Therese nodded.

"Dan O'Leary," he said. "Am I right? I'm good with names too. He told me his wife used to live in the Mattioli mansion. Her and her sister. Quite a coincidence, huh?"

"How so?"

"The man who built the mansion was a liar and a murderer. He built that mansion on the mining claims he stole from men like William Kenmore. And your employer, Tracy Crosswhite, is also a liar and a murderer. Maybe not such a coincidence."

He kept grinning, belying the spite in his words, like a predator who had trapped its prey and now toyed with it. He turned to the beach towel and the Tupperware bowls on the patch of flat ground. "You look like I interrupted your lunch. Don't let me stop you from feeding the little one. You don't want her to get cranky; am I right?"

"We were just getting ready to leave," Therese said.

"Doesn't look like it."

"She's cranky. I think she might be sick. She has a fever."

"You better get out of the water, then." The man stepped forward as if to help her, and this time both dogs lowered and lunged forward. The man seemed unworried and stepped toward them. Both dogs scooted back but stayed between the man and Therese and Daniella, continuing to bark.

"You should call off your dogs," the man said. "I'd hate to kill them."

Therese quickly swung Daniella to her other hip, farther away from the man, and took another step back.

He raised his hands. "Just trying to help." He grinned. "I've had a lot of experience with helping young women."

———

Roy Calloway radioed Finlay and told him he was going out to the game trail outside of Silver Spurs—the trail along Racehorse Creek leading up to the falls. Finlay, an accomplished backpacker, knew of it. Calloway told Finlay to check the library first, then meet him at the trail. If the car was there, Roy would not be able to hike far up the trail or do so quickly, not on his bum ankle.

Calloway raced along the county road toward Silver Spurs, thinking déjà vu. He couldn't drive this road without remembering the morning he'd found Doc Crosswhite's truck, the one Sarah was supposed to have driven home, parked along the side of the road. He had fully expected to find Sarah asleep in the back, safe. But his joy at having found the truck dissipated quickly when Sarah was not in the back, and concern replaced his joy, though not panic. Things like that—a woman disappearing—didn't happen in Cedar Grove. Not then. Not unless she'd gotten lost in the mountains. He thought maybe the car had broken down and Sarah had tried to walk home, that she'd still walk into the house, tired but safe.

A subsequent inspection had revealed the truck's fuel tank had been punctured and the truck was out of gas. Not an accident. A deliberate act of sabotage. That was when panic set in.

Roy slowed his SUV when he sensed he neared the turnoff. In winter, trails like this one couldn't be easily located when the snow built up along the edge of the road from the snowplows that worked hard to keep the county road open—the only access in and out of Cedar Grove and the other small towns nearby, like Silver Spurs.

Calloway saw the rock and, just past it, the road leading to the trailhead. Turning, his SUV bounced and pitched, jostling his back and his neck, which now always felt on the verge of going out. He slowed over ruts in the road, and the car's front end dipped down, then bounced back up, like a ship in a storm navigating the troughs and crests of waves.

He came around a bend to a small clearing and saw Tracy's Subaru parked against the fence railing made from tree limbs. He almost breathed a sigh of relief, but he'd been down this path before. He wasn't after the truck—or the Subaru. He was after Therese and Daniella.

He radioed Finlay. "I found Tracy's car parked at the trailhead up to Racehorse Falls. How far out are you?"

"Five minutes," Finlay said.

Calloway hung the mic in the clip and called the number Tracy had given him for Therese. It rang several times, meaning she had her phone turned on. Then it went to voice mail instead of the call failing. He didn't know crap about cell phones but deduced that meant she had service, which meant she couldn't be far. He called Tracy. She answered on the first ring.

"I can't reach Therese," Tracy said.

"I found your car at the trailhead to Racehorse Falls."

"Are they there?"

"They're not here, but Finlay will be here in two minutes, and I'll send him up the trail. I also tried calling her but I got voice mail."

"Are there any other cars parked there?"

"One. A Suburban. Hang on. I hear someone coming down the trail."

"Is it Therese?" Tracy said.

"Hang on." Two hikers came around a final bend to the trailhead. "No. It's a man . . . and a woman. I'm going to get out and talk with them."

"Put me on speaker," Tracy said.

Calloway did. He exited his SUV and approached the hikers. They looked anxious. Calloway in uniform could have that impact on people.

"Did you see a young woman and little girl hiking?" Calloway said.

They both nodded. The man said, "Yeah. We passed her on the trail as we were coming down. She was taking a water break and debating whether to go further."

"She had a little girl?" Calloway asked.

"In a hiking backpack," the woman said. "Did she take someone's baby?"

"No, nothing like that," Calloway said.

"Did you pass anyone else on the trail?" Tracy asked over the phone.

"A man," the woman said, looking to the phone, then back to Calloway. "A hunter. At least, he was dressed in camouflage and had a rifle on his back and a sidearm. He also had a knife."

Calloway looked about but didn't see a third car.

"What did he look like?" Tracy asked. She sounded panicked. Calloway repeated her question.

"Hard to tell," the man said. "I'd guess he was about my height, six feet. Lean but muscular."

The woman interrupted. "He was dressed in camouflage pants and a tank top, with one of those floppy hats. Looked like Army-issued fatigues."

"And he wore tinted glasses," the man said.

"Was he going up or coming down the trail?" Calloway asked.

"He was going up," the man said.

"Alone?" Calloway asked.

"Didn't see anyone with him."

"How long ago did he go up?" Tracy asked.

The man spoke to his wife, then said, "We probably passed the woman and little girl half an hour ago, so . . ."

"Twenty minutes," the woman said.

"Did you speak to him?" Tracy asked. "The man. Did you speak to him?"

The man and woman both shook their head. "Just said hello in passing."

Tires crunched gravel and Calloway turned. Finlay Armstrong's SUV skidded to a stop. Roy told Tracy of Finlay's arrival, then spoke to his deputy. "They're up the trail at the falls, the nanny and little girl," Calloway said when Finlay exited. "A man went up after them. Armed. Rifle and sidearm. He's dressed in camouflage."

Finlay went back to his truck and unlocked the dash-mounted rifle rack. He removed his department-issued BCM Recce-14 carbine and worked the charging handle to chamber a round from the magazine, then slung the rifle across his body and headed to the trail.

"You have your sat phone?" Calloway asked. Finlay held it up. "Call me as soon as you find them."

"Finlay," Tracy said over the phone.

Finlay stopped. "Yeah?"

"He's an excellent shot. He's trained. He won't miss."

Finlay gave Roy a look, then went up the trail at a fast jog.

"Officer," the man who had come down the trail said to Calloway. "I don't know if this matters but . . . it was odd, seeing him in camouflage and armed."

Calloway knew what the young man was about to say, because he'd thought the same thing.

"It's too early for deer or elk season; isn't it?" the man said.

―――

Therese took another step back. The water level now reached her knees.

"You go much further, you're going to have to start taking clothes off," the man said, his grin now more of a leer.

Therese did not respond. Her phone again rang in her backpack.

She was thinking now about what to do with Daniella, and she realized going into the water had been a mistake. If the man came for her and she dropped Daniella, the little girl would drown. She looked about her for any place to which she could swim, with Daniella on her back, and possibly climb out on the other side. She could, but the man could just as quickly circle the pond and wait her out. Right now Rex and Sherlock, who refused to give ground, were her best defense.

"People around here sure are jumpy," he said. "And not very friendly to strangers. It's almost as if something bad happened around here, and people have never been able to get over it."

Therese felt on the verge of tears. She knew what had happened to Tracy and to her sister Sarah.

"I told my employers where I was going. They know exactly where I am. And they can ping my phone at all times," she said, though she could hear fear in her voice.

Again, the man grinned. "Well then, you better not lose that phone," he said. "Thing is, knowing where you are, and getting here in time to help you, are two separate things. Looks to me like I'm your only resource."

"What do you want?"

"I told you. I just want to help you pack up and head out."

"We can pack up on our own, thank you."

A voice came from the trail; Therese's name echoing off the mountainside. The two dogs alerted to the sound but did not leave their positions.

Therese turned to the voice, then back to the man standing on the shore.

"Aren't you going to answer him, *Therese*?"

Therese yelled, "I'm here. Up by the falls." She saw movement on the trail, brush shaking, then the top of someone's cowboy-style hat. "Someone is . . ." She turned to the man but said the last word to herself. "Coming."

William Kenmore was gone.

CHAPTER 30

Tracy stopped the truck in her driveway behind Roy Calloway's SUV. Another police SUV was parked across the street, a deputy sitting inside the vehicle. She felt an unbelievable sense of relief but also a burning anger.

Erik Schmidt had crossed the line. He'd threatened her family. Twice.

She pushed from the cab, fumbling from the safety strap, and sprinted across the lawn, leaving the driver's-side door open. She ran inside the house, her eyes searching the room for her little girl.

The two dogs rose quickly and rushed to her, but she stepped past them to where Roy Calloway had gotten up from a chair.

"Where is she? Where's Daniella?"

Roy pointed to the sofa, where Daniella lay beneath a blanket, sleeping. Therese sat right beside her.

Calloway raised both his hands. "She's fine, Tracy. Fast asleep. And perfectly safe."

Tracy went to her daughter, but she resisted the maternal instinct to pick her up and hug her. Therese, hands folded in a prayer position beneath her chin, looked up, and Tracy could tell from the redness of her eyes, the moisture on her cheeks, that she'd been crying hard.

"I'm so sorry, Mrs. O. I'm so sorry," she said softly. "I should have asked you if it was okay for me to take Daniella hiking."

Tracy sat beside the young woman who had become like a member of the family, wrapped an arm around her, and hugged her fiercely. "No. No, Therese. Mr. O'Leary told you about the hike. You had our permission. Of course you did." She would not allow anyone to take the blame for this, to feel guilty. This was Erik Schmidt's doing, and she was determined it would not go unpunished. "Are you all right? That's the important thing. Are you all right?"

Therese nodded and wiped additional tears. "Scared more than anything," she said softly. More tears flowed down her cheeks. "Rex and Sherlock . . . I don't know what I would have done without them. They got right between him and me and Daniella, and they weren't about to let him get near us."

Tracy turned to her two dogs and called them over. She rubbed and kissed both their heads. Then she pulled Therese's head to her shoulder, holding her. "Thank you for taking care of Daniella," she said softly, looking down at her daughter.

Therese raised her head. "I would have done anything to protect her," she said. "You have to know that."

"I know it, Therese. I know you would have. Of course I do. And I love you for it. Mr. O'Leary and I love you for it. And I love the two of you," she said to her dogs. "God how I love you."

Calloway motioned for Tracy to step out the sliding glass door into the backyard. Tracy rose and followed him, expecting Rex and Sherlock to come with her, but the two dogs remained beside the sofa, where Daniella slept. She smiled at them both, then shut the slider behind her.

"She gave us a description," Calloway said, "and the man told her he *had* met Dan at The Daily Perk, *and* his name was William Kenmore but his friends called him 'Wild Bill.'"

"He's not trying to hide his identity anymore, Roy. He wants me to know he's here."

"For what purpose?"

"I don't know yet, not for certain," she said. "To scare me. To threaten me." She saw again that stare in Schmidt's eyes in the shooting video, the same stare he'd given Kins in the courtroom. He wanted the same confrontation with Tracy he'd had with Kins. He'd accosted Dan, a shot over the bow. He'd likely been the car that followed her Friday night after she dropped off Lydia. Now he'd accosted Therese and Daniella, and maybe would have taken them but for Rex and Sherlock. The person he really wanted was Tracy.

So be it.

"Something else your nanny said he told her," Calloway said. "He said he knew all about the people who lived in the Mattioli mansion, that Mattioli stole miners' claims and used their money to build his mansion. You ever hear anything like that?"

"No," Tracy said.

"He also said Mattioli was a liar and a murderer. And he said you were as well."

"I don't know anything about Mattioli, but Schmidt believes I lied to get House out of prison so I could kill him. We need to get ahold of Atticus and see what he's found out about William Kenmore. If there is any sort of connection, and what that might be," Tracy said.

That afternoon, Tracy stood at her Subaru holding Daniella. She'd spoken to Dan, told him what had happened, though she knew the impact it would have on him. She tried to temper what had happened by telling him that Therese had taken Rex and Sherlock with her, and the two dogs did not allow Schmidt anywhere near them. She also told him she'd made arrangements to get Therese and Daniella out of Cedar Grove. They would stay at Faz's house until things were resolved.

Dan wasn't satisfied, and she didn't expect he would be. He wanted Tracy to leave Cedar Grove with them. But Tracy knew better than to be anywhere near them or Dan. Erik Schmidt had made it clear he wanted her, and he'd go after her family to get to her. Getting her family as far from her as possible was the only way to ensure their safety.

The Subaru had been loaded with Therese's and Daniella's suitcases. Finlay would drive the car, with Therese and Daniella, to Bellingham. A second deputy sheriff would follow close behind. In Bellingham, at a prearranged location, they'd make the switch. Faz would drive Tracy's car, and Del would follow him. Therese and Daniella would stay with Faz and Vera for as long as necessary, with a police presence.

When Therese came out from the house, Tracy again told her the plan. Therese seemed nervous but also determined. "I won't let anything happen to Daniella," she said to Tracy. "That's the thing I remember most about today. I was scared, but I would have done anything to protect her." She'd started to cry again.

"You're safe now. No harm is going to come to you. Faz and Vera will take good care of you both until I get this resolved."

"What about you?" Therese said.

"I'll be fine," Tracy said.

Therese gave her a wan smile, exhausted, worried, and scared.

Tracy had no doubt Schmidt would have taken Therese and Daniella but for the two dogs, and Finlay getting to them quickly; that he would have used them to make Tracy come to him—for what, exactly, she did not yet know. But she knew Schmidt wanted to scare her. In that regard, he had succeeded.

But he'd also pissed her off.

In that regard, he'd regret it.

She heard Tim Herman telling her revenge could be a powerful motivator.

Schmidt was going to find out how powerful.

She kissed her daughter, then strapped her in her car seat, fighting back tears. Daniella was patting Tracy's face, saying, "It's okay, Mama. Don't cry. I'll say hello to Uncle Faz and Auntie Vera."

Tracy smiled through her tears. "You be a good girl for Tasey," she said. "And for your uncle Vic and aunt Vera." She kissed her again, nuzzling her check. Then she stepped back, afraid if she lingered too long, she'd change her mind and have them stay—or go with them. Getting them away was the best thing; she knew it intellectually, but letting them go was about the hardest thing she'd ever done.

Finlay stepped to the driver's seat. "I'll guard them like I would my own," he said.

Tracy had no doubt Finlay, a widower and a father of three, would do so.

She stood at the end of the driveway with Roy Calloway, and together they watched the cars depart.

It was time to go to work.

"You have your service pistol?" Calloway asked, still looking at the street.

"Always," Tracy said.

"Shotgun and rifle?"

"And my single-action revolvers."

"Because it sounds like this guy is going to come for you."

"You might be right," she said.

"Do you have any idea when or where?"

She shook her head, watching the cars until she could no longer see them.

"I can have a deputy sit in your driveway until Finlay gets back. I don't mind staying either."

"No," she said. Calloway had nearly died because he'd once tried to protect Tracy from Edmund House. This wasn't his fight any longer. It was hers. "You go home to Nora, Roy. Watch over your town. Finlay has kids to care for when he gets back. I'm locked and loaded. And I have Rex and Sherlock. Nobody is getting in that door if I don't want them to. And I can take care of myself if he does."

"That's what worries me. Don't try to do this on your own, Tracy."

She did not respond.

After Calloway had departed, Tracy went inside the house. She wore her Glock 23 service pistol in a Kydex concealment holster on her hip, and she carried a spare Glock magazine on her other hip. She went from room to room closing the window blinds. With Daniella and Therese out of the house, she staged the shotgun beside her bed, loaded with one round in the chamber and six more shells in the magazine tube. She put the rifle just behind the refrigerator, easily reachable, also fully loaded, and she stashed one Colt pistol in the bathroom and another under a seat cushion in the living room. Then she sat on the sofa, Rex and Sherlock at her feet, heads on their paws, looking up at her with worried expressions.

Whatever Schmidt intended, Tracy sensed it would happen quickly now. He was no longer trying to hide and had set things in motion. Given the chance, Tracy would do as Kins had said. She wouldn't hesitate to end him.

Dan called, and she told him Therese and Daniella were both safe and on their way to Faz and Vera's.

"What about you? You told me you wouldn't do anything to put yourself in danger, but you're still there."

"I don't intend to do anything stupid, Dan. But I can't run back to Seattle. You know that. Look what happened to Kins."

"That's what worries me."

"Anyone around me is in danger. The smartest thing to do was to get Therese and Daniella as far away from me and Schmidt as possible. I've done that."

"Can't Roy arrest the guy?" She heard the frustration in his voice.

"First, we don't know where he is. Second, he hasn't done anything warranting an arrest."

"Not yet," Dan said. "I don't like this, Tracy. I don't like the tone of your voice. It's your pissed-off voice."

"I don't like the situation any more than you do, Dan, but I also can't say anything more to make you feel better. Schmidt is currently holding all the cards, but he'll make a mistake. These guys always do. And when he does. I'll get him."

"You or Roy?"

"Same thing."

"Not to me. What if you're the card Schmidt slips up on?"

"Then I'll handle it."

"I'm getting on a plane. I'm coming back."

"No," she said, more forceful than she intended.

"No?"

She softened her tone, but only a bit. "Don't come here, Dan. Roy Calloway would tell you the same thing. In Cedar Grove, near me, you're a target. That complicates things for Roy and his officers and makes it more difficult for me to do my job. If you want to help, go home to Seattle, to Daniella and Therese, and do what Faz tells you. You come back to Cedar Grove and you put me in greater danger."

"I can watch my own back, Tracy. I'm no longer the fat little kid who needed your help."

"I didn't mean to imply you were. I'm just explaining to you that Schmidt wants to get to me. You come back here, and you become someone he can use to do that. You want to keep me safe, stay away."

Dan remained silent.

"Dan, please. Roy and Finlay and every other police officer in every town up along the county road is looking for Schmidt. I'm locked and loaded, and I have both dogs with me."

"But you somehow always end up in the middle of the shit."

"Not by my doing, Dan."

Dan sighed. "I know, Tracy. I know. I'm just frustrated and angry and worried about you. What are you going to do?"

Tracy had been thinking of the video games Lydia had been using to train her. She didn't know what was going to happen before she'd played those games either. She'd learned to act and react on instinct, based on what she saw. She'd learned to solve each puzzle as it was presented, before she moved to the next level. She'd learned to stay present and not look ahead. She needed to keep the same mindset now. She couldn't focus on killing Erik Schmidt. Not yet. She just had to solve the next puzzle, whatever it turned out to be, and learn as she went. Schmidt chose the name William Kenmore, a miner, for a reason. He said Mattioli had been a liar and a cheat, and a murderer. That he'd stolen the miners' claims. That was the first puzzle.

And the first place to look for answers was Atticus Pelham.

CHAPTER 31

Tracy jumped into her truck for the short ride to the *Towne Crier*'s offices on Fourth Street. The old building that housed the newspaper had always reminded her of a Lincoln Logs cabin, mortar oozing from between the cracks. It had been a miner's cabin, first built in the late 1800s, and the town had eventually designated it a historical landmark.

The office had a thick, musty smell that reminded Tracy of the smells inside an antique store. Given the late hour, the desks were empty. Pelham sat at his desk in his glass-enclosed office, working on his computer, his jacket on. Tracy had reached him by phone as he prepared to leave, but he agreed to wait for her. He saw Tracy enter and waved her over as he stood from his chair.

Tracy deadbolted the door behind her.

She'd also been cautious on the drive over, checking her surroundings, making random turns, and looking for anyone sitting in a car.

"Thanks for waiting for me, Atticus."

"Not a problem," he said.

Perhaps five foot six, Pelham had thinning red hair showing flecks of gray.

"On the phone you said you found something on William Kenmore?" Tracy asked.

"I found the paper for the date Roy provided on microfiche, then checked those issues published before and after that date. I made you copies of the articles." Pelham held out the pages. "They're hard to read and limited in what was written."

"Just tell me, Atticus, if you would, please."

"It's an obituary. It says William Kenmore was a prospector from California who moved his wife and two daughters up to Silver Pines. It was a small mining town high up in the North Cascades, near Mount Shuksan."

"I know of it," Tracy said. "I remember talk of it growing up. A ghost town. So, what happened to him and his family?"

"The obit says they all died in a house fire."

"That's it? Anything else?"

"Nothing. Can I ask what this is about?" Pelham asked.

In a town where everyday news stories were scarce, Pelham hunted for anything to fill the paper's pages. "The Kenmore family is buried beside my mother and father's plot, and I noticed they all died on the same day. Could I ask another favor?" she said, not fully answering his question.

"Sure. If I can help, I will. You know that, Tracy."

"I was wondering if your archives might have any articles on Silver Pines."

Pelham made a face and blew out a breath. "Maybe something tangentially, like how Christian Mattioli owned both towns, but otherwise, I'm doubtful. What are you looking for?"

Tracy didn't know, not exactly, but she also didn't know Mattioli had owned Silver Pines.

"He owned both towns?"

"Eventually." Pelham explained that both towns were established after miners found silver and gold, though mining those precious metals and getting them out of the mountains proved more difficult than some were willing to suffer. "Silver Pines was even more remote than Cedar Grove. That's one of the reasons the town, unlike Cedar Grove, didn't survive after the mines stopped producing."

Pelham was not from Cedar Grove, having arrived after Tracy left. "How do you know this?"

"I did do some digging through the larger newspapers for the same time period—the *Bellingham Herald* and the *Cascadia Daily News*—to see if they had anything else on William Kenmore. I didn't find anything, not about Kenmore, but I did find an article about Silver Pines during my search in the *Herald*. It was much more recent and tweaked my memory."

"What was it about?"

"It reported on the forest service performing a toxic cleanup of contaminated mining tailings in Silver Pines. That was . . . maybe a decade ago. I remember because I saw it as an opportunity to determine if Cedar Grove suffered the same toxic fate. It didn't. Anyway, the article said a historical society had at one time tried to preserve Silver Pines, what's left of it, and someone appeared at the hearings to comment on the cleanup."

"Why would they want to preserve the town?"

Pelham shrugged. "I don't know, but my guess is the historical society would have the most information about the town. If it even still exists."

"That's a good point. Any idea how I might find them?"

"The name of the gentleman who appeared and spoke is in the article I mentioned. I'd start with him."

"Would you mind printing it out for me?"

"I did." He pointed to the pages he'd handed Tracy.

She shuffled them until she found the article on the forest service hearings and noted the man's name who spoke on behalf of the Silver Pines Preservation Society. Stan Bleeker. She skimmed the article. Bleeker said the society was started by his father, and that the society had tried to turn Silver Pines into a resort destination, restoring and refurbishing several buildings, including the general store, the hotel, and the saloon.

Tracy and Pelham went to the computer terminal in his office, and Pelham pulled up the society's website, though it didn't look to have been updated in years. Tracy read how the town was established at the base of Mount Shuksan and named after the pine trees that grow at high elevations. Mount Shuksan was one of multiple peaks in an area capped by glaciers and surrounded by rugged terrain, waterfalls, alpine lakes, meadows, and smaller peaks with names like Mount Triumph, Mount Despair, and Mount Terror. Given the terrain, the town was not easily accessed, as Pelham had said, reachable only by traveling a twenty-three-mile stretch of forest roads off the Mount Baker Highway near the Nooksack River's North Fork and White Salmon Creek.

The society—Stan Bleeker, she assumed—listed a phone number and a mailing address. Tracy first tried calling the number on her cell phone but found it no longer in service. That did not bode well.

"Like I said. This guy Bleeker might not even still be alive," Pelham said.

The address on the website listed a street off the county road. Tracy recognized the street name from the years she lived in Cedar Grove and had driven the road frequently. "One way to find out."

"I'll let you know if I learn anything more about William Kenmore," Pelham said as Tracy got up and moved toward the newspaper office's door. "This is turning into a real mystery; isn't it?"

"Maybe," she said. "Thanks, Atticus."

She drove from downtown, checking again to determine she was not being followed. Fifteen minutes later, she turned onto High Mountain Road, continuing until she reached an A-frame house at the end of a cul-de-sac. The weathered mailbox with worn and chipped paint looked like a *Wheel of Fortune* puzzle: _LE_K_R.

That could be good news or bad.

She waited in the cab for a minute, checking her rearview and side mirrors to determine if anyone came over the crest in the road. No one did. She exited and climbed the stairs, looking down again for cars or anyone following on foot. Atop the stairs she disturbed an ancient black Labrador lounging on the extended porch in the late afternoon–early evening sun. The dog rose dutifully, though slowly and seemingly with difficulty. He managed a hoarse bark that sounded more like a croak.

"Hey there, old boy," she said. "Did I disrupt your nap? Are you going to be good and let me knock on the door?"

The dog stopped barking. Its tail swept slowly back and forth.

"You're an old boy; aren't you?" The dog leaned his side against her jeans for a good scratching.

Tracy knocked on the door, which caused the Lab to bark again. After a few moments she knocked a second time, then cupped a hand and looked in a window to the side of the door. An older man approached and pulled open the door, speaking first to the dog. "It's okay, Oscar. You did your job. Good boy. Go lay back down." The dog complied. The man looked at Tracy through thick spectacles on a friendly face. He had a monk's ring of white hair with long sideburns and a heavy five-o'clock shadow. "Can I help you?"

"I'm looking for Stan Bleeker."

He smiled. "Well, you must be a detective, because you found him."

She smiled and showed him her SPD credentials. "Actually, I am a detective."

"Well, hell. Maybe I'm a psychic. I should buy a lottery ticket." Bleeker raised his spectacles to his forehead to glance at her credentials. "Crosswhite. You related to Doc Crosswhite, used to live in the Mattioli mansion a long time ago?"

"I'm his daughter, Tracy."

"You don't say," he said. "I haven't heard that name in decades. Thought you all had moved away." Bleeker slid his thumbs behind red suspenders he wore over a long-sleeve white shirt to hold up his khaki pants.

"I did," she said. "But my husband and I kept *his* family's home just outside of town. We get up every so often with our daughter to escape the city."

"Smart move. Cities now are way too crowded for me. Heck, Cedar Grove is becoming too crowded for me."

"I know what you mean. It's changed a lot since I was a kid here."

"What brings you out here to see an old man?" He smiled. "Am I under arrest? Wouldn't mind you handcuffing me. You're a lot better looking than Chief Calloway."

Tracy chuckled. "No arrest today. I'm here, I hope, for some history about Silver Pines, and I'm told you're the man who knows more than anyone."

Bleeker beamed. "Maybe the *only* man who knows anything anymore. Why the interest?"

"I have an interest in William Kenmore," Tracy said.

Bleeker's eyebrows arched. "William Kenmore? Buried in the Cedar Grove Cemetery along with his wife and two daughters?"

"That's the one. You know of him."

"I do. How do you know of him?"

"The family is buried next to my parents' grave, which sort of sparked the interest. His obituary said they all died on the same day in a house fire but doesn't offer anything more."

Bleeker gave Tracy a serious stare. He looked almost stricken. After a moment he stepped aside. "Best you come in and sit. There's a story here. But I can't tell it without also providing a bit of background on the town."

"That's exactly what I'm looking for."

Minutes later, Tracy sipped a cup of chamomile tea and sat on a couch covered with a blanket that showed Oscar's hair. The house and furniture, though dated, was otherwise spotless. She didn't see a speck of dust. The carpet was clean, the windows free of smudges, the kitchen counters clear. The house also smelled of a lemon-scented disinfectant. Someone was caring for Bleeker, or he was doing very well on his own.

Bleeker sat in a La-Z-Boy chair, facing a television on a rolling cart. On a side table, looking like they could teeter at any moment, stood a stack of books, mostly nonfiction. Beside the tower of books rested a remote control and a lamp with a magnifying glass. Bleeker had retrieved an eleven-by-seventeen black-and-red scrapbook and set it in his lap. The corners of yellowed newspaper articles peeked out from the edge of the book.

"Can I get you anything besides tea?"

"This is fine, Mr. Bleeker. Thank you."

"Stan," he said. "Makes an old man feel young to have a woman call him by his first name."

"How old are you, Stan?"

"I'll be eighty-one in a month."

"You don't look it."

"You're kind to say so, but I do have mirrors, and I feel it on long walks with Oscar. Neither of us can go as far or as fast as we once did."

"Do you live alone out here?"

He nodded. "I lost my wife just about a year ago."

"I'm sorry."

"It was a blessing. Louisa went peacefully and had dementia the final years of her life, and I didn't want her to suffer. And I'm not really alone; I have two sons and a daughter and seven grandchildren, and one or the other calls me daily and frequently comes for visits. My son sends in a lady once a week to clean the house and make me dinners in Tupperware bowls for the week. He thinks I might starve." He patted his belly.

"It's nice you raised such caring children."

"Louisa did the heavy lifting in that department, but I'm reaping the benefits. They want me to move to a retirement home in Bellingham to be closer to them. They don't like me living out here alone, especially in the winters, but this is all I've ever known. That day is coming, I know. But it isn't today."

"So . . . Did you know my parents?"

"If you lived in Cedar Grove, you knew Doc Crosswhite. I recall he was a competitive shooter, and your mother a gardener."

"You have a good memory."

"It isn't what it once was, but after what Louisa went through, I'm just happy to remember to get dressed in the morning. And, of course, I know all about Christian Mattioli—in whose home you once lived—but not from memory." He tapped the scrapbook. "From the newspaper clippings in here and the stories my grandfather told."

"You don't sound like you cared for Mattioli."

"I don't," Bleeker said. "Not after learning the truth about the man."

"That's why I'm here—to find out what you know," she said, now more curious than ever.

"Can I take you back a few years? I've given this talk a few times at local schools, and it's easier for me if I start at the beginning."

"Please do," she said.

"I apologize if it sounds rehearsed, because, well, it is." He laughed and Tracy laughed with him.

Bleeker explained what Atticus Pelham had learned, that Silver Pines came into existence in the late 1800s when prospectors discovered gold and silver deposits in streams in the mountains. Much like Cedar Grove, claims quickly followed, despite miners having to hike miles over rugged mountain terrain. He told her how the miners overcame isolation and difficult winter weather in search of their fortunes. "This is the moment where I bring out a hunk of gold and a glass vial of silver my grandfather obtained from his claim and show it to the kids."

"I'll bet they love it," Tracy said.

"Their eyes get as big as saucers," Bleeker said.

"Your grandfather was one of Silver Pine's first miners back then?"

"He was a young man determined to make his fortune, like so many others who tried and failed."

Bleeker got back to the story and explained how the gold and silver strike, as was the case in Cedar Grove, attracted the deep pockets of Christian Mattioli.

"Mattioli bought several miners' claims, then established both the Silver Pines and Cedar Grove Mining Companies to process the ore. Not long after, he formed the Cedar Grove and Silver Pines Railway Company, and he extended an ore car line that ended at the Cedar Grove Smelter outside of town, where they processed the dirt and rock before shipping it by train to Bellingham."

"Gold fever," Tracy said.

"For certain, but the euphoria of those moving to Silver Pines caused them to overlook or underestimate the North Cascades' inhospitable and severe mountain weather."

"I can only imagine," Tracy said.

"No offense, but I don't think we can imagine what it was like back then for those miners and their families. We put on a down jacket just to walk to the mailbox to get the mail."

Tracy smiled. It was true.

Bleeker told her that miners worked long hours, day in and day out, in all kinds of weather, wearing nothing more than wool clothing. They slept in homes heated by a stove or a crude fireplace—if they could find or buy enough dry wood. He said in the winter and the spring, slow-moving, moisture-laden storms blew in off the Pacific Ocean and dumped piles of snow and torrents of rain that caused the rivers in the narrow canyons to overflow their banks and destroy everything in their path—hastily constructed roads, bridges, and homes. He said the steep peaks were also susceptible to avalanches that wiped out entire families at once.

Tracy shook her head. "Must have been horrific," she said.

"The natural topography wasn't the only problem. The miners and geologists brought in by Mattioli were unfamiliar with the North Cascades. They misjudged the mineral wealth, basing the mines' potential on the rich surface deposits. They believed the deposits would extend far underground like in the Sierras and the Rockies."

"They didn't?"

Bleeker shook his head. "Add to that a severe depression when banks failed, demands for goods collapsed, and credit markets dried up. Those miners who'd taken advances on equipment, clothing, and other supplies based on estimated mining profits couldn't pay back the bank loans."

Bleeker paused here and Tracy thought it a dramatic one.

"Mattioli?" she said.

"Christian Mattioli was desperate to save his investment and his fortune. He saw opportunity where others saw demise. He was also the only one with money, and he bought the foreclosed claims from the miners who went bankrupt."

Based on Bleeker's dark tone, Tracy had a sense what was to come was far worse.

"Mattioli bought miners' claims for pennies on the dollar, then hired the miners to work the claims for minimal wages. When some of the miners refused to sell, Mattioli stopped making needed railroad repairs and sharply raised the costs of mining supplies in the businesses he owned."

"He strangled them," Tracy said.

Bleeker nodded. "They, too, eventually went into bankruptcy, and Mattioli took their mines and their businesses until he owned just about everything. Well, you can imagine, unrest among those miners who'd stayed in Silver Pines grew. The miners tried to form a union, called for strikes, and, in some cases, sabotaged the mines. Mattioli sent out a gunman named Trey 'Treat' Crane and other gunmen to protect his interests, but Crane was the most infamous."

Bleeker said Crane had been a lawman who had lived and worked in Tombstone, Arizona, where Wyatt Earp and Doc Holliday had once lived. He said Crane met Mattioli when he was looking to get into business, much like the more famous Wyatt Earp.

"Silver Pines became a town as lawless as, though far less known than, Dodge City, Kansas."

"Lawless how? Killings?"

Bleeker nodded. "Murders."

Erik Schmidt had told Therese that Mattioli had been a liar and a thief and a murderer.

"To make the killings legal, Treat Crane and his gunmen, charged with upholding the law, forced the miners to duels, which allowed the gunmen, and Mattioli, to argue the killings were in self-defense. Not that Mattioli needed help in that regard. He owned the town, including the law and the politicians. Silver Pines became a killing ground."

Tracy had focused on the word "duels" and thought again of Schmidt, his shooting ability, and his glare into the camera. He'd likely learned from House of Tracy's shooting prowess. Is that what he was looking for? A duel?

"Now, to your specific question. Two of the miners who tried to organize the miners into a union were William Kenmore and his mining partner. They had one of the more lucrative claims and had stubbornly refused to sell to Mattioli. Crane caught them in the saloon one night with other miners making plans to sabotage the mines and shot Kenmore's partner dead in the street. He then told Kenmore if he and his family weren't gone at sunrise he'd shoot him too."

"How do we know that's all true, Stan, and not just urban legend?"

"That account comes straight from my grandfather, who was there that night and watched William Kenmore flee with his wife and two daughters and only what they could carry on their persons."

"What happened to him and his family then? Did Mattioli send someone to have him killed?"

"In a sense," Bleeker said. "Bill Kenmore worked as a laborer in Cedar Grove, but he refused to give up his claim. He'd filed suit in court to recover it and thought it just a matter of time before he would win it back and Mattioli got what was coming to him. What little money he'd made went to his legal fees and court costs. What he didn't know was that Mattioli owned the judge and the lawyers. Kenmore lost. Some said his claim was worth hundreds of thousands of dollars, which, today, would be millions. At some point after the court ruling, William Kenmore had nailed shut the bedroom door to the house he lived in with his wife and daughters, poured kerosene all around, and set the house on fire."

Tracy sat in stunned silence.

After a pause, Bleeker said, "You know the rest, I'm sure. Mattioli extracted what gold and silver existed from the mines, then abandoned the claims, leaving behind tons of pollution from the mine tailings. Silver Pines became a ghost town. Some, like my grandfather, said that all the natural disasters the town suffered were caused by the evil Mattioli spread there. They might be right."

"You don't believe that; do you?" Tracy said, though Bleeker's comment made her think of Roy Calloway's statement to her about the devil, in the form of Edmund House, walking into Cedar Grove and spreading evil. *So much evil.*

Bleeker raised his eyebrows. "My father was behind the effort to refurbish the town. He wanted people to experience how the miners and their families lived, dressed, and worked back then. He had the fire road and the lone bridge into town refurbished. The day after Christmas, 1980, after he used his own money to also refurbish several of the buildings to accommodate the workers and the would-be tourists, a massive mudslide washed out the lone access bridge into town, and the county opted not to fix the road or the bridge. It bankrupted my father. The preservation society, what remained of it, agreed it best to let the town die and not give it a chance to cause any more deaths."

"What motivated your father to try to refurbish it, Stan?"

"I think my dad did it for his dad. For his memory. It's why I have this. All the books and articles about the town."

The story explained why Schmidt told Therese that Mattioli had not just been a cheat and a liar but also a murderer, but it didn't fully explain why he'd taken the persona of William Kenmore, or how he had obtained the information about the town and the mine Kenmore had lost. But she had another thought on what his reason might be.

"You said William Kenmore had a partner in the lucrative mining claim Christian Mattioli stole. Any of those papers document who that partner was?"

"I've got the original mining claims in another book in the back room. You want me to get it?"

"Would you mind? It might shed some light on a mystery for me."

"Be right back."

Bleeker departed, leaving Tracy with her thoughts. He returned, flipping pages in another scrapbook that looked as old as the first. "My father and grandfather kept just about everything. I think when he was trying to re-create the town, my father intended to put up copies of some of these original documents for the tourists to look at. Here," he said. "These are the claims."

Tracy stood and read over Bleeker's shoulder as he turned the pages and used his index finger to scan the names on each document.

"Here it is, William Kenmore . . . and his partner was . . . Charles House." He looked up at her. "Does that solve your mystery?"

Or deepen one.

CHAPTER 32

As Tracy stepped from Stan Bleeker's home to his front porch, the wind had picked up considerably. The trees surrounding the house swayed, and the branches shimmered.

"Looks like Chinook winds," Bleeker said. "Hope nobody gets hurt."

The warm gusts occurred in the North Cascades during the spring and summer, caused by moist air moving inland from the Pacific Ocean. Once the air reached the steep mountain slopes, the air quickly warmed and caused winds to form that could reach speeds exceeding fifty miles an hour. In the worst storms, trees toppled, closing access roads or in some cases hitting cars and homes and doing millions of dollars in damage.

Tracy's cell phone rang. Calloway.

She thanked Bleeker and stepped down his stairs to where she'd parked, answering the call. "I was just about to call you. I have more information on William Kenmore—"

"Tracy—"

"—and it relates to Edmund House."

"Tracy—" Calloway said, louder. He sounded like he was speaking along the side of the freeway, a roar in the background similar to the rush of traffic—which Cedar Grove did not have. She heard other voices, too, voices that sounded rushed, frantic.

"What's going on?" she asked. Then she heard screaming sirens reverberating off the surrounding mountains.

Fire. She thought of their home, and of Rex and Sherlock.

"You need to get out here," Calloway said.

"Where?" She had trouble hearing him. "Where, Roy?"

"The Mattioli mansion," he said, raising his voice above the roar.

Tracy dropped the truck into reverse and left a trail of tire dust as she drove from Bleeker's home. Sirens continued to blare as she drove along the county road. She thought of William Kenmore, burning his house to the ground with his family trapped inside, and of the video game Lydia had used to train Tracy, about the marshal who lost his house and wife to outlaws and had his daughter kidnapped. Whatever was happening at the Mattioli mansion, and she assumed from the sirens it was a fire, she hoped it didn't involve another family. She was glad Therese and Daniella were safe.

She press checked her Glock, ensured it was fully loaded, and replaced it in her holster. Her thoughts kept returning to William Kenmore and to Charles House, the swindled miners. House had to be related to Edmund, a great-grandfather perhaps. Maybe the reason he'd come back to Cedar Grove all those years ago—to determine what happened to him and to his claim, and why he'd been gunned down in Silver Pines.

As she neared the turnoff to the mansion's driveway, a plume of black smoke billowed from the treetops, though the strong winds quickly dispersed it. If they didn't get the fire under control, the scope of the catastrophe could rapidly and tragically spread.

She weaved in and around slower-moving vehicles—some of which had pulled to the side of the road, indicating fire or police vehicles had recently driven past.

Just past the familiar walled yard she hit the brakes and turned the wheel, tires squealing, truck bed again fishtailing. She quickly corrected, punched the gas to straighten the back end, and drove up the sloped driveway, coming to a hard stop behind a police car. Atop the driveway, tongues of fire flickered from the mansion's upstairs bedroom windows, the house already engulfed. There would be no saving it. Glass shattered, and the house popped and crackled, the flames dancing with arrogance, as if alive, turning the sky aglow in orange and red.

Tracy pushed from the truck cab and held out her police credentials to an approaching officer intent on stopping her. Wasn't going to happen. He let her pass.

Police and fire vehicles cluttered the area alongside a fire truck. Their swirling lights lit up the surrounding trees in an array of colors as volunteer county firefighters, more than a dozen, carried two hose lines running down the drive to the fire hydrant her father had paid to have the county install when he purchased the house and property. Cedar Grove's city leaders accommodated her father because they believed the mansion's restoration would symbolize the restoration of their city.

They had no idea.

The firefighters did their best, pouring gallons of water on the blaze, but Tracy knew from the toxic smell making her eyes water and her nostrils burn that an accelerant, most likely gasoline, had been liberally used. Again, she thought of the parallels to the Kenmore fire—Bleeker saying Kenmore poured kerosene around the house. The firefighters soon realized that their best efforts would not save the house, and they redirected their attention to stopping the fire from spreading to the forested hillside around it.

Another explosion blew out the large picture window at the front of the house, sending firefighters and police officers scurrying to the ground for cover.

Not Roy Calloway.

Cedar Grove's stubborn chief of police stood alone, as rigid as a statue near where the weeping willow had once provided an umbrella of shade. Tracy pulled her shirt over her nose and mouth and raised an arm to block the heat from the flames. Calloway wore the expression of a man in mourning, as if witnessing the death of a loved one.

When Tracy reached his side, Calloway glanced at her, but he otherwise did not react. He did not speak. Not a word. He just stood there, resolute, as the mansion and what it had once meant to him and to his town burned, and he lost another piece of Cedar Grove's—and his—past.

CHAPTER 33

Dan's case hadn't settled. Not yet. But it would. The depositions had been productive and informative, and they convinced both sides that settlement talks would be prudent rather than paying the expense of a trial. Their judge, already with an impacted trial schedule, was more than willing to kick the trial date over for a month to allow for those talks.

Dan had packed his bag in a frenzy, checked out of his hotel, and called for an Uber ride to San Francisco International Airport. From the back of the car, he searched the internet for flights into Paine Field, in Everett, Washington. Everett was an hour or more, depending on traffic, closer to Cedar Grove than SeaTac airport. He found a flight leaving San Francisco at 7:30 p.m. and arriving in Everett just after 9:00 p.m., if the flight was not delayed. With the time it took the plane to taxi to the gate and for Dan to deboard and get to a car rental counter, it would be closer to nine thirty.

The flight had several open seats. Dan checked his watch. He had an hour before the plane took off. The Uber had to maneuver through heavy Bay Area traffic, and he had to then get through security. It would be close, but he made the reservation.

He then called Everett, found a rental car company, and booked one of the new Ford Mustangs. He'd drive to Cedar Grove from Paine Field—ordinarily close to two and a half hours, but Dan had no intention of obeying the speed limit. He estimated he'd arrive around eleven, if all went smoothly and the stars aligned. They rarely did. It wasn't fast enough to ease his worry about Tracy, but it was the best option he had, under the circumstances.

After securing the car, he called Therese, who said she and Daniella were in good hands and in good spirits. Daniella, already adept at using the phone, was excited to see and talk to her daddy, but preoccupied with Vera's French toast sticks, which she dipped in syrup. Not exactly the dinner Dan and Tracy allowed, but he wasn't about to complain. When he couldn't get much more out of Daniella, he asked to speak with Faz.

"Have you spoken to Tracy recently?"

"Not since I called to tell her Therese and your daughter arrived safely. Have you?"

"I've been in a deposition and settlement discussions all day. Anything more on Schmidt?"

"Nothing definitive. No reports of anyone seeing him, and I'm told his Corvette remains in the driveway, and the chalk mark I put on the tire indicates it hasn't moved. Of course he could have taken another car. Tracy knows Schmidt's girlfriend drives an older Jeep, and I provided the make and model and the license plate number to Roy Calloway in Cedar Grove. Other than that, we're just waiting for that SOB to do something wrong."

That's what Dan was worried about. He knew his wife, and he knew she was not about to wait. He thanked Faz and disconnected the call.

Traffic was moderate for the Bay Area, and Dan reached the curb at SFO at 7:09 p.m. He headed to the CLEAR entrance and found just a few people in line ahead of him. His bag bordered on too large for carry-on, but he had no intention of missing the flight to check it.

He went through security in just under four minutes, grabbed his bag on the other side of the metal detector, and hurried down the terminal toward his gate as fast as he could, pulling his suitcase and his work briefcase behind him. He reached the gate just as they were closing the door.

He'd made it. He caught his breath as he passed down the gate tunnel and hurried onto the plane, the last passenger to board. He found space to accommodate his bag, and he settled in his seat as the plane rolled back from the gate and the flight attendants went over safety protocols. He pulled out his phone and debated again whether to call Tracy, then went to settings and put the phone in airplane mode.

Calling would not be productive. His wife would only tell him again not to return to Cedar Grove. She'd tell him again to stay in Seattle, to pick up Daniella and Therese and take them home, that Faz would arrange to have the police watch the house and them.

Fat chance.

He knew his wife. Too well. He knew when she was angry the color of her eyes changed from blue to gray, and the tone of her voice became deceptively calm. It belied an intensity that churned inside her. Most people would fear Erik Schmidt—by all accounts a psychopath who had already had killed two women, tried to kill a police officer, and now had shown up in Cedar Grove to psychologically torture Tracy and her family.

But Tracy wasn't most people. She didn't scare easy. She wouldn't fear Schmidt. She hadn't feared Edmund House, the Cowboy, or the other psychopaths she'd killed or put behind bars. Schmidt was a predator. Like most, he preyed on the weak and the vulnerable. Two words that had never been associated with Tracy.

He'd picked the wrong person to mess with this time when he'd crossed a very big line and accosted their family. Dan knew the reason Schmidt had done so was irrelevant.

The act alone was enough.

Rather than be intimidated, Tracy would be irate.

Rather than be afraid, she would become determined.

Tracy would do anything and everything to protect her family, even risk her own life.

And that's what worried Dan most, and what he hoped to prevent.

Tracy had a family now. She had a little girl to raise. She had to think of Daniella and Dan. Which was why Dan was headed back to Cedar Grove. During their years of marriage, he had become his wife's conscience when she needed it most. He was the voice in her ear talking sense. And he would bring her home before she did something that would impact him and Daniella for the rest of their lives.

This flight would be the longest flight of his life.

CHAPTER 34

As darkness descended, the flames died, then were extinguished. All that remained of the once-grand mansion were smoldering embers. Tracy couldn't help but consider the irony of Christian Mattioli having ordered a third-story addition to the original structure, to ensure his mansion would be taller than any other in Cedar Grove, and now firefighters walked atop it, poking shovels through the blackened debris. The men and women had done a heroic job preventing the flames from spreading to the surrounding trees, despite the Chinook winds having picked up in intensity. All around the property, treetops swayed, and their branches, some singed from the flames, danced and shimmered as if in protest.

Calloway spoke without diverting his eyes from where the mansion had once stood, keeping his voice soft. "We got lucky, given the wind."

"Just thinking the same thing," she agreed. "I talked to Atticus. He said William Kenmore locked his wife and two children in a house and burned them all alive."

Calloway turned to her, speaking above the rush of the wind. "Do you think there could be . . ." He stopped before saying it.

"Bodies in the ruins? I hope not. I think this was intended to be symbolic."

"Another message to you?"

She nodded. "In part."

"What's the other part?"

"To destroy the last remaining image of Christian Mattioli."

"Why? What purpose does it serve to burn down something that could never be replicated? That mansion was a spectacular piece of this town's history."

"And mine. Which is why he burned it—to destroy Mattioli's history, and to destroy mine."

"What did he care?"

"He didn't do it for himself. He did it for Edmund House."

"How could it be part of Edmund House's history?"

Tracy braced her legs when another strong gust rushed over and past them. She told Calloway what she had learned at Stan Bleeker's home, about the rich claim Charles House and Kenmore had shared, and how Christian Mattioli's gunmen shot House dead and stole his claim.

"Okay, that explains what he had against Mattioli. What about you? What was his intent in burning the house as to you?"

"Schmidt sees me as an extension of Christian Mattioli—a liar and a murderer who also lived in the mansion, which I'm sure, in his warped mind, isn't a coincidence. He thinks it will hurt me, to burn down a part of my past, where I was raised."

"Doesn't it?"

Yesterday she might have said yes, but after what she had learned about Christian Mattioli, about how he had obtained his money to build the mansion, no doubt to serve as a testament to his power and wealth, she saw the fire as a fitting end to his presence in Cedar Grove. One that came far too late. She shook her head. "No."

Calloway's brow wrinkled. "No? You were raised in that house. Your family lived there."

"And died there," she reminded him. Not that he needed reminding. Calloway had been first to find her father's body after he shot himself in his study, and he had done his best to visit her mother, who rarely left the mansion after the sorrow that consumed her will to live. He had also been the one who called to let Tracy know her mother had died in her sleep in the home after suffering from cancer. She also believed her mother had simply lost her will to live.

"Maybe my father's restoring this house wasn't such a good thing to begin with."

"Why would you say that? There were the good times also, Tracy," Calloway said. "Many of them. Don't forget them."

"I haven't. But the good times were because of the people—my father and mother, you, everyone who lived here. Not because of this house." Another gust of wind blew some of the charred debris into the air and intensified the smell of gasoline. "This town is better off without this house hovering over it like some feudal castle. I'm relieved it's gone, Roy. You once asked me what happened to your town when Edmund House arrived. Do you remember?"

"I remember."

"Maybe evil arrived here long before House did."

"Mattioli?"

She nodded. "What really did this house represent, Roy? It was a symbol of ostentatious wealth and of power and greed—from the moment Mattioli insisted a third story be added to ensure it would be more grand than any other." She told him of Stan Bleeker and said, "He knew the history of Christian Mattioli, and it wasn't grand or beautiful. It was dark and ugly. He stole claims, had miners killed, stripped the mines of every ounce of precious minerals, then fled and left behind poison. Erik Schmidt did me, and this town, a favor."

Calloway sighed and ran his hand through his thinning hair. "Maybe you're right," he said. "Maybe it's for the better. Maybe it's best not to hold on to the past."

They walked back to her truck. The nighttime temperature had warmed thanks to the winds, which felt as if they were continuing to increase in intensity.

Calloway said, "Are you being careful?"

She lifted her shirt to reveal her Glock in an appendix holster.

Calloway nodded his approval. "The fire captain said there's little doubt the fire was deliberately set."

"Pretty hard to miss the smell of gasoline," Tracy said.

"I can get him on arson now."

Calloway could, if he could find Schmidt and prove he set the fire. Tracy knew Schmidt wouldn't let that happen. Not before he confronted her. It now seemed inevitable.

"I'll have a deputy follow you home and check the house, just to be sure he isn't waiting for you."

"I appreciate it," she said, not interested in arguing. "But if he tried to get in, Rex and Sherlock would tear a hole in his ass."

"Humor an old man, Tracy, especially tonight."

━━━

Finlay followed Tracy home, and together they went through each room and each closet and looked beneath beds and other possible hiding places, Rex and Sherlock close at her side. After Finlay had left, Tracy got the dogs out into the yard to run around for a bit. The wind continued to howl and the trees swayed ominously. She then fed the two dogs and settled on the couch where she'd left her cowboy gear when she returned home from training. Rex and Sherlock lay on the carpet staring up at her, sensing something wrong. "I don't mind admitting I'm glad to have you two," she said.

She was beat. The events had taken a lot out of her.

She thought again of William Kenmore and of Charles House, and of the miners who'd been forced to duel Mattioli's gunmen. She wondered if that was how Erik Schmidt, a trained speed-and-accuracy shooter, planned to even the score for Edmund House. If he saw this, too, as a battle between good and evil, with Tracy and Mattioli on the side of evil.

Her cell phone rang. She looked at her watch. After nine o'clock. Probably Dan.

She checked caller ID, a 206 area code—Seattle, but not a number she recognized, nor that caller ID identified.

Likely a burner phone.

Not traceable.

Schmidt.

She sat up, sensing she was about to find out what he intended. She took a deep breath and answered.

"Do you see how easy it would be?" Schmidt said. "I could have taken your little girl and her nanny while in the mountains. I could have put them in that mansion before I burned it to the ground."

Tracy laughed, and she sensed from the silence on the other end of the phone call that her unexpected response caught Schmidt off guard. "What are you supposed to be, Erik, a dime-store villain? Didn't you do any research?"

"What I did—"

"You burned down a tired, old building that stood empty for decades and represented the very worst of a human being. You did me and everyone else in this town a favor by burning it down. As for my daughter and nanny, you never would have got past the dogs."

"What I am . . ."

"Is pathetic," Tracy said, hoping to goad Schmidt into the confrontation she knew he wanted, and soon. She didn't want to sit around worrying when he'd appear. "You got kicked out of the AMU. You got court-martialed and dishonorably discharged from the Army. You went to prison, where you worshipped a psychopath and a murderer who manipulated you with false tales and bullshit. You've built a hell of a resume. You're a three-time loser, Erik."

Schmidt said, "I did my research too, Detective Tracy. I know you went to the newspaper, and that you spoke to Stan Bleeker."

He had followed her. It concerned Tracy that she hadn't noticed.

She moved to one of the blinds covering the window and looked out at the street as Schmidt continued speaking. "So I'm assuming you know Mattioli had Charles House murdered. You know that if things had been different, had Mattioli not stolen his claim, House would have owned Silver Pines and Cedar Grove. You and Mattioli are cut from the same cloth. You're a liar and murderer. That's why you lived in his house. You're both the same."

Tracy moved to a sliding door at the side of the house and peered into the darkening backyard.

"It's time to pay for past sins, Detective Tracy. That's why I burned down the mansion, that symbol of stolen wealth. I can't avenge Charles House's murder. Mattioli is long since dead. But I can avenge Ed's."

"You crossed the line when you went after my family," Tracy said.

"I was hoping you'd feel that way."

Tracy moved to another window in another room. "If you've followed me, then you know where I am. I'm not running, Schmidt."

"We'll pay tribute to history then, Detective Tracy, and we'll end this where it all started."

"Silver Pines?" Tracy had no intention of meeting Schmidt on foreign turf, where he could set booby traps and stage his weapons. "I don't think so, Erik."

"Oh, you'll come."

"Yeah? Why would I come to you?"

"Because I have something you want."

"Doubtful."

"That's right. You sent your family away. Tucked in all nice and safe. Or did you?"

Tracy felt her blood run cold.

"Tracy?" A woman's voice.

Her knees weakened.

Lydia.

CHAPTER 35

Momentarily struck dumb, Tracy quickly recovered. "Lydia? Lydia!"

Schmidt took the phone. "Still don't think you'll come, Detective Tracy?" he asked.

"If you harm her, Schmidt. If you do anything to her, I will—"

"Now who sounds like a dime-store villain? What? No Erik anymore? I thought we were friends, Detective Tracy."

Tracy struggled to get her emotions under control. Lydia's life depended on her remaining calm, thinking rationally. "This is between me and you, Schmidt. Let her go. I'll meet you in Silver Pines—if that's what you want. You know I'll come."

"Oh, you'll come. The girl is my assurance you'll come. You just can't help yourself, can you?" He paused then said, "She looks like you; don't you think? She could be your sister." Schmidt laughed again.

Tracy clutched her phone and bit back her emotions.

"Just me and you, Schmidt," she said again. "Let her go."

"You're not giving the orders here. So shut up and listen because here's how this is going to go. You have two and a half hours to get to Silver Pines. You contact that big-shit chief of police or anyone else, bring them with you—and I'll know if you do—I will kill the girl and them too."

"And when I get there, then what?"

"I'll be waiting to give you additional instructions. Two and a half hours, Detective Tracy. Not a minute more. When we disconnect, the sand begins to slip through the hourglass, so you'll need to leave immediately, and you'll have to hurry. Wait—to plan, scheme, or to get help—and you won't make it in time. Crash that truck of yours and you'll fail. And you'll be responsible for what happens to the girl. You know I'll do it. I killed Julia Hoch and I killed Bridgette Traugott, and I'll kill this one, too, and her death will be on your conscience for the rest of your life. Time is running, Detective Tracy."

He disconnected.

And in that frozen moment of time, Tracy heard nothing but the sound of the wind, howling outside, moaning and whistling through the cracks of the house. A gust caused the windows and doors to rattle.

She pulled up the timer on her watch and hit "Go." If she hurried, she'd reach Silver Pines between eleven thirty and midnight. She had no idea what she might encounter between here and there; what impediments she would hit, but she heard Lydia's voice in her head, training her not to consider the variables she could not control. To think in terms of completing just one level one at a time.

First level. Gather what she would need.

She stood so quickly, Rex and Sherlock bolted backward, out of her way. She grabbed Sarah's Stetson off the table, and her long duster, and shoved the red bandanna and bolo in the coat pocket. She'd need as many weapons and as much ammo as she could carry. Her weapons were spread throughout the house. Shit.

She raced from room to room, gathering her guns, then hurried to the door. Rex and Sherlock looked at her, wanting desperately to go with her, sensing, no doubt, something was wrong. "You stay this time. You've done your job. Time for me to do mine. Watch the house until I get home."

If she got home.

She rushed outside to the garage, fit the shotgun, rifle, and Colts in her rugged cart, and confirmed her gun belts were fully loaded with ammunition. She wheeled the cart out but stopped when she spotted headlamps hanging on a peg alongside her and Dan's reflective running vests. She grabbed a headlamp, pressed the button to ensure it worked, and put the lamp in the rugged cart box. She used the two-by-tens to wheel the cart into the bed, secured it with the bungee cord, then jumped down and tossed the two-by-tens onto the lawn alongside the driveway. She slid behind the wheel and backed from her driveway.

Level two. Make it to the Mount Baker Ski Area.

She raced through downtown Cedar Grove, the businesses shut down for the night, the parking stalls empty. Antique streetlamps illuminated swirling debris. She felt the truck shimmy from a strong wind gust and hoped the winds didn't topple trees in her path. She took the exit onto Mount Baker Highway and drove east at a high rate of speed; the truck shuddering with each successive gust. The trees lining the road bent and swayed with a controlled fury. Branches already littered the road, causing her to swerve around the larger ones, as well as slower-moving traffic. As she drove, her eyes constantly searched the edges of the road for other variables—deer and animals—a precaution bred in her by her father. Hit one and it was game over.

She checked her watch. It would take her half an hour to reach the Mount Baker Ski Area. Once there, she'd start level three—Stan Bleeker's website said she'd have to drive forest roads for twenty-three miles. She'd then be on foot, level four.

She had no idea how much time it would take to hike the remainder of the way to Silver Pines.

Or whether she could make it in time.

But she wouldn't think about that. Couldn't think about that.

She thought of Lydia, which made her think of Sarah, whom House had kept a prisoner in a room in a mine shaft. Tracy hadn't solved that puzzle. And her sister had paid with her life.

She wasn't about to fail her again.

The minute Dan's plane landed in Everett, he turned on his cell phone and tried to reach Tracy. He'd told himself he wouldn't tell her he was driving to Cedar Grove, but while in flight, his anxiety from not speaking to her, not knowing she was okay, was worse than enduring another lecture telling him not to come back.

His call went immediately to voice mail.

She could be talking to Daniella, checking in on her.

He tried texting her.

No immediate response.

He called Faz. He hadn't spoken to her.

He told himself not to overthink it. Not to panic.

He grabbed his luggage from the overhead compartment and waited, impatiently, for the people in front of him to deboard. When the line moved, he hurried down the ramp to the terminal, excusing himself as he rushed past and around those ahead of him, then through the tiny terminal to the rental car counter, where he presented the agent with his license and credit card.

He took out his cell phone and again tried Tracy. Again, his call went to her voice mail.

He called the Cedar Grove Police Department and asked to speak with Roy Calloway. The answering service told him the chief was not on duty and asked Dan if it was an emergency.

The rental car agent asked Dan if anyone else would be driving the car. "No."

"No?" the woman on the phone said.

"I mean. Yes. Yes, it is an emergency." He provided his name and was put on hold.

He continued the rental car transaction. As the agent provided him with his rental agreement and directions to his car, he was connected to Roy Calloway.

Phone pressed between his ear and shoulder, he said, "Roy, it's Dan O'Leary. I can't reach Tracy on her cell phone. Do you know where she might be?"

"Slow down, Dan. You sound like you're running a marathon. Tracy's at home," Calloway said.

Dan felt a wave of relief. He stepped out the airport doors and looked for his car beneath the umbrellas of light from the parking stanchions.

"I had Finlay escort her home about half an hour ago, and he went through the house to make sure it was clear. I'm sure she's fine."

Dan felt his adrenaline kick back in. "What do you mean you had a deputy escort her home? Why? What's going on?" He rushed down the aisle looking at the poles with the stall numbers.

"We've had some things happen, Dan, but Tracy is safe."

Dan found his Mustang, threw his bags onto the back seat, and slid in behind the wheel. "What kind of things?" he asked, backing from his stall.

Dan's anxiety increased as he listened to Calloway tell him about the burning of Mattioli mansion. "I insisted Finlay escort her home, Dan, and that the house be checked. I wanted to post a deputy outside the home, but she declined. She said she was fully armed and had both dogs as her alarm."

That was all very comforting, but: "Then how come I can't reach her?"

"I don't know. Look. If it makes you feel better, with everything going on, I'll head over there right now and call when I get there."

"I appreciate it, Roy. I would feel better if you could get eyes on her."

"I'm already out the front door. I'll be at your house in about ten minutes. I'll call you when I get there."

"Roy, you know her. You know what she's like."

"She's not stupid, Dan. And so far, this guy, Schmidt, has shown no inclination to confront her directly."

Dan used the automated kiosk and pulled from the airport, listening to directions to the freeway. The Mustang had the horses he'd hoped it would. He just hoped he had enough.

Tracy reached the fire trail near Mount Baker. Second level completed.

The third level would be navigating the fire trail. Variable one, she had never driven the road before. Variable two, she'd be driving in the dark. Variable three, the road could be littered with downed trees or limbs that would stall or halt her progress.

Tracy couldn't control the variables, only her performance.

She dropped the truck into four-wheel drive and, about to proceed, noted the odometer setting on the car, then the stopwatch she'd activated on her phone. She'd lose time having to proceed cautiously on the rugged, winding, uneven dirt road to ensure she made it. The county did not regularly tend to these fire roads, and the forest service prioritized those roads leading to campgrounds and cabins where people lived.

Her phone rang. Dan. She had one bar.

Just seeing his name made her remember that Dan was her family now. Daniella was her family. Their little girl. Dan had been right. She needed to think about both of them. She had responsibilities and obligations to them.

She answered the phone. "Dan."

"Tracy, thank God, I got a—"

"Dan? Dan, you're breaking up."

"Tracy?"

"Dan? I don't have much service, and we're having a storm—"

"What do you mean . . . service? Roy said . . . home." Dan was breaking up and it was getting worse.

"Dan, just listen, please. Schmidt has Lydia."

"Tracy?"

"Can you hear me? Dan?"

"You're breaking . . . again."

"Schmidt took Lydia to Silver Pines," she was nearly shouting. "I'm going to get her. If I don't, Schmidt will kill her."

"Tracy?"

"Dan? Can you hear me?"

"You're breaking up."

"Call Roy. Tell Roy I'm heading to Silver Pines. Schmidt is there."

"Roy . . ."

"Dan?"

The phone beeped. The call failed.

She hoped he'd heard her, because she had no bars to call him back.

She drove as fast as she dared—the potholes not insignificant. Hit one going even thirty miles an hour and she could snap an axle, possibly pop a tire. Again, game over. The only thing was completing this level.

The truck lights bounced and pitched up and down the swaying tree trunks and branches. The thick canopy served like a blackout curtain, preventing even what little ambient light the starlit sky provided. The road was pitch-black, even with Tracy using the truck's high beams. Where the road narrowed, branches slapped and scraped against the side of her truck, the windshield, and the side mirrors on aluminum extenders.

The truck began a steep ascent, further slowing her progress. She dropped the transmission into low and heard and felt the engine gear down. She had no way to know for certain how long the twenty-three miles would take, given the unknown condition of the road, but hoped to have enough time to hike the trail leading the final distance to Silver Pines. She didn't doubt for a moment that Schmidt would kill Lydia if Tracy failed to arrive on time. She feared he would kill her anyway, if he hadn't already.

Whatever he intended, Tracy had no intention of making things easy for him. She hoped to arrive with time to acclimate to her surroundings, determine what she could use for cover, and where she might best stage her guns.

She might not get it.

The truck came to a horseshoe turn. She pumped the brakes hard and spun the wheel sharply. Coming out of the turn, the road narrowed; portions of it appeared to have been washed out. It looked like the forest service had made rudimentary repairs, supporting the road with large rocks to minimize further erosion. Tracy had to slow her speed to almost a crawl and peer out the driver's-side window, searching the drop-off of several hundred feet. She told herself Schmidt had driven up this mountain. He hadn't walked to Silver Pines.

If he'd made it, she'd make it also.

With her head out the window, she eased down on the accelerator and watched the front wheel inch over what remained of the road. She made sure the back tire also found a perch. When it too cleared the repaired section of road, she gave the truck more gas and continued her ascent.

A loud crunch on the passenger side of the truck made her brake hard but not quickly enough. The side mirror had struck a rock protruding from the side of the hill, snapping off the aluminum extension arm and mirror.

She checked her odometer; she'd traveled just eleven of the twenty-three miles. If the conditions didn't improve, she'd never make it to Silver Pines in time.

Don't think ahead. Control what you can. Deal only with what is in front of you.

She continued on.

At a clearing she hit the brakes, grabbed her cell phone, and got quickly out of the cab, leaving the door open. She climbed into the bed of the truck then onto the cab's roof, holding the phone high overhead. She got a single bar.

Her phone pinged and buzzed, indicating incoming text messages, emails, and phone messages.

She checked her texts first. Dan. He'd also made several calls after their initial call had dropped. She hoped that meant he had heard enough of their phone conversation to seek Calloway's help.

She hit her voice mail messages. Dan. Then Calloway. One message after the next, but their voices broke up and the calls had failed.

She dialed Roy Calloway's cell phone. The call failed.

She tried leaving a text message. Again, it failed to go through. She hit "Try Again." It failed, a second time.

She looked again at her phone.

She had no bars.

And no time.

Time to move.

CHAPTER 36

Roy Calloway picked up the microphone from the radio mounted in the center of the SUV alongside a mobile command post computer. "Finlay? This is Roy. Are you there?"

After a moment Finlay responded, "I'm here, Chief. What are you doing out here?"

"Got a call from Dan O'Leary. He can't reach Tracy on her cell phone. I'm heading over there. You followed her home, correct?"

"Correct. Cleared the house with her. She declined when I offered to stay. Given the size of her two dogs, and all her guns, I didn't question her reasoning."

"Okay. She say anything about turning off her cell phone?"

"No, and under the circumstances—"

"I hear you. Dan said she isn't answering her cell phone, that his calls are going straight to voice mail, and his text messages aren't being delivered."

"That doesn't sound like her."

"Where are you?"

"I'm just arriving at Mason Pettibone's."

Calloway immediately alerted. "Why?"

"He said his granddaughter, Lydia, didn't come home from work after her shift at Cedar Grove Market this evening."

"When was she expected?"

"The mother, Celia, picks her up outside the market after her shift ends, right around eight o'clock. She said she was a little late arriving, that something came up at work, and Lydia wasn't there."

"Shit," Calloway said, getting a bad feeling. "Why didn't you radio me sooner?"

"Just got the call, Roy. And you're off duty. The mother said she thought Lydia might have gotten confused and walked home. She drove home, looking for her. Mason confirmed Lydia wasn't home."

"What about a cell phone?"

"Lydia doesn't have one. The expense and, well, she tends to lose things."

"Did Celia try contacting Lloyd Cunningham?" he asked, meaning the store owner.

"Store was closed. She finally reached him at home. He said Lydia clocked out at eight as per usual."

"Okay, get over there and figure out what's going on and keep me posted if Lydia arrives. I'll meet you at Pettibone's house after I check in with Tracy."

"Roger that, Roy."

Calloway disconnected and replaced the microphone in its clip. His bad feeling intensified. He punched the gas. The SUV roared over the railroad tracks at a high rate of speed. Tree branches and other debris littered the road from the high winds. Calloway swerved around them.

Minutes later, he pulled into Tracy's driveway. The garage door was open. The truck was not in the driveway or in the garage.

"Where did you go, girl? Please tell me you're home." Calloway swore and pushed from the SUV. A strong gust of wind nearly pulled the door from his grip. He left the headlights on and the engine running and approached the front door. Inside the house, Tracy's two dogs, alerted by the headlights and possibly the engine, barked furiously. Finlay was right. The two dogs were protective. Calloway tried the door handle. It turned, the door unlocked, but no way those two dogs were about to let him in the house. That was both good and bad. Bad, because if Tracy was inside and injured, he couldn't easily get to her. Good, because it made that scenario unlikely, given the dogs would not have allowed anyone else inside. The person would have had to shoot them first, putting Tracy on guard.

He banged hard on the door, then tried the doorbell several times, calling out Tracy's name over the sound of the howling wind. The dogs were now apoplectic, leaping up to put their feet on the door, barking as he peered through the windows. He hurriedly walked the one-story house's perimeter, shining a small but powerful flashlight through the windows into darkened rooms while calling out Tracy's name. Can lights illuminated the living room, dining room, and kitchen. He didn't see her. The dogs patrolled the inside, matching Calloway's movements, continuing to bark and growl.

At the back of the house, he shone the flashlight through a sliding glass door into the master bedroom. The dogs leapt against the glass, putting their paws as high as Calloway's shoulders, their barking more frantic. Calloway feared they'd bust through at any moment.

Tracy was not inside the bedroom.

He turned and did a quick search around the remaining perimeter before retreating to the front door.

He tried calling her cell phone, but his call went straight to voice mail, as Dan had said. He put his ear to the door and dialed again but could not hear her phone inside over the dogs barking and the howling wind. Not that he thought she was inside, not with the garage door up and the truck not there. She'd gone somewhere, and since it was unlikely she would have turned off her phone, the only logical explanation was she was out of cell phone range. In the mountains, it happened more than people imagined.

He hurried to his SUV, picked up the radio, and called Finlay, speaking over the gusting winds, advising him Tracy was not home. "And her truck is also gone, meaning she's driven someplace."

"I think you better get over here to Pettibone's, Chief," Armstrong said.

Something in Armstrong's tone cut off any further debate. "On my way," Calloway said.

As he raced down the road, Calloway's cell phone rang. Dan O'Leary. "Dan. I just came from your house. Tracy's not there and her truck is not in your garage or the driveway, but both dogs are inside the house."

"I know. She called me."

"She called you? When?"

"Just a moment ago."

"Where the hell is she?"

"Her call was breaking up. I couldn't hear everything she was saying, but she mentioned Schmidt and Lydia."

Calloway felt himself go cold. "What else? What else did she say?"

"I don't know. She was breaking up and then her cell died. I wasn't able to get her back."

"Finlay got a call from Mason Pettibone's daughter, Celia. He said Lydia did not come home from her shift at Cedar Grove Market."

"Ah shit, Roy. He took Lydia. Schmidt took Lydia to provoke a confrontation with Tracy. He knows her history. Sarah's history. He knows Tracy will do anything to get that young woman back."

"Slow down, Dan. Where are you? How far away are you from home?" Calloway asked.

"Still about thirty minutes out, but the high winds have downed branches along the county road, slowing my progress. If a tree falls, it could take me hours."

"The Chinook winds picked up here just after dark and are raising havoc. Do you have any idea where Tracy could have gone to meet Schmidt?"

"None."

"Has to be the mountain," Calloway said. "That . . . or the storm are the likely reasons she doesn't have cell coverage. Listen, I'll meet you at your house. Keep me posted on your ETA, and if you think of anyplace else Tracy might have gone, call me and let me know."

Calloway disconnected. Tracy was somewhere in the mountains, which would explain why Dan's call had dropped. Calloway looked at the outline of the North Cascades against the night sky.

She could be just about anywhere.

———

After nearly forty minutes of intense concentration, her senses on heightened alert, and her extreme concern about Lydia, Tracy felt mentally exhausted. She fought to maintain focus, to concentrate on the road, avoid what potholes she could, and watch for further washouts as well as possible deer. *Solve the next puzzle,* she kept telling herself. *One level at a time.*

She checked her odometer. She had to be getting close to the end of the twenty-three-mile road. She studied the road as far as the headlights revealed it, uncertain what she would see—if the road would simply end, if there would be a turnout or a roundabout.

She came around another bend to a straight stretch. An incline followed another decline. She shifted the transmission into low to give the brakes a chance to cool. The road flattened out and she saw what she'd been looking for: a circular turnaround large enough for fire and emergency vehicles, though she doubted any could make it this far, given the road conditions she had just traversed. But a parked car had made it. A red Jeep. Schmidt's girlfriend's car.

She turned the truck around and checked her watch. Ten twenty. She had an hour and ten minutes to reach Silver Pines.

She shut off the engine and the lights. Pitch-black enveloped her. She was glad she'd thought to grab her running headlamp.

She stepped down from the cab; the wind, howling through the trees, made an eerie moaning and clicking sound. The thick canopy shielded her from much of the wind, but the tips of the trees swayed violently across the starlit sky. Tracy slipped the headlamp over her head, turned it on, then hurried to the bed of her truck, lowering the gate and climbing up. She wished she'd brought her armored T-shirt, but she couldn't lament now about what she didn't have. She heard Lydia again, telling her to focus on the resources she did have. She'd be well armed. She draped the ammo belts over each shoulder. One belt carried her shotgun and rifle shells, the other held rounds for her revolvers. Her Glock held fourteen rounds. She had it holstered in an open-top Kydex holster on her hip. While she was sacrificing the security of the pistol in an open-top holster, she would be quicker on the draw, and having witnessed Schmidt's shooting abilities, every split second could be the difference between living and dying.

She slipped a spare magazine in the deep pocket of her duster and clipped her six-inch switchblade, a gift from Sarah decades ago, to her duster's inside pocket.

She took out her cell phone. Still no bars. She'd try again if she came to a clearing, in the unlikely chance she could get another signal.

For now, she was on her own.

She stepped down from the truck bed and grabbed her rifle and shotgun. She wished she had a sling for one or for both, but in Cowboy Action Shooting, a sling would be an unnecessary encumbrance. She'd carry one in each hand, using her headlamp to scan the area until she found the foot trail Stan Bleeker said Silver Pines miners had walked to stake their claims and eventually to leave them, carrying what little they owned on their backs. She bent down and checked the ground, detecting hiking-boot tread and tennis-shoe prints.

Schmidt and Lydia.

She put on the duster, as well as Sarah's Stetson, pulling it low on her head so it was secure. Then she started up the trail, an incline, following the beam of light. Though she was in good shape from running multiple times a week and lifting weights in the police gym, within minutes her labored breathing mixed with the moaning wind, clicking tree branches, and the rush of water flowing in the creek. It would take time to catch her breath. She'd have to do so on the move. No time to spare.

Occasionally, the branches and thick foliage rustled, causing her to turn her head quickly, the dark making every sound ominous. Black bears and mountain lions were present in the North Cascades, along with deer, elk, and other wildlife. Tracy kept up consistent chatter to alert the animals to her presence; they would avoid her if she didn't surprise them.

As the trail ascended, the conifer forest thinned, and she felt the wind, particularly the gusts, more acutely. At times she had to grip her Stetson to her head, driving forward in the wind. Overhead, free of ambient light, the Milky Way's band of millions of stars stretched across the night sky.

Tracy had no time to consider any of it.

She was singularly focused. Finish this level. Reach Silver Pines.

Then worry about the next level.

If she solved this one.

———

Dan had lost additional time getting home due to fallen tree limbs and a small fir tree that had toppled across the county road. An en route truck driver arrived, carrying a chainsaw, and quickly cut the trunk into manageable logs that Dan, with the help of other stranded motorists, rolled onto the shoulder. In the mountains you learned quickly to adapt to and prepare for any emergency. He pulled into his driveway at just past eleven thirty, delayed but in one piece. Dan started toward the house, stumbled, and nearly fell over something on the lawn. The motion sensor over the garage alerted to his movement, kicking on. He looked down at the two-by-ten ramps with the bed clips he'd made to help Tracy load and unload her rugged cart. He looked to the garage. As Calloway had said when they spoke on the phone, the door was open. The truck gone.

Dan checked inside the garage. Tracy's rugged cart was also not there. Nor were her shooting clothes.

She wasn't at Pettibone's. He knew that from Calloway.

And she was out of cell range.

"Shit," he said. "Where did you go?"

He made his way to the front door and took out his key to unlock the deadbolt. Inside Rex and Sherlock barked incessantly; their tone meant they were happy to see him. Dan spoke to them, soothing them. They whined and pranced. He stuck the key in the lock. The deadbolt had not been engaged. He tried the door handle and found it also unlocked. Tracy had been in a hurry.

Where did you go?

Inside, he did his best to fend off Rex and Sherlock, who sought his attention. Rex picked up a chew toy and shook his head vigorously, the toy squeaking. Dan petted them as he moved quickly through the house, calling out his wife's name, knowing she would not respond. She was not in the rooms at the back nor on the outdoor patio. Dan moved back to the family room and saw headlights pierce the windows. Calloway's SUV. Dan had called the chief when he'd reached Cedar Grove's town limits.

Dan opened the front door and stepped out. Rex and Sherlock bolted outside like two prisoners on a prison break, racing across the lawn in a large circle, one chasing the other, barking.

Calloway pushed from his vehicle and lumbered from the car, leaning forward into the wind as he approached. The dogs, alerted to his presence, started in his direction, but Dan called them off. They obeyed.

Dan met Calloway halfway across the lawn. A gust of wind was strong enough to blow them both off balance. He raised his voice. "She's not home. Wherever she went, she took her rugged cart and her guns. What did Mason have to say?"

"His granddaughter's still not home. They haven't heard from her."

"Did you tell them?"

"No. Not until we know for certain. You said Tracy's phone was cutting out before the call failed."

"We have to tell them, Roy."

"When we know. I told them we're doing everything in our power to find Lydia, and when we do, we'll bring her home. I have two deputies looking all over town for them."

"Tracy isn't home, and she isn't in Cedar Grove. Not if her phone is out of service." Dan's stomach gripped. "Do we have any idea where she might have gone?"

"No, but I know she spoke with Atticus at the *Towne Crier* late this afternoon. He called and said he had additional information on William Kenmore and told me that Tracy came in to talk about it. He said he has copies of the articles he gave her at the paper and will meet us there."

"Let me change quickly and get the dogs inside." Dan called Rex and Sherlock and rushed back inside the house. He threw kibble in two bowls, changed out of his khakis and dress shirt into jeans, hiking boots, a long flannel shirt, and slid on a black down jacket. The dogs followed him to the door, thinking he was going to take them out.

"I can't do it now, boys. I'm sorry. You guard the house while I'm gone."

It killed him to lock them back inside, but he had little choice.

He jumped into the passenger seat of Calloway's SUV, and the chief drove to downtown Cedar Grove. Minutes after they had arrived, they greeted Atticus Pelham outside the *Towne Crier's* office. Pelham looked like he'd just gotten out of bed.

"Thanks for coming down, Atticus," Calloway said. "Sorry about the late hour."

"Not a problem, Chief. If I can help, I will. You know that."

Pelham unlocked the newsroom door, and they all stepped inside, out of the unrelenting wind. Pelham flipped on the fluorescent lights. "It's really blowing; isn't it?" he said, straightening his thinning hair. "I hope we don't lose power."

"Tracy came to talk to you today. What about?" Dan asked, not bothering with pleasantries.

"She did," he said, taking off his jacket and laying it over the back of one of the newsroom desk chairs. "Initially she wanted to talk about William Kenmore. I found an obituary online and gave it to her, but I kept a copy of what I gave her here in the office. Do you want me to get it?"

"Can you quickly fill us in?" Dan said.

"Kenmore was a miner in Silver Pines," Pelham said. "Tracy wanted to know how he died."

"How did he die?" Dan asked.

"The obituary said a house fire. Nothing more. Then she asked about Silver Pines, the mining town out by Mount Shuksan."

"Did she say why?" Dan asked.

"No. She just said she wanted to know what more the paper had on the town's history."

Dan asked, "What else did you learn?"

Pelham explained about finding the article detailing that the preservation society was set up to save Silver Pines. "She tried to call the guy, but the number was not in service. She said she was going to take a drive out there to talk to the guy."

"Do you still have that address?"

"Sure. It was on the website. Let me pull it up."

Dan and Calloway followed Pelham into his office. He tapped the keyboard to awaken his computer and pulled up the preservation society's web page.

"Did you talk to Tracy after she went out to this guy's house?" Calloway asked.

"No. I haven't talked to her since she left here. Don't even know if the guy is still alive."

Dan was almost out the newsroom door before Pelham finished providing Roy Calloway with Stan Bleeker's name and address. Hopefully he remained alive and had information on where Tracy might have gone.

CHAPTER 37

Sweat dripped beneath Tracy's shirt and made the fabric stick to her back, and she wiped beads dripping down her face from the inside band of the Stetson. Her pace had left her winded, but adrenaline had fueled her climb. She wished she'd thought to bring along water. She estimated she was at roughly 3,500 feet, given the tree line. The temperature remained warm from the Chinook winds.

When she had climbed higher than the tree line, the wind, no longer impeded, howled over the rounded mountain surface like the blast of air from a hair dryer. She feared a strong enough gust might blow her off the mountain.

She'd been walking for nearly forty minutes, which meant she had roughly forty-five minutes to reach the town, scout it out, and determine where to stage her weapons. She didn't want to confront Schmidt in a duel if she didn't have to. After viewing his shooting video, she didn't believe she could beat him, at least not that version of him, despite her recent training, were it to come to that. And she suspected it would. She held out hope that Schmidt, having served a long prison sentence, wasn't the shooter he had once been either. She also hoped an element of surprise might help to disarm him. Her intent wasn't to kill him if she didn't have to, though she recognized that thought was naïve.

One of them was unlikely to get out of Silver Pines alive.

The trail led to a domed rock clearing, and she looked across it to the snowcapped granite peaks illuminated beneath an iridescent moon and starlit sky. The beauty must have made all those miners and their families feel as though they'd found the Garden of Eden and were about to make their fortunes. Then, as Bleeker had described, the November rains came, followed by the winter storms, and those who had survived those harsh and inhospitable conditions must have thought the garden had been but an illusion, and the lure of precious metals like the apple into which Adam and Eve had bitten, paying a very heavy price.

Tracy checked her phone. Still no bars.

She pushed on, over the windy ridge, and descended the back side, eventually coming to what had likely once been the supports for the lone bridge leading into Silver Pines. Heavy rains and time had reclaimed the planking, leaving only the two cedar logs, six feet apart, bridging a twenty-foot span across a steep ravine. On the far side of the gap, the two logs spanned the final five feet over a rock ledge just a couple feet below the mountain's surface. Tracy squatted and, in the light from her headlamp, she saw holes in the logs where the wood planks had likely once been secured. The log surface was slick to the touch, but Tracy could see where someone, Schmidt and Lydia, had recently crossed.

She walked up and down the ravine looking for another potential way to cross, not finding one.

Next, she considered whether she could toss her shotgun and her rifle to the other side, not having a sling in which to carry them, but she was anything but certain she could throw them the required distance, or that they'd survive hitting the granite mountain surface. The rounded slope of the mountain also made for the very real possibility that the weapons could skitter down the granite and slide off the mountainside.

She had no choice but to balance them in each hand, crossing in the dark with gusting winds, and only her headlamp to lead her. She put her boot on the log, testing the surface before she stepped up with her other foot. She took a moment to regain her balance, then stood for a moment. The log remained secure, without give. One small positive.

She put one foot in front of the next, proceeding slowly, being certain of each step before she moved the next step, using her arms like wings. Wind gusts kicked up, playing havoc with her balance.

Halfway across, she lost her balance, but she was able to regain it. She paused and caught her breath, then recalled a Pilates instructor's advice that the best way to maintain one's balance was to stare at a distant, immovable object. She looked across the river at the moonlit mountain and focused her attention on a small rock atop another, roughly in line with her crossing.

She took another step. Better. Then another. And another.

She had crossed two-thirds of the way, just past the ravine where the river ran below her, and three feet from the rock platform on the ravine's far side.

She lifted her foot and felt a strong wind gust. It hit the duster, causing it to billow, like a sail, pushing her further off balance. Her body teetered forward. She fought to retain her balance but lost that struggle. Needing to free her hands, she tossed the shotgun and the rifle forward onto the mountain as she pitched from the log, managing to push off with her legs so she fell far enough forward to land on the rock ledge. The stone, moist and slick from the river's mist blown by the wind, caused her boots to again slip, but she grabbed a small tree growing from a crack in the granite, holding on to it to keep from tumbling off the ledge and falling into the ravine.

Her body swung in an arc and her side hit the mountain. The jarring impact popped her Glock from the open-top holster. Unable to release her grip on the tree without falling, she had no chance to grab the pistol. It tumbled onto the rock platform, ricocheted off the stone, and skidded over the side, where it would plunge into the river.

She got her feet beneath her and, using the tree for support, pulled herself to an upright position. After doing so, she picked up the Stetson from the rock ledge and put it back on her head, then used gaps and footholds in the rocks to climb up to the mountain surface. She rose from her knees to her feet, pacing to catch her breath and let her adrenaline calm, trying not to think about how close she had come to dying.

But she was running out of time.

She needed to determine if either her shotgun or rifle had landed safely and where. She sidestepped to the direction where she'd tossed them, hoping at least one had caught on a bush or shrub growing from the cracks and crevices, and that she could reach it. When she had stepped far enough to peer over the edge, her hopes vanished. The mountain sloped at a precipitous angle. Anything skittering on the surface would have picked up speed as it went, eventually bouncing and tumbling over the side.

No rifle. No shotgun. No Glock. Just her Colt revolvers. More variables she couldn't change. She'd have to make do if she wanted to reach the next level.

She looked at her watch.

If she got moving, she'd make it to the town in just about the time Schmidt had given her. She no longer had to worry about staging her weapons.

Her Colt revolvers would have to be enough.

CHAPTER 38

Roy Calloway pulled up to the front of Stan Bleeker's house at the end of a cul-de-sac. He and Dan quickly ascended the steps—as quickly as Calloway's bad ankle allowed—to a large porch with a single bulb over the front door.

Calloway called to Dan, who had beaten him up the stairs. "Dan." Dan turned. "Let me go first so you don't get shot off the porch."

Dan stepped back, and Calloway knocked hard several times. Inside, a dog barked, though it sounded more like a croak. Calloway stood to the side of the door.

"Who is it?" a man's voice called from inside the door.

"Mr. Bleeker, it's Police Chief Roy Calloway. I need to talk to you about Tracy Crosswhite. I understand she came out to speak to you."

Bleeker answered the door with one leg positioned to keep back a black Labrador. He looked at Calloway through thick lenses, then at Dan. Apparently satisfied he wasn't going to be robbed, he opened the door further, and Dan saw him set a shotgun down against the window.

"It's the middle of the night. I'm assuming this must be important," Bleeker said.

Calloway assured him it was, explained the reason for their presence, and Bleeker stepped back and invited them inside his home. They remained standing. "Sure, she came to see me," Bleeker confirmed. "She was very interested in Silver Pines, especially one of its miners."

"William Kenmore?" Dan asked.

"That's right."

"What did she want to know?" Dan asked.

"It's a bit of a story," Bleeker said.

"We don't have a lot of time," Dan said. "We think maybe my wife could be in some trouble."

"I'm sorry to hear that," Bleeker said. "Okay, here's the *Reader's Digest* version." He told them what had happened to the miners when Christian Mattioli arrived. "If they complained or tried to organize, they were either sent packing or ended up dead."

"By this guy Treat Crane?" Dan asked.

"Crane was the best known of the group."

"A hired gun," Calloway said.

Bleeker nodded. "Crane would put a pistol in the miner's hand and challenge him to a duel. They fought at sunrise. My grandfather was one of those miners, and he told my father Crane would draw a line in the dirt road in town and make the other man wait for the sun to rise over the mountain range. When the sunbeams crossed the line in the ground, the shooters drew."

"Nobody stopped this?" Dan asked.

"Who?" Bleeker said. "Crane was the law in town. And if anyone left Silver Pines and tried to go to the law in Cedar Grove, Crane and the others who worked for Mattioli would say the killing had been in self-defense, that the miner had taken up a pistol. But it never got that far. Mattioli had all the police and politicians in his pocket and, that far out, Silver Pines was likely not considered worth the effort for law enforcement to get to."

"How many miners did he kill?"

"No way to know for certain, but my grandfather said a dozen were gunned down in the street. It could have been many more."

"I thought Kenmore died in a house fire," Dan said to Calloway.

"He did," Bleeker said. "In Cedar Grove."

"I don't understand," Dan said. "Did she ask about anything or anyone else?"

"She was interested in Kenmore's claim, and in his partner, Charles House."

Dan felt his limbs go numb at the mention of the name. "Did you say 'House'?"

"He and Kenmore had one of the richest claims, and both had resisted Mattioli's overtures to buy them out. They tried to organize the miners into a union, and Crane shot House dead and forced Kenmore to flee, but Crane might as well have killed him, too, and his family."

"What do you mean 'and his family'?" Calloway asked.

"Kenmore moved to Cedar Grove, but when he lost his lawsuit to get back his claim, he nailed his family inside a house and set it afire."

Dan gave Calloway a knowing look. He felt nauseated. "Tracy told me Erik Schmidt was in the Army Marksmanship Unit; that the unit produces some of the best shooters in the world."

"I don't exactly follow," Calloway said.

"If he lured her to Silver Pines, he did so for a reason. A purpose."

"Such as?"

"Mattioli took Charles House's claim and killed him. Tracy said Schmidt believes she lured House from prison to kill him."

"And you think he chose Silver Pines for . . . what?" Calloway asked.

"I don't know, Roy. The history. To even the score for Charles House's murder."

"By a duel?" Calloway said.

"What other reason could there be to go to such elaborate measures to get her to Silver Pines?"

"You don't think Tracy would take on someone like that by herself; do you?"

"A gunfight? Maybe not under ordinary circumstances, but if Schmidt took Lydia, Tracy would move heaven and hell to get her back. You know that."

"If she's looking to move hell, she's going to find it in Silver Pines," Bleeker said.

"Can you tell us how to get there?" Dan asked.

"Hold on, Dan," Calloway started.

"You heard him, Roy. That town is abandoned. We're it. We're all Tracy has. And if Schmidt intends to play this out, then he's most likely to do so at sunrise." He turned to Bleeker. "How do we get there?"

Bleeker gave them directions, after which Dan said, "How long will that take?"

When Bleeker told them it would take a few hours just to reach the end of the fire trail, if the road hadn't been closed by a downed tree or broken limbs, then longer still to get to the town on foot, Dan said to Calloway, "What about a helicopter?"

Calloway shook his head. "We've used the park service for rescue operations in the mountains before, but they won't fly in winds this strong, which will be even stronger atop the mountain."

"Anyone else?" Dan asked.

"I can try Snohomish County Search and Rescue, but same problem. Puget Sound Energy may be our best bet. Those pilots can fly in anything and sometimes will."

"Make a call," Dan said. He turned to Bleeker. "Do you know of any other way to reach the town? A faster way?"

"Maybe. Mattioli expanded the ore rails to bring the ore down the mountain in cars so it could be crushed before being sent by railcar to Bellingham for processing. If you can access those ore car tracks, if they even still exist, it would be a more direct route up the mountain, though still difficult—steep. And there's no way of knowing if the tracks still exist."

"Why wouldn't they?" Dan asked.

"Mudslides, collapsed tunnels, any number of things."

Dan figured they'd cross that bridge if, and when, they came to it. "How do I access the ore tracks?"

"I'd start at the processor," Bleeker said.

"I know it," Calloway said. "It's just outside of town."

Dan knew it too. He'd seen the ore tracks while hiking the mountains.

"That would be your fastest route," Bleeker said.

Dan thanked Bleeker and hurried down the porch steps to Calloway's SUV. When he looked back, Calloway lumbered down the staircase, step by step on his bad ankle. If the ore car line remained passable, Dan would be on his own.

"I'll call Finlay," Calloway said when he reached the car.

"No time," Dan said, checking his watch. "Sunrise is around 5:40. I need to leave now. Just give me a gun and get me to the ore tracks."

"You can't go alone, and I can't go with you. Not on my bum ankle. Finlay knows these mountains like the back of his hand. I'll radio him to meet us at the processor and tell him to bring supplies. If he's coming from Cedar Grove, he'll arrive at around the same time we do. While you two are hiking, I'll get on the horn to Search and Rescue and figure out when we can anticipate getting a helicopter airborne."

"We can't wait that long, Roy. The winds are supposed to continue until morning. She might be dead by then."

"Tracy can handle herself. She's good with a gun."

"No doubt," Dan said. "But eventually someone better always comes along, Roy. You know that. Always."

CHAPTER 39

Tracy climbed back up to the trail that continued just across from the bridge. She'd taken only two steps when she heard the explosion and felt the concussive blast hit her in the back. The force tossed her forward, like riding a powerful wave, and she landed hard on the granite, felt her body bounce across the ground, and hit again, knocking the wind from her. She struggled for air while trying to get her bearings. Bits and pieces of debris rained down around her like hail. When it stopped, she rolled onto her back and immediately felt a searing pain in her right arm and shoulder that made her cry out. The pain was so intense she fought to remain conscious, afraid she might pass out. She managed to breathe through her agony, taking slow, deep breaths, careful she didn't hyperventilate.

She reached up with her left hand to the front of her shoulder and felt a bump beneath the skin, indicating she'd likely snapped her collarbone in the fall. She shrugged her right shoulder and heard a loud pop. The blinding pain returned, stars bursting behind her closed eyelids. She rolled to her side and vomited.

She'd dislocated her shoulder before. This felt like the shoulder had dislocated, then popped back into place. She couldn't move her right arm and felt a burning pain running up and down the limb.

When she opened her eyes, she could no longer see out of her right eye. She reached up and felt blood trickling from a cut on her forehead above her brow. The blood obscured her vision. She removed her bandanna from the pocket of her duster and wiped at the blood, then pressed the bandanna to the wound to stem the flow. She did a quick further assessment. She felt bloody scrapes on the right side of her face where she'd hit and skidded along the ground, but she didn't believe she'd suffered a concussion, though everything felt dull. Nothing, beyond her collarbone, appeared to be broken.

She sat up slowly, cradling her right arm in her lap. Dust particles danced in the moon's blue-white rays, filling the air where the two logs had once crossed the ravine, but where now she saw only a wide expanse.

Schmidt had blown the bridge.

She had no easy way back, and no one could follow, at least not on foot. The high winds would prevent access by helicopter.

Schmidt wanted Tracy alone, isolated.

Tracy removed one of her Colt pistols from its holster and cocked the hammer, searching the darkness for any moving shadow, seeing none. In the blast, she'd lost her headlamp.

She set the gun in her lap and considered her watch, but the lens had also cracked in the fall. The watch face remained dark.

She pulled out her cell phone. The screen, too, had shattered.

It didn't matter. Tracy knew instinctively Lydia was running out of time.

She gave herself one minute to catch her breath and to slow her rushed breathing caused by pain. Then she got to her feet, keeping her right arm bent at a ninety-degree angle. She inhaled and exhaled deeply, squeezing her eyes shut to clear her vision, fighting the pain and the nausea. She bent to the side, overwhelmed by another wave of nausea, and she wondered again if she could be concussed.

She no longer had multiple weapons or even her service pistol. With one arm, she was down to a single Colt revolver, and she couldn't use her right hand to fan the hammer.

She willed herself to straighten. She had to get to the town.

She slid her right hand beneath one of her ammunition belts around her shoulders. The rudimentary sling would keep her arm in place while she walked but do little to relieve her pain. She picked up her sister's Stetson, shook the dust from it, placed it on her head, and stumbled forward.

The trail descended into the pine trees. Woody shrubs grew along the path. Tracy stepped around a large boulder and discovered a meadow of tall oat grass, the tips whipping furiously, like waves across a stormy sea. The wind carried a sorrowful wail that sounded almost human.

She took a moment to let her eyes adjust to the dark. Across the grass meadow, moonlight reflected on the buildings of Silver Pines, ghostly, blue-white silhouettes. Surrounding the town were the snowcapped mountain peaks. It was a thing of beauty, like a high-mountain Montana cattle ranch.

A deception then and now.

Nothing beautiful awaited the miners or, she feared, her.

Tracy got off the trail and approached the town in the tall oat grass, staying in what shadows she could. As she neared the road leading into town, she came upon a modern, brown, forest service sign mounted on a pole, welcoming visitors to Silver Pines. The sign, a likely remnant of the attempt to turn the town into a tourist attraction, rattled when hit by the wind. Tracy picked her path and moved behind what looked like abandoned, rusting mining equipment. Her eyes searched the empty street for shadows that didn't belong, the glint of a light between the vertical slatted boards that made up the buildings' sides or reflecting in one of the windows.

With her eyes adjusted to the dark, the town came into sharper focus. Buildings were positioned along both sides of a wide street, with wooden walkways running the length of both sides. Some buildings looked in better shape than the others, and Tracy recalled Bleeker telling her that the preservation society had been in the process of making repairs when another disaster struck, extinguishing the final flicker of hope.

She advanced to a dilapidated wooden wagon that listed hard to the side, missing a metal wheel. From there she moved to the closest building, placing her back against the wood siding. She took a moment to breathe and again swallow her pain. Then she slid to the edge, squatted, and peered around the corner, searching up and down the street. A wind gust kicked up, swirling dust devils that twisted and rotated down the street like ghosts who'd come outside to greet her.

Just as quickly as the wind had picked up, it died again, and the devils collapsed.

Tracy knew she couldn't stay hidden, not forever, if she was hidden at all. Schmidt could very well be watching her through night-vision goggles, or a night scope on a rifle.

And she'd run out of time.

Time to call her own variable.

With her left hand, Tracy pulled one of her Colts from the holster and stepped out into the street. She called out. "Schmidt? You wanted me. I'm here." The only response was the moaning wind. "Schmidt? Let the girl go. Come out and face me."

For another few moments she heard only the wind.

Then something squeaked.

The swinging doors to the saloon down the street pushed open and a figure stepped out, letting the doors swing shut behind him. He stood for a moment atop the steps before he descended to the wooden sidewalk. He crossed from the sidewalk to the center of the street, stopping fifteen yards away—too far for Tracy to ensure accuracy with her Colt, especially injured.

She needed to get closer to have any chance of hitting Schmidt. She took a step forward.

Schmidt lifted his head from beneath the bill of a black baseball cap. He'd cut his hair. In a black T-shirt and black jeans, he looked very much like the young man in the shooting video sent to Tracy. His hands dangled at his sides, empty. Tracy did not see a gun, but she knew he could have one wedged at the small of his back or concealed under his shirt.

"I'm unarmed," he said. "Put the gun back in its holster."

"And if I choose not to?"

"The girl," he said.

She put the gun back in its holster. "Let her go. You got what you wanted. I'm here. This is between you and me."

Schmidt grinned. "It will be. The girl is my insurance. It stays that way."

"That wasn't the deal, Schmidt. The deal was if I came, you'd let her go."

Schmidt grinned. "I lied. You can relate; can't you?"

"Let's get on with it, then."

"What's wrong with your arm?"

"Nothing."

"Doesn't look like nothing."

"What do you want?" she asked. "Why am I here?"

"I told you. Time to pay for past sins, Detective Tracy. Yours and Christian Mattioli's."

"Cut the dramatic bullshit, Schmidt. Just tell me why I'm here so we can get on with it."

"You're a liar. Just like Mattioli. You got Ed a new trial to get him out so you could kill him."

"I got House a new trial because I believed he'd been framed for my sister's murder. I was wrong."

"You got him out to kill him, just like Christian Mattioli lied to all those miners he killed. He killed Charles House. Ed could have been rich. Things could have been different."

"Edmund House was a psychopath. All the money in the world wasn't going to change that fact. You have no idea what you're talking about. You're making shit up to justify what you intend to do."

"House told me everything."

"Then he lied to you. He manipulated and used you, and you fell for it. Is that why we're here, in Silver Pines, to pay for what you perceive to be past sins?"

"Don't perceive anything. You see the parallels. Ed said you and your family tried to pass yourselves off as better than everyone else in town, living in Mattioli's mansion, but you weren't."

"You've created a fable. You and House are the same. You prey on the weak, kill young, vulnerable women. You're a psychopath, just like he was, Erik."

"Am I?"

"Prove me wrong. Let the girl go."

"Not done with her yet."

"Where is she, then?" she asked. "I want proof of life. Before I agree to anything, I want to talk to her."

"You're not in a position to be demanding anything. But you'll have time to ask her yourself. We're going to settle this with a nod to history. We're going to settle this the way Treat Crane settled things with the miners, with Charles House. But this time, the miner will be armed."

"A gunfight," she said. "You and me. I get it."

"Do you, Tracy Crossdraw?" He grinned. "Ed told me all about you and your sister's shooting ability. The Washington State Championships? Well, at dawn, we're going to find out who's really the best."

The longer Tracy kept Schmidt engaged, the greater the chance, though it was minimal, that help might arrive. She had no assurances how much Dan had heard during their telephone call. "Name the time then."

"Sunrise is at 5:36 a.m. That's when Crane did his killing. The sunlight comes over those mountains." Schmidt stepped to the side and used the heel of his boot to draw a line in the dirt. "When the light comes over the building peaks and crosses that line, we draw, and we'll find out who really is the best. Don't try to run. The jail is wired with enough C4 explosive for me to blow half this town, the girl with it."

"I don't intend to run, Erik."

Schmidt smiled. "Get a few hours of sleep, Detective Tracy. Tomorrow's your last sunrise."

CHAPTER 40

Dan stood on what had been the ore car tracks cut into the mountainside above the processor. A stream, largely dried up, had powered a wooden waterwheel that turned the heavy stamps that crushed the ore brought in the iron railcars. The wooden wheel had rotted away long ago and the heavy metal stamps removed and likely sold for scrap metal, along with the ore cars. The trail, illuminated by Calloway's headlights, was wide enough for two men to hike side by side, but not wide enough for a modern car. That, and the trail's unknown condition above the processor, as Bleeker had said, meant any off-road vehicle could also have difficulty. They'd have to go on foot.

Dan paced and checked his watch as he and Roy Calloway awaited Finlay's arrival. He knew waiting was the prudent thing to do, but also the hardest. He was not equipped for the North Cascades—were anything to go wrong, and that was almost always a given in the mountains. To go up an unknown trail in unknown condition, alone, in the middle of the night would be impetuous and stupid. Two verbs he was currently using to describe his wife's decision to go after Erik

Schmidt on her own, though he knew why she had done it. Tracy saw Lydia the way she'd once seen her sister. It wasn't just the physical resemblance to Sarah, or that they were roughly the same age as when Edmund House took Sarah, or even that they were both excellent shooters. Lydia, from everything Tracy had told him, was innocent and trusting. She'd done everything Tracy had asked of her, including getting the job at the market, which gave Schmidt the chance to snatch her. Tracy would hold herself responsible if anything happened to the young woman, the way she held herself responsible for Sarah's disappearance and death.

She wasn't about to let Sarah die again.

And given that Schmidt had already killed two young women, that was not a bluff Tracy could call. She didn't have much choice but to go alone. Schmidt would know if she did not, given the limited foot access, at present the only way into town. Dan hoped, at least, Tracy was well armed and that her rifle wouldn't require her to get close to Schmidt, that she could pick him off at a distance.

He saw headlights in the tree line across the dry riverbed, a car winding its way toward them. Calloway saw it also, and together they watched Finlay's SUV pitch and bounce over the uneven road, cross the shallow riverbed, and pull up alongside Calloway's SUV.

"What took so long?" Dan said when Finlay got out. The deputy stepped to the back of the SUV, opened the tailgate, and removed two ready backpacks.

"These." Armstrong tossed one of the packs, which had **CEDAR GROVE PD** stenciled on the front pocket, to Dan and advised they contained needed provisions: rain gear, a tarp, energy snacks and dehydrated meals, water, and a filtration straw to purify creek water if needed.

"Sorry," Dan said.

"Don't be. I'd be anxious to get going too."

Dan slid on the backpack, adjusted the pack on his hips, and tightened the straps.

"The hike is roughly seven miles from here," Finlay said to Dan, "but it's steep, with an elevation gain of about 3,500 feet, and we're hiking at night. I'm estimating it will take us roughly four to five hours—if we don't run into any unforeseen obstacles or problems—maybe less, depending on the pace we set. But remember, we don't want to be the hare and burn out halfway up the mountain. We want to be the tortoise—steady—especially at the start. Allow yourself to catch your breath. A consistent pace should put us in Silver Pines roughly between five and five thirty in the morning."

"Sunrise," Dan said.

They'd be cutting it close.

Dan and Finlay pulled on their headlamps and turned them on to test the batteries, then pointed the light at the sky so they could talk without blinding each other.

"I'll stay in contact with Snohomish Search and Rescue," Calloway said. "I've also put in a call to PSE. I'm waiting to hear back from them. When they tell me they can fly, we'll fly."

"When are they predicting that might happen?" Dan said.

"Winds atop the mountain are gusting anywhere from thirty to sixty miles per hour at present, and they aren't expected to lessen until early morning."

"How long will it take once they get clearance for a helicopter to reach Silver Pines?"

"About forty minutes."

Dan looked at Finlay. "Looks like we're Tracy's best bet. Let's go." He lowered his light and started up the trail.

"Keep your satellite phone on," Calloway said.

"Will do," Finlay said, and he and Calloway did a test as Finlay followed Dan. The phone also had a GPS function that would provide

Calloway with Finlay and Dan's precise location on the mountain, should anything go wrong.

The first couple miles were brutal hiking. The trail inclined from the processing plant at a steep pitch. The footing, too, was treacherous. Dan's feet would slip on the loose shale and rock, and he'd stumble and nearly fall. For every foot forward, he felt as if he was taking a step back. He could hear his breathing and feel the lactic acid burn in his legs. An experienced hiker and trail runner, he knew he'd eventually catch his breath, but Finlay was keeping a brisk pace, using his watch to determine their ETA.

Darkness added to their difficulty. With tree roots across or under the ground, they couldn't look too far ahead and risk tripping and hurting or breaking an ankle. Dan's field of vision was the sphere created by his headlamp. As much as he wanted to break into a run, Dan had to hold himself back until that moment when he could sprint to the finish line.

Hopefully in time.

CHAPTER 41

Tracy walked down the street, the pain in her shoulder getting worse as her adrenaline rush faded. She felt nauseated, and her forehead was burning up. She passed refurbished signs hanging over buildings, some askew from the harsh winters and high winds. **GENERAL STORE**, **POST OFFICE**, **HOTEL**, and **SILVER NUGGET SALOON**. It reminded her of Pettibone's shooting scenarios in his backyard, and she felt, for a moment, like she was in a video game, about to tackle the highest level.

The jail was a detached one-room building at the end of the street. Moon rays shone through the open door and two windows, one beside the door and one in the jail cell. Lydia lay on a wooden bunk inside the cell. When she saw Tracy she stood quickly and came to the bars, stuttering and repeating herself. "Tracy Crossdraw. Tracy Crossdraw."

"Hey, Lydia." Tracy tried to keep concern out of her voice, though she was not completely successful. "Are you all right?"

Lydia was rocking back and forth from her heels to her toes repeatedly. She spoke rapidly, as if she were experiencing a meltdown. "I'm tired. And I'm hungry. And I want to go home. Who is that man?

What's going on? Why did he make me hike? Why did he make me cross that log? Why am I here? This place is like *Westworld*. That man is like the robot in *Westworld*."

Tracy needed to find a way to calm Lydia down, but the adrenaline rush that had fueled Tracy's nearly two-hour drive in the pitch-black, her hike up the darkened mountain trail, and her confrontation with Schmidt had evaporated. She felt fatigued, physically and mentally drained. The pain in her shoulder and collarbone had become more acute. She no longer worried she could be concussed by the blast. She now feared the pain could be causing her to slip into shock. She shivered though sweating profusely and felt as though she was running a fever. She needed to lie down.

Tracy looked around the room for a camera, something Schmidt could use to watch them throughout the night, not seeing one.

She tried the jail cell door but found it locked. "Is there a key, Lydia?"

"The key is on the hook by the door," Lydia said, pointing. Then she started again with the same questions and rocking from her heels to her toes.

Apparently, Schmidt was not worried about Lydia taking off once Tracy arrived.

Tracy found the single iron-barrel key on a round metal loop on a peg near the door and unlocked the cell. Lydia rushed forward before Tracy could stop her, giving Tracy a bear hug. Tracy moaned, feeling a fresh wave of nausea and pain. The room spun.

"You're hurt," Lydia said, pulling back. "I'm sorry. I'm sorry. You're hurt. I hurt you. I'm sorry. I'm sorry."

Tracy couldn't hide her pain, not completely. She grimaced, taking short, rapid breaths of air as she stepped forward and angled to drop on the bunk, afraid she might pass out if she didn't. When she caught her breath, she said to Lydia, who had continued lamenting, "I'm okay.

It's all right. Lydia. I'm okay. I'm okay. You didn't hurt me. I got hurt coming here." When she'd gotten Lydia to calm, at least partially, Tracy asked, "Did he hurt you?"

"No," Lydia said, shaking her head. "He tied my hands and put a gag in my mouth to keep me from talking. I had to cross a log. He said we were going to meet you in Silver Pines. He said you would come and rescue me. This is like *Westworld*. It's like the movie."

"It is," Tracy said. "Just like it."

Lydia started speaking without pause again. "When do we go home? I have to go home. I have to take care of Grandpa when my mother goes to work. And I have to work. I have to work at the supermarket. I'm a bag girl."

The poor girl was rambling, stuttering. "We can't go home. Not just yet, Lydia." She tried reasoning with her. "It's dark out. We won't find the way in the dark. But soon."

"In the morning? Will we go home in the morning? Do my mother and grandfather know I'm here? Did you tell them? My mother will worry. I told her I'd meet her after I finished at the grocery store. We were supposed to drive home together."

"I'm sure she knows," Tracy said, then thought it best to give Lydia something to do, something maybe to occupy her mind. "Help me take off my guns and my coat."

The process of removing her coat, even with Lydia's help, was slow and painful. Tracy tried not to audibly grunt or to show her agony, but at times she couldn't help it; the pain was almost blinding. Her coat removed, she asked Lydia to help her take off the gun belts across her chest and hang them across the back of the chair. She then instructed Lydia to extract the knife from inside her duster and to cut a long strip of canvas from the bottom, approximately six inches wide. Lydia did so, then helped Tracy fashion a sling for her right arm, tying the knot at the base of Tracy's neck. When they had finished, Tracy pushed up against the wall, and Lydia helped her lift her legs onto the bunk. Tracy put her head back against the wall and closed her eyes, the exertion and the pain making her weak and sick.

After a beat, Lydia asked, "Are we in Westworld?"

"What?" Tracy asked, opening her eyes. She wondered if Lydia was shutting down, maybe trying to escape reality.

"Are we in Westworld?" Lydia slipped into her infomercial voice, her hands rubbing her thighs as she began reciting facts. "*Westworld* is a dystopian science-fiction Western television series created by Jonathan Nolan and Lisa Joy that first aired on October 2, 2016, on HBO. It is based upon the 1973 film written and directed by Michael Crichton. The story begins in Westworld—"

Tracy reached out her good arm, wrapping it around the young woman's shoulder. "Lydia. Lydia, it's okay. It's okay. Everything is going to be okay."

Lydia calmed, though continued to rock.

"This place is like Westworld, Lydia. But it's not Westworld. You understand; right?"

"I understand."

"You know the man out there is not an outlaw android. But he's like one."

"Do we have to kill him to go home?" Lydia asked.

Tracy was losing steam. "He and I are going to have a gunfight at dawn. When it's over, you'll get to go home."

"With you; right? I'll get to go home with you. We'll go home together," Lydia said.

"That's right. We'll go home together. It's going to be okay, Lydia. I don't want you to worry."

Lydia's face pinched for a moment. Then she said, "But you can't have a gunfight. You're hurt. Your right hand is in a sling, and you cross draw."

"I still have my left hand."

Again, Lydia paused, seemingly deep in thought. "When is the duel?"

"Tomorrow morning," Tracy said. "At sunrise, when the sunlight comes over the buildings and crosses a line in the street, he and I will draw."

"But—"

"I have to talk to you about something else, Lydia. Something important."

"But if you draw and he's faster than you—"

"I need you to be brave. Can you be brave, for me?"

"Yes. I can be brave for you."

"You taught me to take the video games I played one level at a time. Do you remember telling me that?"

"Yes. Yes, I remember telling you that. You can't look ahead to what hasn't happened or back at what already has happened. You have to stay in the moment. Solve one puzzle at a time. Move up one level at a time."

"That's right. One level at a time. The puzzle we now face is how to get out of here and move to the next level. Tomorrow morning. After I go out that door to duel, I want you to go out behind the building. I want you to stay behind the buildings and run behind them back to the tree line. Try to get down the mountain and find someone to help you."

"But you said we were going to leave together, after the duel?"

"I'll come after the duel," Tracy said, knowing that would not be likely. Beating Schmidt at full strength would have been difficult. Hurt, she had little chance. She needed a miracle. She needed Dan to have heard her and to have found some way to reach them. At the moment, those prospects, in these winds, seemed bleak. She tried not to think about never seeing him or Daniella again, but her eyes watered nonetheless.

She pushed that thought away. Still unwilling to give in. She needed to stay in the moment. To give herself a chance to reach the next level. Lydia's life depended on it.

Tracy felt herself growing weaker. "I want you to get away, Lydia. Tomorrow when I go out for the duel. I want you to be brave. Be brave and go down the mountain. Promise me you'll run behind the buildings and go down the mountain."

"But what if you don't win the duel? What if he kills you? You have Daniella at home."

"Run, Lydia. Promise me you will run and get down the mountain. Don't let the man find you."

Tracy had one last level to conquer.

Beat Schmidt.

She had no idea how she would do so.

CHAPTER 42

Dan and Finlay had been hiking in the dark for almost four hours. The trail, after the initial steep ascent, had leveled out, and they'd made better time. They stopped once to refill their water bottles in the creek, but otherwise they ate their energy bars and drank while on the move. Dan had just filled his bottle and slid it into the side pocket of his backpack. Finlay had slipped his backpack on and was adjusting it at his waist.

"How do you feel?" Finlay asked.

"I'm good," Dan said, throwing on the backpack and similarly adjusting the straps. He took off his wire-framed glasses and cleaned the lenses with the tail of his shirt.

"We have a few more miles. I think we're going to get there, Dan."

"Then let's get going," Dan said.

They set out again at a faster pace. Though they kept their headlamps on, the sky above the tree line had turned from black to navy blue, and Dan's night vision had improved, and his sense of urgency had increased, pushing him to pick up their pace to a slow jog. They continued around a bend in the road and came to an abrupt stop. The trail ended at what looked to have once been a tunnel through the mountain, but which had collapsed. Getting around it would be steep and arduous.

Dan's heart sank, though Finlay had told him of this exact possibility. "Shit," he said.

"The forest service likely collapsed it," Finlay said. "It's too dangerous to have these tunnels around with people out here hiking."

Dan's eyes searched the mountain. "We go up and over," he said. "There's no other way. It's steep, but it's not that much higher. We can hike over the top and down the other side."

"Footing is going to be treacherous," Finlay said. "A lot of loose rock and shale on the hill. We'll take two steps up and slide one step back."

"Any other options?"

Finlay shook his head. "No good ones."

"Then we go up and over."

They searched for a place to climb. Dan noticed an animal trail that looked manageable. "I'll go first," Finlay said. "Stay below me but to the side, in case I lose my footing and slide backward. I don't want to take you out with me."

The footing was indeed treacherous. Dan's feet slipped out from under him on several occasions. A few times he fell hard, landing on his side. He held on to every shrub he could find to keep his feet from sliding down the mountain, the shrubs cutting up his hands. Half an hour after starting, with his hands aching and bleeding and his pants torn at the knees, he reached the summit. Bent over, hands on knees, breathing heavily, he looked down on a meadow in a valley ringed by mountains. In the center of the valley, illuminated by the moon, Dan saw buildings.

"Silver Pines," Finlay said, his hands also on his knees, his chest heaving. He checked his watch. "It's 4:58 a.m. We can't get there. Not before sunrise. It's too far. It will take thirty minutes just to navigate a path down this hill, which is mostly loose rock and shale."

Dan felt a rush of adrenaline. "Not if we go straight down."

"How can we go straight down?"

Dan removed his backpack and unzipped it. He pulled out the blue plastic tarp to be used in case of rain. "With this. We slide on our asses, feet first."

It would be no different than when he'd been a kid, tobogganing out of control down ungroomed slopes—except he wouldn't be on snow or riding a toboggan or even a saucer.

"It's a risk, Dan. We'll be sliding on loose shale . . . If one of us is injured—"

"The other goes on without him. Look, it's not perfect, but it's the only shot we have. And we have no time to waste. I'm going. If I get hurt, go on without me." Dan folded the tarp in half and sat atop it. He pulled the front corners between his legs, like a sled.

"I'll push you," Finlay said. "Then I'll follow. Controlled descent, Dan. Use the heels of your boots to control your speed and maintain control to avoid getting hurt."

Dan nodded, but he also knew he didn't have time for a controlled descent, not if he was going to have any chance to make it to the town by sunrise.

Dan lifted his feet, scooted forward on his ass to the edge of the slope, and peered down. It was steeper than it had first looked. Finlay shoved him from behind. His slide began slowly, but as he progressed down the mountain, the shale and rock gave way, and he quickly picked up speed, like what he imagined riding an avalanche would be. He felt every rock on his butt as he careened over them, heard the tarp ripping, and had to fight the urge to lower his boots to the ground to serve as brakes. It was a calculated risk. He'd be of no use to Tracy if he was hurt, but he'd also be of no use if he was too late.

Near the bottom, Dan approached the tree line at too high a rate of speed and had no way to control his direction. If he hit a trunk or one of the large boulders at the bottom, he could die. He released the tarp and rolled off it, tucking into a ball. He pitched, bounced, and skidded in the loose rock until eventually coming to stop. He hurt all over his body. He'd ripped his clothing and had more cuts and scrapes on his arms, some bleeding. He did a brief assessment. Nothing felt broken.

He turned to his right and saw Finlay also careening down the mountainside. He, too, dropped the tarp and rolled, stopping not far from Dan and a bit too close to a large boulder.

"You all right?" Dan asked, rushing over to help him to his feet.

Finlay stood. "We have to run," he said. "Go."

Dan took off through the shrubbery, an arm raised to protect his face from tree branches as he ducked and stumbled forward. He heard Finlay similarly rampaging through the brush, but he didn't look back, and he didn't dare to glance down at his watch for fear he'd miss a tree branch and knock himself out.

He already knew he didn't have a minute to spare.

CHAPTER 43

Erik Schmidt considered his watch: 5:25 a.m.

He'd kept an eye on the jail from the hotel across the street. The hotel was empty of furnishings, but Schmidt didn't need any. He had no intention of sleeping, not being this close to completing what he'd set out to do.

He'd slid a wooden box to the second-story window and sat facing the jail, watching to make sure Crosswhite entered and neither she nor the girl tried to get away. Not that there was anywhere for either of them to go with the bridge blown, and not that Crosswhite was in any physical condition to go anywhere.

She was clearly hurt. She'd barely moved her right arm when he confronted her in the street. She had no doubt injured it when he'd blown the bridge using C4 explosives.

A part of Schmidt was disappointed. The competitor in him wanted to kill Crosswhite when she was at her best. Based on her shooting time on the range when she arrived in Cedar Grove, that would not be a problem. He'd drop her. Then he'd stand over her with his Beretta and make sure she knew the bullet that killed her was from Ed.

He'd settle Ed's score, as he'd solemnly promised he would do. For Charles House, he'd burned down Mattioli's mansion, erasing a structure intended to glorify the man. This morning, he'd kill Crosswhite for having killed Ed, and finish what he had set out to do. Then he'd climb down the mountain using a longer, circuitous route, bypassing Cedar Grove, and slip quietly away.

The only thing he had yet to figure out was what to do with the girl, Lydia. During the time he'd watched Crosswhite, he initially thought the two were somehow related. The girl looked like the image Ed had described when Crosswhite had been young, and how he had described her sister, Sarah. He could tell the two were close. Crosswhite had taken the girl grocery shopping and brought her home to watch a movie in the front room.

But he sensed something different about her the moment he'd picked her up outside the supermarket. Something was out of whack, and he thought that, maybe, she was retarded or something. Whatever it was, she clearly didn't comprehend her situation. Just kept talking to him about video games, about something called "Westworld." He finally had to gag her just to keep her quiet. He wasn't sure how he'd get her to cross the log, but she went across without a problem.

Schmidt stood from the window and stretched the fatigue and the tightness from his joints, cracked his neck and his knuckles. He put on his holster and press checked his customized 9 mm Beretta M9A1 semiautomatic pistol, the same pistol he'd used during AMU competitions. During the weeks leading up to this moment, he'd taken the pistol to the shooting range and ensured it was finely polished and tuned for a light, smooth trigger pull, enhancing his speed and his accuracy.

He pulled back the slide to ensure a 9 mm cartridge was locked and loaded, then slid the gun back into its holster. He wasn't as fast as his days at the AMU, but he didn't need to be that fast. He only needed to be faster than Crosswhite.

This morning, he would be.

He checked his watch: Five twenty-seven a.m. Time to go.

He'd planned for this moment while still in prison, formulated how he would avenge Ed's and Charles House's deaths. Ed had told him all about Silver Pines, his great-grandfather, William Kenmore, and Christian Mattioli. He'd told him of the fortune Mattioli stole and how his father had died. Ed told him how everything could have been different; how it could have been his grandfather, father, and his family who lived in a mansion above the town, instead of Mattioli and then, Crosswhite. Schmidt knew he had to burn that mansion to the ground.

He didn't want to ambush Crosswhite or kill her from a distance with a rifle shot. He wanted to look her in the eye, make sure she knew who had killed her. He got the idea of a duel, just like the duel in which Charles House lost his life. He wanted to see how good Crosswhite was when the target was shooting back.

That had required careful planning.

When he got out of prison, Schmidt had read every article he could find in the newspapers and on the internet about Silver Pines: its history, its location, and its geography and weather. He determined how to get into and out of the town, and that meant waiting for good weather. When it came, he'd done a reconnaissance trip to learn everything else he could. The last piece was figuring out how to isolate Crosswhite and prevent her from bringing a posse. He knew he could blow what remained of the bridge after she crossed it. That eliminated anyone following on foot. But people could still come by helicopter. He did more homework and learned about the Chinook winds in the spring and summer that blew atop the mountains at gusts of sixty miles per hour. The winds would prevent the use of a helicopter, the only way into the town other than on foot.

Then it was just a matter of his being patient and setting down necessary breadcrumbs on the trail. As he predicted, she brought her family to Cedar Grove after Kinsington Rowe's car crash, no doubt thinking she could keep her family safe there. His initial plan had been to take the nanny and the little girl, but Crosswhite had the police in town keeping an eye on her house. He had a chance when the nanny went into the mountains, but he had to first wait to ensure the other two hikers descended the mountain and would not be a problem. He had a moment, but the damn dogs wouldn't let him anywhere near the little girl or her nanny, and then the sudden appearance of the deputy sheriff on the trail had required him to abort that plan altogether. With the winds in the forecast, he had to act fast or miss the opportunity, maybe his only one. That was when he'd hit on the idea of taking the girl.

Everything fell in place from there. This morning, he would finally right the wrongs inflicted on Ed and his family.

He turned from the window and left his room, descending the stairs. He pulled open the front door and looked across the street in the predawn light, imagining for a moment what it had been like, all those years ago, when Treat Crane gunned down Charles House and other miners. He wondered if there'd been a crowd of people-watching, or if Charles House had died alone.

He looked to the jail at the end of the block. No sign of Tracy Crosswhite.

She'd come. She wouldn't risk Schmidt killing the girl.

He walked across the street and faced north. The winds that had whipped through the town all night had finally died down, though not completely. Every so often a gust would kick up the dirt, then just as quickly die. Clouds overhead blew quickly across the early morning sky.

He checked his watch—5:30 a.m.

The sun would rise in six minutes. He shifted his gaze again to the jail door.

No sign of her.

Maybe he was wrong.

Maybe Tracy Crosswhite wasn't the heroine everyone made her out to be.

Maybe that, too, was a façade.

Maybe Tracy Crosswhite was a coward.

He saw her in the building doorway—a shadow in muted, dawn light. She wore her duster, a red bandanna around her throat, her Stetson hat pulled low on her brow to block the wind. Her shooting clothes. Her Colt pistols were in their cross-draw holsters just below her waist, grips facing inward. He had to give her credit for the dramatic entrance.

Not that it would change anything. She wasn't fast enough. She wouldn't get the guns out of their holsters, let alone get off a shot, before he'd fatally wounded her.

She stepped from the wooden walkway and slowly crossed the street, each step deliberate—whether to protect her injuries or just her demeanor.

Schmidt didn't know or care.

She stopped approximately twelve feet from him. Shooting the Colts, she needed to be close.

She squared her shoulders, her head tilted forward, Stetson blocking the wind and the dust it kicked up, casting a shadow over the lower half of her face. Her blonde hair fell to her shoulders.

"I didn't think you'd come," Schmidt said.

She didn't respond. Fine. The time for talking was over. Time to get on with it.

"When the sun comes over the rooftops and crosses that line in the street, we draw." Schmidt swallowed and felt it stick in his throat, which surprised him. He was nervous. He never got nervous shooting his guns. He held his right hand at his side, near his firearm, and felt a small tremor in his hand.

Crosswhite tucked her duster behind her holsters, then rested her hands near the grips of each gun. She looked calm. Relaxed.

She tilted her head to the side to better see the line he'd drawn in the street.

"Say hello to Ed for me, Detective Tracy. You'll be seeing him for all eternity."

CHAPTER 44

Roy Calloway had been in contact with SnoHawk, the North Cascades National Park Service, and a pilot who worked for PSE. The SnoHawk and the park service–operated rescue services both were well versed on rescues in the North Cascades National Park. They had been monitoring the wind conditions on Mount Shuksan and said the gusts throughout the night remained too strong to send up a bird.

At 4:32 a.m. the pilot for PSE called Calloway and told him although wind conditions remained "dicey," he'd flown in worse, and if Calloway was willing, "he'd give it a go," given the dire circumstances. Not exactly comforting words from the man who would be his pilot, but it was the best Calloway and Tracy were going to get. If the pilot was willing to man up, Calloway would also, despite having a fear of heights and a healthy respect for helicopters. He'd known of too many people, like the basketball player Kobe Bryant and his daughter, who had met their ends in helicopter crashes.

Couldn't think about that now.

"Let's give it a go," he said, and he told the pilot he'd meet him in a field out near Mason Pettibone's home.

The pilot touched down in the meadow at 5:18 in the morning. Calloway quickly jumped on board, carrying his Recce-14 rifle with an ACOG 4x scope. He strapped into a rear seat. The pilot motioned for Calloway to put on a headset with a microphone.

"Are you good?" the pilot asked in a muffled voice. He told Calloway to give him a thumbs-up if he was good to go.

Calloway finished buckling in and returned the thumbs-up gesture, though he was anything but fine. He got the willies in a high-rise commercial building if he got too near the windows. Whenever possible, he preferred driving to flying.

As the helicopter lifted, a gust of wind caused it to shudder. Calloway shut his eyes and took several deep, controlled breaths to calm his nerves and even said a few prayers.

"Just a little wind," the pilot said. "We may encounter stronger gusts en route."

Calloway nodded and managed to ask, "How long?"

"About twenty minutes if the wind is favorable. We might make it a few minutes before that."

Calloway checked his watch. It was going to be close. Very close, if Schmidt did intend a duel at sunrise. "Let's try to shave off a few minutes," he said.

Then he shut his eyes and said another silent prayer they made it in time.

He couldn't bury another Crosswhite.

Couldn't bear that pain.

Not again.

Dan cleared the tree line and burst from the forest into a meadow of tall, golden grass. In the near distance, maybe a quarter of a mile, he saw the rooftops of Silver Pine's buildings lining each side of a wide street. In the center of that street, stood a man, though Dan was too far to see any detail.

As he ran, another person came out of a doorway to one of the buildings, pausing for a moment. She wore a cowboy hat and what looked like a long coat. A duster.

Tracy.

She stepped into the street and walked across it, stopping with her back to Dan, facing the man in the ball cap.

"Tracy!" he yelled. "Tracy!"

The distance and the wind swallowed his words.

A noise to his left drew his attention. Finlay had fallen and grunted in pain.

Dan stopped. Finlay held out the rifle.

"My ankle," Finlay said when Dan reached him. "Go. Take the rifle and go."

Dan grabbed Finlay's rifle and started running again through the grass, sprinting while he looked for a boulder, a downed tree stump, anything on which he could rest the rail of the rifle and take precise aim through the scope. He saw nothing in the meadow but the stalks of grass.

He looked back to the town, back to Tracy and the man standing in the street as sunlight peeked over the roofs of the buildings and spilled into the street, then inched forward until Tracy and Schmidt moved, each lightning fast, their movements followed by the retort of pistols discharging, multiple shots echoing across the valley.

Dan felt his legs slow, and he stumbled to an abrupt stop.

Numb. Stunned.

Everything came to a standstill, the only sound his raspy breathing.

He watched and waited.

To see who fell.

CHAPTER 45

S chmidt flexed the fingers of his right hand as the first sunlight spilled over the mountains and flowed down the snowcapped mountain range like liquid gold. It crossed over the grass meadow, seemingly gaining speed, then disappeared, momentarily, behind the buildings. It reemerged over the peak of the saloon roofline, spilling over it and onto the ground, creeping now toward the line he had drawn in the dirt.

"Any last words?" he said.

Crosswhite raised her chin, the shadow over her face receding, revealing her features.

"Best get off the range, boys. There's a Lightning Strike coming."

The light crossed the line.

Tracy startled awake.

The realization of everything that had happened came at once—where she was, the injuries she had sustained, the fatigue that had overcome her, and what awaited her. She looked across the cell. Lydia was not on the bunk. She was not in the cell. Not in the room outside the cell. Had she gone? Had she fled as Tracy had instructed?

Tracy sat up and felt immediate pain. She shut her eyes and groaned, taking a second to catch her wind.

She opened her eyes and looked about.

Her duster was gone, along with her Stetson and her cross-draw holsters holding her Colt revolvers. All that remained were her gun belts that held her rifle and shotgun rounds.

Realization hit hard.

"No!"

She threw her legs over the side and stood from the bunk.

Morning light, sunshine, crept past the jailhouse door, crossing the street.

Dawn.

Sunrise.

"No!"

She flung herself from the cell to the doorway, bracing her left arm on the door frame. The sunlight crossed the line Schmidt had drawn in the street.

"Lydia!" Tracy shouted.

The burst of gunfire happened in the blink of an eye; the retort of guns discharging drowned out her final cry of anguish and echoed across the valley.

———

His shock. His realization that it wasn't Crosswhite cost him a fraction of a second.

And in that fraction of a second, she moved with lightning speed, left arm swinging the barrel of the Colt at him, right hand fanning the hammer, cylinder rotating, smoke obscuring her face.

His Beretta flew from his hand, sending his first shot off target.

The second bullet hit him in the shoulder, disabling his right arm.

The third bullet exploded his kneecap, buckled his leg, and dropped him to the ground. He writhed in pain. Blood flowed down his right hand from the stump that had once been his index finger. The digit now lay in the dirt, along with his Beretta.

He stared at it in disbelief, the realization that he had failed overwhelming him. He'd planned it all so meticulously. He'd owed that to Ed. And he'd failed. Only this time, he hadn't lost. He'd been beaten. She'd been faster—lightning fast—and more accurate. He looked up, still disbelieving, still stunned at having lost, at having failed.

"What are you?" he asked. She spun the revolver by the trigger guard and shoved it back inside its holster, resting her palms on the grips. Then she smiled down at him, though not a belittling grin. Nor did her grin hold any air of superiority at having beaten him.

Her smile looked to be of utter and complete joy.

"Good game," she said.

CHAPTER 46

Tracy stumbled across the street as quickly as her injured shoulder allowed, grimacing with each step that jarred her broken collarbone. She moved first to where Schmidt lay in the dirt, swearing, his face a mask of pain, shock, and disbelief.

She bent and picked up his weapon, stood, and shoved it in the waistband at the small of her back. Without handcuffs, she couldn't cuff him.

"You didn't come," he said, looking up at her from the ground, nearly spitting the words. "You lied. Again. You said we would end this here. We were supposed to end it here . . . Everything."

Tracy took a step back. "We did end it here."

"You sent a girl to fight your battle."

"I didn't send her." Tracy glanced at Lydia, who was looking to the side, rocking again from heels to toes. "She came on her own."

Schmidt looked past Tracy, to the young woman. "What is she?" he asked.

Tracy smiled. "Lydia? She's a lightning strike."

She kept an eye on Schmidt and stepped down the street to Lydia, positioning her body between Lydia and Schmidt, so Lydia wouldn't see the injuries she had inflicted or the blood that colored the ground.

"I won," Lydia said, matter-of-fact.

"You did," Tracy said. "But you were supposed to run and hide."

Lydia shrugged. "I wanted to go home together. Now we can go home together; right? You have Daniella to take care of."

Tracy tried to hug her with one arm, but Lydia stepped away, her eyes shifting from side to side. "We can go home," Tracy said. "To Mason and your mom. You can go back to work at the supermarket."

Lydia nodded. "I want to go home. I want to see my mother and my grandfather. And I want to go to work."

Tracy saw movement in the grass field behind Lydia, something so incongruous she could hardly believe it was real. She shut her eyes and shook her head.

Dan?

Dan charged through the waist-high blades of grass, a rifle in hand, and a look of utter terror on his face, as if being chased by something lethal.

And hobbling behind him and to his right, Finlay Armstrong.

The whir of helicopter blades drew Tracy's attention to the snowcapped mountain peaks behind them, a deafening, thumping sound like the inside of a car when someone in the back seat lowers a window. A helicopter appeared over the tree line and shot quickly toward them, nose and front struts lowered slightly toward the ground. When the helicopter reached them, it turned, hovering. Tracy raised her one good arm to shield her and Lydia against the tornado of dirt and dust the blades kicked up.

Moments later, the helicopter struts touched down at an angle, and the pilot cut the engine. Inside the helicopter sat Roy Calloway, wearing a headset and holding a rifle barrel out the window, aimed at Schmidt.

When the noise from the blades dissipated, Tracy heard Dan shouting her name and turned again. He'd reached the town edge and raced down the street toward her.

"Tracy! Tracy!" Reaching her, he gasped for air.

She put up her hands to stop him before he hurt her.

In between those gasps, he said, "Are you okay? Are you all right?"

"I'm okay. Dan, I'm okay. We're both okay. Thanks to Lydia."

Lydia did not respond. It was as if she'd shut down.

"What happened to your arm?" Dan said to Tracy.

"I broke my collarbone and dislocated my shoulder . . . so no hugs. But I'm okay."

Roy Calloway stepped down awkwardly from the helicopter and walked forward, rifle still leveled at Schmidt. He handed the rifle to Finlay, who had also arrived, then rolled Schmidt over onto his belly and cuffed his hands behind his back. He straightened, standing over Schmidt, and stared down at him. "Mr. Schmidt. I'm Roy Calloway, chief of police. I'm the law in Cedar Grove, and you, sir, are under arrest."

Calloway retrieved his rifle from Finlay, then shifted his gaze between Tracy and Lydia, no doubt recognizing Tracy's clothes and guns. "What the hell just happened?"

Tracy glanced at Lydia, then at Calloway, giving him a look not to press the issue. Then she looked down at Schmidt. "Lydia won. Game over."

CHAPTER 47

Search-and-rescue helicopters arrived after the winds had ceased. They airlifted Tracy and Schmidt separately to St. Joseph Medical Center in Bellingham. Calloway accompanied Schmidt while Finlay remained behind to fully process and document the crime scene. When they got in cell phone range, Calloway contacted Mason Pettibone and his daughter, Celia, and told them Lydia was safe and he would bring her home to them later that afternoon. The two would not wait, however, and said they would meet them in Bellingham.

After Schmidt's wounds were treated, Calloway would have him taken to the Whatcom County Jail, where he would await arraignment on charges for the crimes he'd committed in Cedar Grove and Silver Pines, including arson, kidnapping, assault with a deadly weapon, and attempted murder. After being charged in Whatcom County, he'd be taken to King County, where he'd be arraigned for the murders of Julia Hoch and Bridgette Traugott—having admitted the killings to Tracy.

Tracy refused any pain medication until she'd given a full statement to Calloway of everything that had happened, while the events remained fresh and her recollection uncompromised. After providing a statement, she was taken into surgery to have her shattered collarbone repaired.

When next she opened her eyes, Dan stood at her bedside holding a bouquet of flowers.

"Did you bring chocolates?" Tracy asked.

"No," he said.

She frowned. "Edible flowers at least?" She remained a bit woozy from the anesthetic.

"Don't make jokes," he said.

"Sorry. How bad was it?"

"The collarbone? Shattered it. They fixed it with metal plates and screws."

"Going to make getting through airports interesting," she said. Then, when Dan didn't smile: "Sorry."

"Doctor says you're going to be in a lot of pain. The good news is your shoulder popped back in on its own. The bad news is you might need surgery to tighten the muscles to keep it from dislocating again. Both injuries will take ten to twelve weeks to heal, but the doctor is optimistic that, with physical therapy, you'll recover full range of motion."

"How are Therese and Daniella?"

"They seem very happy living at Vera and Faz's. Therese says she's never eaten so well."

"We may not get her back . . . the way I cook," Tracy said.

"Just the opposite. She says if she stays there much longer, she won't fit into any of her clothes."

"How's her mental attitude?"

Dan shrugged. "I think we should pay to have her get some counseling. We should at least present her with that option."

"I think that's a good call. And Daniella?"

"Happy as a lark, though I'm sure she misses her mommy." The last word caught in Dan's throat, and she realized he was fighting his emotions.

"I miss her too. And you," Tracy said. "Have you spoken to Lydia?"

"No," he said, shaking his head. "She's at home with her mother and Mason. I didn't get the chance to speak to any of them, but Roy says they're just glad to have Lydia back, safe."

"Did Roy interview Lydia, take a statement?"

"He says he tried, but she wasn't answering his questions. Wasn't saying anything. Mason told Roy that she'd shut down from the level of stress she experienced. Do you think she comprehends what happened? That she shot a man?"

Tracy nodded. "She went out there for me, Dan. And I think she knew exactly what she was doing. She knew I was hurt, that I couldn't draw my pistols, that I have Daniella to care for."

"My God," he said.

"She didn't know what she was up against—that Schmidt was a trained and skilled shooter—but that doesn't really matter; does it?" Tracy asked, a tear rolling down her cheek. "She was willing to risk her own life to save mine."

"What did happen, Tracy?"

Dan had refrained from asking Tracy too many questions on the flight to the hospital. She had been in no real condition to tell him much beyond the basic facts she had provided Finlay and Calloway.

Tracy sighed. "Help me to sit up and have a drink of water?"

Dan did so. The water soothed her throat. When she lay back, she told Dan about the phone call from Schmidt telling her he had taken Lydia and his threat to kill her, unless Tracy made it to Silver Pines in a certain time, alone. "I couldn't bring anyone. You saw how isolated the town is, how limited the access. Schmidt would have killed her. But then, when I reached the access road and you called, I realized that I had a responsibility to you and to Daniella; that this is no longer just about me."

"No. It's not. That little girl deserves to grow up with her mother."

"I know," Tracy said. "Lydia made that abundantly clear. And I love her for it and I love you both, more than anything in the world. But I had my job to do also. Lydia was innocent in all of this. And she needed me. She needed my help. I couldn't let her die because of me, Dan. I couldn't allow that to happen again."

"I know, Tracy. I know you still feel guilty about what happened to Sarah and likely always will. I'm not happy about what happened, but I understand why you did what you did, and I'm trying to come to terms with it. But it isn't easy."

Tracy knew it wasn't, but that was a longer conversation. "I'm just glad you heard enough of our phone conversation to know where to find me."

"I didn't," Dan said, and he told her how he and Calloway pieced it together talking to Atticus, then to Stan Bleeker.

"But how did you get there, Dan? Schmidt blew the bridge, the only access into town."

Dan explained about the ore car rail line and his and Finlay's hike over the mountain. When he'd finished, they sat in silence. Tracy knew he wanted to ask her more questions but was holding back. Finally, he said, "What would you have done, Tracy? What would you have done had Lydia not gone out there?"

Tracy also knew Dan did not want to hear her answer. "What do you want me to say, Dan?"

"Tell me you weren't going to go out there."

She sighed and shook her head. "I love you, Dan. I love you more than anything in this world. You and Daniella."

"But . . ."

"But he blew the bridge, Dan. I wasn't expecting any help. And he would have killed Lydia." She felt herself becoming overwhelmed and took a moment to get her emotions under control. "I couldn't live with someone else dying because of me. Not Lydia."

"You would have gone out."

"I would have gone, not for me. Not to feed my ego. Not because I hate Erik Schmidt and all the things he's done. I would have gone out for Lydia. Just as she went for me."

"With one arm?" Dan asked.

"With no arms, Dan."

"Because it's your job."

She nodded. "And because I love that girl."

"Maybe it's time for another job," he said.

She didn't answer. Not right away. She wanted to absorb what he had said, not dismiss his concerns out of hand. Things had changed. She was a wife now. A mother. And no matter how many young women she saved, it wouldn't bring back Sarah, wouldn't erase everything that had happened. After a moment she said, "When I first took this job, I admit that I did so to determine who killed Sarah. I saw every case that involved a murdered young woman as a chance to do something good, to redeem myself, ease my guilt, so my sister's death wasn't in vain. I thought if I could bring a family comfort, or at least closure, Sarah's death would have a purpose, that something good would come from something horrific."

"And help you also find closure?"

"Of course, Dan. I don't deny that."

"You have a family now," he said.

"I told you; I know that, too, Dan. And it's the reason I haven't pushed to go back to active homicide investigations. I'm happy in cold cases, finding closure for the victims and their families."

"Are you?"

"What does that mean?"

"You went to Mason's because you anticipated this."

"I could not have anticipated this."

"Maybe not exactly, but . . ."

She paused, again gathering her emotions. "I went to Mason's because I failed the shoot/no-shoot course."

Dan gave her a puzzled look. "*You* failed?"

"I had a hallucination while I went through the course."

"Your night terrors?"

"I saw Edmund House and I saw Erik Schmidt, and I pretty much eviscerated a target."

"I take it that wasn't a good thing?"

"No," she said. "The target was a civilian with a walkie-talkie."

"Why didn't you say anything, Tracy?"

"Because you had enough on your plate to worry about, and I didn't want you to worry that your wife and the mother of your child was losing her mind."

Dan sighed and shook his head. Then he leaned down and put his head beside hers, whispering. "I will always have room for you, Tracy. Always."

"And I will always have love for you," she said. "So, to answer your question, I went to Mason primarily to get my edge back to pass the shoot/no-shoot course. But I also went to try to get rid of my demons. If it meant I would be better prepared for a moment like this, or something else down the road, then . . ." She shrugged her good shoulder.

"Did you?"

"Did I what?"

"Did you get rid of your demons?"

She thought about his question for a long moment, and about what her counselor, Lisa Walsh, had told her. Then she said, "I'm not sure any of us ever fully gets rid of our demons. I think we just learn to better live with them. It's what makes us human, Dan. All of us."

CHAPTER 48

The day the hospital discharged Tracy, Dan brought her back to Cedar Grove. Nolasco called to tell her she was free to come back to work, whenever her injuries healed. She'd be out of commission for several months and decided she wanted to recuperate in Cedar Grove and enjoy the summer with Daniella.

Dan and Tracy had a long talk with Therese, asking her if she wanted to come back or wanted some time away.

"Don't be daft," she said. "Of course I want to come back."

They all agreed it would be best for the whole family to get some counseling, after their ordeals in the mountains. Dan learned from an ad in the *Cedar Grove Towne Crier* that one of the work-from-home residents who had moved to Cedar Grove during the Covid pandemic was a counselor taking new clients. Tracy felt comfort knowing Therese and Dan would be there with her, so none of them would have to go through their recoveries alone.

When they arrived in Cedar Grove from Bellingham, Tracy asked Dan to drive her to Mason Pettibone's house. Faz and Vera would be arriving with Therese and Daniella later in the afternoon and would spend the weekend relaxing. Faz loved Grandma Billie's, and Dan had promised him and Vera dinner for taking care of Therese and Daniella.

In the interim, Tracy wanted to check on Lydia. She also wanted to apologize to Mason Pettibone and Celia for what had happened.

When they reached Pettibone's driveway, Dan said, "You want me to come in?"

"Sure. You can talk to Mason while I talk to Lydia."

Dan knocked on the door and Pettibone answered it. "Dan. Tracy."

"Hey, Mason," Tracy said.

"How are you feeling?" he asked her.

"Better. Though still a bit dizzy from the pain meds."

"Come on in and sat down."

They sat in the living room, Lucille running from one person to the next, dancing and prancing on her two legs, pawing at the air. Tracy said, "Mason, I'm so sorry about what happened." He waved off her apology, but she persisted. "I should have done better protecting Lydia."

"You told me about Schmidt," Pettibone said. "I was aware. And none of us could have known or predicted what that crazy son of a bitch would do. Roy told us everything about what happened, and we're just so glad and thankful you brought Lydia home safe."

"Don't thank me," she said. "Lydia saved my life. It's because of her I came home safe to Dan and Daniella. I'll never forget it, Mason. I'll never forget what she's done. Whatever I can do to help her, I will."

"Roy said she took down Schmidt, though he didn't provide many details, and Lydia still won't talk about it."

Tracy heard the sliver of pride in Pettibone's voice, knowing Lydia had been quicker than someone who had once been the best of the best. "Probably best for you and Celia to keep it simple. But she was fast, Mason. Lightning quick, and more accurate. You named her well, and you trained her to live up to her name."

Pettibone gave her a satisfied smile.

"How is she?" Tracy asked.

"She's okay. She's coming around. We'll have her in counseling and that will help," he said. "Still determined as ever about whatever she puts her mind to. She wants to get back to work at the supermarket—Mr. Cunningham said to let her take her time, that her job will be waiting, but you know Lydia, she's adamant about not missing a day, and the counselor thinks it best to get her back to her routine. She's also been asking about the shooting lessons, whether you were going to continue. I told her you were injured and wouldn't be shooting anytime soon, but I was sure you'd come by and see her."

"I'm happy about the job," Tracy said. "And I've decided to stay in Cedar Grove while recovering. Since I'm going to have time on my hands, I thought I could work with Lydia, teach her to drive, take her places, help her to socialize. I made a phone call to Grandma Billie's; they can use a prep cook in their kitchen and would love to give Lydia a chance. Do you think she'd be willing?"

"I don't know, but if you suggest it, she might. As I said, I think she misses not seeing you. Why don't you go on down and say hello? Dan, can I interest you in a cup of coffee?"

"You can interest me, and I will say yes."

Tracy walked down the hall, put her ear to the door, knocked, then said, "Lydia?"

The door flew open quickly, before Tracy had time to pull back.

"Tracy!" Lydia took a step forward but caught herself. "You're hurt," she said, sounding as if she didn't recall Tracy's injuries.

"I hurt my shoulder. Broke my collarbone."

"Does it hurt?"

Tracy nodded and made a face. "A lot. Can I come in?"

"Are you here for training?"

"I'm afraid I won't be training for a while, at least not on the range. The doctor said up to twelve weeks. But maybe I can do some computer training."

"That would be totally great. I liked training with you. I liked being your teacher. We can find new games to train on. I have—"

"Lydia," Tracy said raising a hand. "We can decide the games together, another time. I'll have to be getting back to Seattle after my collarbone heals—"

"And be a homicide detective?"

"And be a homicide detective. But I'm going to spend the summer in Cedar Grove, and while I'm here, I want to give you driving lessons. Would you like that?"

Lydia's smile broadened. "Like your sister. You taught your sister to drive, and she was younger than me. A colt that couldn't be broken."

"Yes, just like my sister."

"Grandpa got me the driving book. I've read all the rules."

And no doubt Lydia could recite them verbatim. "I also heard that Grandma Billie's is looking for someone to help them in their kitchen and would like you to give it a try. I told them you would be perfect for the position. If you want to do it. You would be paid very well, and you could learn how to cook, for when you live on your own."

Lydia didn't immediately answer.

"You can think about it," Tracy said.

"Would I have to stop working at the supermarket?"

"No. Not at all."

"Okay. I'll think about it."

That was enough pushing for now. Tracy looked at Lydia's computer screens. "What are you playing?"

"*World of Warcraft*. It's my favorite game. I've logged over nine thousand hours."

"Wow. You must be very good."

"I am. I'm very good."

Tracy laughed. "How do you play?"

"It's a multiplayer online role-playing game set in the world of Azeroth. You create an avatar and you and your team fight monsters, complete quests, and . . . Do you just want me to show you?"

"Sure. That might be easier."

Lydia kept up a running dialogue as Tracy pulled up a chair and sat beside her. She explained how she and her team of avatars moved all over the fictional realm. Tracy stayed silent, watching her, enjoying the beauty of what Lydia did so well—and seemingly so effortlessly. And in that moment, she understood the art of the game, what Lydia had been explaining to her but which, like so many things in life, you had to experience to truly understand the beauty. Behind all the lasers and the lights and the bells and whistles was a puzzle, a quest, a conquest. It was much like climbing mountains, painting, writing novels. Any artistic craft. The satisfaction came in achieving what you set out to accomplish, despite the struggles you endured along the way.

"Which one is you?" Tracy asked, confused by what seemed like a dozen avatars advancing on a monster.

Lydia pointed. "That one."

"You don't have a weapon."

"I'm a healer."

The answer gave Tracy pause. "What does a healer do?"

"My job is to ensure my team members remain alive and healthy during battles and quests. I can use spells to heal wounds, cure ailments, and revive fallen team members."

Tracy wondered if that was what had motivated Lydia to take her place in the duel with Schmidt. If the young woman was, innately, a healer. "You're a hero, Lydia."

"No," Lydia said. "Not hero. A *healer*."

Tracy smiled and quietly watched, enjoying the artistry in what the young woman did. After a while, she said, "You know you were my healer, Lydia. You kept me alive in Silver Pines."

"I know," she said matter-of-factly, eyes focused on the game, fingers moving swiftly and with a purpose across the keyboard. "You were hurt. You needed time to heal."

Lydia's honesty nearly took Tracy's breath away.

She fought back tears. "Why did you go out there, Lydia, knowing it wasn't a game?"

The girl's eyes darted all over her screen, her avatar moving swiftly but efficiently, swirling, twisting, turning, sending out spells to heal her team members and restore their lives. She shrugged one shoulder. "Because you couldn't."

"Because I was hurt?"

"You had to heal. He would have shot you. And then I would have lost my friend, Tracy Crossdraw, three-time Single Action Shooting Society champion and Seattle Police Department homicide detective. We wouldn't have had any more training sessions, or girls' nights."

Tracy didn't know what to say, continuing to struggle with her emotions.

Did Lydia also comprehend that she could have died? Tracy didn't want to ask. She didn't want to know. Maybe it had simply been instinctual—an impulse or predisposition genetically ingrained in Lydia's DNA. Maybe she truly was a healer.

But as Dan had said, the reason didn't matter.

What mattered was that Lydia had gone out—for Tracy.

It had been an act of complete and total selflessness. Something to be cherished, not analyzed. She had saved Dan's wife and Daniella's mother. Because of Lydia, they would continue as a family. Because of Lydia, Tracy and Dan would get to see their daughter grow up.

My God, she said to herself, as Dan had said in the hospital.

My God.

Tracy stood as Lydia moved her avatar across the computer monitor. She wanted to hug the young woman. She wanted to hold her tight and tell her she loved her, but she knew Lydia didn't like to be touched, that touching made her uncomfortable, unless she initiated it. Tracy would respect that.

She walked to the bedroom door.

"Hey, Crossdraw."

Tracy turned back. Lydia had swiveled her chair, facing her. Behind her, the game continued in a blur of movement, colors, and flashes. "Yes, Lightning Strike."

"Do you think I could still be a homicide detective?"

"I think, Lydia, that you can be whatever you put your mind to."

Lydia smiled. "Cool," she said, and turned back to her game.

EPILOGUE

During the three months she recuperated from her injuries, Tracy and Dan invited Kins and Shannah to Cedar Grove, where they ate good meals and relaxed in the warm sun and gentle breeze. Kins was getting better each day. He showed no cognitive issues resulting from the crash, and physically, his body was healing. He'd even lost ten pounds and put on a bit of muscle.

Nolasco had advised Tracy during a call into the office that Schmidt's arrest and arraignment on an assortment of charges both in Whatcom County and King County had also changed the media's focus pertaining to Kins's invalid search warrant. The brass, too, had changed its narrative and now spun it as an aggressive tactic to take a killer off the street. Fernandez had also come forward and told Nolasco and the prosecutor's office what had happened. Cerrabone said it wouldn't rectify everything; prosecutors would still be reluctant to put Kins on the witness stand when defense attorneys could so easily impeach him. But outside the courtroom, what Kins had done elevated him in the prosecuting attorney's office and at SPD, including the brass.

Tracy had started physical therapy, and while she couldn't say she'd lost ten pounds—she told Kins she hated him for telling her *he* had—she was recovering full use of her right arm and building back her strength. She'd also spent a lot of time with Lydia. The young woman had easily passed the written portion of her driving exam, receiving a score of 100 percent, and was now preparing for her road test. All Tracy had to do was liken driving to a video game. Lydia's focus became much more intense, as did her determination to succeed.

Lydia had also taken the part-time job at Grandma Billie's Bistro, working in the kitchen with Hannah several nights a week—chopping vegetables, measuring out ingredients, and otherwise doing the busy work so Hannah could focus her time and energy on cooking. Hannah told Tracy on one of her and Dan's visits to the bistro that Lydia, a stickler for details, meticulously followed Hannah's recipes down to the last kernel of pepper and grain of salt, ensuring Hannah's dishes tasted the same each time ordered.

This morning would be another step in Lydia's progression to live on her own. She had another job interview, this one in Redmond, Washington, not far from Tracy and Dan's home. She'd spent the weekend at their house, as she had done on several other weekends.

Early Monday morning, Tracy and Lydia drove to the headquarters of the gaming company, LegendCraft of America. Lydia looked like a young professional in one of Tracy's blue pantsuits with a cream blouse. It had been a bit of a challenge finding something Lydia liked and would wear. Lydia gravitated toward loud colors, and Tracy had to explain that during job interviews, Lydia didn't want her clothes to stand out, just her gaming abilities. That seemed to make perfect sense to her.

Tracy parked in a designated stall. "Are you nervous, Lydia?"

"Why?"

Tracy smiled at the young woman's confidence—or naïveté. Or maybe it was simply optimism. Sarah, too, had the same outlook on life. "No reason," Tracy said.

They walked into the building together, but Tracy took a step back as Lydia approached the receptionist. She had told Lydia that she would have to go through the job interview—with some rehearsal—on her own, without Tracy present. She didn't tell Lydia the person she was about to meet was the husband of a fellow police officer whom Tracy had trained to shoot.

"Hello," the receptionist said.

"Hello," Lydia said. "I have an interview appointment with Mr. Giovanni Tallino, senior vice president of product development and publishing for LegendCraft of America."

"And your name?" the receptionist asked.

"My name is Lydia Johnson."

"If you'll have a seat, Ms. Johnson, I'll let Mr. Tallino know you're here."

Lydia sat next to Tracy. Tracy and Dan had brought Lydia home to Redmond to further expose her to different people and different environments. Some, like the receptionist, recognized Lydia's idiosyncrasies and responded with kindness. Others acted like they did not notice or care, though they did and usually responded with discomfort. Only a few had been rude or unkind, and Tracy had made those into teaching moments, telling Lydia those people usually had deeper problems unrelated to Lydia, and that she should respond to them with kindness and politeness.

A few minutes after they'd taken their seats, a man with a tapered white beard, glasses, and a wide smile approached. "Hi," he said extending a hand toward Lydia. "I'm Giovanni Tallino. You must be Lydia."

Lydia stood and extended her hand. "Hi. I'm Lydia Johnson."

"I've heard a lot about you, Lydia. Detective Crosswhite tells me you are a pretty incredible video game player."

Lydia smiled at Tracy. Then she said, "I do my best, Mr. Tallino."

"Would you like to play some of our video games today, games that aren't yet out to the public, and tell me and my colleagues what you like and don't like about each game?"

"I can do that," she said.

"I'm sure you can."

The job, if Lydia were to get it, would require her to come into the company office every few weeks to receive her assignments, and to provide the management team with her assessment of each game before they took it to market, what they might highlight and what they might change, and in some instances, what to scrap entirely. Because Lydia's opinion would not be filtered—tempered neither by the creators' feelings nor by the amount the company had invested in marketing a game—LegendCraft would be getting a completely objective product assessment from a high-level gamer. If it worked out, they said Lydia could be hired full-time.

And they would pay her handsomely.

At present, the plan was to help Lydia learn to take the train from Bellingham to Seattle the Sunday before she was expected at the LegendCraft offices. Dan and/or Tracy would pick her up, and she would stay a couple nights with them. She'd then take the train home with her assignments for the week, further acclimating her to change. The eventual plan, which would take time, was for Lydia to live independently, likely in Cedar Grove, so she could continue to help her grandfather.

After all, she was a healer.

"Okay. I'll take you back and get you set up." Tallino directed his next comment at Tracy. "This will be a few hours, if you have some errands or things to do."

Tracy smiled. "I have a shooting course to complete this morning."

Crazy Joe Mazy and another instructor had set up a new Hogan's Alley, given that Tracy was already familiar with the original one. "I'm going to head over to Seattle and complete that course, then come back here this afternoon."

"The timing sounds perfect," Tallino said. "If you get hungry, the company cafeteria is just across the hall. You can get something to eat and relax."

Tracy held up the copy of *Charlie and the Chocolate Factory* Lydia had loaned her. She'd seen the movie but realized she'd never read the book. Lydia smiled.

"We'll see you in a few hours," Tallino said.

At the door, Lydia turned back. Fear knotted Tracy's stomach, but Lydia smiled. "Hey, Crossdraw."

"Yes, Lightning Strike."

"Good luck on the shoot/no-shoot course."

Tracy smiled. "Luck, Lightning Strike, has nothing to do with it. This time, I'm prepared to succeed because I've had perfect practice with two of the best instructors in the state."

"Stay in the moment, Crossdraw. Don't think about the shots you've taken or anticipate the shots you will take." She sounded just like Mason.

"I remember. One level at a time."

It was, Tracy had come to realize, a way to live her life, not to dwell on past mistakes, regrets, or losses, and not to anticipate what could or might be—things that had not yet happened and might not ever occur. She would stay in the present, living each moment fully, handling whatever problem she might encounter, and enjoying every blessing she received.

That was enough for anyone.

It was enough for her.

Lydia beamed. "Cool," she said, and stepped through the door.

ACKNOWLEDGMENTS

People ask where I get my ideas. "All over the place" is my usual answer.

For *A Dead Draw*, the idea started when I read an article in the local paper that a consultant on my books, someone I greatly respect, was excoriated in court because of a technical issue on an affidavit for a search warrant. The result was that the search warrant was thrown out, and a violent drug dealer walked free to continue to distribute his drugs despite being clearly guilty. This is a tough issue with no easy answers. I know it can be a highly charged political issue, but that is not my intent. I understand that on the one hand, if our constitutional rights are not protected, we all suffer. On the other hand, when a drug dealer is out selling heroin and fentanyl, we all suffer the consequences of addiction—including rampant homelessness, crime, and needless deaths. In one month, I watched three families from my children's grade school each bury a child who overdosed.

Tough issues make us all think.

On a much lighter note, my father loved classic movies, and I loved to watch them with him. He wasn't great about keeping the mystery a mystery. He'd prod me and my siblings. "Did you see that? Did you hear what he just said?" And we would cringe and tell him not to spoil it.

But I don't think there has ever been a person whose company I enjoyed more than my dad. If I could have him back, just for a few hours, we'd watch *Casablanca*, *Trapeze*, *On the Waterfront*, *The Dirty Dozen*, *The Guns of Navarone*, or any of the other hundreds of movies we watched together. He was a big fan of Clint Eastwood and the spaghetti Westerns like *The Good, the Bad and the Ugly*, *A Fistful of Dollars*, *For a Few Dollars More*, and *High Plains Drifter*. I never met Clint, but I did have the pleasure of meeting "Big" George Kennedy, as my father referred to him, who starred in some of those movies. He was well into his eighties, had lost his wife, his dog, and much of his hearing, but he remained affable and thrilled when I told him how much my dad and I enjoyed his movies. And I got his autograph.

I was a big fan of the Western growing up. I loved the original *True Grit*, *The Cowboys*, *The Man Who Shot Liberty Valance*, and *Rio Lobo*. My dad and I watched *Butch Cassidy and the Sundance Kid*, the Sam Elliot movies, Jimmy Stewart's Westerns, *Unforgiven*, *Tombstone*, and many, many more. Who can forget Val Kilmer as Doc Holliday in *Tombstone*? Legendary. I think about and miss you, Pops. Every day.

I have been fascinated with stories of Dodge City and Tombstone and other legendary frontier towns. When I read Larry McMurtry's *Lonesome Dove*, it hit my emotions like few books can. It was hardscrabble living for some very brave people who ventured west in search of a better life and found some of the most beautiful and some of the most inhospitable land on which to carve out an existence. It brought into play the conflict between these settlers and the Native Americans who had lived in these areas long before those settlers arrived. It was a lawless time in many places, where scores were settled with the bullet, not the law.

Living in California and the Pacific Northwest, I have traveled to many of these old Western towns in Washington, Arizona, California, and Colorado. Some still exist, others have become tourist destinations, and some are ghost towns. All are fascinating. A part of me wonders if I could have existed then. I'd like to think so, but the reality is, I doubt it.

I also had the pleasure of attending a Single Action Shooting competition here in the state of Washington to learn a bit about that sport and those who participate in it. It is not just shooting. It is a re-creation of a way of life that has long since gone. That day I spent observing in the mountains, I asked one of the champions about the future of the sport. The Rattle, his cowboy name, told me the future was in the young people who honed their speed and accuracy playing video games.

Luckily, I have another very good friend who spent his career in the gaming industry, advising a company which games would sell and why—or why not. He spent an afternoon showing me his craft and explaining to me why the games are not about violence but more about strategic thinking at a very high and very fast level. Yes, the news reports of mass shootings will often reference the impact of certain games and the dehumanization of the people in those games. But the vast majority of serious gamers are more about solving puzzles in order to advance to the next stage, about outsmarting the computer, about teamwork with those they play with in a community, and about fun. I finally understood what my friend had been telling me, and I wanted my protagonist, Tracy Crosswhite, to find herself not just a player but someone who finds herself sucked into a video game–type setting and having to find a way to survive.

I'm also not a shooter, but I was blessed to have my good friend Dan Brzusek introduce me to someone who does shoot competitively. Carl Kleinknecht spent his career in law enforcement as a police officer and assistant police chief and now is spending a second career ensuring that citizens are safe in a very large Seattle-area public space. Carl was kind enough and generous enough to spend an entire afternoon teaching me and my son proper gun safety rules and protocol, as well as the proper technique for drawing and firing various weapons at different distances. I have no desire to hunt. I just wanted to feel safe around weapons and to understand the incredible responsibility we must undertake each time we pull a trigger. Carl also put my son and me through the qualification test police officers must annually pass and helped me to create a shoot/no-shoot course. I'm proud to say I passed the qualification exam—by the skin of my teeth. Thank you to the Bellevue Police Department for allowing Carl to use their shooting range to do this instruction.

Thanks also to Alan Hardwick, who spent his first career as a Boise, Idaho, and Edmonds, Washington, police officer and detective and who now works as private investigator for Hardwick Consulting. Alan has been through many combat shoot simulations and was terrific about showing me some of those that were recorded and walking me through them. He helped me to create a scenario that Tracy Crosswhite would likely face in her job as a detective, and he showed me the likely places and moments where she might slip up and the reasons behind those mistakes. Alan is always available and willing to help . . . usually with a big smile and chuckle.

Thanks to Jennifer Southworth, retired Seattle Police Department Violent Crimes detective. Jennifer has been helping me with Tracy Crosswhite since book one, *My Sister's Grave*. Like Alan, she has always been willing to make sure I get police procedure as accurate as the story will allow. Things like the timing of events have to be condensed in novels, but I always ask, "What is beyond the realm of fiction?" Jen helps me to find it.

With Tracy being a shooter since her childhood, I wanted to bring her back to her shooting roots, back to those movies I used to watch with my dad. I wanted her to face a lawless situation where she stood isolated, on her own, and had to either kill or be killed, to put her shooting to the ultimate test—take a life or lose her own.

I hope you enjoyed it.

Another quick note. I have a character in the novel, Lydia, who is on the spectrum. I hope I captured her accurately. I did a ton of research to try to get it right, then had two epiphanies when I met two individuals, one from my childhood and one I met fortuitously, who were clearly on the spectrum and told me so. It was fascinating to hear them tell me what they understood without any embarrassment or self-consciousness. I've tried to conduct my own life similarly, talking openly about my stroke and the anxiety that resulted from it. It is a part of who I am. I hope I handled Lydia fairly and accurately. I have a brother with Down syndrome and have a heightened awareness of characters in books who are different. My intent was to portray Lydia as an accomplished, high-functioning human being but one who must deal with something over which she has no control. I hope I accomplished this.

Thanks to Meg Ruley, Rebecca Scherer, and the team at the Jane Rotrosen Agency for all they continue to do for me. It's a lot.

Thank you to Thomas & Mercer, Amazon Publishing. They put an awful lot of time and energy into ensuring the quality of each of my novels, then getting them out into the world to readers all over the planet.

Thanks to Andrea Nauta, production manager, and Jarrod Taylor, art director. Thanks to Allyson Cullinan at Amazon Publishing with all the promotion and assistance with travel.

Thanks to the marketing team, especially Andrew George, Erica Moriarty, and Andrea Mendez for all their dedicated work and incredible new ideas. Thanks to Julia Sommerfeld, publisher of Amazon Publishing, for a team that has brought millions of readers to my novels.

I am especially grateful to associate publisher Gracie Doyle for all that she does for me, from the initial idea to the books in the bookstores.

Thank you to Charlotte Herscher, developmental editor. She handles all my books deftly and makes each better.

Thanks to Scott Calamar, copyeditor, who I desperately need. Grammar has never been my strength, so there is usually a lot to do.

Thank you to Megan Beatie of Megan Beatie Communications, who has designed and executed some brilliant publicity and marketing campaigns for my books and for me. She's helped me to secure reviews in top newspapers and magazines around the United States and events that bring in thousands of dedicated readers. I'm grateful to Megan for all her efforts and her team's hard work to get my books into the hands of readers.

Thanks to Tami Taylor, who creates my newsletters. Thanks to Pam Binder and the Pacific Northwest Writers Association for their support.

Thanks to all of you tireless and loyal readers for finding my novels and for your incredible support of my work all over the world. Hearing from readers is a blessing, and I enjoy each email. I can't respond to them all, but I do read them.

Thanks to my mother and father for a wonderful childhood. Thanks to my mom for a love of reading and my dad for a love of old movies. I can't imagine a world without those books or those movies when acting had to carry the script.

These stories, characters, and words are mine. But the finished product belongs to all of these terrifically talented people, and the sum, what you read, is so much better than the individual parts.

Thank you to my wife, Cristina, for all her love and support, and thanks to my two children, who make me so very proud.

I couldn't do this without all of you, nor would I want to.

ABOUT THE AUTHOR

Robert Dugoni is the *New York Times*, *Wall Street Journal*, *Washington Post*, and Amazon Charts bestselling author of several series, including Tracy Crosswhite, Charles Jenkins, David Sloane, and Keera Duggan. His stand-alone novels include *Damage Control*, *The 7th Canon*, *The World Played Chess*, and *The Extraordinary Life of Sam Hell*, which was named *Suspense Magazine*'s 2018 Book of the Year and won Dugoni an AudioFile Earphones Award for his narration. The *Washington Post* named his nonfiction exposé *The Cyanide Canary* a Best Book of the Year. Dugoni is the recipient of the Nancy Pearl Book Award for fiction and a multi-time winner for best novel set in the Pacific Northwest. He has been a finalist for many other awards. Dugoni's books are sold in more than twenty-five countries and have been translated into more than thirty languages, reaching over ten million readers worldwide. He lives in Seattle. Visit his website at robertdugonibooks.com.